THE JACOBITES' PLIGHT

MORAG EDWARDS

BLOODHOUND
— BOOKS —

www.bloodhoundbooks.com

Print ISBN: 978-1-916978-51-5

FOREWORD

The Herbert family suffered decades of persecution for their Catholic faith and Jacobite sympathies. William, the 2nd Marquess of Powis (1665-1745), was not a loyal Jacobite but helped his beloved sister, Winifred Maxwell (1672-1749), escape to France in 1716. Winifred had committed treason against George 1st through rescuing her husband from the Tower of London, on the eve of his execution. Mary Herbert (1686-1775), William's daughter, lived in Regency Paris with a widowed aunt and was one of the earliest known female entrepreneurs and a professional gambler. These three members of the Herbert family share one ambition, to have enough money, whatever 'enough' means for each of them.

This family lived real, well-documented lives. While the most important events happened as I describe, some names, details and dates have been altered to suit my purpose as the author. Their personalities, motives, desires, and conversations are entirely fictional and bear no resemblance to how they may have actually thought, acted, or spoken.

Morag Edwards
October 2023

CHAPTER 1
1716

William Herbert paused to watch a little girl standing alone on the other side of the street, a pretty little thing despite the torn, adult coat and oversized boots. She reminded him of his own eldest daughter as a child, his beloved Mary, but he felt sure she was lost, or disoriented, or both. The girl looked about three years old, but these abandoned children were always small. And then a heavy cart thundered past, too fast for a narrow street of trading shops and hawkers, driven by cocksure apprentice boys who should have known better.

He stared at the space where the child had been, a gap immediately filled by a woman selling asparagus, bellowing to passers-by. William glanced from left to right, and with foreboding saw a pile of rags a few steps from where the child had stood. His only duty was to find a safe passage out of the foreign territory of Moorfields and make his way back to Great Ormond Street. He had just committed an act of the deepest betrayal against the king and should not draw attention to himself. But watching the busy throng of Londoners step over what he guessed was the girl, he crossed the street and approached the crumpled body. She looked unhurt, perfect in fact, except that she lay oddly, like a snapped peg doll. He knelt to inspect the child, sure that she was dead, but pulled back from the rank odour of raw sewage. The little girl was covered in cakes of faeces, dropped by the night soil men. William pushed against his knees to stand, his gloved hand covering his nose, and looked around at the crowded street. Was anyone searching for a missing child? The hordes of men and women hustling around him seemed indifferent, intent only upon their own survival until the end of the day. The nearest shopkeeper, the owner of a tripe shop, came out with a broom to sweep the offending bundle into the gutter. William spoke to him.

'Where does this child belong? She needs to be taken to her family for burial.'

'Family?' The shopkeeper snorted, leaning on his broom handle. 'You could try the parish nurse.' He pointed over William's shoulder. 'First left, then a right into the courtyard, ground floor. You can't miss it. The sound of bawling will tell you when you've arrived.'

Somehow, this dead child had become his responsibility. Reluctant to remove his rough cloak, worn to disguise his rich man's clothes, William lifted the child with his hands, horribly aware of blood oozing from the back of her head, smearing his gloves and sleeves. The crowd parted as William, holding the child's body in front of him, followed the shopkeeper's directions through houses and shops thrown up without regulation or planning.

He found the house, once an ancient manor from the days when the area had been fields and orchards, but surrounding the old, crumbling walls, every alleyway and court was crowded with new buildings. He could hear infants crying and peered through a dirty window to see if he could find the nurse. A movement inside revealed an old man lying on a thin mattress, his clothes so torn that he must be condemned to a life indoors, reliant upon the charity of neighbours. Seeing that William was not a person who would provide food, the man snarled and shook his fist, showing only one tooth in his purple gums.

William listened again for the sound of babies mewling. Easing himself through a gap in the wall, into what once would have been the formal courtyard of a wealthy farmhouse, William found an open door and above the harsh sound of a woman yelling, heard children wailing. He pushed the door ajar and before his eyes could adjust to the absence of daylight, his stomach retched from the smell of bodily fluids and sour milk. Three babies were lying in cots, trying to shield their eyes from the unexpected shaft of sunlight, and four ragged children sat in a circle on the dirt floor, naked apart from a vest, chewing on what looked like pieces of filthy cloth. The parish nurse wore only a stained shift without stays. She swept around them, her breasts swinging loose as she used her broom to mix dirt with the urine that trickled out from under the children's legs. Hearing his knock, she turned to the sound and William held out the dead child.

'Is this one of your charges? I'm afraid she's been hit by a cart.'

'Oh no, not Miriam!'

'I'm afraid so. I'm sorry to bring such bad news.'

The woman pointed accusingly at Miriam's body and glared at William. 'Do you know how much it costs me to get one of these to the age where they can beg? The first day I send her out, look what happens.'

'Where can I put the child?' he asked.

The nurse gestured to a corner of the room. 'The parish will pick her up later and bury her.'

William hesitated, reluctant to enter. 'It wasn't my fault. I just found her on the pavement.'

She raised her eyebrows in disbelief and moved closer to the entrance. William guessed he should drop the body and run but some misguided sense of responsibility for Miriam made him carry the child inside. He propped her in a corner, being careful to support her head, and in the half-light, she seemed alive, waiting for whatever would come next in her short life. William's eyesight adapted to the dim interior and he paused to look inside the cots. The stench of thin blankets soaked in urine made him nauseous, but he tried to catch the attention of one of the babies. At first, the infant turned towards the sound he made, its eyes dull, but rolled away to bury its face into the soiled bedding.

'Who do these children belong to?' he asked.

'The parish. I'm paid to look after them. They don't live long. That's why Miriam was special.'

The nurse used her body and the broom to block William's exit. He would be unable to escape without making a financial gesture, even though the child's death had nothing to do with him. It was wise to travel without money in these parts and everything he carried had been handed over to his sister Winifred, to help her escape. Searching in his pockets, he found his gold snuff box, a present from the Prince of Wales. He tracked the crenelated ridge with his thumb and hesitated, but the woman's eyes fixed upon the object in his pocket. There was no option but to hand it over. From her sweaty pallor, whatever she sold the snuff box for would be spent in a gin house and not on the children. It was pointless, but he couldn't give up something so valuable without a lecture.

William swept his hand in a gesture that encompassed the cots and the children on the dirt floor.

'This is worth a great deal. Don't sell it too cheap. Promise me you'll spend the money on these little ones.'

The woman snatched the snuff box from William's open hand and stood aside, allowing just enough room to let him pass through the door. Forced to squeeze against her body as he made his escape, he heard her whisper: 'Bugger off.'

From Moorfields to his home in Great Ormond Street was no distance on foot but worlds apart in society. He had hoped to throw off any of King George's men who might have followed him to his secret meeting with Winifred, but after the incident with Miriam, he felt his legs would not carry him. Instead, he flagged down a sedan chair, confident that no chair owner would turn down a gentleman, even one wearing a hairy cloak and without a wig or money. One of the servants could pay his fare once he was safely returned home.

William was proud of Powis House, so much improved after the French ambassador had carelessly allowed it to be destroyed by fire. The refurbishment, paid for by Louis XIV, had created an exquisite space of light and beauty, into which he tramped the smell of blood and faeces on his clothing and shoes. He stripped off to his linen undergarments in the entrance hall, dropping his coat and breeches onto the polished parquet floor, to be carried away and burned on the kitchen fire.

It was July and the fires had been left unlaid. Dressed for dinner, William walked through his empty rooms, picking up objects of value to his ancestors and felt his skin tighten in an unexpected shiver. His solitary meal in the dining room, its furniture sold to him as the epitome of modern French design, gave no comfort. The death of the child, and his near escape from the parish nurse, had been truly ghastly but were a distraction from the real threat of this day. He had assisted Winifred and her family to leave the country in a boat from Gravesend. He felt his bowels grip; this was treason, of the highest order. Beneath his wig, something crawled across his scalp. Perhaps he had been spotted in Moorfields, maybe his sister had already been caught? She would be imprisoned and executed, that was for certain, but what would happen to him? He would face another spell in gaol but not in the comfortable rooms of the Tower of London.

Suddenly, being alone no longer felt tolerable and William called for his carriage to take him to the Cocoa Tree. The coffee house was unusually quiet, and he found a place by the fire, always lit in the evenings to liven the dark rooms. Unlike his contemporary home, this place had comfortable wing chairs and carved furniture, without fashionable gilding or marquetry. The wood was allowed to speak for itself. William sipped his chocolate, watching each time the door swung open, hoping for the welcome smile of a friendly face. The scent of woodsmoke and the crack of shifting logs soothed the tension in his tight chest, his eyelids closed, and gradually he drifted into sleep.

The weight of a hand on his arm shook William awake and he startled. Could this be his arrest?

'Well, well, well, if it's not the Marquess of Powis.'

Still groggy from sleep, William struggled to recognise the grinning expression of Sir William Wyndham, leader of the Tory opposition in the House of Commons. Wyndham sat down in the chair opposite and adjusted his wig.

William tried to keep the irritation he felt from his voice. 'Very funny, you know I haven't been given back my titles. I'm regarded as a commoner.'

'But I heard you'd been over in Wales, restoring the castle gardens and getting the lead mines up and running.'

'The Earl of Rochford found he couldn't afford to run the place, so he sold it back to me.'

Wyndham laughed and slapped his thigh. 'Typical of our bloody monarchy, whether it's Anne or George. They steal a man's titles and pass them on to someone who can't afford to manage the estate. I expect Rochford made a profit though?'

'He certainly did, although we tied him up with so many legal challenges it was no surprise he couldn't afford to go on.' William fell silent and reached for *The Spectator*. He felt better for an old friend's comfortable presence but wasn't ready for gossip.

Wyndham ordered coffee, and taking his cue from William, took his own news-sheet from the rack. The two men settled into a companionable silence.

William tapped on his newspaper and Wyndham looked up, his eyebrows raised.

'What do you think of this fellow John Law? It says here he's setting up a new banking system in Paris, funded in part by his own fortune. He's using bank notes instead of silver or gold.'

'He's a Scot by all accounts,' Wyndham added, 'and a convicted murderer.'

'More fool those who invest in his schemes. It says here that he's caught the interest of the Prince Regent. How did Law make his money?'

'I think it was through financial dealing and gambling, and now he's trying to buy a pardon from our king for the murder, without any luck, I might add.'

'Well, he can get behind me in the queue... for a pardon, I mean.'

The men continued to read in silence until William felt Wyndham's eyes on him and glanced across to encourage his friend to speak his mind.

'Are you well? You seem troubled?' Wyndham asked.

'My sister Winifred's gone... I helped her escape. I've been waiting all day to be arrested but nothing has happened so far. I'm starting to believe she may actually have got away.'

'You know my views,' Wyndham replied. 'She was nothing but trouble, no matter how brave she might have seemed to others. You've suffered from her actions and those of her husband. How many times have you been in prison because of your family's misplaced loyalty?'

William hesitated, trying to find the balance between disloyalty to Winifred and disloyalty to King George. 'You're right. I put up with another spell in the Tower because the king refused to believe I wasn't implicated in her husband's escape, but that was luxury compared to my imprisonment in Newgate. I'm fond of my youngest sister... she was the baby of the family and spent so much of her childhood separated from our mother. My daughter, Mary, reminds me of Winifred. A few, rare women have a quality that might be considered reprehensible in a man, a certain recklessness, which is immensely appealing to me.'

Wyndham frowned. 'I disagree. Women should stay at home, care for their families. If Winifred had done so, she'd still be safe in Scotland. I'm a Jacobite too, remember, but I fight political battles, not with a blunt sword and a useless banner. That's where her husband went wrong. As Earl of Nithsdale, he was a fine young politician and could have gone far.'

'Winifred believed that too,' William answered.

'Forget them. Rebuild your life here.' Wyndham tapped the arm of his chair to make his point. 'Get those titles back and think about your own future. You're lucky to be in favour with the Prince of Wales. Capitalise on it.'

'I've no idea why George Augustus likes me. Perhaps it has something to do with my captivating personality?'

Wyndham laughed. 'Or simply because his father hates you.

Seriously, you'll come to no harm if they believe you helped Winifred escape. The king wanted her gone. He had little appetite for executing a woman.'

'I think I might be better off in Paris, a city where even a murdering Scotsman like John Law can dine with princes. I could openly practise my faith, my daughter Mary lives there with my sister Anne, and in Jacobite France, I'm a duke.'

'If you must run off, what about Ghent? Be with your wife?'

William frowned and fell silent, stroking his finger across his top lip as embers shifted in the grate. Sensing that his companion was waiting, he gathered his thoughts and spoke again.

'There's no feeling between us now. Because of my family's faith and political allegiances, I had to send her off to Flanders for safety, and I was away from home too much, fighting wars or battling to hold on to my estates here in London. My wife made sure our sons had no time for me and I hardly know my other daughters. To be close to Mary, that's what I want. I'm almost sixty, and family becomes more important as you age, don't you agree?'

'Yes, I'm lucky. My wife and I are amicable and our two young boys adore me, but they're only six and three, their judgement isn't sound.'

'I hope you have a little girl one day,' William said. 'Let me tell you what I saw earlier and then you might understand why this city no longer feels tolerable to me.'

Wyndham listened, his fingers steepled under his chin, to William's account of Miriam's death and the neglect of the other abandoned children.

William finished his tale, aware of his clenched fists and the crack in his voice. 'It's 1716, for goodness' sake. These children are in the care of the parish. How can a civilised society treat its children so cruelly?'

'We've recently had a report on this very matter before parliament,' Wyndham replied. 'Legislation won't be far behind.'

A servant staggered towards them with a basket of logs, ready to replenish the fire, and both men stood to allow him space to work. Wyndham laid his large hand upon William's shoulder.

'The problem of the poor will never leave us, old man, especially as they flood into London from the countryside. Each one of us lucky enough to be born into wealth must do what he can. For now, we should rid ourselves of this melancholy. Send your carriage home and come with me to White's. Let's lose our shirts on the gaming tables.'

CHAPTER 2
1717

William's favourite daughter, Mary, closed her eyes and raised her face towards the sun. She tried to ignore her friends, Olive and Fanny, sitting alongside her in the Tuileries Garden and talking, talking, talking. Mary allowed her mind to drift, shutting out their voices, absorbing the fragrant smell of roses and feeling the soft touch of a breeze against her cheeks. She congratulated herself, as she did every day, for living as an unmarried woman in Paris, a modern city where women were free to roam as they pleased, along safe, planned boulevards, or through gardens such as these. How glad she was to have escaped her mother's home, where her sisters whined and pined for a suitable man to marry. Mary had dismissed suitor after suitor. It was unfortunate, but nonetheless true, that she was prettier than her sisters.

If the price of this freedom was to live as companion to an elderly aunt, it was a sacrifice she was only too willing to make. Lady Anne Carrington was her father's sister, widowed for sixteen years, a woman who enjoyed intrigue and imagined herself at the heart of the Jacobite community in France. The Earl of Mar, Secretary of State to the exiled James III was a frequent visitor to their apartment, whispering in corners with Anne and asking her to carry secret information to sympathisers in London. Anne would duly set off in her carriage, unaware that Mar had already sent the information by courier.

Mary had no interest in politics and even less in Jacobite affairs but chose not to draw her aunt's attention to Mar's pointless flattery. Their trips gave her the chance to show off her Paris fashions to the dowdy Jacobite women in London and she would also visit her father, if he wasn't in Wales. She had no intention of ever visiting Wales, and with her father planning to settle in Paris, she might never have to.

Olive and Fanny were talking about men. Both younger than Mary, who was now thirty-one, they were preoccupied with finding titled husbands of singular beauty and great wealth. To fill the tedious interregnum before they married, they were happy to occupy themselves with lovers. Mary found their conversation dull and decided to ask about their work at the Jacobite court. This conversation would also be dull, but less so than their talk about men. Both Olive and Fanny spoke and wrote fluently in English and French, and this gave them access to information they should not have shared.

'They're a sad lot really,' Fanny sighed, 'living on miserable pensions from the Jacobite king's mother, Queen Mary Beatrice. If they can't find an apartment in the palace, they're helped to find furnished rooms in the parish. They're too old to come to the palace, so I help them read and sign documents in their homes.'

Fanny pulled her mouth downwards in an expression of disgust and continued. 'You should see how they live.'

Mary would do no such thing, but it fascinated her to hear the details of other people's lives, especially those less fortunate than herself. Her interest wasn't born out of sympathy but confirmed her belief that wealth was everything.

'But they're all expected to leave,' Olive interrupted. 'Haven't you heard?'

'No... tell me.' Mary leaned across Fanny to hear Olive better. Aunt Anne would be shocked by this news if it were true.

Olive sounded breathless, enjoying a rare chance to share something not already known to Fanny. 'The Prince Regent, our Philippe, has made an agreement with the British government. The entire Jacobite court must go because they're a risk to peace. It's nonsense, they're a risk only to themselves. They have to follow James to Italy, every one of them.'

'But Queen Mary Beatrice is far too old to travel.' Fanny was the only one who had met the elderly Jacobite queen mother and never wasted an opportunity to remind her friends of this.

'No, I've heard she's staying on,' Olive continued, 'but it's pandemonium in the palace. The government has decided to withdraw all their funds, so they'll lose their pensions.'

Mary stood and brushed down her new gown, a style designed to shock women who still preferred to wear the tight, fitted gowns of previous decades. She hoped her friends would notice how the informal, loosely fitted robe swung with her movements.

'Come on,' she said, 'let's talk while we walk.'

Mary never tired of walking since Aunt Anne rarely offered to come with her. Her aunt spent most of the day lolling in her dressing robe, writing letters, or playing cards, since an enthusiasm for food had long outlasted her interest in clothes. The new boulevards of Mary's local area, the Faubourg Saint-Germain, had been laid out with pavements made for strolling arm in arm and designers had styled women's clothes, shoes and even hair, to make walking comfortable.

Fanny linked arms with Mary. 'I don't think you were listening earlier,' she whispered, 'did you hear, I'm having an affair with Richard Cantillon.'

Mary kept her gaze level, trying to hide her surprise. 'I thought he was involved with Olive?'

'We're both Irish,' Fanny added, as if that might make more sense of the arrangement. 'He's from a titled family in Ireland. Anyway,' she lowered her voice, 'Olive's having an affair with the Prince Regent.'

'My goodness, that's unexpected.' Mary glanced over at Olive, who seemed unaware of their attention. 'So that's why she knows so much about royal business. Poor Richard was tossed aside by Olive and you saw your chance. He must be handsome,' Mary commented drily, 'since he's satisfied you both.'

Fanny squeezed Mary's arm. 'I want you to meet him. He's a banker, already very wealthy, and he knows the millionaire, John Law. You'd like him.'

'I doubt it,' Mary sighed, 'but I'll meet him if I must.'

In fact, Mary felt a quiet pleasure to have this chance. Anyone who knew John Law and understood his methods would be worth her notice. One thing was crystal clear, if a woman wanted to stay single, she needed independent wealth.

The three women lifted masks over their faces, hoping to discourage a man who first stared, then paused to bow as they passed. They were not concerned for their reputation, but the mere sight of him and his unwelcome attention made them feel irritated. Increasing their pace, the women gave the merest incline of their heads, and soon the intruder was behind them.

To their departing backs, the man shouted: 'Faro, ladies?'

Now they were interested.

Their guide led them to a townhouse, built in a similar style to every other palace on the boulevard. After the shade of the gardens, their eyes were dazzled by light reflected from the white stone used to construct this avenue. They plunged into the shady interior, lit only by a square of sunlight from an inner courtyard garden, just visible through gates at the end of a tiled passageway. Despite the building's recent construction, the shared entrance already smelt of damp. Their footsteps echoed as they climbed a curving staircase of polished mahogany until they reached an apartment. The man indicated that this was where they would find the game. The women tapped on the door and waited. They felt no fear; playing Faro was illegal and finding a game always meant taking risks.

Inside, the room was even darker than the entrance hall, with drapes pulled across tall windows and only a few lit candelabra on the panelled walls. The room smelt of smouldering wax, stale sweat and women wearing too much perfume. Mary covered her nose with a handkerchief, until she was no longer aware of the odour. As her eyes adjusted to the low light, she saw four tables separated by screens. A few armchairs were scattered around the edge of the room, but the gamers preferred to stand at tables, absorbed by the pace of the dealers. The three women separated, and Mary found her place at a board, laying stakes on three of the thirteen cards facing upwards. She watched the dealer closely, suspicious of his speed, and tried to gauge the success of the other players. Time and again, she won nothing, but the others were doing no better. Something wasn't right.

She left her table and found Olive, and then Fanny, whispering to each in turn. 'The probabilities aren't working out. I'm going to make a scene. You should leave if you don't want to be embarrassed, or worse. I'll meet you at the first café in the Tuileries.'

Mary strolled back, taking time to watch the other three games, so that the cheating dealer was not alerted. Once Olive and Fanny left, she studied the play for five more minutes. It was important to be sure.

Moving back from the game, Mary addressed the room. 'Excuse me, this dealer is cheating.'

The players froze, and then a murmur spread through the room as everyone checked whether they had heard correctly. Two men and one woman called for their cloaks and left.

Mary spoke again, louder this time. 'The dealer at this table is cheating.'

From a door beyond the gaming room, a man appeared and pushed his way through the crowd. He bowed and snatched her elbow, as if offering to escort her from the salon.

'I think you should leave, mademoiselle,' he hissed.

'Lady Mary Herbert,' Mary corrected him, tugging her elbow from his grip.

'I think you should leave, Lady Mary Herbert.'

Another man appeared at her side, and both gripped an arm, hustling and pushing her towards the open door. A third man stepped from behind a screen and neatly blocked their way. Light from the open door fell upon his face and Mary saw he was younger and better dressed than her escorts. Her guards released their hold and stepped back.

'My name is Count Gage,' the stranger said, bowing to Mary before addressing her captors. 'I was watching that table myself and Lady Mary Herbert is correct. Sort this out or we'll make sure that no one who's worth anything will play here again. I will escort Lady Mary Herbert outside.'

On the landing, Mary adjusted tendrils of hair that had slipped from under her cap and Joseph Gage brushed down his coat. Behind them, the door to the salon slammed shut. Gage bowed again and held out his arm, asking permission to escort her home. Mary agreed, only because she wanted a better look at him, in full daylight.

'You may walk with me as far as Aubert's café,' she said, once they were on the boulevard. 'I'm meeting friends there.'

Joseph turned towards her, his long face transformed by a grin that contrived to be both flirtatious and provocative.

'I hope you didn't mind me rescuing you back there.'

'I didn't need rescuing. They'd only have turned me out. After all, I can't report them since I shouldn't have been there either.'

'I'd also noticed the sleight of hand. I was planning to say something discreet to the manager, not shout about it to everyone present.'

'I didn't shout, I spoke with clarity.'

They walked on in silence, Mary studying the man at her side, only just as tall as she was but with a face and body that pleased her.

'Are you a count?' she asked.

'No, I'm afraid not, but people here have started calling me Count Gage, so occasionally I take advantage of the nickname. The Gages are a well-known family from Sussex and Oxfordshire. My older brother inherited the title by renouncing his Catholic faith. Younger sons like me are expected to live on our wits.'

'And how do you live?'

'By playing... gaming. I'm afraid I play for profit, which is not expected from a gentleman. I behave like a hooligan but dress like a nobleman, which confuses most people. I've done well out of gaming; I like to win and expect to keep my earnings. But it's not all about winning on the tables. I'm about to get involved in some pretty big financial deals. I can't say much, not yet.'

Mary thought before answering. 'I'd like to do well from gaming. Will you teach me?'

'Nothing would give me greater pleasure, Lady Mary.'

Joseph paused, his eyes wide with curiosity and interest. 'I feel I know you,' he said. 'I was with your brothers at the Jesuit College of La Flèche. How are William and Edward?'

Mary shrugged. 'I've no idea, we don't keep in touch. They live between my mother's home in Ghent and my father's house in London. I never see them.'

As they neared the café, Mary hesitated.

'Thank you for walking with me, *Count* Gage.'

She smiled to reassure Joseph that her use of his nickname was intended to be gentle, not critical, then lowered her eyes, glancing up at him from under her eyelashes. She had seen Fanny and Olive do this with men and although they looked ridiculous, their lovers always seemed impressed.

'I'd prefer to part here,' she said. 'My friends are renowned gossips, and I don't want them to talk. If you contact my aunt, Lady Anne Carrington, and arrange to call on us, we'd be delighted to make your acquaintance.'

Mary watched Joseph walk away until he turned back to give her an exaggerated bow from the waist. She felt no embarrassment and continued to stare, barely acknowledging his ironic gesture. This man was young, fashionable, and a gamer too. He would suit her very well.

CHAPTER 3
1717

The coach rattled through the featureless countryside of the long and expensive journey from Lille to Saint-Germain-en-Laye. Winifred's mind sifted through her grievances against her husband, who now chose to refer to himself by the family name of Maxwell. The list was long. His borrowing and spending, the loss of their home and family because of his treason and worst of all, his ingratitude. He had enjoyed the luxury of escaping from Britain in relative dignity and comfort while she had endured a storm at sea. Due to her premature labour, the captain had been forced to land in Sluis and she had lost the child she carried. With her companion, Grace, her daughter, Anne, and Anne's nursemaid, Alice, they had turned up at her sister's convent in Bruges, Winifred prone on a farmer's cart, their garments bloodied, ragged, and crusted with vomit and sea salt. She had not been expected to live. Maxwell was ignorant of this. He had not asked, and her pain was still too raw to tell him. If she spoke of her ordeal, the blame and accusations would flow, and she did not have the strength to face the consequences.

The coach dropped the Earl and Countess of Nithsdale at

the inn where they would stay the night. Once settled, they planned to walk to the palace and try to see the queen mother. Their room at the inn was clean but basic, a compromise that Winifred was always happy to accept, but would not suit her husband's expensive tastes.

As Winifred unpacked, Maxwell paced the room, inspecting the bed for bugs and peering into the mean, unlit grate.

'I'll tell the owner to set a fire for later and air this bedding. I'll also ask him to prepare us some dinner. What would you like?'

'Oh, Maxwell, it's July, let's not add the cost of a fire. We can buy some provisions in the town and eat in the room.'

'I refuse to behave like a pauper. We'll sit down to a decent dinner and wine. We should celebrate our gains.'

'All right, do as you please, but no wine,' Winifred said, skirting another pointless argument. Her husband had no idea how difficult this meeting would be. As a young woman, Winifred had been employed as part of the exiled queen's household to assist with the care of the young Prince James, but through some miracle, Mary Beatrice had singled her out as a companion, almost a friend. For him it was all about money, but for Winifred there was trust and respect, both of which might well be lost.

The palace grounds were overgrown and unkempt but here was the empty fountain where Winifred had once sat with the pregnant queen, their fingertips catching drops from the tumbling cascade. Here was the path where Princess Louise fell and grazed her knee. Everywhere, there were uncomfortable memories of Winifred's passion for the grim man at her side, but they had drifted far beyond any hope of sentimental reminiscence.

Inside the courtyard, they reached stairs that led to where the queen mother still had her apartment. A servant reclined on the bottom step, a man barely troubled by his sole occupation, which was to screen Mary Beatrice's few visitors. Winifred gave their names and Maxwell barked at the man to hurry. Although she wore her best gown, it was so darned, she decided to copy the manservant and rest on the bottom step, confident no difference would be made to the fabric. Maxwell paced the courtyard, pausing to adjust his wig and brush down the tails of his coat with a ferocity that Winifred found increasingly irritating. He had failed to notice the disparity in their clothing, that the robe his wife was forced to wear was threadbare, while he wore a well-made wig and tailored coat and breeches, suitable for a courtier in attendance at the exiled royal court in Avignon, a position he had chosen to leave.

The palace was silent, its tiers of windows blank and staring. Insects droned in the heat but there were no birds. Someone had planted flowers in the giant urns that sat on either side of the steps, but they were limp and faded from lack of water. Only weeds grew between the paving slabs where courtiers and ministers had once hurried on royal business.

Winifred waited, feeling the sun burn her neck. At last, the servant returned and pointed at her.

'Only you,' he said.

'Have you no manners?' Maxwell shouted.

Winifred laid a hand on her husband's arm. 'This is my business,' she said. 'I worked for the queen, it's my pension. It's right that I should go alone.'

Winifred paused and pressed her palms against her chest to steady her pattering heart. The drapes around the windows were drawn, but even through the thin light Winifred gasped at the sight of worn gilt on the wall panels and chipped, faded frescoes. She walked towards the queen's bed, a high wooden platform with open curtains falling to the floor from a deep canopy. Winifred trailed her fingers down the walnut frame, finding the memory of carved fruit, cherubs, and animals. This was the same bed where Princess Louise was born, witnessed by her father and other senior men of the court, although she herself had been refused permission to attend. Winifred shivered; the room felt chilled, despite a small fire, and there was a smell of mice and mildewed fabric.

There was nowhere to sit, so Winifred stood by the queen mother's bedside, fidgeting, unable to stop her eyes from searching the features of this old woman, who appeared to be asleep. Where was the person who had terrified her, the one she had grown to love? She was only fifty-nine. How ill she must be, Winifred thought, to look so aged.

Mary Beatrice opened her eyes and stared, her gaze finally settling on the woman at her side.

'Ah, the Countess of Nithsdale,' she said, her voice hoarse and rasping, 'I hope life has treated you well since you scurried off to Scotland.'

Winifred had rehearsed what her first words must be. 'I'm sorry you lost your daughter, dear Princess Louise,' she replied. 'The news did reach us, and we felt great sadness.'

'She's with God, as I will be soon. Death doesn't separate us for long from those we love. You would do well to remember that lesson, Winifred.'

It was as if she had left the room only moments before and not been absent for over thirty years.

'I'm still keen to learn from you, Your Majesty. You taught me so much. Did you hear how I humiliated the British king and why I had to escape to France?'

Mary Beatrice patted the bed. 'We heard something but not the whole story. Why don't you sit down and tell me?'

Winifred perched on the counterpane and recited her tale,

watching the elderly woman's expression change with each twist and turn and hearing her gasp of pleasure at the final moment of triumph.

'You always were impetuous. I saw it from the moment you met that young earl. You rushed into marriage, just as you rushed to save your husband from execution. It's in your nature... rush, rush, rush.'

Winifred struggled to answer this unfair accusation. The queen mother had lost none of her acerbic humour. If her sense of fun was intact, so might her temper be, and this was not something she could risk.

Mary Beatrice interrupted her thoughts. 'And where is Nithsdale now? Is he with my son in Avignon?'

'He was there but he left to meet me at a convent in Bruges. I think the abbess, my sister Lucy, must have written to him. Our young daughter, Anne, has experienced too much loss, too much fear during our pursuit by the king's men. In her lessons at the convent, they found she would not conform. My companion, Grace, and my daughter's nurse resented the menial tasks they were given by the nuns, and we were four extra mouths to feed. It was best that we left but I wasn't ready. I'd lost a child, you see.'

The queen mother reached across the counterpane and took Winifred's hand.

'That pain is like no other. I will pray for you,' she said.

Winifred squeezed the sick woman's thin fingers, remembering the many babies that Mary Beatrice had lost, even before she reached adulthood. The half-light thickened. There was no sound other than the sick woman's shallow, laboured breathing.

Winifred broke the silence. 'We've taken rooms in Lille. Maxwell's downstairs in the courtyard.'

The queen's eyes glistened, alert but feverish.

'Let him stay there; I don't allow men in my apartment. Now what did you really come to see me about, apart from sharing your adventures?'

'Your Majesty, it's about the pension that you generously provide for my past service. It hasn't increased for many years, and since he left James's service, Maxwell has lost many benefits. I wouldn't ask but we simply can't live on such a small allowance.'

The queen mother plucked at the bedding. 'I'm so sorry,' she said at last, 'I can't help.'

This wasn't the reaction Winifred had hoped for.

'But I worked with Princess Louise too, even though I wasn't her governess.'

'I can't fault the care you gave my children, and I'm grateful for the sacrifice you and your family made for me and my late husband, but I don't have any money.'

'How can that be?' Winifred questioned, hating that she couldn't accept the answer and leave. The thought of her husband's anger forced her to press her case.

Mary Beatrice lifted both hands and allowed them to drop back onto the bed, her gesture conveying the futility of any further argument.

'You know more than anyone else that my relationship with the French king, Louis, was exceptional and the Jacobite court would not have survived in France without his generosity. Since his death, it's all gone. The new king is a child and the Regent's priority is peace with Great Britain. My own pension from the French Government has gone, so those directly supported by me will lose everything. Philippe has promised I won't starve. I'm told his mother wouldn't allow anything else, thank goodness.'

'Are you saying my pension will cease?' Winifred felt her stomach turn to liquid. This couldn't be true.

'That is indeed what I'm saying. The small amount you had this month is the last payment. It's finished.'

A tight band wrapped itself around her skull. 'I came to ask for an increase and I'm going away with nothing, not even what I had before. That is a shock.'

When the queen mother did not reply, she spoke again, her voice trembling: 'Is there any chance I could join your household and help care for you?'

Mary Beatrice stared at Winifred. 'I have all the staff I need but thank you,' she said, her breathing quickening.

Winifred knew she must leave. This conversation had been too much, had deprived a sick woman of precious reserves of energy. She must allow Mary Beatrice to sleep. If she died, she would not be able to forgive herself, or Maxwell.

'Tell your husband he must go back to Avignon at once,' Mary Beatrice gasped. 'The royal court is on its way to Italy. I'll write to my son and ask him to find Maxwell a post, but he must hurry, before every job is taken.'

'Thank you, Your Majesty, thank you. You will write to the king tonight?'

'Of course... I want to help, but first I must rest.' The queen mother lay back against her bolster and closed her eyes. 'That man of yours needs to work,' she whispered. '*He* should provide for his family.'

Maxwell had been gone for about six weeks, taking the queen mother's advice to leave their home in Lille immediately and join the wandering Jacobite court in Pesaro. Money had to be found to hire a horse and provide sustenance for his journey and Winifred was left with nothing. Once Anne was in bed, she asked Grace and Alice to join her at the fireside.

'I'm afraid we cannot stay here,' she said. 'We're owing a month's rent and I will have to sell my bridal jewellery to pay. They're the last few tokens I possess of any value.'

From attending to the fire, Grace looked up at Winifred, the deep line between her eyebrows emphasised by shadows. 'But that's so sad to part with those.'

Winifred shook her head. 'There's no alternative, we must live. Besides, what do those jewels mean to me now?'

Grace glanced at Alice and back towards Winifred, giving a brief shake of her head. Winifred looked over at Alice, who stared straight ahead, as if she had heard nothing of her employer's indiscretion.

'Where will we go?' Grace asked. 'Should we find less expensive rooms in Lille?'

Winifred paused before answering, afraid of trespassing once again upon Grace's view of what was suitable for Alice to know but decided to favour truth over decorum.

'My husband took these rooms having left the employ of the Jacobite court, without any other source of income except my pension, which has now ended. The cost was always beyond our means, a decision typical of the earl. I'm sure my honesty is no surprise to either of you. Now he has gone, we can live where we choose. There might well be somewhere suitable here in Lille, but I have a better idea...'

Alice clapped her hands. 'I think I can guess. We should go to La Flèche, in France, where Will is at school...'

'What a wonderful idea,' Grace interrupted. 'How many years can have passed since we last saw Will?'

'Too many for any mother to be separated from her son,' Winifred said, enjoying the approval of her companions. 'It is settled. We will all move to France.'

$\approx$

Winifred found two simple rooms in La Flèche overlooking a street where local people shopped, met their neighbours to gossip, or sat on stone benches under street trees already tinged with the burned ochre of early autumn. In one room they slept, Anne and Alice sharing one bed and Grace and Winifred sharing the other. The second room had a plain fireplace with a mirror above, panelled cupboards and an oak table with four chairs. In this room, they lived.

The women kept a low profile in the town. Winifred gave Anne lessons at home and earned money by writing letters for the townspeople, introducing herself as Winifred Herbert. Grace and Alice took jobs at the Jesuit college where Will was a student, Grace in the kitchen and Alice in the laundry. They didn't complain about the work, as they had at the convent, because this time they were being paid. Any money, no matter how pitiful, made the difference between having food or missing another meal.

Will was almost eighteen, very nearly a man, finding his future amongst the sons of British peers of Catholic faith. They did not shame him by visiting the college, given their reduced circumstances, but he had been an occasional visitor.

Winifred turned to the sound of the door opening. Her daughter cupped a fresh loaf to her chest and held out a letter. Anne dropped the bread onto the table and passed the letter to her mother. 'This might be news from my father.'

Winifred passed it back. 'You read it to me. It can be your practice for today.'

Anne tore the seal and frowned as she scanned Maxwell's words, his rushed handwriting a test for her seven-year-old reading skills.

'He's in Ur... Urb...'

'Urbino,' Winifred prompted and nodded at her daughter to continue.

'He can't send us any money because he has to pay for his loggings.'

'Lodgings. Carry on, Anne, you're doing well.'

Anne looked at her mother, her expression wary. 'He wants to come home.'

'What was that?' Winifred snatched the letter from the child's hand and ferociously read the offending paragraph, disregarding the fragrant loaf and the hunger in her belly. She reached for paper, pen and ink and scratched out a reply, impressing upon her husband that his only hope of earning a respectable income was to stay near James and make himself useful. To soften her words, she suggested that if the king took a bride, and there were children, she would offer to be their governess. Until then, they were better to live apart.

Sealing the letter, Winifred passed it to Anne with a coin, shooing the child with a flap of her hand.

'Take this to the courier. Be quick.'

Anne gave the bread one wistful glance and reluctantly moved towards the door.

Winifred laughed and said: 'Don't worry, you'll be back soon. Your meal will be waiting.'

Heavy footsteps thumped on the stairs, followed by insistent banging on the door. The women paused from their repair of worn linen shifts by candlelight, hardly daring to breathe, eyes searching each other's faces for reassurance. All three had known the anger of strangers in Scotland, shared memories of being vulnerable and unprotected from a mob.

Winifred whispered to Grace and Alice, asking them to hide with Anne. Only when she heard the heavy oak trunk dragged across the inside of the bedroom door, did she dare to answer, pretending to call out for her husband, 'Maxwell, who is there?'

The hammering continued and she crept to the door, her heart pounding so hard her throat hurt.

In a pause between blows, she whispered, 'What do you want?'

'It's John Dalrymple, the Earl of Stair.'

'I don't know who you are. I can't let you in.' This was a lie. Winifred knew exactly who Stair was; the most powerful British man in France, envoy to King George and reputed to be the most handsome man in Paris. She pressed her back against the door, feeling her breath settle. This was not a violent mob, out of control, but an ambassador for the British government. He would not harm them.

'Let me in,' Stair bellowed from the other side of the door. 'I'm here on behalf of the Earl of Mar.'

Winifred turned the key and slid the two bolts Grace had recently fitted. A tall man, one who was accustomed to using his height to intimidate, pushed his way past her, followed by two guards.

'They must stay outside,' Winifred commanded. 'I will only talk to you.'

'They'll leave after they've searched. How many rooms?'

'Just one other. There are two women in there,' Winifred indicated the bedroom with a tip of her head, 'and one little girl.'

The guards easily forced the chest back. Winifred heard Anne cry and words of comfort murmured by Alice. The men emerged from the bedroom after less than a minute, followed by Grace, wrapped in her nightgown and robe.

'Win, do you want me to stay with you?' Winifred nodded and reached for Grace's hand.

Stair instructed his men to remain outside the apartment

and pulled a chair towards himself, straddling backwards on the seat, as if mounting a horse. Winifred and Grace remained standing, Winifred staring at the rough beams on the ceiling, using the trick of imagining the person she feared as vulnerable, emptying their bowels or vomiting in public. As for this intruder, the Earl of Stair, she lowered her gaze and searched his pale, hooded eyes and high, arched brows for any remnant of the eight-year-old boy who had accidentally killed his older brother and been banished from his home. It was a cautionary tale often repeated to small boys in Scotland, who might be tempted to handle their father's pistols.

With a wide sweep of his arm, Stair indicated the other chairs, exposing lace cuffs that belied the military cut of his jacket. 'Sit, sit, for goodness' sake, I mean you no harm.'

Winifred and Grace lifted their mending from the seats and sat down.

'Now,' Stair continued, looking around with mock concern, 'where is that traitor, the Earl of Nithsdale? I heard you call his name.'

'You are mistaken. He's in Urbino with the rest of James's court.'

'I knew that... just wanted to check he hadn't sneaked back to France. The thing is, Lady Nithsdale, neither you, nor your husband, is welcome here. My advice to you is to move on, join him in Urbino.'

'I understand your job is to protect British interests,' Winifred replied, 'but we're welcome in Jacobite circles, of which there are many in Paris. I have the protection of Queen Mary Beatrice.'

Stair gave a yelp of mocking laughter. 'Ha... I'm sorry to disappoint you, but stories about you sniffing around the queen for money have not been well-received. You're right, those of a Jacobite persuasion are unfortunately tolerated in France, but you two are different. Your presence is a thorn in the relationship between the Regent and King George. It was the Earl of Mar himself who tipped me off.'

'But the Earl of Nithsdale fought with Mar's army at Preston, less than two years ago,' Grace protested. 'Mar is a disloyal turncoat. He can't be trusted.'

Stair nodded, acknowledging Grace's words. 'True, but he's a useful source of information, as turncoats usually are. I know everything that happens in the Jacobite camp, my spies cost me almost my entire budget. I live amongst them, eat with them, game with them. Almost everyone you know is in my pay.'

He turned back towards Winifred, spreading his legs wide to show off firm thighs wrapped in tight breeches. 'Two years is a long time. There's a new king in France, only five years old, who hasn't even learned to say the word Jacobite. Neither Britain nor France can afford any more insurrection, plotting or uprisings. My advice to you all is... leave.'

Winifred raised herself to speak. She had heard enough and wanted to face down this bully.

'I will not leave,' she said. 'I can't, not right now. My son is still at school here.'

Stair swung his leg over the chair and stood to tower over the women.

'I have warned you, Lady Nithsdale, and can do no more. Whatever happens, don't allow your husband to return. While King George despises you, because you made a fool of him, those of us better versed in politics understand that the Earl of Nithsdale is the real threat. Be careful who you trust. Those titled Jacobite acolytes who hang around Faubourg Saint-Germain only want to gamble, sleep with each other, and indulge in maudlin tales of past glories. They'll betray you before you're out of their door.'

Stair bowed, managing to convey disrespect in his exaggerated gesture. He slammed the door and the vacuum he left behind rang with the echo of his domineering presence. The women sat in silence, knowing what each other was thinking but too afraid to speak the words.

Grace placed her hand on Winifred's arm and gripped her wrist. 'What will we do, Win?'

Winifred sighed and shook her head, raising her other hand to cover her lips. 'Stair spoke the truth. We're not safe here. It won't be long before others come looking for me, people who do not share the envoy's principle of abiding by the law.'

'We have to run... again?'

Winifred lowered her head and nodded. 'I'm afraid so.'

The next morning, Winifred sent a courier with a note for Will, asking him to visit her as soon as possible. She sat with Anne at their table, trying to teach the child some simple arithmetic using buttons but her attention drifted to the sounds from the street below, carried through the open window. Living near her son, in a safe, dull little town like La Flèche, had held out the possibility of an ordinary life. Money, fine dresses, or rich food were of no value compared to the chance of raising her own children. Political ambition was worthless compared to freedom.

'Mother, Mother.' Anne touched her cheek. 'You're not looking; I've done the sum.'

Winifred dragged her attention back to the buttons laid out in rows across the table.

'Well done, Anne, that's correct.'

The child frowned. 'What are you thinking about?'

'Nothing, my darling, I'm listening out for your brother, that's all.'

There was a tap at the door and Winifred smiled. 'And here he is!' she said.

Will made a face at his sister, as he eased his tall, ungainly body through the narrow door. Hoping to be chased, Anne giggled and ran away into her bedroom. Winifred poured her a cup of milk and asked the child to stay where she was. Ignoring Anne's wails of frustration, she firmly closed the door on her daughter.

'Sit down, Will. We haven't long to speak. Anne is not the most obedient of children; she won't stay in there for long.'

Winifred turned her back and poured her son some ale. 'I must leave La Flèche, very soon. The Earl of Stair was here last night. He warned us we're in danger.'

Will was silent and she turned around to face him, surprised to see his head bent, masking flushed cheeks.

'What's the matter?' she asked.

'I know I should protest. I should beg you to stay, but I can't. You must go. It is right.'

Winifred felt his words like a blow to the chest.

'But we've only just found each other again. You're becoming a friend to Anne. I'd no idea you felt like this. Is it our poverty? Are you ashamed of us?'

'I am ashamed of you, Mother, but not because you are poor. My friends at the college say that many good men died, some members of their own families, because you stopped my father's execution. I am embarrassed to be known as your son. It would be best for me if you followed Stair's advice.'

Winifred swallowed, feeling the injustice burn in her temples. Would she be forever haunted by this untrue accusation, made even more painful when repeated by her own child? When she spoke, her voice was calm but empty of warmth.

'I am grateful for your honesty, although I cannot accept your argument. We will be gone, very soon. I intend to join your father in Urbino and will write to you from there. Please leave me alone... right now.'

Will stood to bow to his mother, awkward, hesitating, his small movements betraying his uncertainty whether he should hug her. Seeing her son's conflict, Winifred felt a rush with love and drew his head into her neck, feeling his cheek damp against hers.

'My beloved child,' she whispered. 'Live well, in peace and safety. Be loyal to your family. Never try to be a hero.'

Winifred steered Will to the door, and without allowing him to turn back, closed it behind her. She heard a faint sound, as if he had pressed his brow against the wood, followed by his footsteps descending the staircase. Tonight, he would mask his sorrow and laugh with his friends but once alone, sadness would crowd him. What had happened between them was the worst any mother could experience, short of the death of a child but for her son, it was for the best. Any pain he felt now would slowly turn to relief as he grew into adulthood and found a life free from his family's reputation. She breathed deeply and pressed her fingers into the hollow between the corner of her eyes and the bridge of her nose. Anne should be freed from her room. There was a lesson to finish. She must not cry.

CHAPTER 4
1717

It was early afternoon, on a misty December day. Wisps of smoke were the only evidence that people still lived on the open scrubland separating the new developments towards Leicester Fields. All the northern side of Leicester Square was occupied by the magnificent Leicester House, and William's carriage first entered the gates through the Prince of Wales's formal gardens, before arriving at the gilded entrance to the palace itself.

His plans to leave Britain had been slow to materialise. Finding a reliable tenant for Powis House had not been easy. There had also been trouble with his lead mines in Montgomeryshire; the tenant farmers objected to the fumes and effluent and were refusing the miners access to their land. He'd had to spend most of the year in Wales but was now ready to leave.

William's relationship with the Prince of Wales was friendly but formal, as befitted a future king and his subject. He was kept waiting on an uncomfortable chair in an anteroom, wondering whether his plain brown wool coat and old-fashioned, high-parted wig would make him look shabby next to the prince. A servant led him through tall, double-panelled doors to a fine room, full of light, where George Augustus waited for him at a table set with two glasses and a decanter of wine.

George rose in greeting and William bowed. The prince wore a fine grey suit, embellished with silver thread around the buttons and cuffs, matching the intricate pattern on his waistcoat. He felt dowdy by comparison.

'Ah, Powis... at last. Where have you been? We've missed you at our gatherings.' The Prince of Wales gestured to a chair and nodded to the servant to pour the wine.

William cleared his throat and took a sip, touching his lips before speaking. The Prince of Wales dismissed the servant with a flick of his hand.

'I've been in Wales, Your Majesty, settling the business. I'm planning to leave for France in January, so I've had to make sure my estate managers are sound.'

George Augustus echoed William's words: 'You're leaving?'

'My mind is made up, but first I need to check a couple of things with you.'

'Ask away.'

'Nothing happened after I helped my sister flee. Either the king doesn't know it was me who gave her assistance, or he doesn't care.'

'It's the latter,' George replied. 'He wasn't pleased but you solved a problem for him. He was persuaded to let the matter drop, by me and many others.'

William tilted his head. 'Thank you, Your Majesty, but might I be arrested at the port when I try to leave? Will I be allowed to return to this country?'

'It's unlikely you'll be stopped. Most sensible people have forgotten all about it. There's too much going on, what with splits in government and your lot plotting to restore the

Pretender to the throne, publicly brawling in the streets with the Whigs.'

William stared at the leg of the fine mahogany table before him, aware he must control his frustration. He weighed his words before speaking.

'Your Majesty, for clarification, what do you mean by my lot?'

George squinted at William and shifted in his seat. 'Jacobites, of course. Look at those riots last year. Five men executed.'

William hesitated. 'I'm from a Jacobite family, Your Majesty, but I'm no Jacobite myself. I thought you knew that. I have no interest in helping to restore an exiled Stuart to the throne.'

'Then why not stay in London? Take the oaths and renounce your faith.'

'I'm a Catholic, Your Majesty, but not a Jacobite, they're not the same thing. I can't renounce my faith. That's why I'm leaving, or at least one of many reasons. Will I be allowed back into the country?'

'When you return, let's hope my father is dead and I'm king. I can't promise more I'm afraid. I've had a serious falling out with the old man.'

A silence followed, and to his horror, William realised that the Prince of Wales was crying. He felt panicked, wanting to put his hand on the young man's arm, but terrified by a breach of etiquette. Instead, he pretended to admire the room, and found himself taking an unexpected interest in the moulding on the wall panels. French in style, he thought... the use of gold leaf was the clue... overdone as usual. He heard George give up the effort of stifling his tears, until he openly sobbed, like a child.

William waited until the prince had gained control and turned his head to look at him, his gaze mirroring his genuine concern.

'My lord, what has happened? Is it Lady Caroline or the baby prince?'

George shook his head. 'It's the girls. When we were forced to move here after my quarrel with my father he wouldn't let our children leave Saint James's Palace. My three little daughters are living with their grandparents, and we're forbidden to see them.'

'But that's so cruel. Why would he do such a thing?'

'Because he can.' George spat out the words. 'Because he's a bitter old man.'

Both men fell silent, William's mind inspecting the paradox of modern society. Those who wanted children lost many at birth or rarely saw them, while those who didn't want children had too many and abandoned them on the streets. He felt great sadness for George Augustus and his wife, who had adored their children.

'I pray that you, and the king, can resolve this,' he said. 'I cannot imagine how you can bear such a separation. Your quarrel with your father sounds like one of passion, so not too far removed from love. Perhaps he has taken those you love because he wants you to love him more, but he despairs it will never happen. You should make the first move.'

The Prince of Wales stared at William, his eyes red and glistening as he fought back more tears.

'You're the only man I know, Powis, that I have been able to speak to freely about my girls being stolen from us. You're a man of good advice and a sound heart and I will miss you.'

William's journey back to Powis House was in darkness. The enclosed carriage smelt of old leather and something else, not so pleasant, which he suspected was many years of his body odour. Within minutes the scent was lost in familiarity, and his thoughts drifted to the advice he had given the Prince of Wales. He weighed up his own attempt at fatherhood and wondered if resentment at his father, who had always put faith and politics above his family, had poisoned his chance of successful parenting. Now, of his six children, only Mary spoke to him.

Thank goodness his role in Winifred's escape had been forgotten, if not forgiven. It was a relief to learn from her last letter that the mysterious John Law had paid all the debts of the exiled queen mother. Whatever Law's motives, this meant that the pensions of former ladies of the bedchamber had been restored, including Winifred's. He wished he could help his youngest sister with money, but he had no income except for the small amounts he could cream off the estate. Like most, he survived on an ocean of debt and if he was to leave anything to his sons, he had to maximise his profits. That meant abandoning his London home and Powis Castle into the care of capable employees. With reassurance from George Augustus about his personal safety, the last piece of the puzzle was in place. He would now leave for France and see his beloved Mary.

Mary curled her naked body against Joseph's warm back. He was asleep, making soft grunting sounds in his throat. She was beginning to feel cool, since the fire had burned low, and the drapes were no defence against the early hours of a December morning. She lifted her foot and rested it on Joseph's thigh, causing him to murmur, before his breath settled back into the rhythm of sleep. Mary ran her hand across his scalp, freed from his wig, feeling the close-shaved stubble against her palm. Closing her eyes she tried to doze but sleeping with another body was hard. Of course, she had shared beds with her sisters, but Joseph was different. The imbalance of weight and temperature was the first hurdle, but then there were smells and sounds she did not find agreeable.

Mary rolled onto her back and pulled the heavy covers across them both. It would soon be time to leave. Her aunt had been charmed by Joseph, who was surprisingly happy to spend time playing cards with an elderly woman. Anne soon trusted him to keep her niece safe late at night when the pair trawled the gaming houses, and since they weren't expected back until two or three o'clock in the morning, they could comfortably steal a few hours at Joseph's house. It wasn't as if there was any more money to earn. By midnight, most gaming houses showed them the door, their losses already too great, and it was becoming hard to find establishments who would admit them at all.

Far greater than the pleasure Joseph gave her, and he was as expert a lover as he was a gamer, Mary found satisfaction in thinking about the money she had won, stored in the lockable console in her bedroom. But how could she capitalise on this and join the world of serious finance, where she belonged?

Joseph stirred and rolled towards her, using one finger to lift a strand of loose hair that had fallen across her cheek. His eyes roamed over her face and he smiled, not a smile of passion but one that was tender and loving. Mary smiled back, trying to copy Joseph's expression.

'I suppose we'd better dress,' he said and sighed. 'And I'll take you back.'

One thing that Mary did appreciate about Joseph was that he insisted on accompanying her home. If they had been in her bed, instead of his, she knew she would roll over under the warm covers and allow him to leave on his own.

As they dressed, so familiar there was no longer any need to steal glances at each other's naked bodies, Mary grasped at a thought that had troubled her for weeks.

'Joseph, I need to properly understand how John Law's banking system works. Tell me again.'

He sat down on the edge of the bed to pull on his breeches and stockings and Mary waited, seeing he was thinking about her question.

'At present we exchange goods for coins, whether you're buying a loaf of bread or a mansion, and the coins are kept under your bed or in a bank. John Law thinks that we should write a note for the bread or whatever. The baker pays the carpenter with a note, the carpenter pays the farmer with a note, we all pay our taxes with notes. The notes become as valuable as coins.'

'Surely there must be enough coins in the bank to back up the notes?' Mary asked.

'Exactly. Or at least, the buyer promises there is enough. Someone might pass a note based on income they're expecting.'

Mary joined Joseph on the bed to pull up her stockings. 'The Prince Regent is backing this? It seems risky to me.'

'Law has created his own bank, secured by his personal fortune, and he's willing to bankroll the Regent. I think Philippe sees him as a magician who might make our national debt disappear. Law's idea is to get trade flowing again by providing cheap money for farmers, tradesmen and merchants. Once men are working, they're paying taxes. He's willing to invest his own money to make this happen. I agree it's risky but it's also ingenious.'

'How will this system affect people like us?' Mary said.

'It's not just a new model of banking and finance, he plans to exploit our territories in Louisiana. Both he and the Regent have invested a large amount of their own money in this venture and those owed money by the government have been paid back in shares. It's a clever plan.'

Mary paused in her dressing and turned fully around on the bed to face Joseph.

'I thought Louisiana was over. These days, no one seems interested in colonies, at least no one I talk to.'

Joseph picked up his wig from the floor and stood to check in the mirror whether his newly fashionable locks, tied at the ends, were hanging correctly over his shoulders and down his back.

'I don't mean to be critical of your friends,' Joseph said, grinning at Mary's reflection in the mirror, 'but I can't imagine that finance is their first choice of conversation. I thought you spent your time gossiping about other people.'

Mary picked up her shoe and threw it at Joseph.

'Be serious,' she shouted, 'I want to understand.'

The shoe glanced against the mirror, just above Joseph's shoulder. He bent to retrieve it, and pretending to study its construction, turned sharply, his arm raised, as if to hurl it back at Mary. She laughed, ducked, and hid behind the drapes.

Joseph tossed Mary's shoe onto the bed and continued his explanation. 'He wants to encourage people to invest by selling shares cheaply. It might work. I'm wondering if I should get involved.'

Mary pushed on her shoes and stood next to Joseph to check her clothes in the huge mirror, framed by gilt moulding, which filled one entire wall of the bedroom. She lifted the lace streamers trailing from her cap and tied them onto the crown.

'So, you've met him, this John Law?' she asked.

'Law and his wife, Katherine. She chooses to mix with the Jacobite women in Faubourg Saint-Germain and knows your friend Fanny, so you might meet her too.'

'I'd rather meet her husband.' Mary caught Joseph's eye in

the mirror, checking whether her intent may have been misunderstood.

'That's unlikely. He's too busy for social meetings with anyone who does not have significant influence, but I've heard he easily finds the time for those connected to the royal family.'

Joseph took both of Mary's hands in his, turning her around to face him. 'I have an ambition that we'll be like the Laws someday. They're so rich and fashionable but still in love, with two beautiful children. That could be us, once we're—'

'Once we're what?' Mary interrupted.

'Married of course. I love you and hope that one day you'll be my wife.'

'I love you too,' Mary said, uncertain whether this was true, 'but I'm not ready to marry or have children. If you want to take a wife, you must look elsewhere. It's your choice whether you decide to wait for me. I cannot promise that I will ever change my mind.'

Mary had no intention of prolonging this awkward conversation. She reminded Joseph that it was time to leave, hustling him out of the bedroom and down the staircase, only to pause in the entrance hall to collect her outdoor clothes. A solitary servant, one who had lost the household lottery to see Lady Herbert from the premises, stifled a yawn as he passed Mary her gloves. She noticed Joseph frown at his servant's behaviour but knew he would not make a scene. From his solemn expression, her lover was trying to manage hurt feelings far beyond the importance of any minor breach of etiquette.

Their carriage was already waiting, the horses venting hot steam into the frost and tossing their heads against the restriction of the bridles. The couple journeyed in silence, sitting far apart, unlike on previous nights when she had rested her head on Joseph's shoulder and enjoyed lingering kisses in the dark. Mary felt satisfied that her behaviour had been fair. Joseph had let himself down by selfishly raising the matter of marriage; if he felt rejected, that simply wasn't her responsibility.

She watched her adopted city through the carriage window, the familiar route made magical by the glow of street lighting, cloaked in a veil of fog. She felt something like love for Paris but that wasn't what she felt for Joseph. She enjoyed his company, and he was useful to her, but a marriage had to be a contract where there was mutual gain. Unlike many of the women here, whose titles were only recognised in Jacobite circles, she was a member of the British aristocracy and had no need of a title. She wasn't wealthy yet, but she was perfectly capable of making money on her own and would never demean herself by marrying for money. As for children, she had no interest. They made their mothers fat, and the few she had been unlucky enough to meet had bored her with their endless demands. Marriage was important for women like Olive and Fanny, but she was different. Lady Mary Herbert had other plans.

CHAPTER 5

1718

T t was early June and Mary, Olive and Fanny drank coffee in the garden of Aubert's, under the shade of a trellis smothered with swags of early roses. Sitting out of the sun mattered, not only for their complexions but also because they were dressed in black. Queen Mary Beatrice had died the month before and since both Olive and Fanny worked at the palace of Saint-Germain, dark fabrics were expected. The French court was also in mourning, Olive announced, but only because the Regent's mother had insisted. Aunt Anne had dressed for mourning, in a gown obviously made in London sometime last century, so Mary decided that if it was expected to wear black, a new gown was essential. She glanced down at her sleeves, embroidered in fine silver thread, and if she hadn't been so hot, might have felt more pleased with the effect.

Richard Cantillon was with them, being fussed over by Fanny. Joseph was there too, watching her across the table. They had seen little of each other since that awkward moment before Christmas and Mary had missed him, finding the days long and empty without their salon visits and the hours in his bed. From the way Joseph looked at her she guessed he still struggled with her rejection. He turned away whenever their eyes met.

'Who made your gown, Mary?' Olive asked. 'It's exquisite.'

'It's from Magoulet's new shop on rue Saint-Benoit,' Mary replied. 'You should go... the fabrics and threads are laid out for inspection and there are comfortable chairs where customers can wait. The assistants bring chocolate in the most delicate cups.'

Olive laughed. 'Sounds like it's worth a visit, even if I don't need a new gown.'

Mary turned to Fanny. 'How are the residents of Saint-Germain coping with their loss?'

'It's chaotic. There are rumours circulating that most of them will lose their pensions for the second time. With the queen mother gone, the Regent will want to shut down the palace, so they'll lose their homes too—'

Richard Cantillon interrupted his lover. 'That's unlikely, Fanny, don't exaggerate. I've already explained that John Law agreed to help the Prince Regent by bankrolling Mary Beatrice's court, and he won't stop paying just because she's dead.'

Everyone turned to stare at Richard, except for Fanny, who looked down at her hands. It was the first time Fanny had brought her lover to meet her friends and Mary knew she would not have enjoyed a public rebuke. The trouble with Fanny was that she never listened. Perhaps Richard might show more respect for a woman who was truly interested in his expertise?

'Richard, as a banker, what is your opinion of John Law?' Mary asked. Joseph frowned at her, as if, by asking this question, she had trespassed into an area that was not her concern.

'I'm keeping an open mind...' Richard paused, waiting to gauge the reaction of his audience before he continued. 'As someone with experience in finance, I'm intrigued by his motives. He's supporting the Regent by clearing government debts, so he's obviously in favour at court, but I think he's using much of his own money. I suspect his intention is for his private bank to become the national bank of France.

Fanny put a hand on his arm. 'Tell them about the Mississippi Company.'

Mary sat back, aware of the drone of insects above their heads. Everyone fell silent, keen to hear what Richard had to say.

'He's bought up as many trading companies in Louisiana as he can and merged them. Everyone's calling it the Mississippi Company, but Law prefers the title Company of the West. It's financed the same way as his bank, with Law injecting most of the funds at present.'

'Richard's bought shares.' Fanny smiled broadly, sounding like a proud parent.

Richard leaned forward, as if about to share something confidential, and glanced at Joseph, trying to draw the other man into the conversation. 'Shall I tell them the rest?'

Mary noticed Joseph's cheeks flush. He hadn't expected to reveal this news, at least not right now.

Cantillon didn't wait for Joseph to reply. 'Gage and I are in discussion with John Law to enter a partnership, one that will encourage settlement in the colonies. We're not sure it will happen.' Richard tapped the side of his nose. 'So don't breathe a word to anyone.'

No one spoke, as if their vow of silence had already begun, but Mary could not hold back.

'Should we be investing too?'

Richard frowned. 'My dear, I'm not your financial advisor,' he replied, looking over her shoulder instead of into her eyes. 'If you need an answer to that question, visit me at my offices.'

Mary felt as if a hand had squeezed the back of her neck. She rose, her movements sudden. A strange sensation, as if her head was floating above her body, forced her to clasp the table and their coffee spilled into the saucers.

'Are you well?' Olive asked, reaching out for her elbow. Mary nodded, spreading her parasol to demonstrate that for her, this meeting with Richard Cantillon was over. She glared at Joseph, who remained seated.

'I intend to stroll in the Tuileries before lunch,' she said, holding Joseph's gaze. He understood, gathering his cane and three-cornered hat, before bowing to Olive and Fanny. Olive also left, claiming an urgent appointment, leaving Richard and his lover alone to enjoy the privacy of the bower.

They walked on alone, Mary spinning her parasol above her head in a manner she hoped would display her irritation. Joseph walked alongside her, silent.

'Richard Cantillon is an Irish peasant,' Mary hissed, glancing at Joseph for a reaction.

'That's not true. He's from an ancient and respected Irish family.'

'He was rude to me. He had no right to treat me as if I was a... a nobody.'

'To be fair, you did ask him for specific financial advice. He was trying to enjoy coffee with friends, not work.'

'Why are you defending him? Is it because you're now in his pocket, investing in the Mississippi Company? You should have told me. I might want to invest too.'

'It wasn't any of your business. You made your feelings about me perfectly clear.'

'About marriage, yes,' Mary said, 'but nothing else. We were the very best of lovers, why can't we be the very best of business partners?'

Joseph sat down on a nearby bench, shading his eyes with his hand.

'Are you serious?'

'Of course I'm serious. If you haven't met anyone else, I would be more than happy to be by your side, in every possible way, except as your wife.'

Joseph brushed the skirts of his coat, and linked his arm through Mary's. 'Then my carriage will call for you tonight at nine. I've found the most elegant and discreet club. It will suit you well.'

Mary turned towards Joseph and squeezed the crook of his arm between hers. 'Good, that's settled. Here's to our ambition... we'll be as rich as Richard Cantillon, as famous as John and Katherine Law and ignored by no one.'

They stood up and walked on, stopping to watch other couples, trying to guess whether they knew who they were and sharing gossip about those they recognised.

'And later, Joseph, after the club,' Mary said, 'does our business plan include later?'

'Of course, with your consent our evening will not end at the card tables. Speaking for myself, I can't wait.' Joseph did not turn to face her, but Mary saw from the curve of his lips that he was smiling.

Lady Anne Carrington could not wait to share her news, learned at her weekly card game with three other Jacobite matrons. One of these women was Anne's eldest sister Frances, Countess of Seaforth, stranded in Paris after her husband's early death. Mary had never met this aunt and had no intention of doing so. One widowed aunt was enough.

Puffing with excitement, Anne sounded so breathless that

Mary and a maid had to help her squeeze into one of their generous, overstuffed armchairs before she could speak. The story slowly emerged, between sharp intakes of breath and much panting, but eventually, Mary understood that the Jacobite king, the exiled James III, had found a suitable bride at last – Maria Klementyna Sobieska. Not only was she rich and pretty but she was royalty, the youngest daughter of the king of Poland. But would you believe it? Here, Anne rolled her eyes for effect, James's bad luck with women had struck again. On her way to join her future husband for the wedding, Klementyna had been kidnapped and was being held prisoner in the castle at Innsbruck. She might never escape, and everyone was wondering who might take her place, since James had to marry. With the weight of this dilemma shared, Anne fell asleep, snoring loudly.

Mary found the ivory box containing pieces for the game Reversino, a sweet gift from Joseph to her aunt, and tipped the tiles onto a card table. She had no focus, picking up the pieces, prettily decorated with birds and flowers – not her taste at all, but Anne loved them – and placing them down in rows. Instead of practising her moves, she thought about Klementyna. Perhaps the princess had engineered her own imprisonment and was relieved to have escaped an arranged marriage with a much older man. Everyone knew that James yearned only for his cousin, and poor Klementyna would not have been ignorant of this. A simple idea took hold, one that at first seemed ridiculous and quite impossible, but the more she tried to push the thought away the more real and practical it became. Who would, indeed, take Klementyna's place? Mary asked a servant to ready the coach and fetch her cloak.

The Duke of Powis was asleep. He preferred to rest after lunch, not entertain visitors, and resented being interrupted mid-snore and without his wig. Both failings mattered, even though the visitor was only his daughter.

'Dearest, it is lovely to see you, but I wish you had waited until I was ready.'

Mary sat in a gilt chair on the other side of the fireplace, held out for her by a servant. 'They asked me to wait, but this is too important.'

'Claude, bring us some wine and a few more logs,' William instructed the man.

Once the fire was blazing, candles lit around the room and the table between them covered with a cloth to protect the veneer from their wine glasses, William asked Mary what on earth troubled her that couldn't wait until morning.

'Have you heard that this woman, James's bride Klementyna, has been kidnapped?'

'The Princess Klementyna,' William corrected Mary, 'yes, I had heard that.'

'What will happen if she's never freed? James will need to find someone else.'

'And how does this matter involve us?' William questioned, aware of a growing unease that he might already know the answer.

'He could marry me, of course. Why haven't we thought of it before?'

William choked with the effort to stop himself from laughing. He took another sip of wine and pretended to consider what Mary had said. The poor girl was serious. He must be careful.

'But what could you bring to such a marriage? You're not royal or wealthy and I'm afraid your reputation as a gambler is well-known. What of your relationship with the younger Gage? I do hear things.'

William could see that his daughter was close to tears. 'This is my only chance to be a queen. It might seem impossible,' she continued, 'but I still want to try. As you say, I'm a gambler.'

'What do you want me to do?' William raised both hands and let them drop onto the arms of his chair.

'Write to James and make the offer. It must come from you, my father.'

'You could do worse than marry Joseph Gage. I know he's a younger son but from a good family, and he's Catholic. He's doing well financially, I believe.'

'He'll only ever have a title if his brother dies,' Mary wailed. 'Never mind about doing worse, I could do better, in fact, I could be the best. Anyway, I don't want to marry.'

William gave a bark of protest. 'You've just asked me to write to the king, asking him to consider you for his bride.'

'For his queen, Father, not his bride. There's a world of difference.'

William agreed to write the letter. Mary stared into the fire, her features softened, and slowly sipped her wine. After another half an hour passed with not a word spoken, William risked saying aloud that her aunt would be expecting some company at dinner. She roused from her daydream and lifting her eyes, gazed around as if surprised to find herself in this room, with her father. William rang for her coach and the servant brought her cape and gloves.

Mary adjusted her hood in the bronze mirror, set above the fireplace, and spoke again. 'Don't let Joseph find out about this, the thing we've agreed and, Father, do something about your wig if you want to be seen in company.'

William was startled. Even for Mary, this was a strange change of tack.

'What on earth do you mean?' he said. 'What's wrong with my wig?'

'Yours is so old-fashioned, all high and long. Look around you; the younger men are wearing smaller wigs, set back on the crown, with a ponytail and bow at the back.'

William rolled his eyes. 'If you think I'd be seen dead in a ponytail and bow, you would be mistaken.'

Mary sniffed. 'It's your choice, of course, but I thought you had more style.' With those cutting words, Mary was gone.

Once alone, William rested at his sloping writing table, his fingers tracking the gold inlay, before drawing down the lid to lift out his writing materials. His daughter's knowledge of him, his frailties and weakness, was forensic, meaning that she knew exactly how to wound him. What he would never understand was whether she acted out of spite, which was needless given he had just agreed to her request, or did she simply not understand how her observations hurt?

He poured himself another glass of wine and sighed, knowing he would have to write this letter. The gossips would soon learn of his request, and they would both be mocked in Paris and Urbino, but if he tried to avoid his daughter's demand, she would ask again and again whether he'd had a reply. Could Mary not see that her plan was utter fantasy?

Chewing on the end of his quill, he scratched out a letter and blotted the ink. It felt sad to collude with Mary's deception of young Joseph, who clearly loved his daughter. Any young man would be heartbroken to discover that his beloved was seeking marriage with another, no matter how preposterous the idea. From his own experience, love in a marriage was worth having, never mind wealth or titles. His daughter wasn't like his sister Winifred after all. Yes, she was intelligent, beautiful, and reckless but unlike Winifred, Mary had little compassion for others.

Two months later, William had a reply from the Earl of Mar, thanking the duke for his interest and the generous offer of his daughter as a bride for King James Francis Edward Stuart but thankfully, Klementyna had escaped and was now on her way to meet her future husband. For weeks, he carried the letter in a pocket, unable to guess what Mary's reaction might be. To his relief, she accepted Mar's answer with a shrug, as if the entire scheme had nothing to do with her.

'Father, that was sweet of you to write to the king, but I've told you, I never want to marry.'

CHAPTER 6
1718

Anne had fallen ill. The ailment had started in January as no more than a feverish cold, so her mother had not felt unduly worried. But as grey February turned into a cold and blowy March, the child seemed no better. The glands on her neck were swollen and she complained of a sore throat that prevented her swallowing even tiny spoonfuls of meat broth. A fire they could ill afford was kept burning in the bedroom, where Anne lay for hours each day, consumed by fever. Grace, Alice and Winifred took turns to sit by the child, bathing her skin with damp cloths. When Anne woke, her eyes bright and cheeks flushed, they told her stories remembered from their own childhoods, wishing for the day their little girl would return.

As the child tossed and murmured in a fitful sleep, Winifred's thoughts drifted to her own mother, a woman skilled in nursing the sick. She tried to recall her mother's still room and the rows of jars, feeling angry with herself for not being able to remember which potion would have helped, or how it was concocted. Her mother had encouraged her to watch and listen, but Winifred had refused, preferring to play with Grace.

She fell asleep, her head resting on the child's legs, until Alice shook her awake. Winifred felt the thin covers damp below her open mouth and sat up, confused, wiping her lips.

'It's Anne, my lady, she's burning up,' Alice cried.

Winifred placed a hand on her daughter's brow. The child was so hot, a doctor had to be called at once.

Alice pulled on her clothes and ran out into the night while Grace and Winifred stripped the child and used wet cloths to soak her legs, arms, face, and neck. They worked in tandem on Anne's body, soaking rags, wringing them out, stroking her skin and taking turns to replace the water. The repetitious, mechanical task helped Winifred stay calm and she said aloud: 'I wish I still had her notebooks.'

Grace knew exactly what she meant. 'There was much we had to learn from her. Your mother left us too soon.'

The bedroom door slammed open and the doctor elbowed Winifred aside to kneel at Anne's bedside. The other two women slipped into the kitchen to warm some wine while she waited with her daughter. His hands assessed the naked child, beginning with her eyes, ears and neck, his expression blank and impossible to interpret. After the examination, the physician remained kneeling, his hands clasped as if in prayer. He stared at Anne, as if the answer lay behind her swollen eyelids.

'You should have called me sooner,' he said, pushing up against his knee to stand. He looked at Winifred as he spoke, but his expression communicated neither reassurance nor despair. Alone with Anne, Winifred pulled the soaked sheet from under the child's frail body. Her daughter's head lolled against her shoulder while she used her free hand to spread a clean sheet over the mattress. The child's veins tracked blue streaks underneath her almost translucent skin. She was too thin, too fragile. Winifred stroked Anne's brow and whispered: 'Please stay with us.'

In the kitchen, Grace had laid out soap, a basin of water and a clean cloth for the doctor's hands. Winifred joined the women at the table, waiting for him to finish washing. He reached for his wine, his eyes focused upon some inner thought, and as he took long, thoughtful sips, the wait became interminable. Winifred's heart pattered, missing so many beats, she was forced to take deep breaths to prevent a faint. This must be bad news.

'The child will recover,' the physician said, studying a distant point through the window. 'This high fever could well be the end of the infection, but she'll be listless for a month or two and not herself. I'll ask the apothecary to prepare something. You can collect it this afternoon.'

'I'm afraid I can't pay you,' Winifred said, these shameful words flowing from her wave of relief. 'At least not right now. Can I owe you the money?'

The doctor's eyes drifted once again into introspection and there was an uncomfortable pause before he spoke.

'I believe you are the Countess of Nithsdale, a former lady in waiting to Queen Mary Beatrice, God bless her soul.' His gaze returned to the present and travelled over her worn night-robe and loose, greying hair. 'Yet you say you can't pay me?'

'The evidence is before you, sir. This is how we live. I will pay... I just need more time.'

'Forgive me,' he said, 'but I wonder how you have fallen on such hard times? Many people refuse to pay me, claiming poverty, but your circumstances are surely different.'

'We have nothing except the small amount we earn and no savings for emergencies such as this. If you wait, a month perhaps, I will ask my brother to help. He is the Duke of Powis.'

The doctor nodded and reached for his hat and cloak, held out by Alice.

'I've heard of the duke,' he said, turning back to Winifred. 'I'll wait one month but no longer. Keep the child quiet, even if she wants to be active. Feed her whenever she's hungry. If you're worried, send for me again, but I think you'll be surprised how quickly she recovers.'

When the door closed behind their visitor, Alice left to take her turn watching the child.

Grace rolled her eyes and said, 'Thank goodness for brothers.'

Winifred smiled. 'Not any old brother. Only a duke will do, even a penniless one.'

By early summer, Anne had regained some of her former energy, although she was not yet the same child who had passed the time jumping between their two beds. Winifred had not been able to pay the doctor's fees and his reminders were becoming more frequent and less respectful. No money had arrived from her husband and in his letters, he persisted with demands that she join him in Italy, convinced that she had more financial worth in the exiled court than he did, given her family ties to the king's father. Maxwell wanted her to join him as soon as possible, before all posts were snapped up. Winifred replied that there was no money for travel, which was the truth, hoping this undeniable fact would buy her more time. There was no option but to turn to William for help and she wrote asking to meet him in the company of her sister, Lady Anne Carrington. Only when she had heard from her brother, a warm letter expressing his delight at seeing her again, did she dare to ask if he would send his carriage.

Winifred and Grace were escorted through room after room in William's apartment, each one revealed through double doors that reached the height of the painted cornice. She was reminded of the day when she had first entered her parents' apartment in the palace of Saint-Germain-en-Laye, how over-whelmed she had felt by the expanse of panelled walls, high windows framed with heavy silk drapes and mirrors every-where, which she had once loved, but now hated.

'Glad to see that Louis' style endures,' Grace whispered. 'I'd miss it somehow.'

Winifred glanced at Grace, to check her meaning, but smiled when she saw that Grace was joking.

'Personally, I prefer our shabby little place,' she replied.

Grace grimaced. 'Oh, me too. Provincial authenticity wins every time.'

The final pair of doors opened into a small library with armchairs covered in silk, next to a lacquered writing desk. William, her sister Anne, and a younger woman she didn't recognise, were already seated. From the way they fell silent, Winifred knew they must have been talking about her. The young woman was introduced as William's daughter, her niece Mary. Winifred had not seen Mary since she was a child of about two years old and said so, which brought no reaction at all, apart from a widening of her niece's grey eyes and a stare held for too long. Winifred introduced Grace as her companion, in case there was any question of her being sent to the servants' hall.

Conversation was polite and safe: each other's health, the old queen's death, and James's planned marriage to Maria Klementyna. Tea was served with tiny portions of lemon cake crumbled on delicate, glazed porcelain.

~

William listened to the women talk, not trusting his voice to speak. He had last seen Winifred in London and had believed he would never see her again, but here she was, in his home, looking horribly dowdy for Paris but still tall and proud. Lovely Grace too, forever at his sister's side, her kind face lined with too much sorrow.

After the table had been cleared and the women offered, but had refused, a small glass of sweet wine, William swallowed hard. Winifred was not on a social visit and must be encouraged to speak out before his daughter became bored and restless. He had already seen Mary try to catch Anne's eye, as his sister began another long and rambling anecdote about the Prince Regent's behaviour. Reluctantly, he knew he must help Winifred share the true reason for her visit.

He caught his younger sister's attention. 'Winifred, it has been wonderful to see you, but I know that you must soon return to La Flèche. Was there something you needed to ask us?'

William noticed Grace give Winifred a slight nod of encouragement.

'My daughter has been very ill, for months,' Winifred said. 'She's growing stronger, but I had to call a doctor. I can't pay him, and I can't afford the food she needs. I'm here to ask for your help, your financial help.'

A glance passed between Anne and Mary, who bit her lower lip and frowned.

'What about your husband?' Anne said. 'Can't he send you some money?'

These words should have been enough, but Lady Anne Carrington ploughed on. 'What about his family? They should help you. Why is it always us?'

'I have asked them; they have refused,' Winifred said.

'Anne, please listen,' William interrupted. 'It isn't always us. When was it you last helped your youngest sister? Wasn't it more than thirty years ago?'

He turned towards Winifred and saw that shame had drained her cheeks of colour.

'Ask your doctor to send his bill to me. I'm afraid that's all I can do. I know it looks as if I live in luxury, but income is hard to find.'

'Look here, I know I sound harsh.' It was Anne's turn to interrupt. 'None of us has it easy. William is right.'

Grace spoke quietly, her voice almost a whisper but her calm, still presence held the attention of the room. 'No, Lady Carrington, *you* listen. You don't have to worry where your next meal comes from. When you need a new gown, you buy one. If you need to go out somewhere, you order your carriage. You do have it easy. Only a small amount would make great difference to our lives. Winifred's daughter is your great-niece. The child deserves a chance. As you once helped us, when we were little more than children, we're asking you to do the same for her.'

Anne sniffed. 'I'm not unfeeling. If the child is suffering, then I will have her here, to live with me. That is my offer.'

Mary sat up, as if someone had shaken her awake. 'What? What are you saying?'

'There are rooms vacant next to ours,' Anne continued, frowning at Mary. 'Send your daughter and her nurse to me. I'll pay for her education. Take it or leave it.'

Anne's offer felt like revenge and in the carriage home to La Flèche, Grace wept, apologising for her outburst, fearing she had made the situation worse. Winifred reassured her; nothing could make their situation worse. She watched the sky grow pink and then darken, lights from passing cottages becoming bright as evening drew into night. Winifred pulled down the blind, and they continued their journey in silence, Grace drifting into a restless sleep. She must say nothing for now, but the choice was clear; accept her sister's offer and follow her husband to Urbino.

The day their life in La Flèche ended, William sent his coach to take Anne and Alice to the apartment where her daughter would pass the rest of her childhood. It was the second time in the child's short life she had been abandoned by her mother, but this time she would understand what was happening. Winifred lost courage, fearing that if Anne begged to come home, she would not be able to stand firm. Instead of taking the child to Paris herself, she asked Grace to accompany them. After hours of absence, hours where she paced their silent rooms imagining heartbreaking scenes of distress, Grace returned.

'How was she?' Winifred asked, before Grace had even removed her cloak.

'Sick of course, from the movement of the coach,' Grace replied, 'and your sister made a huge fuss about how pale the child looked and plied her with confections, which made her vomit. Anne was quiet but she didn't make a fuss when I left.'

Winifred reached into the cupboard and brought two glasses to the table, but before she poured their wine, she sat down and massaged her brow between the fingers of both hands.

'My child was sick. I wasn't with her. She's gone. I should have tried harder. What more could I have done?'

Grace turned from the mirror, where she had paused to adjust her cap. 'There was no choice. Anne will come to no harm with Alice at her side. Alice has been with your daughter every day of her life. This is another adventure; one they will face together.'

'You are right, as always,' Winifred whispered. 'Anne cannot come with me to Urbino, but I hate this... I hate that I had to hand over my daughter, to my sister of all people, a woman with no children of her own and little sympathy for others.'

Grace placed an arm around Winifred's shoulder. 'Have no regrets. Leave this doubt and heart-wringing anguish behind. It does no good. Anne is gone, our hearts are broken. It is over, and we must accept our fate.'

After Anne and Alice left, any hope that Winifred and Grace might remain in La Flèche, even for a short time, became impossible. Queuing for their bread in the village, Winifred became aware of whispering behind her. The baker wrapped her loaf in a cloth, but there was no amiable chat during their transaction. A woman at the end of the queue waited with her daughter but dropped her eyes as Winifred passed. This was a mother she knew, someone she had helped to read a legal letter from her landlord while the child played with Anne.

'Excuse me,' Winifred asked, standing right in front of the mother, refusing to be ignored. 'What is everyone whispering about?'

The woman raised her head. 'Surely you have heard. A servant girl changed places with the Princess Klementyna. She was smuggled out of her prison in the dress of a visitor.'

'But what has that to do with me?' Winifred asked. 'Why is everyone staring?'

The woman shook her head, as if Winifred was being deliberately obtuse.

'My lady, you're the Countess of Nithsdale. You did the same thing for your husband.'

All became clear. The Earl of Stair was right, she couldn't hide from her past, not even in a small town in France. To some she was a heroine, to others an undesirable presence, but she could no longer pretend she was invisible.

The kitchens at the Jesuit college were full of the same gossip but the maids and cooks were without embarrassment and pursued Grace for details throughout her shift. She returned to their rooms, pink with anger.

'Will warned me,' Winifred said, after hearing her account. 'The boys at the college have been unforgiving in their judgement of my family. It was for the best he stayed away from us. I encouraged him.'

Grace stopped folding clean stockings and looked across at Winifred. 'I wondered why he hadn't visited, not even when Anne was ill.'

'Will was so young when he was sent to school in France, ties were broken. You will understand this, from your own experience of being taken into service when you were a child. He must make his own way in life, without the burden of my history. He has no need for false responsibilities to family, faith, or political affiliation.'

Grace bent her head over the laundry. 'That was brave,' she said. 'No wonder parting from Anne hit you so hard.'

'Not brave,' Winifred replied, 'only realistic. It's likely I will never see my son again.'

Without raising her head, Grace whispered, 'Nor will I see you.'

∾

They did not ask the Earl of Mar to sit down or offer any refreshments on the day he visited with money to pay for Winifred's journey to Urbino. He could not resist a lecture that she must not disgrace them at court by wearing darned rags and boasted that his gift included money for new clothes. Once in full flow, he pointed out that there was no role for Grace in Urbino.

Winifred's dignity collapsed and she shed unwelcome tears, hearing this bald statement of a truth they both already knew and understood. Grace remained strong, their voice of reason.

'Of course, I cannot accompany the Countess of Nithsdale to Urbino,' she said, her tone ringing with authority. 'We had planned to part in London before we fled for France. The Duke of Powis has promised me a cottage on his estate in Wales.'

Mar bowed to Grace but hesitated, as if expecting gratitude or even some thanks. Winifred held the door ajar and both women returned to their packing. The earl left without acknowledgement or even a curt farewell, only the sound of the door slammed behind him. For the remaining days, both found solace in practical tasks, scouring their tiny home and sharing whatever of value could be carried on their separate journeys. They would never again spend their days together, but by silent agreement, nothing more was said.

Through her daily, solitary walks into the hills around Urbino, Winifred escaped from Maxwell and the quarrelsome community of the Palace Ducale. Her journey from La Flèche had taken almost two months and it was now early November, but this was Italy, not northern France, and the middle of the day could still be warm.

From her seat upon a fallen log, she looked across the valley at the palace, burnished a warm terracotta in the autumn sunshine. The countryside around the walls fell away in shades of sepia and brown, framed by a sharp and perfectly blue sky. Piles of fallen leaves strewn at her feet smelt of fungus and decay, but insects still hovered around her head, attracted by her scent. From here, she could just see the small window of the tiny room she shared with her husband, right at the top of the palace, housed amongst the simple rooms reserved for employees. She could hear voices, carried on the breeze, as men worked to prepare the olive trees for winter. Apart from these walks, she chose to spend most of her time at court, confused by the winding narrow streets of the town. While her French was close to perfect, she struggled with Italian and was not yet confident to roam alone.

Maxwell had settled comfortably within the exiled court, mostly Jacobite supporters from Scotland, his own people. She was soon accepted, given her years in Dumfries, and found they could make savings from their tiny pensions by cooking and eating with other residents. Often, too much wine was drunk, and everyone grumbled about their reduced circumstances, comparing the cold and draughty Palace Ducale to their homes in Scotland. These fortified castles and keeps were likely to have been freezing in winter, but Winifred knew that absence bred a nostalgic hindsight, one she shared. Their own home in Scotland stood empty and cold and that hollow thought brought a loneliness that was almost physical.

Mar had given Winifred two tasks to carry out on his behalf, to justify the expense of her journey. The first had been to carry the old queen's jewellery, a worrying responsibility given how often they broke down in remote countryside. He had spared no expense on their coach, a Berline carriage with four wheels, fast and light on the well-kept French roads, but unsuitable for the rough state of the roads in the Italian states. Rumours about brigands and robbers were whispered in every inn, and she was grateful for their armed footman at the rear. The new design of their coach attracted too much attention, both admiring and suspicious, and she took to tucking the royal jewels into her stays, never removing them, even while she slept.

The earl had chosen to spend money on a carriage, but he had scrimped on their accommodation and food. The inns were little more than farm buildings with earth floors and stone walls in alpine pastures. Animals lived below the accommodation, creating unusual but comforting sounds through the night, but less pleasant smells. Winifred had been careful to keep to her room in these inns, afraid to use her voice or accent with the women who brought her water, cloths and simple meals of bread and local cheese. She spent her nights propped on a chair behind her locked bedroom door, listening for footsteps in the corridor beyond.

In the early morning, eating breakfast on her wooden balcony, she smelt early dew on grass and listened to the jangle of goat bells, trying to find the strength for the ordeal of hours on the road, hidden from view. They travelled in semi-darkness, the blinds drawn against dust and insects. Exhausted from lack of sleep, her head lolled onto her chest in snatched moments of rest, as the carriage tossed and rolled along rutted tracks. She was poor company for her travelling companion, although he appeared not to notice.

George Mackenzie was her second task; to accompany him from the college at La Flèche to join his parents in Rome. He was at the unfortunate age where his voice was breaking and his skin had erupted in both lesions and stubble. Winifred tried to ask him about her son, Will, whether they had met or were friends, but he remained determined not to look at her nor speak. This was especially awkward within the confined interior compartment, where they had to face each other, rather than sit side by side. She never found out why he had left the Jesuit college, whether he had disgraced himself, or his parents could no longer afford the fees. Once, when a broken harness forced them to stop in the mountains on the border between France and the republics of Italy, she climbed down from the carriage to escape the rank odour of a teenage boy in close quarters. The air outside was so pure, it felt almost impossible to breathe. In every direction, the valley floor was circled by jagged peaks, already sprinkled with a powdering of snow, piercing a bright, evening sky of the deepest blue, a colour she had only seen before in sapphires.

Winifred stepped up to the carriage door and saw George's skin glistening in the heat. Their enforced isolation had caused him to break out into multiple blemishes, which looked hot as well as itchy.

'Come down and get some air,' she tried to persuade him. 'Look at the scene before us.'

George shook his head. 'Haven't they finished yet? I'm hungry. I want to get to the inn at Bardonecchia. How far away is it?'

This was the longest speech she had heard from George. Encouraged, she tried again.

'Please look... at least open the blinds.'

'No. Thank you for asking, Lady Nithsdale,' he said, 'but I won't.'

George turned to his book, one he had been reading for the entire journey, but it was obvious he had made little progress.

That had been their last conversation and now, whenever they passed each other in the Palace Ducale, George pretended they were strangers.

Feeling stiff and damp, Winifred stood and stretched, brushing leaves and twigs from the back of the cloak she had spread over the log, to protect her new robe. She could hear church bells ringing out from the town, travelling across the distance from the palace, reminding her that she ought to be helping the residents to pack. No matter that she had just arrived, the court were readying to move on to the Muti Palace in Rome, a gift from the Pope to the exiled king.

It had been right not to bring Anne here, Winifred thought, as she walked. The Palace Ducale was no place for a child and finding extra money to feed her would have been impossible. Anne Carrington had taken the child into her care, as she had once taken Winifred and Grace, and would do her best with food, clothing, and a place at convent school. The daily love the child would need had to come from Alice. Separating from her daughter had been unbearable but she was certain they would meet again.

The loss of Grace was harder to bear, because it was forever. In the mornings, when she woke, the shock knocked her backwards onto her bolster and every day, she fought to hide her tears from her husband. She had known Grace since they were ten years old, playing and fighting like sisters, even though her friend had been a housemaid. Through the trials of their shared adulthood, there had been times of bitter resentment. Without Grace's daily, forgiving presence, memories of her selfish behaviour crowded out happy memories.

She wanted to talk about the women who had once protected her, the children, the home she had left behind but no one here cared. Everyone had made the same sacrifice, giving up their families to the Jacobite cause. There were no new stories to tell. Her husband, who at least shared the loss of their children, seemed obsessed only by a future in Rome where his wife was chosen over all the other Jacobite women to be a governess. She was not a wife, Winifred thought, but an asset. It did not even cross Maxwell's mind that a living child born to James and Klementyna was not something they could rely upon.

CHAPTER 7

1719

The Jacobite community of the Fauborg Saint-Germain showed only mild interest in the news that the teenage Maria Klementyna was finally on her way to Urbino and were even less interested to learn that instead of welcoming his bride, James Stuart was in Corunna, planning to invade Scotland, with the support of the Spanish Government. Invasions had not gone well for James in the past, and his earlier bad luck persisted. Storms meant that most of the frigates had to return to Spain and only three hundred Spanish marines and Jacobite men landed in March at Loch Duich, close to Eilean Donan Castle. Apart from a few, the clans stayed in their glens, leaving the Jacobite army to be defeated at Glen Shiel by government forces. This time, James did not even set foot on British soil.

William shared the disinterest of his colleagues in the exiled king's miserable showing but knew there would be consequences. It was not long before gossip circulated that the Earl of Mar had been arrested in Geneva for his complicity and was now under interrogation by the Earl of Stair. William waited, anticipating his own meeting with this bullying emissary. He did not expect a polite, written invitation, having heard from Winifred about Stair's methods, but guessed there would be a thump on his door, a demand for admission, his men first threatened, then forced to comply. When a servant tapped on his study door, timidly stating that John Dalrymple, the Earl of Stair, was waiting in the entrance hall and refusing to leave, William agreed that Stair be escorted immediately to his study. A carafe of wine and two glasses should be brought at once.

The very atmosphere of the room changed as Stair's size and energy brought the outdoors into William's peaceful sanctuary. He studied the younger man as he crammed his bulk into the chair indicated, taking a deep draught from his glass as if he had spent days in a desert. William was not afraid, having survived many accusations of Jacobite treachery, but made sure his most recent letter from the Prince of Wales lay visible on a table at Stair's elbow.

Stair leaned across to remove the wine bottle from William's new side table, one which had a useful compartment where bottles and glasses could be stored. He poured himself another generous glassful and tipped the bottle towards his host. William shook his head.

'Look, Powis, I won't waste your time.' Stair spoke as if addressing an audience outdoors. 'I'm checking up on all those hiding in Paris who were out in the 'fifteen. France is not keen on harbouring men, or women, who might scheme to overthrow the British royal family. I've just come from questioning the Jacobite traitor Charles Radclyffe. Now it's your turn.'

William tapped his steepled fingers against his lips before replying. This man had the power to have him arrested and he must answer with care.

'Firstly, a small correction if I may. I took no part in the 1715 uprising. I have never met Charles Radclyffe. This is the first time I have heard his name spoken.'

'He's guilty of treason, escaped from Newgate Prison before he could be punished. Now he's hanging around here.'

William played to Stair's pride. 'He must be well-hidden in Paris, since he's unknown in the Jacobite circles I move in. You did well to root him out.'

'You were imprisoned after the 1715, like your sister's husband and the Radclyffe brothers?'

'Yes, a mistaken assumption that because my sister and her husband were involved, I must be too. This has been my misfortune over many years. I was soon freed, legally I might add.'

'But you have Jacobite sympathies?'

'Actually, I don't. I'm keen that Catholics in Britain should be free to practise their faith and hold office and I live here only because of that discrimination. I'm close to George Augustus, the king's son, who will one day be king himself.'

William edged the letter with its royal seal closer to Stair, who picked it up and studied its contents, his lips moving as he read.

'He thanks you for your help... says that you gave him courage to try a reasoned discussion with his father. They now have access to their children. You must feel proud to receive such a letter.'

'Thank you, John, may I call you John? I have no quarrel with King George and only wanted to see two men who are opposites in temperament, but who love each other deeply, try to see eye to eye. I am a peacemaker, not a warrior. I have never met the Pretender, and only know of him through my family's connections.'

'Your sister has wasted no time in joining James's court in Italy.'

'Yes, but only due to pressure from you and financial necessity. She has suffered greatly for her husband's decisions.'

'Your other sister, Lady Anne Carrington, and your daughter, where do they stand?'

'Their interests are the same as everyone else in Paris – a shared obsession with John Law and his financial schemes. They do not care for politics. It seems as if France is in the grip of a money-making fever, from the lowliest butcher to our Prince Regent. My family want to make money, not war.'

John looked hard at William, as if trying to decide whether the older man could be trusted. A tense energy flowed from the large man's body on the breath of a sigh, and at last his shoulders relaxed.

William was experienced in bringing calm to those who tried to accuse and threaten him. On hearing that outward breath, he knew he was safe.

William took a sip of wine and looked across at Stair, lifting his eyebrows, pretending to be interested in his interrogator's views. 'It feels almost like a religious fervour. Many believe the man will be our saviour, don't you agree?'

Stair nodded. 'I even tried to persuade the British government to pardon him and give him a title, so that he would come home. God knows, we need his financial help in Britain. I must admit, I've succumbed to his reputation and have borrowed heavily to buy shares. Like everyone else, I'm greatly in debt. God save us if John Law doesn't fulfil his promises.'

William was not surprised, having heard from Mary and her friend Fanny Oglethorpe about Stair's reckless approach to money. He wasn't about to reveal his own financial circumstances to his guest, since the information might be used against him, but knew he must share something. Stair was not likeable or trustworthy, but William would work hard to make sure that this arrogant man liked and trusted him.

'My daughter is very keen that I invest in the Mississippi Company,' William said, 'but I'm yet to be persuaded. My sister

Anne has shares, as do my daughter's friends. Everyone is making money. It's hard not to feel left out.'

'I've advised King George to copy Law's idea in our colonies, even if Law can't be persuaded to return. I'm a soldier, not a banker, but so far his system seems to be working.'

'So, you plan to invest further, and would advise others to do so?'

Stair rose, adjusting his wig in the heavily decorated mirror over the fireplace.

'Can't afford to, I'm afraid. Others must spend their money as they see fit.'

They waited for a servant to escort William's guest from the apartment. Stair studied his reflection, turning his head to admire his own profile. His suit was embossed with a dense floral pattern, picked out in gold thread, the quality of the tailoring remarkable outside royal circles. William had heard gossip about the Earl of Stair's coaches, gilded to match those of the French aristocracy, and his demands to be treated beyond his status. Yet the man had no personal income. His excess must rely purely upon profligacy with British taxes.

Stair reached for his cloak, and throwing it over his shoulders, invited William for dinner. William agreed, as if delighted, making a silent promise to himself to ensure this offer was not a token gesture. As John Dalrymple, Earl of Stair, might spy on him, William would return the favour, confident that the Prince of Wales would be delighted to learn about the profligacy of his father's ambassador in France.

William finished the carafe of wine, enjoying his solitude, tracing the gold leaf at the rim of the glass with a thumb. His thoughts drifted to Mary and her recent demand that he become a guarantor for her loans. Her friends, women of independent wealth, had already bought shares in the Mississippi Company but Mary's only chance to do the same was to accept a sizeable loan, one she had already secured from the banker Richard Cantillon. William pulled the legal papers from his bureau and studied them again, his finger stroking his upper lip. Mary was due in half an hour and would expect them to be signed.

~

'You haven't signed!' Mary said. The document lay face up on the side table, the place for her father's signature blank. 'Why are you being so cautious? Everyone I know is a paper millionaire, except me.'

'I understand how much you want this,' William replied. 'You believe my dithering is cheating you of your ambition to become a rich woman. But it's not my money. I must think of the family, the estate.'

Mary groaned, as if indifferent to this mantra, repeated too often. 'It's your duty. How can you waste this opportunity to make a fortune? You might secure our family's future.'

William tapped the legal papers. 'Then I should invest for myself. This document asks me to guarantee a loan, so that you can play the financial markets. You are looking to enrich yourself, not me, or the family.'

'That's nonsense.' Mary snorted, rolling her eyes. 'With Joseph's guidance, I will make money and you will benefit. Do your duty by me, Father, and invest.'

William paused, fearful of her reply but he still had to ask: 'What do you mean?'

'You have betrayed me. You have failed to provide me with an acceptable income, one suitable for my station. I am forced to live on the charity of an aunt.'

Hearing these painful words, no less hurtful for being anticipated, William knew that guilt would force him to agree. But could he manipulate this situation to his own ends? Mary had to be married and there was a suitor in waiting. If he was to stand as guarantor for her loans, might she consent to be wed?

William lifted his quill and dipped its nib in the ink.

'I will only sign this if you agree to meet suitable men, with a view to marriage. I have indeed neglected my duty to you, but you have failed in your duty to me. You have not followed the rules expected of a daughter.'

'Of course, Father,' Mary said, watching William scratch his signature. 'Now we have a clear understanding about my worth to you, and yours to me, there may be fewer misunderstandings between us.'

Mary strolled to the Tuileries, enjoying the sultry July afternoon, feeling pleased with her morning's work. Her meeting with Richard Cantillon had been formal, without social pleasantries, which suited her. She wasn't comfortable with the mannered chit-chat other people seemed to enjoy, and since she didn't like Richard, such conversation would have felt even more false. Through his bank, Richard had offered her a generous loan and she had persuaded both her father and her aunt to stand as guarantors, although both were ignorant of each other's role. Her timing had been perfect, since Cantillon intended to leave France the following month and set up home in Florence, with no date for a return. What she had not disclosed to either her father or her aunt was the size of the loan. She smiled as she remembered her skill negotiating with her father. It had been ridiculously easy.

Once her finance was secure, Joseph had accompanied her to the rue Quincampoix, now populated with buyers and sellers of stock, where she spent all her borrowed money on Mississippi shares. It felt right. At last, she had found a way to join the other players on the stock market.

She was on her way to meet Fanny at Madam la Frenais' boutique on the rue Saint-Honoré, the only acceptable shop for an immensely wealthy bride to order her wedding clothes. Although she had no intention of marrying, it annoyed her that Fanny and Olive's new wealth from financial dealing had brought them to the attention of a different league of admirers. Both women had dropped their lovers overnight and set a date for weddings. Fanny was due to be married in December to Joseph-Francois, Marquis des Marches and seemed to take undue pleasure in reminding Mary that John Law and his wife, Lady Katherine, were to be guests. Olive was marrying the Comte d'Auvergne the following year, allowing Fanny the great satisfaction of beating her friend to the altar.

A young woman, a shop assistant, dressed in clothes designed by la Frenais, opened the glass door for Mary and escorted her to a table where Fanny waited. They were brought lemonade in tall glasses and watched models parade sample wedding gowns. Fanny gasped with pleasure at each one, but Mary caught herself daydreaming, studying passers-by through the high windowpanes at the front of the shop. She reminded herself to pay attention but all she could think about was her new stock. How long before she would see the price rise? Should she cash in or reinvest?

'Mary, Mary...' Fanny shook her arm. 'I like the blue, the one with the gold stitching on the sleeves and hem. What do you think?'

Mary hesitated. 'I'd like to see it again. I may have preferred the green. Shall we ask them to show us both gowns a second time?'

'But should I wear a hoop petticoat underneath? What do you think?'

Mary sighed. 'Fanny, it's your wedding day. Wear whatever you like.'

Fortunately, on second viewing, Fanny also preferred the green, thinking it enhanced her auburn hair and hazel eyes, and thanked her friend for her perceptive advice. As Fanny disappeared into the back of the salon to be measured, chattering with the assistant about whether the gown might be adjusted for a winter wedding, Mary sighed again and wondered why her friend was so keen to marry a man she hardly knew. Was this the reason Richard Cantillon was leaving Paris? Was he too distressed by the thought of his young lover being escorted around the city by her new husband?

The women walked home together, arm in arm, Mary listening to Fanny's endless chatter about flowers, carriages, and hats. The absence of detail about the man who would stand by her side on the actual day, or any thoughts about her future as a wife and mother, was only too apparent but Mary decided to stay quiet. Asking questions might suggest an interest she did not feel and would only prolong the conversation. Her silence was interpreted as sadness by Fanny, who tightened her grip on Mary's arm.

'Don't worry, Mary,' Fanny said, 'you will find someone. Perhaps you'll be next... after Olive?'

Mary considered her answer. This wasn't the moment to tell the truth, to say that she had decided never to marry. Happily, she was able to share a very satisfying nugget of gossip.

'Don't tell anyone, Fanny, but my father has promised to find me a suitor.'

'No!' Fanny gasped, 'tell me more.'

'That's all I'm saying.' Mary laughed and said, 'You'll find out soon enough.'

~

Meeting a prospective husband was clearly important to other people, requiring a bath, and the use of her aunt's carriage. Aunt Anne and their maid fussed around her dress and hair, and even Aunt Winifred's ghastly child, her cousin Anne, seemed excited. Mary sat at her dressing table, allowing the girl to play with her crystal perfume bottles and her tortoiseshell eyelash comb. From her low chair, she watched her maid tie up her hair with ribbons that matched her dress. She wasn't beautiful but had the high cheekbones and long neck of her father's family. Presented like this, she would never be short of admirers.

Mary had heard rumours about the man she was meeting and guessed that the evening would not end well, but this did not seem to matter to anyone else. Her father had upheld his side of the bargain and she must do the same, even though the man she was expected to meet was reputed to be hideous. Because she was thirty-three, her father must have thought she would be grateful for a debauched old drunkard, and she felt a swell of resentment that he had considered such a match. In the three months since she had invested in shares, she had become a wealthy woman. There was no reason to marry, not for love, money, or a title. Since she knew she would turn her suitor down, Mary enjoyed being made to look her best. He must experience the full hurt of rejection, as she was being punished with the shame of humiliation.

Mary was escorted into her father's formal dining room, the polish from its long table reflecting the light from gilded, bronze candles, set in clusters of three around the walls. Philippe de Bourbon, Chevalier de Vendome, was already seated at the table, next to her father. They were introduced and de Bourbon grasped her hand, bowing low to kiss the tips of her fingers. Mary immediately wanted to remove her hand from the infection he was certainly spreading, and once seated, pulled a handkerchief soaked in oil of cloves from the pocket underneath her petticoat. Below the table, she wiped her hands clean.

The men made small talk and Mary listened, watching her reflection in the vast mirror above the fireplace. Her claret gown, split to the waist, revealed a tantalising flutter of embroidered lace at her cleavage, which would taunt her proposed husband to a pitch where his disappointment would be almost painful. Her father ploughed on, raising topics of conversation that should have given de Bourbon every chance to present himself in a positive light, an opportunity that he failed to grasp.

'I hear you've given up your position as Grand Prior of the Order of Malta?' William asked, trying not to look at the chevalier dribbling soup from his mouth onto his breeches.

'Yup, can't be bothered with the oath of chastity. Need a son you see. That's where this beautiful maiden can help me out.'

Mary stared at de Bourbon, biding her time. He must be the same age as her father but beyond that there was no comparison.

'It must have been hard to relinquish the role, after all your commitment?' William added.

'Not at all, it was a bloody nuisance. Sold it actually, to the Prince Regent. That fellow, Law, put in a word for me. Always need more money...' De Bourbon leered at Mary across the table and winked. 'Another way this very wealthy young lady can help me out.'

Mary swallowed another spoonful of soup and dabbed the corners of her mouth with her napkin.

'Since you want me for a son and for my money, what will be my recompense? What will I gain from marriage to you?' Mary ignored her father's almost imperceptible shake of his head.

De Bourbon snorted, as if this was a stupid question. 'You'll be a married woman, my dear. Isn't that what all women want?'

Mary smiled, turning her grey Herbert eyes towards Philippe de Bourbon, fixing him steadily in her gaze.

'I won't have children, I'm afraid. If you marry me, there will be none. I would rather...' Mary paused to think of a vile enough comparison. 'I would rather be intimate with a dead animal.'

Her father raised his voice. 'Mary! You've gone too far.'

'Ha... so you think!' De Bourbon leered at her father and winked. 'As my wife, you'll have no choice. A married woman has duties to her husband. Something I'm sure you're keen to try. You've waited long enough, and you won't be disappointed.'

The conversation paused while a servant cleared their plates. As they waited for the fish course, her father tried to change the topic, although Mary noticed that the thought of sex was not easily shaken from his mind.

'Once you're married, where might you honeymoon?'

Mary interrupted him before de Bourbon could reply. 'If you believe I am a virgin, sir, you are mistaken. I regularly enjoy sexual liaisons with Joseph Gage.'

De Bourbon turned on William, his scarred face speckled with red and white blotches, like an ill-mixed compote. 'You have tricked me. I believed she was untouched. No wonder you're desperate to offload her. You've chosen the wrong person. I'm not a fool.'

William placed his hand on the man's arm, as if to stop him leaving, but his attempt to soothe was roughly pushed aside. The door slammed behind Philippe, and father and daughter sat together in silence, avoiding each other's gaze. The clock on the mantel announced the passing seconds.

William spoke first: 'That was appalling. I can't believe you've let me down in such a way.'

'And I can't believe you thought that such an abhorrent man was right for me. What does that say about you?'

'All you had to do was marry him, produce an heir, and then inherit all his wealth after he died. From the look of him, that wouldn't take long. Surely that wasn't too great a sacrifice?'

'Why, Father? I'm making enough money by myself. You heard that he's after my money, so he can't be as wealthy as you think.'

William rested his temples against both palms. 'He has properties and land, the kind of wealth that is long-lasting and secure. God knows, our family needs solid, financial security.'

'We must put our faith in John Law. Joseph tells me that his company now controls all trade with America, Africa, China and the West Indies. He's soon to be the Comptroller-General of Finances for France, the most powerful man in the country next to the Prince Regent. How can such a man be wrong? Once we are all rich, this country will have no need of men like Philippe de Bourbon.'

A servant tapped on the door, asking if they wanted the rest of the dinner. William lifted his hand, about to refuse, but Mary interrupted.

'Yes of course, let's eat. I'm hungry. Why forfeit a meal that would only have been wasted on that boor? We can have a good dinner together, just the two of us, and talk.'

In fact, they ate in silence. Mary felt delighted by her victory and rehearsed every angry word and haughty action for her own pleasure, embellishing moments where hindsight permitted her to be even more cutting. In turn, William harboured a secret relief that he would not have to watch his favourite child make such a bad match. He felt a degree of shame for trying to palm her off with such a husband, but suitors were not beating a path to her door. As he chewed on his rather tough breast of duck, he wondered again why she

83

wouldn't marry young Gage. After tonight's outburst, it was now fact, rather than gossip, that she and Joseph were physically intimate, so what on earth was the barrier to marriage?

As he tipped the last of the wine into their glasses, William dared to broach this.

'I hear Joseph is doing well. He has a sound business with Law and Cantillon. His new residence, the hotel de Tavannes, would not disgrace a prince of the realm. If you and he are truly... erm... behaving as man and wife, why don't you wed? You won't get a better offer.'

'Father, I'm tired of explaining. I don't want to be anyone's wife. I have everything I need.'

'Doesn't Joseph want more?'

'You know he does, but that's not my problem.'

William frowned and drew a letter from his pocket. 'So, I may as well destroy this?'

'What is it?'

'It's a letter from the Prince Regent, proposing you consider the Duc d'Albret as a husband. Albret has already written a most passionate and admiring letter, I might say. He's a widower, so at least he's been married before, and your friend Olive is marrying his younger brother. You would be sisters-in-law.'

Mary opened her hand to receive the letter, but instead of reading it she leaned towards a candle and touched a corner with the flame. The edge browned, curled, and then flared, at first blue then yellow. As the document twisted and burned, father and daughter watched Albret's proposal turn to ash.

CHAPTER 8
1720

William made his way on foot along the tree-lined boulevard behind the newly completed Place Louis-le-Grand. On one side of the boulevard lay undeveloped fields, with woods beyond. On the other side, closed off behind imposing entrances, were overpriced town-houses owned by financiers and those rudely referred to as 'nouveau-riche' by the old aristocracy. William mused that he was typical of the old aristocracy, encumbered with crumbling castles and estates, but without the money to support them. He could not help but feel left out from this new world, where money was made with ridiculous ease, creating millionaires from young men with little education or skill. Everywhere you looked, developers created new neighbourhoods, including his own of Faubourg Saint-Germain, filling every vacant plot with residences to house these upstart financiers.

Unlike London, where building was piecemeal and goatherds lived alongside wealthy neighbours, these were grand homes, built to look like palaces, where a few rooms could be let by those who needed a prestigious address. The surrounding streets were wide, planned for carriages as well as those who chose to walk, and lined with elegant shops, selling everything the newly affluent thought they needed. Strolling felt best at dusk, stepping out in anticipation of a good dinner, with shop windows glowing and the lamplighters stripping the night of hidden threat. William saw bats dart from their roosts amongst the trees, ready to catch insects attracted by the street-lights, just as the birds fell silent.

But it was a worry that the lure of easy money had brought hordes into the city from the countryside, caught up in the fantasy that a quick fortune was within reach of even the poorest labourer. There were too many beggars on the streets and only last week he had been accosted in the Tuileries, surely the safest place in the city, by a man demanding money. It was rumoured that beggars had been arrested and transported to the colonies, along with prisoners taking up too much room in the gaols. Families volunteered anyone who had become a burden to them. The Regent's draconian measures against this upsurge in crime had backfired, with riots in the rue Quincam-poix. The people were unsettled, practically out of control. Perhaps it was time to go home.

William wondered whether he should have taken his coach, although he only had to walk the length of a few more streets to the Earl of Stair's new residence. He paused to look around at the carriages hurtling past, leaning on his cane, the habit of an old man trying to disguise that he was out of breath and needing to rest.

Walking on further towards Stair's apartment, William counted how many evenings he had spent with John. It must be three, or was it four? The two men could not be more different, in either faith or politics, but both had a military background and that was always a place where men could find common ground. His unexpected friendship with Stair intrigued him, even though he was used to younger men seeking him out for friendship and the reassurance a father might give, one who acted like the father figure they deserved, rather than the parent they actually had. The man was a tangle of contradictions; married, but with no children of his own, and a wife left behind in Scotland. Surely, she would have been an asset in Paris, a partner for his ambassadorial duties?

He arrived at the expected time and was surprised to be met by John in the entrance hall. William was clutched by the elbow, barely finding time to pass his cloak to the waiting servant and hustled into an anteroom. Stair did not ask him to take a seat and William felt alarm. Had he done something wrong?

John spoke in a stage whisper, as if there was a chance he might be overheard. 'We have another guest tonight, the banker Richard Cantillon. He's already in the dining salon. I must ask you to find out something for me, and I don't want him to hear.'

William's anxiety grew into irritation. He enjoyed these intimate evenings and was disappointed they would not be dining alone. He waited for John to continue, lifting his brows as a gesture of encouragement.

'My sources tell me that John Law has travelled to the court of the Pretender in Rome. The Regent is keen to find out what he's up to. Is there anything you can tell me? What about your sister? Would she know?'

William's anticipation of a pleasant evening plummeted. No matter how often he repeated that he was not at the centre of Jacobite intrigue, Stair chose not to believe him. He met Winifred, frightened her, bullied her out of France. He must know that she would not have access to strategic information. He kept his impatience in check and forced himself to nod, as if he respected the importance of the question.

'My dear John, I'm afraid I cannot help. I am ignorant of

everything that happens in the exiled court, and I have never met John Law. My sister struggles to find a role within the Muti Palace, and if she did have a position, it would only be to fulfil domestic duties. She will know nothing about this.'

Finding that a degree of firm authority often worked with John, he added, 'I will not write to her.'

The younger man stared, about to argue, but in a sudden movement, as if he had remembered his duty to his other guest, he hurried William up the staircase to the dining room. Despite his reputation for spending, John's rooms were excessively tidy and lacking in ornamentation. The dining room, like all other rooms in the apartment, was furnished in plain wood of solid design and met with William's approval.

A man warming his backside by the grate was introduced as Richard Cantillon. William handed his gloves and cane to a servant and shook the hand that was offered.

'I heard you were abroad, Cantillon,' he said, 'at least that is what my daughter Mary told me. She owes you quite a sum I believe.'

Richard smiled. 'No more than anyone else. I've been working in the republic of Venice, the low countries, anywhere I can do business, but I felt I'd better come home. I need to keep an eye on my money.'

'I'd be interested in your views. There's a strange atmosphere in the city,' William added.

'Not without cause, my friend—' Richard had more to say but was interrupted by John, rushing his guests to the table.

William was fascinated by John's eating habits, the way he swallowed his food with intensity and speed, attributing this to the man's military background, like his sparse surroundings. Each course vanished from Stair's plate, his friend's expression fierce and determined, not looking at his dinner guests or making any conversation. It was only once all the food had been served, and they moved to sit beside the fire with another carafe of wine, that William was able to revisit his earlier conversation with Cantillon.

'Do you trust John Law's methods, Richard? Is our money safe?'

Cantillon adjusted his position, sitting upright and spreading the tails of his coat behind him, as if preparing to give a lecture.

'Law's approach to finance is that of a gambler and in the buying and selling of currency and shares, I must admit he's been successful. His methods are well worth studying, but a gambler is not the same as an experienced banker and this is where he's coming unstuck. The Regent has invested too much faith in Law's model for financing a national economy, making the habitual mistake of assuming a rich man is a clever one.'

William felt a strange sensation in his head, as if his skull had grown lighter. 'That is concerning. I feel a deep unease for us all...'

'I wouldn't worry,' John interrupted, 'the Regent is a fool and Law's days are numbered.'

Cantillon frowned. 'Be careful, John, they're both powerful men. Such views might be misinterpreted if spoken outside these four walls. Your presence in Paris is tolerated because you're useful to the Regent but John Law is even more useful. He's promised to solve all the government's financial problems. What do you have to offer?'

William expected an outburst of temper, but John's eyes closed, and he appeared to have drifted into an alcoholic slumber. With relief, William thought it unlikely that Stair had heard Cantillon's rebuke. He turned his attention back to Richard and found the man's fixed gaze waiting for him.

'You *should* feel concerned,' Cantillon continued. 'Law's system relies upon the people believing that banknotes can be trusted over gold and silver. I'm afraid that hasn't happened. The economy has been swamped with paper currency, but everyone has continued to hoard coins, jewellery and precious metals.'

Both men paused, listening to John snore. Richard shook his head and spoke again. 'Law has become too powerful. His men have been given the power to raid people's homes, even churches, to find hidden silver or gold.'

'The system relies on trust and the trust isn't there?' William added.

'Exactly. People are starting to sell their shares in the Compagnie des Indes. If too many people try to sell, there will be a run. There's not enough in the bank to pay them all back.'

'What is the Compagnie des Indes, if I may ask?'

Richard swallowed a deep draught from his glass and leaned forward, his eyes never leaving William's face.

'It's Law's new name for the Mississippi Company. I've heard that he's about to fix the rate of interest on shares. He calls it rebalancing, but most bankers think it's fraud.'

'Where is the value of a share if it doesn't rise and fall?' William asked. 'They're worth nothing if they can be devalued overnight by a government bank. Speculators won't think it's worth investing.'

Richard grinned. 'Bravo, you have summarised our national problem with great elegance.' He leaned back in his armchair, holding his glass close to his chest, still smiling at William as if encouraging a particularly bright pupil. 'That, my friend, is why a government should not put a gambler in charge of an economy.'

Both men turned to study their host, still soundly asleep, his only contribution a range of whistling, snuffling sounds best left in the bedchamber. William remarked that perhaps they should leave, and they rang for their cloaks.

On the street, Cantillon offered William a seat in his coach, but he decided to walk, despite his earlier misgivings about safety. The evening's conversation had troubled him. Mary was a gambler too, inexperienced in the world of finance, yet she bought and sold shares as if she had been born to it. But Cantillon was right, the rules of finance are not those of gambling; for a gambler, the chase is all that matters. His daughter was treating the stock market as just another card game, blind to whatever was happening around her. He must talk to Mary and Joseph as soon as possible... warn them of the risks... but would they listen?

CHAPTER 9

1720

Mary's reputation was secure as a woman of independent wealth. She and Joseph were openly accepted as a couple in the Regent's Paris, a city where lovers did not have to hide. Their days of hurrying home late at night, to preserve her reputation, were over. She now had a fine carriage of her own, and most nights she stayed with Joseph.

At breakfast, Mary sipped her coffee and waited for Joseph to say what was on his mind. She struggled to understand other people but one of the things she liked about Joseph was that he was so easy to read. His recent silence, accompanied by a troubled expression, required nothing of her, neither questioning nor interrogation. He would speak to her eventually. Joseph cleared his throat and reached across the linen tablecloth to touch her fingertips.

'Mary, at the risk of repeating myself, I'd like to ask you to marry me. There's no inequality between us in terms of wealth and I wouldn't expect you to have children. We are true companions. I know you don't love me as I love you, but I think you love me well enough to be happy with me.'

Mary wanted to reply with *not this again*, but she was fond of Joseph and knew he was easily hurt.

'I do love you, Joseph, but my love depends upon us not being married. Couples are different once vows have been exchanged. Society expects the woman, and only the woman, to bend to other people's expectations. Look at Fanny, how boring she's become.'

'How can I trust you won't meet someone else, abandon me for a rich old man with a title? A title is the only thing I lack and even that omission I've taken steps to remedy. I met the Earl of Stair and asked him to approach the British government on my behalf. I promised to transfer all my wealth in exchange for a title and an estate. I was refused, of course, but only because I'm a Catholic. You see how hard I've tried.'

Mary sighed. 'It's not about a title, Joseph, a title doesn't matter to me.'

To distract him, she decided to tell the story of her suitors, hoping he would find it funny. She gambled that the whole uncomfortable business of marriage could be laughed away.

'Since we're being honest, my father has already tried to match me with men who own land and have titles. I refused all offers.'

Joseph straightened his back and pulled his hand away.

'You've said nothing about other suitors.'

'There was little to tell. I only met one and he was so vile, I quickly sent him on his way.'

Joseph's skin reddened, as it always did whenever he became anxious. 'What if he'd been young, handsome and titled?'

Mary tried to laugh, aware that her lover was not finding any humour in their conversation. She gazed into the untroubled eyes of the portraits on Joseph's walls, not Parisian style at all, but a misguided attempt to recreate an English country seat in France. She felt a growing irritation with his obsession with marriage. Would it be too cruel, she thought, to tell him the worst thing?

Whether it was cruel or not, she decided to speak: 'My father even wrote to James Stuart, suggesting he take me as a bride. I was proud that my father thought so highly of me, but it was quite ridiculous.'

Joseph looked down at the tablecloth and adjusted the cutlery beside his plate. 'If James had accepted the offer, you would have said yes?'

'Probably, but so what? Perhaps James Stuart was the one person I might have agreed to marry, but he was so beyond my reach, the idea was nonsensical. Please, Joseph, let's leave things as they are. There is no one else for me but you.'

Mary folded her napkin and pushed back her chair, but Joseph laid a hand on her arm.

'Don't walk to your aunt's. I'll order your carriage.'

'You don't think I'm safe to walk in daylight?'

'There are too many reports of robberies, targeting anyone believed to be wealthy,' Joseph said. 'Many have been fatal. I would use your carriage from now on.'

'I heard there was more rioting last week. What's wrong? What do the people want?'

Joseph smoothed out an imaginary crease in the tablecloth. 'They want money, Mary, and they're frightened they won't get any. If they already have money, they're scared they'll lose it.'

Mary sat back and folded her arms. 'It's all so unfair. I didn't have money, but I didn't go around robbing people. I'm scared too, scared we're losing our lovely city. It's no loss to me to have to use my coach but it's time the government took control.'

She stood and kissed the top of Joseph's wig, pressing his shoulder in a manner she hoped might reassure him.

'I need to check on Aunt Anne,' she said. 'Try not to worry.

We should have faith in the Regent and John Law. They won't allow the country to fall apart.'

A month later, Mary pushed her way through the crowd at the Théâtre du Palais-Royal, glad that most fashionable women had abandoned the hoop petticoat. Followed by her servant, she climbed a dimly lit staircase that smelt of warm dust to their box, hurrying to join Joseph, who was always early. They had tickets for a new Italian comedy, but the greatest pleasure of the evening was the anticipation of being seen with her lover, amongst the best of Parisian society. For the benefit of her potential audience, she wore a new robe of claret velvet, hoping that admirers would appreciate how the sleeves had been gathered in tiers to settle just above her elbow.

Joseph sat chewing on a fingernail, frowning with the anxious expression that was becoming habitual and even a little annoying. Mary passed her theatre cape to her maidservant and sat next to him.

'Everyone's saying that John Law has been dismissed as the comptroller-general of the national bank,' Joseph said, without turning to look at her.

Mary leaned across to kiss his cheek. 'Hello to you too, Joseph.' She scanned the pillared auditorium and pointed to a box on the other side. 'There's John Law and his wife, in the Prince Regent's box. It can't be true, or he wouldn't be here. Try to relax.'

'But look in the parterre, at the people standing. The audience is as surprised to see him as we are. There was some hissing and a slow hand clap when he arrived. He's not popular, not anymore.'

Mary lifted her scented handkerchief to her nose to mask the smell of sweat and food rising from below.

'He doesn't have to be popular, just successful. These people,' she wafted her hand to take in the crowd, 'probably think he should be in the bank, counting their money, not out enjoying himself.'

Mary squeezed Joseph's hand but felt her own mood sour. This night was meant for comedy, not troubles. The Laws should have stayed away. Everyone was looking at them, not her... the new dress had been a waste. The orchestra began the discordant sounds of tuning instruments and candelabra were lowered from the ceiling to be extinguished. Smoke and the smell of candle wax filled the auditorium. There was a rumble from backstage, as the first set rolled into place behind the stage curtain. Conversation fell to whispers, followed by silence. The curtain twitched then inched upwards towards the proscenium arch. The audience gasped at the sight of a garden, a bridge over a stream, water rippling over cobbles. The stage was lit by at least a dozen candelabra, light falling across the upturned faces of the audience nearest the stage, as if they had been picked out by the sun.

From the corner of her eye, Mary studied Joseph throughout the first half and saw that he was trying to enjoy himself. His laughter seemed genuine and not just for her benefit. At the interval, the stalls had not yet been lit and the auditorium remained dark. She reached for Joseph's hand, and they made their way towards curtains that separated the balcony from the foyer. In the darkness at the rear of their box they stumbled, and Joseph caught her, kissing her neck.

Mary heard an unexpected scuffling. Someone was trying to find a way through from the other side and she reached out to aid the fumbling hands. Startled and embarrassed, she saw her father's flustered face.

'Ah, you two,' William said. 'I hoped you would be here. Can we find somewhere to sit?'

They were shown to a table and a waiter poured them wine.

Mary spoke first. 'Is there a problem?'

William nodded, looking from one face to the other and tapped the table as he spoke. 'People are saying it's time to sell Mississippi shares. Have you thought about this?'

Mary saw Joseph nod but before he could reply, she interrupted. 'Goodness me, not at all. We'd have to sell at such a low price. I'm sure it's better to wait. Law needs more time.'

'I'm worried about you. If there's a crash, how will you pay back your loan to Richard Cantillon, of which I am guarantor?'

This time, Joseph managed to speak: 'It's more complex than you think, my lord. We have invested in South Sea Company shares and those are still rising. If we allow them to reach their peak, then sell at the highest price, we can pay off any debts.'

William stared into his glass. His skin had the pallor of old meat, with two bright-red patches glistening under each eye. Finally, he spoke, his tone measured but cold. 'I cannot understand how you managed to buy South Sea Company shares without a guarantor. How was it possible for Mary to draw down credit without land or property?'

'It's possible to sell them on, even before you own them,' Joseph explained. 'The profit allows you to pay the seller and you pocket the difference.'

'For God's sake, man!' William exploded, banging on the table, slopping wine over the edge of their glasses. 'I didn't want a lesson on how you're cheating the system. Can't you see what's happening?'

He gestured towards the entrance to the rue Saint-Honoré. 'Out there, a crowd is banging on the doors of the national bank, trying to withdraw their savings. Guards have been sent in to keep control.'

People circled their table in small groups, pretending to chat but pausing in their progress to listen. Mary had rarely seen her father so angry. She lowered her voice before she spoke, adopting a tone she hoped sounded calm and reassuring, for the benefit of her father and their unwelcome audience. There was little point in adding to the febrile rumours already in circulation.

'Joseph's right,' she said, 'we should keep our nerve. I understand your concern but if we sell now, even if it were possible to access a bank or broker, we'd lose everything. The Regent will not allow the finances of the entire country to collapse. We must trust that the economy will recover.'

Her father's cheeks slowly lost their high colour, and when he replied, he sounded more like himself. 'Even your aunt, my sister, has followed your example. If she loses all her investments, how will she maintain the child?'

'What child?' Mary frowned.

'Winifred's little girl, of course. You know full well she lives in the apartment next to yours.'

'Oh her,' Mary replied. 'If Aunt Anne has no money, the girl will have to go back to her mother, which is where she belongs. She tried to borrow from me, by the way. I refused.'

'The child tried to borrow money?' William stammered.

'No, Father. Your sister Winifred.'

'Winifred must be at rock bottom to ask for help from her niece. Surely you could have spared her a little something?'

Joseph had been silent, perhaps reluctant to enter an argument between father and daughter, but took his chance to contribute.

'Don't forget, Mary, John Law says that wealth is for spreading around, not hoarding.'

Blood roared into her ears. Joseph's comment was not only unreasonable but unjust. She glared at him before turning to her father.

'I don't have coins, gold, silver, or anything else I can share with other people. You of all people should understand that. I make money selling shares. I reinvest or pay back loans. When a currency rises, I sell and buy more. I am a financier, not a charity.'

Mary noticed that her father's skin had gained a sweaty sheen. He ran a finger under his cravat, as if his neck burned.

'I should have visited the child more. I hope you are kind to her,' William said, his voice barely audible.

Mary rolled her eyes. 'I'm not unkind, just indifferent. Anyway, I'm hardly ever there. Aunt Anne dotes on the girl, as does her maid. Everything is fine... stop worrying.'

Her evening felt quite spoilt. Why did she have to reassure everyone else about matters that were of no importance? She rose, and held out her arm to Joseph, asking him to call for their cloaks. They would not stay for the rest of the performance.

Mary looked down at her father, slumped over the table, his shoulders rounded in defeat.

'Enjoy the rest of the evening,' she said, as he raised pink-rimmed eyes. 'Remember to laugh. It's meant to be a comedy.'

Following Law's reinstatement as comptroller-general of the government bank, Mary felt a great deal of self-righteous plea-sure when share prices recovered. Why didn't people listen to her more often? She made sure her father, Joseph, and her aunt, understood that she was the only one who truly had her finger on the pulse of financial affairs.

Mary met Olive in a new café in the Tuileries, to share their plans for Fanny's wedding. When her friend arrived, over half an hour late, she looked pale and her eyes darted from side to side, as if she needed to check their surroundings.

'Are you feeling well?' Mary asked.

'I'm worried about returning safely,' Olive answered. 'I struggled to get here. There's a crowd at every bank, blocking the streets. My coach couldn't get through.'

'I've heard that worried customers are even paying apprentices to stand in line for days,' Mary said, hoping that Olive might laugh. When her friend's expression remained grim, she added: 'Now we're here, let's have some coffee, but we can be quick. I think it's all nonsense, little more than sheer panic, but I won't keep you.'

The women sipped their coffee, but any interest in the details of the dresses they planned to order for Fanny's reception had evaporated.

'Let me pay for this,' Mary said, handing over a ten-livre note to the waiter. She felt relief when the note was accepted, but was shocked to be handed some amateurish, home-made notes as change.

'Look at these, Olive.' Mary held out the fake banknotes. 'They've obviously been manufactured in a back room.'

Olive smiled and shrugged. 'That sums it up. People aren't confident about banknotes and don't understand how paper money works. When notes are scarce, why not make your own?'

'I won't complain this time,' Mary said, standing to leave. 'We'll never use this café again.'

Olive took her arm and they walked to where their coaches waited. The gardens were empty of groups of friends or couples, the paths lined with beggars in rags, their faces raw and scabbed, hands outstretched and trembling.

Mary and Olive's coachmen walked towards them as they came into view, and the women hurried to reach the safety of their escorts. At their carriages, Olive turned towards Mary and pulled her into a deep embrace. Olive had never touched her before and Mary drew back, startled.

'You said we won't use that café again,' her friend said, 'but we won't visit these gardens again, at least not for a long time. We've made a great deal of money, but something has been taken from us and that is sad.'

'Nonsense,' Mary argued, 'all this will pass.'

Olive climbed into her carriage and leaned out through the open window. 'I don't think so. Goodbye, Mary. Keep yourself safe.'

For the first time, Mary felt at risk travelling alone in Paris. Held up by a rabble in the rue Saint-Honoré, she drew her blinds to shut out the mob and heard voices surrounding the coach mocking John Law. Relieved to reach her apartment, after hours spent inching through streets blocked by angry Parisians, Mary told her maid she did not intend to journey without company in future. The maid agreed this was sensible in such troubled times. Emboldened by her mistress's unusual sharing of a confidence, she added that their neighbour's manservant had seen Law's coachman pulled down from his carriage. There was a fight and the man had broken his leg.

Her aunt was out, playing cards with her sister Frances and other Jacobite matrons. Hours passed and Mary felt growing concern. When Anne finally reached home, she had to be helped into a chair and brought some warm, sweet wine before she could speak.

'We all got there safely,' Anne puffed out the words, 'but decided to abandon the game. We didn't want to be caught up in trouble trying to reach home.'

Her aunt's carriage had become trapped, like Mary's had been earlier, and the coachman had leant forward to ask a passer-by the cause of the delay.

Anne's bottom lip trembled and before she could continue, she swiped at her watery eyes with a handkerchief. 'He said people had been crushed to death in the queue at the bank. The crowd ahead were carrying their bodies through the streets.'

Mary gasped. 'What an awful thing. You must have been terrified.'

'I feared for my own death,' Anne admitted.

Mary was not a natural comforter of others but tried to calm her aunt.

'This discord is temporary. We must stay indoors for now, but I'm convinced that in a week or two – a month at most – everything will be back to normal. In the meantime, my dear aunt, why don't you take a potion and rest in your bed?'

Late summer progressed, a season unusually hot and sticky, made worse by confinement indoors. On the streets, disorder grew, and the Regent announced a ban on all public assembly. The salons, apartments and palaces buzzed with news that the Royal Bank of France was bankrupt. The price of shares tumbled and those who had lent money, whether to a bank or a friend, sought immediate repayment in gold or silver. By October, John Law's Company des Indes was liquidated. Those who still felt safe to roam the streets, crowds seeking recompense or justice, set fire to millions of worthless banknotes outside the Louvre.

Trapped in the apartment with the shutters closed and the drapes shut, Mary felt the atmosphere thicken with unbearable tension. She waited for Joseph, numb with disbelief at his absence, wanting his comfort and the reassurance of a fellow investor, someone who understood. The last time they met, Joseph had asked her to move permanently into his home, but Mary had decided she could not abandon her aunt; a decision she now regretted.

Weeks passed and still Joseph did not come. The only visitor was her father, bleached, and aged with shock, blaming her for their family's ruin. One afternoon, when her aunt started to accuse her of stealing her money, her voice rising to an ear-splitting wail, Mary ran from the room and demanded her coachman take her to Fanny's. She felt desperate to be with someone who wouldn't be angry with her, who might even have made the same mistakes.

In Fanny's elegant salon, the air fresh with the scent of cut flowers displayed in translucent porcelain vases, life was unchanged. In the tranquil, late-afternoon sunshine, the pastel silks covering the furniture shone with a soft glow. Fanny smiled broadly and held out her arms in welcome. There was no sign of tears, no blotched skin, no wringing of hands.

'Mary, what a surprise. I do wish you had let me know you were planning to visit. Shall I ring for some wine?'

'Fanny, oh Fanny, my dear friend,' Mary blurted out her unplanned speech. 'I came as soon as I could. Have you lost everything too?'

Fanny looked puzzled. 'Do you mean have we lost our fortune? We sold our shares last summer and bought land. Some paintings too if I remember.'

'You sold?' Mary repeated.

'Yes, we sold at the peak of the market. Didn't you?'

Mary slumped into an armchair, grasping her side as if she was in pain. 'How did you know when to sell?'

'Why, Richard advised me of course, before he went abroad.'

Feeling as if she could no longer swallow, Mary accepted a

glass of wine but found she could not drink even a mouthful. She placed her glass on the table at her elbow, struggling to control her shaking hands.

Fanny stood, as if to call for her servant. 'Are you well? Shall I send for some help?'

Panic would not allow Mary to stay still for a moment longer. She rose and pushed past Fanny, slipping across the polished parquet floor of the entrance hall, crashing into a mahogany table, and causing a vase of lilies to topple and smash.

'Sorry, sorry,' she called out, before tumbling down the broad sweep of steps towards her waiting carriage.

'Take me to Mr Gage's house,' she shouted up to the coachman. 'Hurry!'

The short journey between Fanny's palace and Joseph's townhouse seemed interminable. The coach made progress in short bursts, easing through disparate groups of jeering Parisians, blocking the road with fires built with furniture robbed from banks. At every barrier, Mary heard her coachman argue with the protestors, insisting that he conveyed only a terrified young woman, innocent of any financial mismanagement. Usually, this was enough to let them pass, but in one terrifying moment, the carriage door flew open and three men, their faces smudged with soot, peered inside. Mary covered her face with a handkerchief, hoping that the sight of a distressed woman on her own would satisfy. After several tense minutes, the door slammed shut.

At last, they passed through the gateway to Joseph's court, still manned by a guard. The windows of Joseph's house looked shuttered and blank. Mary climbed the steps to his door but no matter how long she battered, or called out his name, no one answered. She leaned her forehead against the polished wood, hearing only the echo of her flat palm thumping against the panels. Turning to press her back against the door, gasping for breath, she looked up towards the rows of staring windows from the townhouses opposite and wept in deep, sobbing gulps. It felt as if the solid granite beneath her feet would open and swallow her into a pit. Her legs buckled and she knelt, her forehead resting against the cold stones. With clenched fists, Mary beat at the hard surface until her hands bled.

The coachman climbed down from his seat and grasped the bridle of the lead horse, calling out to the guard for help. Once the other man stood between the heads of the agitated horses, their bridles secure, the coachman mounted the steps and knelt beside his employer.

'Looks like Count Gage has gone, Lady Herbert,' he whispered. 'The guard said he left days ago. It's time to go home.'

CHAPTER 10

1721

The Muti Palace was a small and undistinguished building, compared to the exiled court's palace in Urbino and already a source of much grumbling amongst Winifred and Maxwell's companions. For those who could remember the palace at Saint-Germain, and the generosity of Louis XIV, the consensus was that their so-called welcome from the Pope had been begrudging.

James's announcement that he could not afford to support their number, and those who could live elsewhere should leave, added to their sense of being unwelcome in yet another foreign city. Unlike the Catholic emigrés, the Protestants had little reason to stay, unless guilty of active conspiracy against the British government. Many took the hint and sought family in other parts of Europe or returned home to their crumbling castles. The Catholic families were less fortunate. To go home, they had to renounce their faith or forfeit their estates.

Winifred and Maxwell were entirely dependent upon James's generosity. Neither had been assigned any regular duties, yet they had to be available in case a request was made. Without a permanent role, they were forced to live outside the palace, but close by, and had to pay for their own lodgings and food. Other Catholic couples still had property managed by family or agents and were able to supplement their pensions with regular payments from home. Let them try living as I do even for a day, Winifred thought, amongst the poorest of the exiled community.

Their rooms were a few streets from the Muti Palace, down a narrow, cobbled lane, never touched by sunlight. The house leaned so close to its neighbours, they could shake hands if they chose with people living on the other side of the passageway. She still felt uncomfortable walking in streets where accents were strange and the smell not always pleasant, and she spent her empty hours listening to the conversations of other women, shouting to each other as they hung out washing.

If the Palace Ducale had seemed a jealous and quarrelsome place, in Rome, the rigidity of the hierarchy between palace insiders and outsiders, made it impossible for Winifred to become known at court and promote her qualities. She tried hard not to feel singled out by her poverty but knew she must look too shabby even to be considered for the queen's service. She also suspected that people were wary of Maxwell, because of his reputation for borrowing money which he could not pay back.

It all felt so unjust; not a single man in this godforsaken place, except her husband, had ever fought on British soil for the restoration of a Stuart king. Her own parents had served James's father as senior members of his court, her father as Secretary of State and her mother as governess to the royal children. The current holders of these posts were a humble Mr and Mrs Hay, but her parents had been a duke and duchess. Such comparisons were petty, but it was more than fair to notice that Mrs Hay had no experience of children, should any be born.

On the rare occasions when Winifred was able to access the

palace workrooms, she was given the task of mending the young queen's undergarments, a task well below her capability. The woman who asked her to help, the mistress of the queen's wardrobe, whispered, 'If you could ease the seams on these shifts, I'd be grateful. Queen Klementyna is gaining weight.'

Winifred's fingers trembled as she tried to thread her needle and her normally deft stitching looked as if a child had made their first attempt. As soon as the last seam had been sewn, Winifred wiped her sweaty palms on her apron and sought a meeting with Mrs Hay. She found her in an anteroom next to the kitchen, supervising maids counting linen.

Winifred spoke softly at first but raised her voice as Mrs Hay failed to turn around. 'Why do you keep me away from the queen? She's expecting a child, isn't she? Why wasn't I told?'

Mrs Hay finished her sentence before turning to Winifred with a smile stretched over her bare teeth like a grimace.

'My dear Lady Winifred, the imminent birth of a royal child is not your business.'

'The news has been deliberately kept from me. You believe I would ask the king to be the child's governess because I'm the only woman at court who has held this position before. You have acted out of jealousy.'

Mrs Hay pursed her thin lips. 'It has nothing to do with me. I follow the king's orders. He has not requested that you care for his child. If you have any quarrel, it is with him.'

Winifred remained standing, fists clenched, heart pounding. Mrs Hay dipped her head to indicate that the conversation was at an end and continued to berate the housemaids.

Before she left the palace, Winifred sought a private meeting with the king, something her former status still allowed. Two days later, she followed a servant past the inner courtyard and upstairs to the principal floor, where the king and queen had their staterooms. This was only her second time in the formal areas of the palace, and she trailed behind the servant, marvelling at the frescoed gallery and ornate console tables positioned between windows that rose from floor to ceiling. James met her in his library, a dark room lined with books stacked high between gilded marble columns.

Winifred curtseyed before the king, who remained standing.

'Your Majesty, I am sorry to be presumptuous,' Winifred stammered, 'but I am the best candidate to be governess for your child. I'm afraid I may have been overlooked. Mrs Hay doesn't know me. It feels like everyone has forgotten my background.'

James listened, his expression polite but distant, as if preoccupied with something else.

'Countess, I had not forgotten, although given my other priorities, such an omission might be forgiven. We cannot afford to take on new staff; Mrs Hay is already employed and will have to manage, despite her lack of experience. Is it so difficult to look after a newborn baby, with the assistance of a team of women?'

The king turned away; his attention caught by a book lying open on the library table. Winifred waited, studying the heavy carving on the desk; scrolls, tumbling fruits, draped human figures tangled together in their descent down sturdy, curved legs.

The king's secretary nodded. It was time for Winifred to leave. She curtsied, hoping to catch James's attention but he remained absorbed, indifferent to her departure.

That night, Maxwell and Winifred quarrelled, as they so often did.

'You did not try,' he barked, 'not hard enough. That was our only chance of advancement and you missed it.'

Winifred retaliated, sparing her husband nothing. 'If you

spent less, I might have been able to present myself as worthy of a position at court. If I had been chosen for the queen's household, I would have been noticed. I'm never there. I'm not seen.'

Maxwell sneered at her, walking backwards towards the door. 'I might have guessed this would be my fault. You're never at the palace because you're idle. What do you do all day except hang around this apartment? When did anyone last see you smile?'

Winifred's voice roared as the door slammed behind Maxwell's departing back. 'I will smile once you are sober, you selfish bastard, but don't expect to see a grin on my face anytime soon.'

It was Grace, not Winifred, who had made friends with their neighbours, even earning respect in the covenanting stronghold of Dumfries. Without her, Winifred was adrift. In her letters, Grace encouraged Winifred to be more adventurous, to explore her new home, learn about its past and try harder to speak the language. In a gentle reprimand, she reminded Winifred that no matter how poor she was, many of her neighbours would be poorer. Why not explore her local shops and discover what the citizens of Rome cooked and ate? Why not find a dressmaker amongst local businesses, who could surely copy a dress or two for little money?

Winifred tried. She visited a convent next to the Church of Santi Apostoli, hoping she might be able to help nurse the sick, as her mother would have done, but when she tried to explain what she wanted, the door was slammed shut in her face. With hindsight, she realised that pretending to rock a baby had been a mistake. With food, she'd had more success. Overcoming her fear of the narrow streets, she entered shops that were little more than holes in the wall. Through dark rooms at the back, which smelt of damp and decaying vegetable matter, Winifred found oils, olives, vegetables she couldn't identify, dried pasta and unrecognisable meats such as oxtail and pig's cheek.

Using her limited vocabulary and much gesture, Winifred explained that she didn't know how to cook such ingredients. Once they understood, the women who served her laughed at first, but then took time to explain. Step by step, they held up each item, demonstrating whether it was for pouring, or chopping, or frying. One woman led her by the arm to her own house across the alleyway, where her tiny mother was cooking the family meal, and left Winifred behind to watch. She was recognised in her favourite shops and called Contessa to her face, but more likely 'the one who can't cook' behind her back. But 'the woman who couldn't cook' was a fast learner and she and Maxwell now ate well, mopping up the delicious juices from the pan with dense, local bread and drinking wine brought out from the depths of the shop by her new friends' husbands.

In time, she tired of staring through the window at her neighbours' washing and found the confidence to explore more of Rome. She wrote to her daughter about the Romans, and it became a project to find their ancient ruins scattered throughout this strange city. One bright day in early spring, as she strolled through streets where buildings huddled together in unplanned chaos, Winifred thought of the financial disaster that had befallen her brother due to the selfishness of his daughter. For the first time, she felt relief her husband had no money. He would certainly have invested, given the chance.

The streets widened out into Winifred's favourite square, the Piazza di Spagna, always an unexpected pleasure. It was hot for the time of year, and she was disadvantaged by wearing the heavy, sombre dress she had bought years ago, to mourn the queen mother. Resting on the railing around the fountain, she trickled some water onto her wrists and dipped a cloth into the multiple jets, wiping her face and neck. She took care that no one was watching; it was not fanciful to imagine that she might be asked to move on, mistaken for one of the beggars who thronged the streets. Winifred felt her body cool, helped by the water's mist and a breeze drifting from the line of trees that climbed the hill towards the church of the Santissima Trinità dei Monti. If she had enough money, Winifred thought, she would buy a house in this square, with its beautiful fountain shaped like a fantastical boat. The houses were solid, well-built residences with tiled roofs, regular rows of windows and arched doorways. Each house was topped by a pagoda with a turret and flags, and one house, the one she most envied, even had an enclosed balcony where she would be cool and able to watch the square in private.

Two young men stood near the fountain, one of them pointing out the church. It was not unusual to hear English spoken, since wealthy young men often spent a year travelling in Europe, but these two had Scots accents. They turned towards the fountain and Winifred could see their faces beneath their broad-brimmed hats. It was a shock to recognise her nephew Linton, the eldest son of her husband's sister, Mary. When they had neighbouring estates in the Scottish borders, Mary had been Winifred's closest friend.

'Linton!' Winifred called out, shading her eyes to see his reaction.

The young man peered through the sparkling haze. Failing to see who had called his name, he walked around the circular railings, his back now blocking the sun.

'Aunt Winifred, how fortunate to meet you.' Linton's colour rose, belying his words.

'How long have you been in Rome?' Winifred tried to make her question sound less like the accusation it was.

'Two weeks, actually, we're staying at the Muti Palace.' Linton gestured towards his companion but did not introduce him. The friend remained firmly on the other side of the fountain, engrossed in the architecture of the square. 'I was planning to visit you, but I couldn't find out where you lived.'

Linton's hands skimmed the rim of his hat, his nose, his beard, and his eyes shifted, avoiding her gaze. She understood how awkward it was for him, to have heard about his aunt and uncle living in such reduced circumstances. People may even have hinted at Maxwell's drinking, his borrowing.

'How are your parents and the rest of the family?' she asked, trying to make Linton comfortable.

He searched in the leather bag slung around his neck and produced a letter.

'My mother asked me to give you this, but only to you. It's lucky I met you today, Aunt Winifred, I didn't know how to deliver it without my uncle knowing.'

Poor Linton had indeed been faced with a dilemma and Winifred immediately forgave him. She watched them stride away across the square, both young men dressed in the comfortable travelling uniform of the grand tour. As they reached a passageway leading into the adjoining streets, Linton turned and waved. She guessed he would leave Rome without any further contact with her, or Maxwell, and that was for the best.

In her rooms, Winifred tore open Mary's letter, standing at the window where there was more daylight. She trembled as she read her sister-in-law describe how Maxwell had written repeatedly to his family, demanding more money. They had sent him what they could spare, Mary said, but there must be no more requests. Any further correspondence would be destroyed.

Winifred felt blood rush to her forehead and to prevent a faint, fell onto a chair next to their rough table. She sat for hours, tracing the surface grooves and splinters with her fingers. It was dark when Maxwell came home but she had lit no lamps.

'Sitting in the dark?' he asked, throwing his cape onto the hook behind the door. 'You were requested this afternoon, at the palace. I had to say you were ill.'

'Our nephew Linton is in Rome. I know you've borrowed money from Mary and Charles.' Winifred's tone was flat; it wasn't a question.

Maxwell took time to light the lamp on the table and she waited for the bluster; first, denial and then lies.

'They owe us money,' he said, licking his thumb and fore-finger to extinguish the taper. 'My brother-in-law earns from our estate but gives us nothing.'

Winifred held her voice steady. 'That is simply not true. How many times must I remind you? Our estate is managed by trustees, and anything earned goes to pay your debts. When the money we owe is paid, our son inherits. You signed the documents.'

Maxwell snorted. 'Under duress,' he said.

Winifred sweated, the heat of the day trapped between the enclosed walls.

'We had no choice,' she said. 'We were bankrupt, because of the life you chose to lead in Edinburgh. How can you so easily forget and twist the story to your own ends?'

Maxwell mocked Winifred's patient tone. 'Oh, here we go again. How many times do I need to hear this?'

'Just stop wasting our money – stop borrowing. We can't pay it back.'

'Why is that, dear wife? Tell me again why you were not chosen to be governess? At least one of us should mix with the people who matter. I must spend money, simply to be included at court.'

Winifred's resolve shattered and she spat out harsh words, words she knew to be true. 'I understand only too well. We're not wanted here. They think we're trouble. And you... you're an embarrassment. You stink of wine, whatever time of day, just like you do now. Who would employ you?'

'And you stink of garlic.' Maxwell reached across the table and grabbed Winifred's wrist, his grip twisting her skin.

'Leave me alone!' she yelled. 'Just go!' The pain caused tears to sting Winifred's eyes and course down her cheeks.

Maxwell released his grip and strode across the room, throwing his cape across his shoulders. Instead of leaving, he returned and brought his face down close to hers. Winifred felt his spit on her cheeks.

'Let me tell you what will happen next. That useless son of ours must stop poncing around in Paris. He will go home and reclaim the estate. I don't care whether it belongs to him or me, I want it back in our family. Then, we will leave.'

Winifred watched the oil in the lamp sputter and flare before it extinguished. In the dark room, the smell of smouldering wick masked the encroaching rancid odour of the street, as people emptied their rubbish into the gulley below. Maxwell would never accept the truth, she thought, rubbing her bruised wrist. Going home will never, ever be possible.

CHAPTER 11

1722

William took advantage of still owning a carriage to visit his sister Anne. In the months since the collapse of the French banking system and the end of John Law's brief but catastrophic reign, he had learned, day by miserable day, the extent of his daughter's borrowing. She had been profligate in buying foreign currency and converting it into French banknotes, now worthless. If any good fortune was to be had from this mess, she had not inveigled him into acting as guarantor for most of her debts, but the money he now owed Richard Cantillon on Mary's behalf was enough to bankrupt him for the rest of his life.

As the streets of Paris passed by unseen before his staring eyes, William thought it ironic that his financial ruin had been brought about by his daughter rather than his own ill-judged investments. For other Catholic exiles in Paris, their lives already ruined by punitive legislation at home, a desperation for money had made them vulnerable to the national fantasy of easy wealth. Many families had been broken forever. The birth of a son last December to the Pretender ought to have led to days of celebration but had barely been acknowledged in his circles.

Anne's only maid led him through to the salon, where he found his sister still in her dressing robe, her face streaked and swollen, her hair dishevelled.

'Dear brother, what can we do? You must help us. If only Joseph were here. Do you know where he is? Mary won't come out of her room. The food we leave outside her door is left uneaten. Perhaps you could try knocking, she might speak to you.'

William slumped in an empty chair and took Anne's damp hand in his, noticing her double chin tremble as she struggled to control even more tears. He could weep himself and had done so many times in private. If he could only keep Powis Castle, he didn't care how many of his other properties he had to sell, but his heart had broken when he'd handed over his mines and the land of his tenant farmers to trustees. This was what Mary would never begin to understand; the money she had borrowed in his name belonged to the miners and the tenants of the family estates. Yet he found he couldn't blame her. She had been drawn into a world she did not understand, led astray by Joseph Gage. In his acidic gut there fermented a deep dislike for Gage and for Mary's brothers, his own sons, who had made clear their intent to sue their sister, on behalf of the family. If anyone was to blame for this mess, it was him. He was her father, and no matter how difficult, society expected him to control an unmarried daughter.

Today, he had to break more bad news to his sister.

'Anne, you asked me to check the extent of your debt and the actions you must now take. I'm afraid you have no choice but to sell the Carrington estates in Britain. I can't advise you about your debts here in France. Are you and Mary being pursued by creditors?'

Anne pushed a pile of letters towards him, still sealed.

'She won't open them. Most are addressed to her.'

'You've not been threatened?'

'We don't go out. The last time Mary tried she was accosted in the street.'

William thought before replying, stroking the end of his nose. 'You will have to move on. Sell what you can and find somewhere cheaper to live. If you can't pay these debts...' he waved towards the letters spread on the table, '... you risk debtors' prison. Are you able to provide for Winifred's child, or shall I look after her until her mother can fetch her? That girl has seen enough trouble without witnessing your arrest.'

His words, blunt but realistic, caused Anne to give way to another bout of weeping. She bent forward and sobbed into the crook of his arm. He waited for her to finish, awkwardly patting her unwashed hair, until her shoulders were still.

Anne gulped and swallowed back a choke before she replied. 'The thing is, William, I'm married. I have a husband. I will sell the estates, but as a married woman, my husband is responsible for my debts. Of course, I won't bankrupt him. What use would he be if I did? But he's a safety net, I suppose.'

William echoed her words. 'You're married? You have a husband?'

His sister lowered her head and clutched her robe tightly around her neck. She couldn't meet his incredulous stare. 'I married a London lawyer, over ten years ago.'

'But why have you told no one? Why aren't you living with this man, your so-called husband? Who is he?'

Anne sniffed and her expression took on some of its former haughty pride. 'There is a difference in status between us. No doubt he saw some advantage in the marriage for himself, but I made sure he kept it secret. I do visit him when I'm in London.'

Of his sisters, Anne had been his least favoured, something

he had always tried to hide, but now his contempt for her felt pure and right. She had engaged in marriage with a man too ordinary to be acknowledged in public but, because of her debts, would now become only too visible. This lawyer, whoever he was, was about to pay a high price for his union. He rose awkwardly, letting Anne's hand fall from his arm. He would try to speak to his daughter, not that she would make any more sense.

'I'll knock on Mary's door now,' he said. 'Remember, you must leave very soon. Find some lodgings and try not to stay in one place for too long. I will give up the lease on my apartment and move in here, to keep an eye on the child.'

William tapped on his daughter's bedroom door. 'Mary, Mary, please let me in.'

The door opened a fraction and William waited before he entered, until he heard the shuffling movements from inside settle. The room was in darkness and the drapes hanging from the canopy were closed. He parted the curtains nearest to the door and dropped down onto the end of the bed, reaching out for what he assumed were Mary's feet under the bedclothes. The rest of his daughter was an indeterminate shape under a pile of bedding.

Without warning, Mary sat up, threw aside her covers, and fell onto his neck, sobbing. The shock was so great, he had to stop himself from jumping aside. Mary's unwashed smell was unpleasant, but he remained still, saying nothing, simply rubbing her back in a manner he hoped conveyed concern, instead of the deep resentment that boiled inside him.

'Father, what will I do? Everyone wants money from me and I can't pay them back. I hate John Law. I hope he's dead.'

It wasn't relevant, William knew, but facts were comforting. He withdrew his hand and tried to look his daughter in the eye.

'No, he's not dead. The Regent is a decent man and stood by

his friend, but in the end Law asked to be released from royal service. I understand he's left the country. Mary, you must listen to me. Law has promised to pay back his debts and has agreed all his properties and land should be sold for the benefit of the people of France. You followed his example when there was a profit to be made. Now, you must follow his example and pay back your debts, even if it takes you the rest of your life.'

Mary wailed, falling back onto her bolster, and threw her arm across her brow. 'Why am I always to blame? No one complained when I was making money for them. Those bankers, Richard Cantillon and goodness knows who else, have done very well out of me and Joseph. I can't pay them back. My life is over!'

William's eyes adjusted to the dark and he gazed around the room. Her marquetry dressing table, the gilded chairs, even the commode, all would need to be sold.

'Anne tells me you're not eating, that you don't ever leave this room.'

Mary lifted her arm and nodded, the glisten from her wet eyes captured in the light from the open door.

'Where is Joseph? Why has he abandoned me?' she whimpered.

'Where did he come from?' William answered. 'The underworld of Paris made him and I'm quite sure that's where he's returned. If you're not safe from creditors, then neither is he. Like you, he's hiding.'

'So, you think I'll see him again?'

William stood to leave; it was time to behave like the father he ought to have been. He would deliver his ultimatum and hurry away before Mary grasped the gravity of his decision. He coughed before speaking, hoping to gain her full attention.

'Your only safe option is to disappear. I can see how unwell you have become, but I hear only anger and self-pity, and no remorse. I am a man with many sisters, who both trouble and delight me, but my most useful sister is Lucy, the abbess of a convent in Bruges. I will ask your Aunt Lucy to take you in. Like many women before you, a life of penitence will be your refuge. In the meantime, I have advised your aunt that you should both leave this apartment, as soon as possible.'

In the few seconds it took for Mary to understand her father's intent, her stuffy room became as cold as a nun's cell. She felt her skin crawl with fear and she no longer trusted her legs to give her support. Her father was kinder and more indulgent than most but he held a ridiculous amount of power when it came to the fate of an unmarried daughter. If he decided to commit her to a nunnery, she could be taken away by force and might never be released, particularly if she was judged not to be of sound mind. She must recover from her trauma without delay, and certainly before her father returned.

Forcing herself to leave her bed, despite weakness from shock and lack of food, within hours Mary had dressed, and within days she and her aunt disappeared into areas of Paris she had never visited, let alone heard of. Her father was well-intentioned but lazy, and if she kept herself hidden, she knew he would not try to pursue her, but her creditors would be more persistent.

To make the flit, they were forced to maintain a carriage, even though Paris had public carriages they might have used, but they could not risk being seen in public. Whether it was the incongruity of the carriage, stabled near their cheap lodgings, or the indiscretion of the maid and cook they had retained, it was not long before the nightly harangue of stones at the window and thumps on the door began.

One outing in public could not be avoided; Mary had to meet with Richard Cantillon. His letters, eventually opened, were more threatening than all the curt correspondence she had received so far, and his bailiff visits the most terrifying. If he saw her again, in person, perhaps he would soften, remembering the days in the Tuileries when he, Fanny, Joseph and Mary had met as friends. She ought to have tried harder to like Richard. Perhaps it wasn't too late?

Richard Cantillon looked as if the financial turbulence, which had rocked the nation's government, as well as almost every individual in France, had passed him by. He was not aged, his eyes were clear, and he retained a calm, professional demeanour as he welcomed Mary into his office in the rue Vivienne.

'You are a most welcome visitor, Lady Herbert,' Richard began. 'I hope you are here to set up a plan of repayment. Your father has made a start at paying back what is owed to me by your family, but it would help us both if you would contribute.'

'You must have suffered great losses too, Richard. Joseph told me how deeply you had invested in the Compagnie des Indes. Surely you can understand how we are all victims of John Law's plan and find some sympathy for my family's position. You will be paid back but give us time... please.'

Mary watched Richard try to smile but his lips stretched across his teeth without any visible warmth and his eyes remained cold.

'There were only three people who truly understood Law's system,' he said. 'One of them was Law himself and he has vanished. The second was the Regent, the Duc d'Orléans, and he is denying that he ever had any real understanding. The third was me, and I used my knowledge to make sure I did not suffer.'

She guessed at his meaning but wanted to hear the words

spoken aloud. 'You chose to warn Fanny and others but not Joseph or me. You sold your own shares at their highest value.'

'Lady Herbert, you borrowed money from a bank. It was not my responsibility to monitor your financial dealings.'

'But you warned Fanny,' Mary repeated.

'Fanny is a friend, and you are not. You were a customer and now you are a debtor. Since your brother is suing me, there can be no question of friendship between me, or any member of your family.'

Cantillon sounded so smug, so certain of his infallibility, a rush to destroy him flooded through her, her disappointment and frustration roaring into the white heat of rage.

'I will sue you!' she shouted. 'It was you who persuaded me to borrow. You encouraged me!'

Richard's voice remained calm, and his eyes never left hers.

'You were desperate to invest. Good advice would have failed to stop you. You would not have listened.'

Mary's chair fell backwards as she stood, stabbing the air with her finger, shattering any remaining hope of a reasonable settlement.

'Richard Cantillon, I am accusing you of being a usurer and a crook.'

Richard walked towards the door and held it open, bowing towards his guest.

'Lady Herbert, I believe this meeting is over. I will see you in court.'

This cramped room, one they used for everything except sleep, was their third lodging. The cook, the maid and lastly the carriage, had gone, their only income Aunt Anne's pitiful subsistence from her husband. Mary paced between the crowded, mismatched furniture, remembering every word of her row with Richard Cantillon. She had mishandled the meeting, that was true. Allowing her temper to speak for her had been regrettable, but it wasn't her fault. Even her aunt had expected too much, had built the meeting into something it could never be. Now she had taken to bed, miserable with the pain of crushed hope. Every snore from the bedroom stoked Mary's resentment. She wasn't to blame for this.

It would be a risk, she thought, but if she took care, she could go out. It wouldn't be difficult to hide her appearance since masks were still widely worn and in this area of Paris, the streets were not yet lit at night. She decided on her black dress, which was elegant enough to allow her admittance to a gaming salon but would not advertise her past good fortune. As she dressed, pinning up her hair and choosing a plain, silver necklace, Mary felt the old thrill of anticipation. She took all the money from the drawer where she and her aunt stored coins used to cover their weekly expenses, but if her old luck returned, she would replace it all and more. In the kitchen, Mary found the knife they used to prepare vegetables, small but sharp, and slipped it into the secret pocket sewn into her petticoat.

To an experienced gambler, the location of local gaming rooms was never a surprise and Mary had noticed three, close to their lodgings. At the first door she tapped lightly, and after a superficial glance, was admitted. The salon was dimly lit, the air thick with smoke from cheap candles, guttering whenever the curtain at the entrance was drawn. The players avoided any social contact, their focus entirely upon the play. There was little conversation, only the rattle of tiles and the click of counters. At first she watched, and then placed cautious bets, anxious to test her old skills of prediction and probability. After winning three games, Mary decided to leave, aware she must not strain her welcome. She slipped the coins into the pocket of her petticoat and with her thumb, stroked the reassuring blade of the knife.

In the second gaming room, there were few players and Mary noticed there were no observers positioned at the tables. As the only woman, and playing alone, she felt conspicuous. The other players seemed to prevent her moving between the tables by blocking her path, and when the dealer refused to accept further bets from her, she decided to escape and move on to a third salon, one she'd noticed hidden down a dark lane.

Gathering her cloak tightly around her shoulders, and dragging her hood over her head, she hesitated in a doorway to check whether she had been followed. She felt for the knife and waited. There were no footsteps behind her, only voices carrying from the salon's doorway, still some distance down the alley. Every time the door opened to admit a new player, a pool of light split the darkness. Taking advantage of another guest's entrance, she ran to the open door and squeezed inside before it closed.

A man held up a lamp to scan her face. 'You are playing?'

'I am indeed,' Mary replied. 'Is there a space for me?'

'Minimum ten-livre spend at each table. You got the funds?'

'Yes, of course I have.'

'Right, you can enter. And no soliciting.'

Mary pushed through velvet curtains into a room where she heard the familiar hum of play. Her eyes adjusted, she found the Faro table and placed her bets. Of course, she won easily and as she counted her winnings, felt a familiar prickle across her scalp, an awareness of being watched. She had made a basic error, advertising her presence as a lone woman, one with money. A player bumped into her from behind and when he squeezed past, she felt his hand grasp her backside. Another man forced his way through the throng and stood too close, offering to buy her a glass of wine, his eyes never leaving the silver pendant that sat between her breasts. Mary refused him and pushed her way back through the crowd towards the refuge of a new game.

She pretended to watch the play, so that she could assess her predators. There were three of them, men who seemed to be working together, each one of them stationed where he could monitor her movements. A trickle of sweat ran down her back and her armpits prickled. The third man moved to the door and touched his hat. It was a signal. Mary scanned the room. Where were the others... she couldn't see them.

From behind, someone grasped her wrist and forced it up between her shoulder blades. She felt his full body weight lean forward, pushing her against the table, and his lips brushed her neck. He tugged her arm higher, and she gasped with pain. She smelt his fetid, meaty breath as he whispered in her ear: 'Don't make a sound. You will come with me.' His hand slid into the purse hidden in her petticoat and she felt him withdraw the knife, sickened as his fingers returned, to explore beneath her undergarments.

Across the table, a fourth man stared. Mary risked returning his gaze, her eyes round with fear, making a silent plea for help. He wore a heavy beard and a workman's cap but there was something about the expression in his eyes, not lustful or greedy but full of wonder.

The bearded stranger called out her name. 'Mary, is that you? It's me, Joseph.' He forced players aside to reach her, causing them to raise their fists and swear.

Mary's captor dropped her arm and before she could face him, he was gone. Joseph grasped her other arm and pulled her close. She rested her head on his shoulder, trembling.

'I'm not safe here,' she whispered. 'Men are watching me. One of them tried to take me prisoner. He touched me.' They both raised their heads and scanned the room, but there was only a sea of bent heads, intent upon the tables.

Joseph lifted a strand of hair from her face and his finger traced her cheek. 'Come on, I'll take you home, I'm tired of rescuing you from games of Faro.'

They walked together, arm in arm, through silent, hazy streets and the darkness suddenly seemed ordinary and safe. Joseph stopped frequently, listening for any sounds behind them.

'Are we being followed?' Mary asked, peering into the mist.

'Unlikely,' Joseph said. 'My reputation goes before me. Once they recognised me, as I'm sure they did, they couldn't be sure I wasn't with... erm... comrades. They wouldn't risk a fight with me, or my friends.'

'Joseph, why did you leave me? Why was there no word?' Mary pleaded, when they stopped at the passageway to her rooms.

'If we'd stayed in contact, I would have led them to you, and you would have led them to me. I had to vanish and make a living the only way I can.'

'Who do you mean by *them*?'

'Cantillon's men, of course. If they'd caught me, I'd be in the river by now with my throat cut. I know too much about him and his methods.'

Mary shivered. 'But what if that was Cantillon's men, back there in the salon?'

'It wasn't. I check out every salon before I start playing. I know every one of Cantillon's thugs by sight... and then there's this.' Joseph pulled back his coat and revealed a hidden sword, his grin asking Mary to be impressed.

'He cheated us, Joseph, but I don't want him dead. I'm suing him and so is my brother.'

'Hmm, I'd rather kill him. But for now, I'll join in whatever legal action you're taking once I've made enough to pay my costs. How on earth can you afford a lawyer?'

'Don't laugh, but my aunt secretly married a London lawyer, years ago.'

Joseph threw back his head and gave a bark of laughter. 'She did what?'

'It *is* shocking, but we live off whatever he can spare and he's advising us on the lawsuit. It's turned out to be the best decision she ever made. Of course, my father has cut me off.'

Joseph scanned the street in both directions. 'My dearest, I will leave you again, but I'll be back, I promise. Never, ever go gaming alone, at least not around here. You were in real danger tonight.'

'I'm always in danger. I'm robbed every single day by lawyers.'

Joseph gripped Mary's shoulders and shook her.

'No, you're not,' he insisted. 'You're being harassed by bailiffs, that's all. You have no idea what real danger means. If I hadn't been there, being robbed would have been the least of your problems. I don't have to explain.'

Mary felt too much relief at having found Joseph again, for his warning to make much sense.

'I promise,' she whispered, her voice deep with yearning, 'I won't try to make money from gaming, but I need you at my side. You saw that for yourself tonight.'

Joseph disappeared into the darkness, his shadow fading as he darted between the street trees, fog dripping from the branches like cobwebs. Her mouth tingled from the pressure of their parting kiss. She touched her bruised lips and held her fingers aloft, feeling the chill of night on their damp tips.

CHAPTER 12

1723

William watched his niece Anne stroll ahead of him, taking a skip every few steps, the back of her simple, pale-green dress flitting between other pedestrians. She stopped for a moment to watch a hawker sell live chickens from a basket strung from a pole. Although she was now as tall and beautiful as her mother, at thirteen she was still a child.

He swung his cane, feeling an unexpected well-being, despite his reduced financial circumstances. Once his daughter and her aunt had disappeared into the Paris underground, a few months spent in London to settle his affairs seemed possible. Of course, Winifred's daughter had to accompany him, leaving the nuns and her convent school behind. She had been delighted to come and her sunny nature brought him great pleasure. The area where they walked in the welcome spring sunshine was called Soho and he had leased a few rooms in Frith Street, a row of fine houses quite unlike the chaotic development of the surrounding streets.

Soho was populated by Huguenot refugees, escaping persecution in France for their Protestant faith, just as he had fled discrimination in Britain for his Catholic faith. He enjoyed hearing French spoken and being able to find the bread, wine and cheese he had become used to in Paris. He felt at home and even better, had found a French school for his niece, although they had made a pact to avoid telling her mother, since she was now being schooled in the Protestant faith. At the door to the school, Anne waited for him. He laid a hand on her shoulder, reminded her to behave, and weighed his body against the heavy oak door, allowing her to push inside under the arch of his cloak.

To add to his lightness of step, his title and heavily mort-gaged estates had been restored, and he was the Marquess of Powis once again. For this unusual act of generosity from King George, William owed a debt to his dear friend the Prince of Wales, who had persuaded the king that the marquess was no Jacobite, and should not suffer for the sins of his family. He had dressed carefully for London, wearing his plain brown coat and breeches and choosing to wear a hat instead of a wig. It was important to mingle with the crowd as a respectable but unre-markable elderly gentleman, to avoid any debt scouts alerted to his presence. It was not his intention to allow himself to be persuaded, by uncomfortable methods, to pay off his daugh-ter's loans.

His first appointment of the day was with his sister's husband, the lawyer Kenneth Mackenzie. William took a sedan chair from Soho Square to Mackenzie's office in Lincoln's Inn. He was shown into a waiting room, the servant indicating one of two high-back chairs. William listened to voices drifting from behind panelled doors. From the exchange of words, he guessed that the conversation was nowhere near its conclusion. Mackenzie had some fine pieces of furniture from the last century, William thought, as he ran his finger along the piecrust edge of a side table made from elm. No shortage of wealth here, at least not until his sister Anne had rummaged through it with her plump fingers. He waited, the rush seat prickling his thighs, and wondered how much revenge Mackenzie had built into this delay.

Finally, the doors opened and the lawyer gestured that William should enter his office. The man was at least twenty years younger than his wife, short but dressed like a gentleman. He was wearing the latest Parisian style of wig, set low on the scalp, with a ponytail. To cover the gap between the wig and his receding hairline, Mackenzie had made excessive use of hair powder. A carafe of wine sat on a table between two chairs and William took a seat, watching Mackenzie make great ceremony of pouring them both a small glass. To fill the awkward silence, William told the lawyer that his eldest sister Frances had also married a Kenneth Mackenzie.

'Two sisters married to men with the same name, who would have thought?' he said.

Mackenzie stared at him and William became uncomfortable, aware he had already committed the sin of the elderly, sharing details that were not funny or interesting, except to himself.

The lawyer waved his hand, as if to dismiss William's observation. 'I am distantly related to the Earl of Seaforth's family. I care little for the connection, other than the business it brings me.'

The lawyer continued, narrowing his eyes and peering at William with contempt. 'I did some work for your father, the first Marquess of Powis. He was an honourable man.'

William felt rebuked. 'I hope that you will not find me wanting in that respect,' he replied.

'Powis, I won't waste your time or mine. Due to your sister's unfortunate financial dealings, on the advice of your daughter I may say, I find myself responsible for her debts.'

William paused before replying, feeling a swift rush of anger he knew he must try to control.

'In this country, and most others in the civilised world, a wife and her property belong to her husband. You, sir, are simply experiencing the downside of this contract, which until now has suited you. Why else would you have married my sister? She had wealthy contacts, which helped your business, and I'm quite sure you saw yourself as lord of the manor in Ashby Folville, once she was dead. Am I right?'

Mackenzie's expression revealed his own struggle to manage his temper.

'How dare you. Not only do I have to pay off my wife's creditors, but I must provide her with an income, which I believe your daughter shares. Why should I support your daughter, sir?'

'Because everything I have is sold or mortgaged. To my regret, I signed a document that left me responsible for a portion of Mary's debts in France, but fortunately not in Britain. But as her father, even in this country I can be pursued for her debts. I live on credit and have nothing to spare. My other children have been ruined by their sister's stupidity and I have been left with the sole care of my niece.'

'I repeat my question, Powis, why should I support your daughter?'

'You should not. Leave her to survive on her wits, alongside her partner, Joseph Gage. Between them they will make enough on gaming tables to live, even if they cannot pay off their loans. Should my sister, Lady Carrington, choose to pay for lodgings and food for her niece, that is her responsibility.'

William could see that Mackenzie was not satisfied, and the younger man's eyes roamed the dark corners of the room in search of another grievance.

'I can't fund all these lawsuits. They're throwing them

around like rose petals at a wedding. It is a complete waste of my time and money.'

William sighed and said, 'The lawsuits are a delaying tactic. By counter-suing, they keep the bailiffs off their backs, if only for a while, and there is the remote chance of winning. Ask yourself this, Mackenzie, what hope does your wife have, alone in Paris, without the protection of my daughter and Joseph Gage?'

The lawyer drained his glass and glanced across at William's, already empty, but offered no more. He stood up and held out his hand.

'Lord Powis, I had hoped for more. A father is responsible for his daughter.'

William removed his hat from the table and raised himself, allowing his height to dominate the younger man.

'I am indeed responsible for my daughter, I need no reminder of that, but her actions have placed her beyond my care. You must decide for yourself what to do about your wife, but know this – all Lady Carrington's properties in England have been sold to help pay her debts. She owns nothing.'

Outside Mackenzie's office, William found a quiet square, shaded by trees. He sat on a mounting block and wiped his forehead, feeling shaken and dizzy. That lawyer was nothing but a rude upstart, quite undeserving of his sister, despite her faults. He felt stung by Mackenzie's criticisms. It hurt most because the accusations were so close to how he judged himself. He wanted to force his way back inside and start arguing all over again but a tight sensation in his chest reminded him that he was an old man, alone in London, with responsibility for a young niece.

William inhaled deeply and focused on the birds hopping between the branches above, until he could breathe more easily. He replaced his hat and thought about walking to Lord Wyndham's new house in Clerkenwell, where he had been invited for lunch. He realised it wouldn't look acceptable to arrive on foot, so decided to walk most of the way and catch a sedan chair for the final stretch. Walking would calm him, and he could pass by Powis House in Lincoln's Inn Fields, seized by bailiffs thanks to his perilous financial state, and see what the new residents had done to his beloved house. Was that a good idea, he thought? Perhaps it wasn't, but he knew that curiosity, envy and perhaps regret, would carry him there.

Wyndham's solid stone residence faced Clerkenwell Green and was one of only a few built during Queen Anne's reign. Alongside, there were still vacant plots facing the green, occupied by goats and their herdsmen, next to small houses built of brick or wood, many of the tenants trading as watchmakers with workshops hidden behind the shopfront. Over lunch, William expressed his surprise to find a member of parliament living in such an area of contrasts.

'It suits me,' Wyndham replied. 'Catherine prefers to remain in Somerset with the children. I like the people around here; they keep my feet on the ground. I'm planning to become a governor of the new Foundling Hospital; a place where women who are expecting a child, but have no means of support, can leave the baby in safety. Since the birth of my daughter Elizabeth, the fate of small children has become more important to me, especially girls. Do you remember that awful death you witnessed the last time we met?'

William felt pleased that Wyndham remembered that dreadful moment. 'I heard you were behind the new workhouses, replacing those terrible parish nurses,' he said. 'Do you think we might see the end of children's deaths on the streets?'

Wyndham gave a shout of laughter. 'A bit optimistic, old boy, but we've made a start.'

The lamb and wine from Wyndham's estate were delicious and it was enough to eat in silence, both trying to avoid the delicate subject of William's financial ruin.

'The other thing I remember we discussed that day,' Wyndham said, after their coffee had been cleared away, 'was that fellow John Law and his Mississippi Company. I hear he had to make his escape, after bankrupting almost everyone.'

'He became overconfident,' William agreed. 'He believed in himself too much. The final betrayal, although I have no proof of this apart from something hinted at by my friend the Earl of Stair, was that he tried to ingratiate himself with the exiled Jacobite king and his court. The Prince Regent had stuck by him, but Law's disloyalty was the final straw. Peace with Britain had to trump support for a banker. Now that the Regent is dead, and young Louis XV is king, I cannot imagine such an unfortunate chain of events ever happening again.'

'How are you managing? The whole financial upheaval must have destroyed you.'

William swallowed before he replied, trying to control the catch in his voice.

'My family is broken. My sons are suing both Richard Cantillon and Mary for deceit and fraud. Cantillon is suing me, as well as Mary. She is suing Richard Cantillon. Everything I once owned is mortgaged.'

'What possessed her? How did she find the means to invest so unwisely?'

'I'm afraid the answer lies with a fellow called Joseph Gage. If she hadn't tied herself to him, been enticed to gamble on the stock markets, none of this would have happened. The galling thing, what really upsets me, is that she refuses to marry him or anyone else. If she was someone's wife, I wouldn't be responsible for her debts.'

'He's not the brother of Thomas Gage... Oxfordshire estate?'

William nodded. 'That's the one. He's the younger son gone wild. It's an age-old story but I wish my family hadn't become embroiled. I can't blame him entirely. Joseph did ask to marry Mary, several times. She's an unusual woman. I always found her difficult to understand and so did her mother. For too long, we both looked the other way, tried not to see her idiosyncrasies but I did love her.'

Wyndham frowned. '*Did* love her?'

'That's how I feel, although I will only ever admit that to you...' William hesitated before continuing. 'Mary has no remorse and blames everyone but herself. She has no idea of the lives she has ruined, nor does she have any intention of trying to make amends. She scurries around Paris, from one doubtful hovel to another, with my older sister and Gage still hanging on to her petticoats. I have given up on her.'

Once again, the men fell silent, and William allowed his eyes to roam across Wyndham's shoulder to the sunny garden beyond. He saw a brick wall, one that would feel warm in the late-afternoon sunshine, and a plum tree covered in blossom. Something about the scene stirred such feelings of loss; he thought he might weep.

'Thank you for lunch, Wyndham, I must be back in time for my niece.'

Wyndham threw down his linen napkin and pushed back his chair. He walked around the table, and in embracing the older man's bent shoulders, helped him to stand.

'Come on, old fellow,' he said. 'I'll send you home in my carriage.'

CHAPTER 13

1724/1725

Debtors' prison was not much different from the rooms they had recently left. As women with titles, Mary and her aunt had been allocated a small sitting room with a fireplace, a corner table with two chairs, and a bedroom they reluctantly had to share. At least Mary felt reluctant sharing, but Aunt Anne clung to her every night, weeping into her shoulder before sleeping soundly and taking up most of the bed. Her snoring was a particular trial. It was not a rhythmic sound that held out any possibility of adjustment, but long periods of silence followed by a crescendo of snorts, designed to shock anyone who had foolishly fallen asleep into a startled panic.

Since women were rarely of independent means, even in Paris, they were also rarely responsible for their own debts, which meant that women were very much in the minority in the prison. The toileting area had to be shared with men and the floor was often wet. Mary worried that the hems of her robes had started to smell, but the horrible necessity of having to use these at night was most troubling. More than once, she had been accosted by one of the male prisoners, attempting to kiss and grope her. Her aunt had no such worries since she generally avoided personal hygiene and used a bucket in their room for her other needs. Despite the lid, it was hard to mask the farmyard odour of urine, or worse, from their bedroom. Fortunately, the prison employed a young boy to empty the pail every morning, replace their firewood and flick a broom across the wooden floors. This service was paid for by Mackenzie, her aunt's unfortunate husband, but he had made it clear he wasn't willing to pay their bail. His mean allowance did not stretch to the best of food, and Mary was tortured by the tantalising aroma of meals delivered to other titled prisoners, from the best of Parisian restaurants.

Joseph was their only visitor, cheerfully bribing guards, or threatening the families of any warders who proved to be less corruptible. He was making money in the gaming salons and was able to help with extra food and small luxuries like soap, but he never won enough to secure their freedom. She waited for him in her sparsely furnished room, playing a game of patience. Anne was asleep in the bedroom after a bout of weeping and an endless rendition of her well-worn lament about their disgrace and fallen status. Mary had tried to explain to Joseph that escape was not uppermost in her mind. They were safer in debtors' prison than anywhere else; their creditors couldn't reach them, and since they were already imprisoned, what further punishment was possible? For herself, she was happy to wait it out, feeling she could breathe at last after months on the run.

There was a tap on the door and Mary ran over to slide the bolt. Joseph entered, accompanied by a man who was a stranger. He stood at least a head taller than Joseph, his face long and gaunt and as he crossed the room towards an empty chair, Mary noticed that he walked with a pronounced limp.

Behind his back she glanced at Joseph, and seeing her frown, he shook his head, warning her not to speak her mind.

Joseph introduced his companion as the Chevalier de Balfe, who tried to kiss her hand, had she not snatched it from his clammy grasp. There were only two armchairs, so Mary and her visitor faced each other in front of the smoking fire, while Joseph sat at the table, inexplicably wiping the surface with his hat. She could not avoid staring at the leg irons wrapped around de Balfe's calf, since his long legs stretched out so far, his boot almost touched the filthy hem of her dress.

'I'm sorry I have no refreshments to offer,' Mary said.

Joseph eased his cloak from his shoulders and draped it across the back of a second chair.

'No apologies needed, I've brought some wine and a rather good cheese, so if you could find glasses and plates, we'll be royally entertained.'

Mary searched for three glasses in the only cupboard, Joseph moving close to help pour the wine, so close their heads almost touched.

'Be careful, Mary,' he whispered, his voice low and rough. 'We don't want to make an enemy of the chevalier. He could be useful to us.'

Once compliments had been shared about the quality of the wine, the unusual depth of flavour of the cheese and the pleasure they all felt obliged to express over making each other's acquaintance, Joseph explained their shared business.

'Mary, the chevalier has a friend, an abbé, also imprisoned in a debtors' jail due to false accusations made by a man called George Mackenzie Quin. I've discovered that he's taken your family to court for fraud and extortion and has won his case. Your father and brothers have been ordered to compensate him for his sizeable losses. You have an enemy in common with the cleric and may want to hear what the Chevalier de Balfe proposes.'

Mary's cheeks flushed and for a moment, her skin lost its grey, prison hue. 'I've never heard of Mackenzie Quin,' she protested. 'Every minor investor is blaming us, yet we were misadvised too. No one is being forced to give us any compensation.'

De Balfe nodded, stroking his poorly tended beard. 'Now, just to check, this Scot is no relation of your aunt's husband, the London lawyer?'

Mary wrinkled her nose and sniffed. 'Not at all.'

'It would be useful for your family to have this conniving upstart reminded of his manners?'

'It certainly would,' Joseph interrupted. 'We should give him a fright. Encourage him, in the gentlest possible way of course, to drop his legal action against the abbé and Mary's family.'

De Balfe nodded. 'I know people who can do that. We'll split the cost?'

'Wait, wait...' Mary covered her ears. 'I'm not listening to any more of this. I already have at least twenty lawsuits against my name, I'm not adding assault, or worse, to the charges.'

'I quite understand, Lady Herbert.' De Balfe used her title with obsequious respect and Mary felt her skin crawl. Since his tone was heavy with menace, she was quite sure he did not understand her position at all. Joseph may be comfortable mixing with renegade, Jacobite outcasts, but they had no place in her circle. She was an entrepreneur, a financier, one who had made understandable errors, but she was not a common thug.

Mary stood and raised herself to her full height, trying to show Joseph that she was in complete command of her own affairs. She stretched out her fingertips towards de Balfe, leaving him in no doubt that the meeting was over. He ignored her, using both hands to steady his rigid leg as he pushed to stand.

'We have no shared business after all,' she said to de Balfe while glowering across at Joseph. 'I am sorry to hear of the abbé's troubles, but it is nothing to do with me. Whatever actions you choose to take with Mr Gage, it is between you two. Leave me out of it.'

Joseph fumbled for his cloak, his expression betraying his confusion. He steered a protesting Chevalier de Balfe from the room, but as he left Mary caught his elbow, stopping him just inside the open door, out of earshot of his co-conspirator.

'If you want to threaten someone,' she hissed, 'how about starting with the letches who harass me in here. Next time, check with me what help I need.'

Joseph left, trying but failing to kiss her cheek. Mary replaced the cork on the remaining wine and sat by the smouldering embers of the fire. She chose not to light any candles and sipped from the wine left in her glass. What possible gain had Joseph thought there might be in involving her with his plan? Had he been trying to inveigle himself into the chevalier's set, using an introduction to the Herbert family as bait? Joseph may have promised that if Mackenzie was frightened off, some advantage might flow from the gratitude of the Duke of Powis. If Joseph believed this, then he had learned nothing about her father.

Mary heard her aunt moving around in the bedroom and the door hinges creaked. Aunt Anne rubbed her eyes, peering into the gloom to find her niece. Her glance flickered from the wine glasses to the bottle and then to the table.

She licked her lips and grinned. 'Ah, cheese!'

They finished the cheese and wine, finding a hunk of bread to make the leftovers into their supper. Afterwards, they lit a candle and sat at the table to play a two-handed game of cards.

When it was time for bed, Mary carried a lantern into the corridor and heard her aunt bolt the door behind her. The narrow, damp passage was lit only by the occasional smouldering rush lamp, but it was bright enough to see the shape of one of her tormentors approaching from the direction of the outhouse. The man tried to make himself invisible, pressing the back of his rotund body against the wall. She hurried past, her lamp held high. Even in these shadows, the deep bruising underneath one of his eyes could not be hidden. Joseph had done what she had asked.

William moved into the apartment in Paris where his niece lived with her maid Alice, the rent still paid for by the long-suffering Kenneth Mackenzie as another of his wife's outgoings. Fortunately, the lawyer hadn't looked too closely at the purpose of these rooms, but William knew they were living on borrowed time.

The Duke of Powis, named in the lawsuit brought by the litigant Mackenzie Quin, was not a vengeful man. Almost everyone in Paris could cast themselves as a victim of misguided financial advice but only the most persistent and resourceful would ever see a fraction of their money again. He believed that most decent people would respond to a fair and honest approach and planned to talk to the fellow. Younger men almost always listened to him, although this was not true of his own sons.

He moved the wine decanter from one side of the small, gilt-edged table, then back to the other side: back and forth. This is old-man behaviour, he thought. Stop it right now! Sitting on his hands, he hummed a tune remembered from his childhood, then stood to look at his reflection in the mirror. The triple candelabra reflected his haunted expression in the glass, as if his face hung disembodied inside a cavern.

'Hurry up,' he spoke aloud, 'don't keep me waiting.'

A tap at the door indicated that his visitor had arrived and Alice showed the man into the room. George Mackenzie Quin looked as nervous as William felt, so he made much of showing him to a chair and begging the Scot to join him in a glass of wine. Seeing that his host was bare-headed, Quin asked if he might remove his wig. William nodded in agreement and saw the short red hair, pale skin with freckles and the sheen of sweat on his forehead.

'Now, tell me, Quin... or may I call you George?'

George nodded, wiping his brow with a handkerchief.

'Are you the same lad my sister Winifred accompanied to Rome? You were meeting your parents there, I believe. That was quite a journey.'

George shook his head and twisted his hands together as if wringing out a damp cloth. The younger man was wordless with fear. William immediately realised his mistake. This man was much older than Winifred's charge would be now. He hated ageing, everyone else looked so young, everyone was called similar names. It was becoming impossible to remember faces, never mind what a person was called.

'I was... I was,' George stammered, 'secretary to the Earl of Stair for a while. That's where you may have heard my name.'

William slapped a hand on his knee. 'Of course, that's it.'

He doubted if Stair had ever mentioned this man to him, but there was no harm in pretending. Anything to relax this not-so-young George.

'I can see you are troubled,' he said. 'You have won your legal action against me and have taken a big risk coming here. Have no worries, I merely want to talk.'

'I wouldn't have come at all but...'

'Spit it out, man.'

William waited.

George's eyes were strangely wide and he blinked with the effort of holding back tears.

'I need you to intercede with your daughter. I'm being followed. Her friend Count Gage and a tall man with a leg iron have offered a large sum to have me killed. They've spread a rumour that I'm a... I'm a...'

William looked away, studying with interest the plain wood panelling, giving the man a chance to compose himself.

George took a deep swallow from his glass and the words came in a rush. 'They're saying I'm a sodomite.'

William tried not to smile. 'Well, there are worse things to be called.'

'But it's an offence, punishable by the rack. If I'm not hacked to death on the street by Gage and his cronies, I'll be arrested and tortured.'

'I apologise, I made a poor joke,' William said. 'I am taking your concerns seriously. I'm afraid I'm not in contact with my daughter but it's unlikely she's behind this. Mary is not vindictive, except to pursue you through the law. I cannot influence Joseph Gage. His actions are beyond me. Your fears may be justified, he has always had contacts in the Jacobite underworld.'

George's sweaty pallor became mottled with pink blotches. 'The Jacobite underworld...?'

'When the Jacobite king decamped to Rome, he left behind many followers at Saint-Germain who could not afford to leave. Some were soldiers, who had fought for James's father in Ireland, and they had few skills except fighting. It is from their ranks that Gage will have found his recruits, if what you say is true.'

George fell silent, pushing his wig down between his knees

and whispered, 'So, you cannot help me? You were my last hope.'

'I cannot help, nor can I afford to pay what the courts say I owe you. I intend to leave Paris, forever, and return to London. The health of King George is failing, and I believe that Britain will be a better place under his son. I suggest you go back to Scotland, where you will be safe. If you stay in Paris, you will forever look over your shoulder.'

'I'm owed so much money,' George persisted. 'I left my Mississippi shares with Joseph Gage in good faith, and your daughter used them to speculate. It was theft.'

'And she deposited shares with Richard Cantillon, which he used to speculate. She was the victim of the same crime, a crime committed by a banker she trusted. A bank deposit ought to be safe, don't you think? Come on, lad, only a fool would trust my daughter and Joseph Gage with money, and I include myself.'

'I must stay in Paris, surely, to see these lawsuits through.'

'You will have heard the saying that a fool and his money are soon parted, and with every respect for your distress, your choice of investment was foolish. You are relatively young and have time to build another fortune if you so choose. Some of us do not have that luxury. Regard this as a life lesson and go home to your family.'

The good sense and patience that William had tried to teach Mackenzie Quin belied the resurgence of contempt he felt for Joseph Gage and his daughter. George's tale might well be true. It was more than likely that Gage was behind the threats and the attempt to ruin a man's reputation.

As he hurried along the banks of the Seine towards Pont Neuf, trying to use exercise to order his tangled thoughts,

William guessed that the tall man in leg irons was not paranoid fantasy. He had spent one night in debtors' prison himself, his arrest paid for by that fool, the Irish banker Edmund Loftus.

On the second day, he had been woken before daylight, by the sound of a knock. Drawing the bolt on his cell door, he had found the warden outside. The man stepped aside to let him pass, bowing low with a somewhat theatrical gesture of respect.

'You're a lucky man, Lord Powis,' the warden had said. 'Your bond has been paid. You're free to leave.'

'I'm grateful of course,' William replied, 'but who paid?'

The warden shrugged. 'I've no idea. He was tall and walked with leg irons. Ugly chap.'

A wind whipped off the river and William wrapped his cape more tightly around his shoulders, stopping to watch the fast-moving water churning below the Pont Neuf. So there it was, a mystery solved. His mysterious benefactor had been the Chevalier de Balfe, his freedom bought by Joseph Gage. William couldn't decide whether to feel angry or grateful, but in the scale of things, it was the very least Joseph could do to make amends.

He felt indifferent to the glances of the hawkers around him; indifferent to their wares and their prurient interest that he might be about to jump. That night, he would tell his niece that her family could no longer pay her school fees. Her education was not at an end but she would have to board at the convent and would be left alone in Paris. Their rooms had to be given up, and soon, on the direction of Kenneth Mackenzie. Alice must leave too. This was the part of the speech he dreaded the most. How could he tell Anne she must be parted from her beloved nurse?

He could not imagine how his sister Winifred persuaded James to part with money to pay her daughter's school fees, given his reputation for parsimony. She would never abuse her reputation at court but may have judged this the perfect moment to remind the king of the debt he owed the Herbert family. Their mother had saved James's life as a newborn baby; an act that had forever changed the course of her own children's lives, as well as British history.

He turned from the parapet and pressed his hat firmly upon his head before walking home, facing directly into the wind. 'Frankly,' William muttered, his eyes watering, 'I can't wait until all this nonsense is over.' What he had not admitted to anyone, knowing that those who pursued him for money had many spies, was that his new mine at Mochnant, one neither mortgaged nor supervised by trustees, was beginning to look profitable. There was still hope of securing his future and providing an income for his other children, but he had to take care. If he stayed, word of his good fortune would soon travel to his daughter's creditors. Paris might dazzle, but in the time left to him, he would return to Wales.

CHAPTER 14

1725/26

The bells of the church where the royal family worshipped rang out to herald the end of morning prayers. Maxwell had been called away early, so at least he would work today, but it was now too late for Winifred to be summoned. She peeled off her only respectable gown and laid it on the bed, wondering how many more months it would last with patching and darning. From her closet she pulled out one of her day robes, made from a coarse, local fabric. It closely resembled the texture of sacking and was of similar colour. Wearing an apron, and a bonnet to cover her hair, Winifred's appearance was indistinguishable from the women who pushed in front of her at market stalls, in competition for the best fruit and vegetables.

A sudden and forceful hammering at the door interrupted her dressing and Winifred ran to open it, pushing a strand of hair under her bonnet. A red-faced boy, no more than seven or eight, stood with his fist raised, ready to knock again.

'Mrs Sheldon said you must come – come now.' The child had already turned away, ready to run back to the palace.

If Mrs Sheldon needed her immediate presence, it was

indeed urgent. Mrs Sheldon was the newly appointed nurse for the queen's second baby, another boy, only two days old. There was no time to change back into her formal clothes. Winifred hurried after the impatient child, who paused only to check that she was following. The approach to the Muti felt dark and oppressive; a tall palace shading one side of the street and the imposing Basilica dei XII Santi Apostoli on her right. As she wheezed behind the running boy, raising the hem of her robe to move more freely, she wondered what she might find. Was the baby ill? Surely, he was not dead. Henry Benedict Stuart had been born a healthy child, a good weight. Klementyna had given birth with an ease many would envy. What had gone wrong?

The four statues on the palace roof appeared to urge her on, their beckoning hands raised in encouragement. The child led her past the columns at the entrance and up steep steps to the left. At the top, they entered the queen's apartments. Even from the anteroom where she was asked to wait, Winifred could hear the young queen screaming. The boy pushed through the next set of high doors to search for Mrs Sheldon and soon brought her to Winifred. Red-faced, dishevelled and barely coherent, the new nurse hurried Winifred into the chamber where the women of the queen's household stood huddled in a silent group, their pale faces reflected in the vast, carved mirrors which filled each wall.

Exhausted from the chase, Winifred sought one of the chairs which crowded the room, but Mrs Sheldon remained standing before her, wringing her hands.

'I couldn't think of anyone else to call, my lady. The queen accuses the king of putting the baby in her bed to spy on her. She thinks the baby looks like his father and won't have him near her. Listen, Lady Winifred – that's Queen Klementyna screaming. She sounds possessed.'

Winifred cast her eyes around the group of waiting women, aware that all eyes were upon her and every word she spoke would be overheard and repeated. 'No, please don't say that, Mrs Sheldon. The queen is not possessed. My mother worked alongside an experienced midwife for many years and I remember hearing them talk about this condition. It is rare but can happen, particularly in lonely young women, far from their own mothers. The queen does sound highly distressed, but the baby must be our priority. Is he feeding?'

'Yes, he's taken to the wet nurses. But the queen won't have him back. She wants to go to a convent. She's begging me to arrange it and demands I go with her.'

Winifred folded her hands and thought. She noticed that the queen's women were listening with an intensity that was almost devout. Many people believed she had inherited her mother's skill to heal the sick and she would be expected to resolve this dreadful situation with hidden, magical powers. She had learned to ignore such expectations. Two lives were at risk, the king's wife, and his second-born son. Caution had to come before misplaced pride.

'I think a convent may be for the best,' Winifred said, at last. 'The queen needs peace and rest. It makes perfect sense that you accompany her. I've heard you are next only to her own mother in her affections. I advise you to follow the queen's request immediately. Remove the baby from her sight and take him to the nursery. I will come later with the wet nurse.'

Winifred was aware she may have acted above her station, but such doubts had to be pushed aside. Mrs Sheldon and the women of the household seemed glad of clear direction and set about making the complicated arrangements needed to move a queen to Santa Cecilia. Winifred took charge of the infant prince. He was a pretty child, much like his mother, and she could see no truth in the queen's accusation that he looked like his father. Even a royal baby smells of newborn perfection, and as she kissed him, quietly humming songs learned many years ago from her Scottish mother-in-law, she fell in love.

The wet nurse, not a woman with obvious nurturing skills, said she was willing to feed a baby but argued that she wasn't paid to occupy children. It soon became clear that Henry was one of those babies who only slept if he was held and Winifred soothed him through the night, rocking the prince in her arms, only handing him over to the wet nurse whenever he whimpered for food. No matter how delightful the child, he could not be held forever. She was aware of a need to bathe, and most of all, she wanted something to eat. Once the household stirred, Winifred eased herself from the rocking chair, feeling her joints ache, and tried to place the baby in the royal crib. The moment his back touched the cold sheets, Henry wriggled and whimpered. She lifted him against her chest, holding his head firm with her free hand. Although it was common practice to leave babies to cry, this was a prince and royalty was never left to cry, even though a little less attention might have helped some of them. On cue, there was a tap on the door and a servant announced the king.

James dismissed the wet nurse with a nod. Winifred tried to curtsey but with a baby in her arms, she stumbled, and he waved his hand for her to be seated. The king stood by the overmantel, staring into the smouldering grate, his long, mournful features even more tightly drawn in the light cast from a single candle.

'She says I'm having an affair, Lady Nithsdale,' James said, without the usual courteous preamble.

Winifred tried not to smile. He lacked any qualities that might make him attractive to women but there were always those who saw the crown and not the man.

'I'm sorry, I hadn't heard that,' she said. 'The queen is

unwell, my lord, and is saying things she may later regret. The care of nuns and her faith will help to restore her humour and in time she will want to be a mother again to her children.'

'She's accused Mrs Hay, the children's governess, of being my lover. Of course, the poor woman and her husband have had to leave, even though there's not a word of truth in the rumour.'

This is indeed fantasy, Winifred thought, picturing the notable but plain Mrs Hay. Poor Klementyna was seeing enemies everywhere.

'I did wonder why Mr and Mrs Hay left, and in such a hurry. Of course, it's nonsense but our enemies will believe anything. Luckily, the queen has quickly grown fond of Mrs Sheldon, which is why I instructed her to accompany the queen to the convent. I hope that decision met Your Majesty's approval.'

'Of course, Lady Nithsdale... Winifred... I trust your judgement. In the interim, you are to be governess for Henry. Charles no longer needs the care of women, so I will find him a tutor. I will make it known that your orders are to be followed, over every detail of Prince Henry's care.'

'Thank you, Your Majesty, thank you. I will look after this child as I once cared for you.' She became aware that the baby's movements were becoming more restless and agitated, as his hunger grew. 'Your Majesty, I must recall the wet nurse, and quickly.'

'One more thing, Winifred, it is not just our enemies who believe Klementyna's falsehoods. The Pope has listened to her nonsense and has cut the income to my household. Tell no one about this, please. You know how much I value your service, and your husband's too, but I cannot make your new position permanent.'

Months passed and the delusions that gripped Klementyna did not diminish. Living within a religious order only seemed to fuel the queen's agitation and she spent her days in a fervour of devotion that Mrs Sheldon was obliged to follow. There were days when Klementyna sent unreasonable demands by messenger about her son's upbringing, each one contradictory, but the days when she fell silent were more ominous. Since Klementyna was her queen, Winifred was obliged to follow her demands, within reason, but the women who worked for her were less agreeable.

Winifred entered the room where the queen's women waited for instructions. The whispering stopped immediately but not one woman lifted her eyes in greeting. It would be a difficult morning. She raised her voice, hoping to speak with an authority she did not feel.

'Queen Klementyna has asked that Prince Henry be fed every four hours. She believes he must learn patience and wisdom. He is to be dressed in breeches and a shirt, not infant gowns. He is to have his hair cut.'

Some of the women tutted, others rolled their eyes. The head seamstress, Mrs Wright, spoke first: 'But we've only just begun making him new gowns. You said he needed another fifteen. I've ordered all the linen.'

An assistant to the wet nurse, a woman whose milk supply was so copious the front of her gown was always stained, was the next to argue.

'That baby is so hungry, three of us couldn't satisfy him. I'm not going to hang around here and listen to his screams.'

Another woman said, 'She's never even seen him, except for the day he was born. He doesn't have any hair.'

This made everyone laugh and Winifred felt she had to reimpose some authority. She clapped her hands.

'Queen Klementyna is Prince Henry's mother. Yes, she is

absent, but she is ill. It is important that in the moments when she is well enough, she is able to contribute to his care.'

Mrs Wright spoke again: 'That's all very well, Lady Winifred, but what should we do?'

'Here is my decision,' Winifred said. 'We will trim the baby's hair, however little he has. We will not reduce his intake of milk or expect him to wait for food.'

'Yes, but what about the baby gowns?' the seamstress argued.

Winifred paused, unwilling to cause more ill feeling. 'Please finish the gowns, but also begin making clothes suitable for a boy who is walking, one of around two years of age. The queen may feel satisfied with this.'

'Shouldn't we just modify Prince Charles's costumes? I've kept them all.'

Winifred hadn't thought of this. 'Yes, of course, a good idea. Thank you, Mrs Wright, for your excellent contribution. I feel the queen's requests can be met, apart from the feeding and I'll take responsibility for that.'

Mrs Wright looked around at her colleagues and rolled her eyes. 'Until the next time,' she said.

The women left to start their duties, barely trying to hide their grumbling. Left alone in the quiet room, Winifred breathed deeply, enjoying her temporary victory. The demands of her new role were exhausting and there was another reason for her team to dislike her, apart from the thankless task of trying to impose the queen's impossible demands. Most knew nothing of her background and believed she had been recruited over the more deserving heads of their friends or daughters. The uniform wasn't popular either. Queen Klementyna was deeply religious, and when it suited her, believed in the simplicity of Christian teaching. She had insisted all the women in her household wear a plain grey robe with a white pinafore and cap. Winifred had been expected to abandon this practice, but she had not. Some of the staff were titled women, others the wives of soldiers, but this inequality of rank was not immediately apparent if everyone dressed the same. She had chosen to wear the grey robe herself, but even this gesture of unity had not endeared her.

There was also the worry of the senior wet nurse, a woman who came with good references but was less than generous with her affections. Winifred had seen the woman handle Henry roughly and decided he could not be left alone while he was being nursed. Her staff had already made a complaint to the king's secretary about her demand that they perform duties on a rota, tasks they considered beneath them and the addition of night-waking duties was the last straw for many. Winifred understood their resentment; a woman who considered herself uniquely skilled in preparing food for a royal child, would hate having to bathe or dress the same child, but she needed time to eat and sleep and the chance to escape for two hours every evening to prepare a meal for her husband. She had been given the responsibility of a royal child, a child without a mother, and to fulfil her duty, she must be fit. The rota would stay.

Henry thrived, and since he had never known his mother's love, he did not miss her, preferring Winifred to any of those who cared for him. At almost five, Prince Charles was different. He remembered Klementyna and never stopped searching for her, his face alert with hope whenever he was brought to the queen's apartments. His father may have believed that the boy was ready to be raised by men, but Charles had other ideas. The palace was not large, and he quickly learned to find his way to the nursery and the mothering that protected his baby brother. As Winifred rocked Henry to sleep, Charles would crawl onto her knee and suck his thumb, burying into her breast, as if by hiding his face he could stay hidden from his tutor.

Winifred decided she must take both boys to see the queen, after finding Charles asleep in his mother's empty bed, and arranged an audience with the king.

'No, I'm afraid not, Lady Winifred,' the king responded. 'The queen has abandoned her sons. It will not be healthy for the princes to see her.'

'Perhaps Queen Klementyna will feel encouraged to return, if she sees how much her sons need a mother,' Winifred argued.

The king stroked his beard and stared at a frescoe on the ceiling. Winifred wondered whether he had forgotten she was there.

'Have you considered that the visit might have exactly the opposite outcome?' he said, after minutes of silence. 'The queen may think she can remain in the convent, with generous support from the Pope, and have the luxury of regular visits from her children. If a woman leaves her family, she cannot be seen to benefit. In fact, she must suffer, as her husband has suffered.'

Winifred persisted: 'Your Majesty—' but James had limited patience with family matters and held up his palm.

'Enough, my lady,' he said. 'A coach will be made available to convey you and the children to the convent. No manservant can be spared for such a fruitless and ill-considered expedition. You will be escorted by your husband, the Earl of Nithsdale. Tell him it's an order.'

The meeting was over.

It was a fine day in early spring, the trees still bare of leaves, but the earth responding with a haze of green shoots to longer days and the warmth of the sun. Prince Henry slept in Winifred's arms, rocked by the rhythm of the coach, and Maxwell entertained Prince Charles. She smiled, remembering how her husband had once played with their own son.

The coach dropped them outside high walls encircling the convent's land. Entering the gate, they passed through manicured gardens, tended by nuns who did not raise their heads to greet them. Henry, who was not yet walking, twisted his body and arched his back, demanding to be put down to crawl on the path. Winifred handed the baby to Maxwell and took Charles by the hand. She looked down into the child's pale face and saw it was his greatest wish to see his beloved mother but also his deepest fear.

Maxwell pulled on a heavy bell, next to a door set into an inner wall. Another silent nun allowed them to enter a courtyard, empty of life apart from the trickle of water from a fountain, made from an ancient urn. They were led through another heavy wooden door into a waiting room with whitewashed walls and a single wooden cross. Here they were brought a bowl of warm water, soap and cloths, with a tray of wine and some bread. Henry screamed as Winifred wiped his face and hands, but Charles held out his hands and lifted his face to be washed, as if he was the best child any mother could want.

Maxwell and Winifred waited side by side on a hard bench, creating a moment of peace to talk by allowing Henry to roam on the spotless floor, with his brother crawling behind him.

'If she won't agree to see Henry,' Winifred said, 'you must go in alone with Charles.'

'But she's never met me. I've heard she's afraid of men.'

'She won't be afraid of you. You have a kind face, at least when you're sober.'

Maxwell started to protest but was interrupted by Mrs Sheldon, looking worn and older than her years.

'I'm so sorry about the delay,' she said. 'The queen's faith means that her prayers cannot be interrupted. She is ready for you now.'

Both boys fell silent, awed by a long walk down a dim, unfamiliar corridor, and up steep stairs to their mother's apartment. Klementyna waited for them on a gilt chair much like a throne, but instead of a queen, Winifred saw a thin girl with dark shadows under her eyes. The queen's women, sewing at her feet, withdrew into the shadows.

Klementyna's eyes scanned both children. She screamed, pointing at the baby. 'I am not having that one. Take him away. I said, take him away!'

Henry buried his face into Winifred's neck. She tried to reason with the distressed woman. 'But, Your Majesty, this is Prince Henry, your son. Please look at him.'

'I don't want him here,' Klementyna wailed, sounding more like a frightened child than royalty. 'Why does no one listen to my orders?'

The queen rose from her chair, her voluminous robe swamping her tiny frame, and pulled Charles towards her. 'I'll take this one.'

The boy reached out for Winifred, his eyes wide with terror, but Maxwell did not release his grip on the child's hand.

He gave a deep bow. 'Your Majesty, I am William Maxwell, Earl of Nithsdale, and I will remain here with Prince Charles. My wife, the Countess of Nithsdale, will remove Prince Henry. You will not see him again.'

Winifred blinked at being so dismissed, but found herself shepherded from the room by Mrs Sheldon, and returned to the waiting room. The queen's loyal companion wiped her brow with a cloth from her petticoat and took a deep draught from the wine left in Maxwell's glass.

'You see how things are, Lady Nithsdale, your husband was right to act as he did. This baby doesn't know his mother, but

Prince Charles needs a chance to be with her. If it goes well today, perhaps he can come again.'

'So, she's no better?' Winifred asked.

'The queen is much improved, as long as her life is ordered by prayer and observance. Our days have a rhythm, and if this is not disturbed, she copes. I remain concerned that she eats very little, and some days has a purposeless energy, but on the whole, we manage well.'

Mrs Sheldon looked towards the door. 'Since no one has come searching for me, it seems that Queen Klementyna is tolerating both her son and your husband. That is remarkable.'

Winifred nodded. 'You are the one who is remarkable, never failing to give caring and dutiful service to that desperate girl. The king ought to be grateful but I suspect he is not.'

Mrs Sheldon shook her head. 'He blames me for conspiring with the queen against him. He has no understanding of what ails her and believes she has a choice.'

'Many think that, particularly in the king's household. He is surrounded by men who encourage his critical judgements. I will do my best, but I do not always have his ear. Now, if you excuse me, I must feed this hungry baby.'

Winifred had asked the children's cook to prepare a pot of mashed vegetables for Henry, which she had mixed with breast milk after his morning feed. The wet nurse had complained about being asked to express milk, saying it wasn't natural, but Winifred had reminded her, more sharply than was helpful, that the woman's time with *this* baby was almost over and with it her salary, meals, and pinafores.

She sat Henry on her knee and spooned the mixture into his wide-open mouth. He ate well at first but quickly became tired, rubbing his cheeks with his fists and spreading the puree into his eyes, which made him howl. By the time she cleaned his face, and his soiled napkin had been changed, over an hour of wailing had passed without anyone checking on them. Through the child's protestations and sobs, Winifred thought about this convent and how silent and empty it felt. She was no stranger to women's religious orders and could remember not only bells and singing, but laughter, quarrelling and sometimes broken crockery. At her sister's convent there had also been the enlivening footsteps and chatter of young children. Perhaps it was the queen's presence that had created this atmosphere of tense solitude. The nuns had drawn deeper into their isolation, terrified of distressing Klementyna, and therefore the king.

Henry hiccoughed himself to sleep, his cheek against her shoulder, and at last a young nun tiptoed into the room, without once raising her eyes, bringing a bowl of soup and some bread. With her free hand, Winifred hungrily dipped a crust into the broth and savoured the flavour of good stock, onions, and cream. She shook her head, as if another person had spoken.

'I am fifty-three,' she said aloud to the sleeping child, 'and getting far too old for this.'

Maxwell returned with Charles and both looked satisfied. He ruffled the child's hair and said how polite the little boy had been, how he had eaten his food without complaint and had even played a game of chequers with his mother. Winifred praised the boy, adding that he had been brave.

Charles frowned and said, 'It wasn't brave. My mother was brave to ask to see me because she had forgotten all about me. I might not have been good enough for her, like Henry.'

Winifred glanced at her husband and saw him wipe tears roughly from his eyes with the edge of a thumb. He's a good man, she thought, despite everything. She wrapped Charles in her arms, holding him close against his brother's sleeping body.

'You are the best little boy in the world,' she whispered. 'Your mother is proud of you.'

'And wants to see him again,' Maxwell added. 'Next week in fact. The queen says I should accompany him, so perhaps I was good enough as well.'

For a few months, life continued in the palace nursery without incident. Henry started to walk, learned to say a few words and acquired more teeth, resulting in both wet nurses handing in their notice. Winifred recorded these details in the letters she wrote to Grace but suspected that Grace was not quite as interested in Henry's development as she was, since in her replies she never once asked about the child. Maxwell became one of Klementyna's trusted courtiers and his visits to her, often with her son Charles, became regular.

It was autumn, and Winifred asked one of the nursery maids to dress Henry for his afternoon walk. His screams of, 'No walk!' gradually became less deafening as he was dragged towards his chamber. Above the child's cries, Winifred was able to hear a quiet tap on the door. James entered, without a manservant, opening and closing the door behind him with the excessive care of someone unused to the task. He spread the tails of his coat and sat next to her, stroking the silk fabric on the arm of his chair.

'We are leaving for Bologna tomorrow,' he said. 'I have found a suitable place in the countryside, which will be better for the princes' health.'

Winifred frowned. She believed that the children were in unusually robust health.

'Your Majesty, this cannot happen,' she protested. 'Prince Charles needs to visit his mother. You should not separate them now.'

The king paused, as if weighing his words. 'You forget who

you are speaking to, Lady Nithsdale. We are not having a convivial chat. This is an order, not a request. If the queen wants to see the children, she must leave the convent and join us in Bologna.'

Winifred felt her skin flush. She had been reprimanded, true, but she was also furious. The king did not even try to hide the worst of his manipulative and controlling nature, almost certainly the cause of his lonely wife's distress, and he was using his children to force her obedience.

She turned her face away, to hide her anger. 'Of course, Your Majesty,' she said. 'I will arrange for the children's belongings to be packed at once. Will this move be for a few months, or longer?'

'Think of Bologna as your future home, Lady Nithsdale. You will accompany us as governess for both children. I have spoken to your husband and he has given his consent for you to leave. He will remain in charge of the queen's household here in Rome.'

This was everything she had hoped for but to gain her happiness at the expense of the queen and her children was a poisonous bargain.

'I can see you do not agree, Winifred,' James added, 'but your family's financial position will now be secure. I expect your willing compliance. Please remember, I do not need your approval or understanding.'

Winifred stood before the king and bowed her head. 'You have my absolute loyalty, sir, and I am proud to be governess for your sons. I will help to raise them as if they were my own and my husband will serve the queen with respect and honour.'

'Yes, yes, he's already promised that, with more haste than you, I might say.'

'I was afraid for Prince Charles, as I ought to be. I fully understand that the queen's happiness is not my concern.'

'Good, then it's settled. Once Queen Klementyna has accepted your husband in his new role, I plan to sack that woman she's grown so fond of. She influences my wife against me, and I can make no progress with our cruel separation while she whispers in the queen's ear.'

Winifred wanted to defend Mrs Sheldon but knew she must not speak her mind. She had no choice but to accept this next phase of her life. The boys would thrive in her care, better than with anyone else, and she had willingly agreed to release her own husband to take care of the fragile queen. While she had not felt his love or affection for years, she knew him capable of doing his best for a young and vulnerable girl.

'There is one more matter, Your Majesty, I need to choose the women who will support me in my role. Not all of those currently employed in the household are suitable and I'm sure you understand that there is a level of animosity towards me amongst the queen's women. I wish to bring an experienced nurse to Bologna from Paris. She is a woman I trained and who helped to raise my own children.'

James frowned. 'There is no money for extra staff. The Pope is so impressed with Klementyna's religious observance, he diverts more and more to her household, at my expense. A move to Bologna is not only about the boys' health, but we will also save money. The house I have taken is a villa, not a palace.'

'I understand,' Winifred said, 'but with our income secure, my husband and I will pay for Alice. I need her at my side.'

CHAPTER 15

1726/27

T he waiting was the worst. Mary and her aunt sat in silence, with travelling bags at their feet. They had chosen not to light any candles, so that a casual visitor might assume they were asleep. After months of pursuit, fear and betrayal, flickering light from the grate exposed deep lines in the pouched skin under both women's eyes.

In her hand, Mary held a letter from a Spanish count, flattering her beauty, wealth, and inexplicably, her family's expertise in mining. She had dismissed the letter as from yet another suitor wasting his time, but Joseph disagreed, believing the contact might be useful and important. Mary had been persuaded that escape from debtors' prison was now essential.

At last, Mary heard shuffling footsteps and woke her aunt. A scratching sound followed and she opened the door to Joseph, unrecognisable in a mask, his feet bound in sacking. He lifted their bags onto his shoulder and beckoned for them to follow. The two women crept along the corridor behind him.

'Stop!'

They halted, turning back towards the direction of the

voice. Through the haze of the rush lamps, a shadowy figure stood, hands on hips.

'You think you can sneak out of here? I'll call the guards,' he bellowed, his voice echoing down the passage.

Joseph hissed: 'Wait here. I'll deal with him.'

She leant back against the damp walls, feeling the chill against her palms, the only sound her aunt's breathing. There was a muffled scream and the sound of a dead weight falling onto the stone flags.

Joseph's shape solidified, and Mary thought she saw a knife, quickly hidden beneath the folds of his cape.

'Hurry,' he said, panting. 'We must get out of here – fast.'

Mary wished her aunt had more speed, but remained behind the elderly woman, who struggled to keep up with Joseph. She glanced behind her frequently, in case the injured man had been discovered.

The guardroom door stood ajar. Joseph hesitated before crossing, and after checking all was clear, beckoned them to follow. Mary pushed her aunt ahead, wondering whether the guards had been bribed, or worse, since the room was empty, even though the fire was lit and jugs of ale waited on the table. Within seconds, they were across the courtyard and through the imposing gate in the barricade, left unlocked by Joseph. Outside the walls at last, they savoured the familiar smell of woodsmoke from chimneys, horses and effluent. It was the wonderful odour of Paris.

Joseph drew a huge key from under his cloak and thrust it into the magnificent keyhole, using both hands to ensure the gate was locked. There was movement in the shadows, a dark figure gripping the neck of a man dressed in the uniform of a prison guard. A gurgling sound from the man's throat confirmed he would never be freed and Mary guessed at the likely fate of the other guards. Joseph threw the key onto nearby wasteland and led them to a waiting carriage, its windows covered with black drapes. Mary helped her exhausted aunt climb inside and paused, her foot on the step while Joseph held up payment for the coachman.

'He knows where to take you,' Joseph whispered. 'There's food and wine inside. Your journey will be long.'

'Where are we going? Will I see you again?'

'No more questions. You must go, right now. I'll follow as soon as I can. Here is money to help you live.' Joseph passed Mary a heavy bag of coins. 'We will meet in Madrid.'

After days of travelling, stopping only to refresh the horses and eat in the back rooms of roadside inns, Mary and her aunt arrived in Spain. Aunt Anne had slept for most of the journey, her head lolling against Mary's shoulder in time with the rolling of the coach, making rest impossible. She heard voices outside the carriage whenever they stopped but only the change of language told her they were safe. She preferred not to think about Joseph's actions to free them, what might have happened in the prison. This was a fresh start.

The door of the coach opened and their driver, who remained masked throughout their journey, indicated that they should step down. Mary supported her frail aunt onto the street, and they saw their future home – a modest but pretty villa hidden behind high walls, with a cool, enclosed courtyard shaded by an ancient fig tree. A maidservant escorted her aunt inside the house and Mary sank onto a rustic bench in the courtyard, feeling the splintered wood catch the thin fabric of her dress. She traced the simple lion's head carving onto the backrest and waited for the maidservant to return with warm water and cloths. She wiped her neck and hands, feeling a cooling prickle from her skin as the water evaporated.

'Is my aunt settled?' she asked the girl, who nodded and curtsied, before hurrying back inside.

Mary breathed deeply, even though the air seemed thick and warm in her nostrils, and studied their farmhouse, its walls rendered a warm, yellow ochre. Upstairs, there were multi-paned windows, but downstairs, closely patterned ironwork grids protected shutters, left open to the air. She leant forward and pressed her fingertips against her forehead.

The coachman coughed and Mary jumped, unaware that he hovered by the gate, waiting to speak to her.

'Yes, what is it?' she asked.

'I am instructed to leave the coach and horses here with you. After I have stabled them, I will remain for one night at an inn. In the morning, I will check whether there is anything you need before I return to France.'

'Thank you, sir, I cannot thank you enough,' Mary stammered, fighting a desperate need to sleep. 'How will we manage for money? Did Mr Gage make any arrangements?'

'The house is rented for six months, and the girl comes with the house. I know nothing else.'

Left alone, Mary spread the remaining coins from Joseph's purse across the bench and counted. Knowing little about the cost of food or clothing in Madrid, she reckoned they could survive for about a month, but there would be nothing spare for the gowns, shoes, and headdresses they would need if they were to be introduced at court. In the morning, she must write a letter and her aunt would do the same.

Like a recalcitrant schoolgirl, Aunt Anne had to be cajoled, then bribed, to write to her husband, asking for more money. Mary herself wrote to the exiled King James, reminding him that they had once considered marriage. She promised to further the Jacobite cause in Spanish royal circles but for this service, she would need to be made a Jacobite duchess, a title essential to smooth her entry into the royal court. If it wasn't too much trouble, she added, she would require enough money to ease her into fashionable society, since she would need to return the hospitality she and her aunt would certainly be offered.

Weeks passed and neither letter received a reply, nor did they hear from Joseph.

As the summer temperatures rose, Mary and Lady Carrington felt their isolation from society more keenly. Aunt Anne was now in her late sixties and her generous proportions meant that she rarely dressed or moved beyond the shade of her upstairs bedroom. Preferring to spend her days outside, Mary sat under the tiled portico that faced the courtyard, its purpose to keep the lower floor of the house cool. The maid did not open any shutters until the evening, and apart from bringing her mistress wine, figs, and local cheese through the day, they did not speak. The air became so sticky and hot that Mary found it hard to breathe, as if her nostrils were blocked with something solid. Her thoughts dwelt upon the progress of the lawsuits they had made against Cantillon and others. It was frustrating to feel so out of control and beyond contact. As regards the many lawsuits others had taken out against her, she was indifferent to their progress.

In the evenings, taking advantage of their temporary relief from the worst of the sun's heat, Mary encouraged her aunt to dress and they would order the coach, driven by their maid's husband, to carry them into the city. They had made one excursion into the countryside but found it windswept, flat and barren, and not worthy of their attention. Mary had been unaware of urban planning in Paris, accepting the well-designed boulevards, gardens, and palaces as no more than her right as a citizen. By comparison, Madrid seemed to be half-formed, with elegant buildings, churches and tree-lined pavements rising incongruously from footpaths and dusty squares, more typical of a rural village. The new buildings had a severity that Paris had managed to avoid, but their doorways and balconies appeared to erupt into a riot of convoluted rosettes, scrolls and shells, as if compensating for the architect's regimented vision. Mary remarked that the new buildings looked as if they'd been designed by two different people who had quarrelled over the design, but her aunt shrugged, as if she had not understood.

Often, Mary and her aunt would sit in the Puerta del Sol, in the shade of the monastery cloisters, where the residents of Madrid stared at them without embarrassment. She enjoyed the attention of younger men and was often complimented on her beauty, or so she assumed from their courteous gestures. Although she was now in her early forties, Mary knew she was still an attractive woman. In turn, she watched the citizens stroll with languid elegance, sharing gossip at a volume that could not possibly guarantee discretion.

Their own conversation rarely diverged from two topics: where was Joseph, and why had he dumped them in this uncomfortable place, simply because of one unexpected letter from a mysterious Count Cogorani?

'Are we expected to wait here,' Anne grumbled, 'for this count to make contact? How will he know we're in Madrid?'

Mary had learned enough about Spanish society to realise that counts were everywhere.

'We should forget about Count Cogorani. He's probably a

minor nobleman, trying to improve his fortunes by marrying the daughter of an English marquess.'

'But if that's the case, what are we to do?' Anne added. 'No one has called on us. Without an introduction, how are we to meet anyone of rank?'

'We should be patient,' Mary said. 'I'm content to wait until I'm sure our litigators have not followed us to Spain. And what about the consequences of our escape from prison? Have you considered that?'

Anne fell silent and shook her head.

'More than one man lost his life that night,' Mary continued, keeping her voice soft to avoid scaring her aunt. 'We might be held responsible. I'd rather stay hidden, for a while.'

Anne's voice trembled and two bright-pink spots appeared below her eyes. 'Men died because of our escape?'

'Of course they did. You witnessed what Joseph has become, what he will stoop to when crossed.'

Anne's voice grew higher in pitch, as she defended her innocence. 'We didn't ask him to hurt anyone. I thought he bribed the guards.'

Mary saw her aunt's distress. 'You're quite right,' she said, 'it was Joseph's fault, not ours. His actions have nothing to do with us.'

Deciding to change topic, she gestured towards the women walking arm in arm in the square. 'Anyway, what on earth will we wear if we receive an invitation? Madrid isn't Paris, but the Spanish certainly know how to dress.'

The invite came only a few weeks later, hand-delivered by a servant in breeches, coat and wig. He stepped down from a well-presented coach, badged with the insignia of the new

British king, George II. Mary had been resting in the courtyard and hearing the approach of horses, ran to the gates. A coach paused further down the narrow street, as if the coachman was searching for a particular house. Abandoning all dignity and protocol she called out, waving her hands above her head, and ran to take the letter from the servant's hand. She woke her tousled and confused aunt, and together they broke the seal and unfurled the manuscript. It was from Sir Benjamin Keene, the British Consul General for Spain, inviting them to a social gathering at the ambassador's residence, only one week later. Mary tumbled downstairs, called the maid from her siesta, and using a combination of gesticulating and shouting in French and English, demanded that she and her aunt be measured for dresses – at once. Unprepared for such unguarded emotion in the middle of the afternoon, the maid screamed and ran away.

The following morning, Mary sought the maid in the shady kitchen, which smelt of garlic and something rancid, like cloths left damp for too long. The girl turned at the sound of her mistress and gripped the edge of the table with both hands, as if she wanted to escape.

This is ridiculous, Mary thought, I'm not an ogre. She smiled, hoping to reassure the maid that she was a calm and reasonable person. She pointed to her robe, frowning theatrically at its shabby folds, then gestured above to her aunt's bedroom, holding up two fingers, meaning that two dresses were needed. This performance was repeated, with cutting movements across the table, where they both frowned at the imaginary cloth. Mary's final attempt brought success, as she laid coins on the table, next to the phantom bolster of fabric.

That afternoon, the maid's sister arrived with a tape measure and pins. Teresa was different; confident, garrulous and with a smattering of English. Mary decided she didn't have to like the woman. Teresa had the one quality that was required; she was a dressmaker.

On the evening of the party, their coach dropped them at the gates of a residence somewhere near the Royal Alcázar. Like their home, it was surrounded by a high wall, but any resemblance to their farmhouse ended once through the gates. Wide, tiled steps, the balustrade mounted with urns trailing early autumn blooms of red and white, carried them upwards towards an open door.

Their invitation was checked inside the entrance, in the cool of a dark, high-ceilinged hallway. Open panelled doors beyond the stairwell heralded music and the murmur of voices. A different servant led them into the salon, a long room decorated in Parisian style but with a lighter, more delicate palette of pale ochre. After the shady hall, Mary blinked in the bright sunlight flooding from floor-to-ceiling windows.

They were loudly introduced, and everyone stopped talking to allow the British residents of Madrid to have a good look at the newcomers – women with titles. Mary surveyed the room and noted with relief that the two gold escudos she had paid to Teresa had not been wasted. Their gowns were of a simple plain fabric, the bodice higher than would be common in France and without embellishment at the neck and cuffs. At first glance, their robes were quite in keeping with those worn by the women of the British community.

A tall man hurried towards them, younger than she was, Mary thought, but already tending to jowls and a double chin. The top buttons of his waistcoat had been left unfastened, to display the frills of his shirt. He held out his hand and bowed low, firstly to the senior woman, Lady Anne Carrington, and then to the younger, Lady Mary Herbert, introducing himself as Benjamin Keene.

'I must apologise, dear ladies,' he said, 'for not welcoming you sooner to our community, but anyone with sense deserts Madrid during the summer months. I only returned from San Ildefonso myself two weeks ago and was horrified to discover you had been neglected. May I ask the reason for your visit to this royal city?'

Mary was prepared. 'I'm here on behalf of the Jacobite court in Rome, to build links and friendships, which may be of benefit to us all.'

She saw the consul general's face cloud and he touched his chin.

'I'm afraid we don't discuss the Jacobite cause here. There was an envoy once, sent by the Pretender. A good chap, so I've heard, but he gave up his post some time ago. We must focus on the future, don't you agree? The important thing is for the Spanish crown to maintain a good working relationship with the new British monarch, if we want to prevent another war. Now, I mustn't monopolise you.' Keene looked over Mary's shoulder into the far distance, as if desperate to escape. 'Ladies, do please mingle.'

It was a warning and one that hurt. Mary had assumed her family's links with the exiled James III might bring some social advantage in Madrid and was cross about her own misjudgement.

Aunt Anne failed to notice their social misstep, and with her antennae honed after years of playing cards in Parisian salons, joined a group of older women at a card table. Mary stood alone, fidgeting with a glass of wine poured by one of the circling servants. She tapped her finger on the rim, in time with the music, and pretended to study the black-and-white-tiled floor. Her ability to mix with others was not a strength, unlike her aunt. Had she already spoiled her one hope of gaining access to the people that mattered?

Mary turned towards a light touch on her arm from a man dressed in the black uniform of the church.

'May I introduce myself? I am the Abbe Paretti. I have been trying to find you, Lady Herbert.'

The nape of Mary's neck prickled, as if a window had been opened at her back. Someone searching for her could only mean trouble. She attempted a gracious smile and allowed the stranger to lift her hand and brush his lips across her fingers, feeling the scrape of his moustache against her skin.

'I am employed within the Spanish court but have been asked to find you by Count Cogorani. We had heard you were in Madrid.'

'Cogorani?' Mary repeated.

'Ah, I can see you recognise the name. I believe he wrote to you earlier this year. Count Cogorani is the director of the Espanola Company. They own three mines near Seville, all in a state of neglect and disrepair. Preliminary investigations suggest that these mines have the potential to become highly profitable. It's a gamble, I admit, but the count is keen that you consider investing, and with your family background in mining, offer us practical help to bring the mines back to life.'

At last, Mary thought. Thank you, Joseph. She frowned and placing her glass on a walnut table at her side, stroked the red velvet inlay with her finger, keen to avoid appearing too interested.

She dipped her head towards the cleric. 'I will consider the count's kind offer, of course,' she said, 'but I need further details. Please arrange a meeting between us.'

Paretti bowed to indicate his agreement, then turning to leave, paused and added, 'You are a stranger to Madrid I believe, Lady Herbert, and alone with an elderly relative. Is there any other matter I can help you with?'

Mary hesitated. The expense of the dresses had left them

almost penniless, and she needed to borrow money, but how could she ask this of Paretti without revealing too much about her financial affairs?

'I need to speak to someone about finance if I am to consider Count Cogorani's proposition. Can you recommend anyone?'

'I will introduce you to the Dutch ambassador,' Paretti replied. 'I am sure he will be amenable to discussing your financial affairs. He has a reputation for helping the hidalgos, of whom there are many in Madrid.'

Mary narrowed her eyes. 'I'm sorry but my Spanish is limited. What is a hidalgo?'

The Abbe laughed. 'Why, it's a member of the impoverished gentry.'

'You are mistaken about me, Abbe Paretti,' Mary blustered, searching for a tone that conveyed both indignation and reproach. 'I need to discuss possible finance for the project, nothing more.'

Paretti frowned. 'I apologise for my indiscretion, my lady,' he said. 'Do you still want me to arrange the meeting?'

'Of course,' Mary agreed. 'As soon as it can be arranged.'

CHAPTER 16

1728

William hurried up the lane towards Welshpool, early morning dew still dripping from the bushes and the air fresh with the scent of new daffodils. In his hand he held a letter from his daughter. For a man of over seventy, there was strength in his grip and a determination in his stride. William had a proposition to discuss with Grace Evans, an offer he had almost resolved to accept, but he needed the encouragement of a friend who never failed to give good advice. He had been delighted when Grace accepted his offer of a cottage on the estate. It was the least the Herbert family could do for a woman who had spent most of her adult life as Winifred's long-suffering companion.

He climbed the steps and paused to admire the distinctive black-and-white walls of the cottage, her well-kept garden and the scrubbed windows and doorstep. Grace was expecting him. William had been warned about dropping in without an invitation and had sent a servant ahead with a gift of warm bread from the kitchen. She curtseyed, holding open the door.

'My lord, do come in.'

In the small, dark parlour, William waited for Grace to bring him a glass of the ale they brewed on the estate. Once they were settled, and enquiries made after each other's health, she fixed her grey eyes upon his face, her lips parted in expectation.

'I've had a letter,' William said, 'from my daughter Mary.' He thought he saw Grace's expression change, but this was quickly hidden. 'She's in Spain, with my sister Anne. Last December, she signed a contract with the Espanola Mining Company to drain one of their mines.'

'Oh, for heaven's sake, whatever next.' Grace lifted her hand to her mouth as if she regretted her words.

'I can understand your reaction, dear Grace, but the contract appears sound. This isn't gambling but a good business investment. Perhaps she has learned from her mistakes. Perhaps she needs a second chance.'

'But, William,' Grace dropped the formalities they both struggled to respect, 'what experience does she have of mining? Where will she find the money to finance this endeavour? Surely no one will lend her more.'

'That's why I needed to speak to you. Mary's relying on my mining experience to guide her and wants me to recruit a manager for the whole enterprise. It seems that Count Cogorani, the fellow who owns the Espanola Company, has heard about me and how well our mines are doing. I am considering helping her, with financial backing too.'

In the silence, waiting for Grace to reply, William heard the song of a blackbird and its energy and persistence spoke for his mood. Perhaps everything might resolve after all; debts paid, marriage settlements found for his other daughters, the castle renovations complete. That would indeed be a legacy worth having.

'I'm sorry,' Grace said, 'but I'm wondering if relief and flattery have caused you to think you must agree. I know how much you regret having no contact with Mary, but she has harmed many people, whose lives will never be the same. My advice is not to trust this proposal.'

'But listen to me,' William argued, 'if this mining opportunity is successful, she can repair the harm. I admit I have lacked good sense in the past but my acumen where mining is concerned, both in operational matters and in the fine fellows I recruit, can be relied upon. Mary's gambling was beyond my control. This is a venture that may well succeed.'

Grace rested her hand on William's arm. 'I can hear you have already decided. If you are looking for my blessing, I will give it, but I feel afraid. I don't want to see you hurt again.'

William paused before replying. 'For the first time in years, I feel capable, as if I have valuable experience I can share. This venture may give me a purpose in my declining years. Perhaps I can learn to love my daughter again and earn the respect of my family. That's worthwhile, isn't it?'

Grace took his hand. 'Of course, and you are welcome to speak to me anytime about its progress, but please discuss this fully with the manager of your mines. He will give you a more informed opinion. I wish you luck.'

William rose and kissed her fingers, his eyes searching her face for permission for more. Instead, Grace led him to her door and passed him his hat and cloak. Walking home, he thrashed at the verges with his stick, beheading last year's flowering stalks and thought of the affection that had always lingered, unspoken, between himself and Grace. If not for their difference in status, he might even consider asking for her hand in marriage, since his wife had been dead for over four years, but of course, Grace would refuse him.

Barely acknowledging the servant who took his outdoor clothes in the cavernous entrance to the castle, or glancing at the paintings that covered the walls, William climbed the staircase designed by his father, taking two steps at a time. On the first floor, he chose to sit in the drawing room, at his Japanese writing table, where he could raise his eyes and look at the mural he had commissioned for the ceiling. This work was intended to show his daughters in their full beauty, as goddesses. It was perhaps unfortunate that Mary had chosen to be portrayed as Minerva, the goddess of wisdom, a quality she singularly lacked but given a chance, it was possible she might still achieve this.

There were two letters to be written, the first to his daughter, expressing his delight. Mary had asked for his help and he felt full of energy and hope for the future. Was this not evidence of her emerging good sense? If only he was younger, he would join his daughter in Spain, even work alongside this Cogorani fellow, who clearly respected him. William briefly considered whether he should send his own superintendent of mines, the very best of chaps, but dismissed the thought. How would he manage without him?

It was pleasing to imagine Mary watching from above as he scratched out the words and he felt the approval of his mother, gazing down at him from her own portrait. The other letter William wrote was to his manager, asking him to find and interview a team of experienced mining engineers for the Espanola project. William himself would be a member of the panel, of course. He intended to be fully involved, at every step. This time, there would be no mistakes.

A manager for the Espanola project was recruited, a man called Donnelly, but there followed a lengthy and frustrating delay in his departure for Spain with their workforce. Mary's letters to her father were full of reproach. She had yet to meet Cogorani but through visits from the Abbe Paretti, had learned of his growing impatience.

Aunt Anne settled well amongst the English matrons of Madrid, but Mary had little to do other than spend her days writing to lawyers under the shade of the portico, or her evenings on the shady, tree-lined avenue known as the Salón del Prado. Here the classes mingled, and it was possible to take a chair and admire the slow, languorous walk of the citizens, the women parading their gowns and headdresses, the men posing in groups, watching the women. One evening, not long before sunset, Mary saw Paretti approach along the Paseo del Prado, in the company of a man wearing an unfashionably high wig, one that exaggerated the already considerable disparity in height between the cleric and his companion. Paretti bowed and introduced Count Cogorani.

'My lady,' he said, 'your maidservant told us you were here. Count Cogorani is keen to make your acquaintance during his brief visit to Madrid.'

The count gave a deep bow from the waist and as he rose, lifted her fingers to make a pretence at a kiss. Such courtly behaviour did nothing to mask his brusque manner.

'Lady Herbert,' he said, without further preamble, 'I can wait no longer. You entered into a contractual agreement with the Espanola Company, but I have seen no progress. Paretti tells me you are managing this situation alone. Forgive me, but I understood you were acting as proxy for your father. In Spain, a woman would not take on such a responsibility without the protection of her husband or her father.'

Mary stared at Cogorani's mean, narrow lips and long pointed nose and felt an immediate dislike. She stood to her full height and stared into his pouchy eyes.

'You are mistaken, Count Cogorani,' she said, 'and the misunderstanding lies with you, not me. I never pretended to be acting on behalf of my father, but he *is* my adviser. My business partner, Count Joseph Gage, will be joining me soon, here in Madrid.'

'I cannot do business with a woman,' Cogorani argued. 'Until this Gage fellow arrives, you must employ a man to act as your agent. Unless I see action within the next two months, our contract is terminated, and I will sue you for the wasted months.'

Cogorani made no effort to lower his tone and a small crowd gathered to witness the pleasure of a public row, even one most could not understand. Paretti stood to one side, twisting his clerical hat in his hands, and glanced around as if searching for a way to disappear.

Into the thick silence between the combatants, he spoke: 'Count Cogorani, if I may remind you, we are due at the palace.'

Cogorani released Mary from his penetrating stare and turned to his companion.

'Thank you, Paretti. It is rude to keep people waiting. Some people would do well to learn that lesson.'

The count gave Mary one further threatening glare and turned away, striding towards the fountain of Neptune, Paretti scurrying behind.

It was now dark. The groups of women had disappeared from the square and Mary felt the stares of the men shift from admiration to threat. She remained seated to allow her pounding heart to slow. It was clear that she must take some action, but what?

A man's shape became distinct, his walk fast and purposeful, scanning the groups of men, searching... searching for her. Her heart lurched. Could this be Joseph, at last? The man's shape solidified and she saw it was her coachman. In the same moment, he saw her.

'My lady,' he called out, 'thank goodness I have found you.

When you didn't return I thought I should search for you. It's not safe here after dark. Let me take you home.'

Mary stood, allowing her rescuer to drape her cloak around her shoulders and lead her towards the waiting coach. She could not swallow or speak but mingled with the disappointment that choked her, was the immense consolation of rescue, even by a man paid to care for her.

A letter arrived the next day from her father, advising that Donnelly was on his way, but the fellow had insisted on sailing for Lisbon, not Cadiz. Mary's frustration with her father's lack of control over this headstrong employee was tempered by relief that she could act at last. She would leave for Portugal as soon as possible and catch her new manager of mines in Lisbon.

Through her aunt's contacts in the community of exiles, Mary found an agent, a young man called Andrew Gallwey, a former soldier who spoke excellent Spanish and Portuguese. She had no concerns about abandoning her aunt in Madrid. The elderly British formed a tight society of gossip and gaming and it was as if Anne had lived amongst them for years.

Their long and uncomfortable journey to Lisbon in an unwieldy, poorly sprung coach passed in a haze of worry about the dwindling supply of money in her purse. There was food for herself and Gallwey, as well as the coachmen and her maid's sister, Teresa, whose presence was required for propriety. Added to that was the cost of accommodation along the way, changes of horses, bribes... Mary could only imagine the scale of her mounting debt.

'All will come right in the end,' she muttered to herself. Once the mine was drained and operational, she would earn two-fifths of its income. It was a sound investment, if only her creditors and Cogorani would be patient.

Once in Lisbon, Mary walked alone under the shade of the portico that hugged two sides of the Terreiro do Paço, wondering how the royal family coped with the hubbub, their palace taking up the third side of the square, with the fourth open to the port. The plaza thronged with people, trade, and traffic. Coaches almost ran over small children, who walked even smaller dogs. Nuns hurried alongside elegantly dressed noblewomen and chattering maidservants in headscarves congregated next to the well.

She was glad it was acceptable for a woman to be alone in Lisbon, at least in this commercial marketplace. Teresa had refused to accompany her to the port, furious at being expected to stay in a room above the stables, instead of at the inn. Andrew had failed to hide his disappointment at their marginally better rooms, complaining that a titled lady might expect to be hosted by the master of the British trading station. How could she have explained about the lawsuits, the fear of meeting someone she knew in a port city dominated by her countrymen?

She had breakfasted on local bread and honey, thankfully with some coffee, learning from the innkeeper that Mr Gallwey had already left to search for the Irishman, Mr Donnelly. She felt dizzy, perhaps the effect of the coffee, and her mind buzzed with the activity around her. Under the shade of the portico, merchants from Portugal's empire squeezed alongside shops built to service the shipping trade, with offices selling tickets to places completely unknown. There were so many languages, different skin colours, women with veils covering their faces, men wearing what looked like dresses. It was all too new, too wearisome. Worse, what should have been a welcome sound in a strange city, felt like a threat. There were too many British accents.

Mary turned her back on the square and walked to the dockside, pausing to watch a line of dark-skinned men, their ankles in chains, heaving boxes and bundles between them before each was weighed by a man with pale skin, his features hidden beneath the shade of a wide-brimmed hat. The cargo continued its journey up the gangway into the hold of a ship, passed hand to hand through the rhythmic movement of another line of black men. As they worked, the men sang, their voices low but in harmony. Three ships were roped to the dock, but further out on the river, multiple ships of different shapes and sizes waited at anchor for their turn to load or unload. Seagulls screamed and swooped over Mary's head to scavenge entrails of fish. She raised her handkerchief to cover her nose and, although it was summer, shivered in the breeze from the water, pulling her cloak across her shoulders. If she waited here, listening to the men in chains, time would pass and Donnelly would be found. But what then?

Someone coughed and Mary jumped, swinging around to see Andrew Gallwey, his eyes creasing at the corners as he squinted at her through the bright reflection of sun on water.

'Sorry, my lady, I didn't mean to startle you. You were miles away, daydreaming I think.'

'Mr Gallwey, I feel...' Mary paused, what did she feel? This city was not hers; she had no compass, no bearings. She felt a well of loneliness so deep that if she looked too closely, there was a risk she might disappear over the edge. Such alarming thoughts could not be shared with an employee.

Her agent waited, his expression alert, expectant.

'I feel... I feel that my father might have made a poor choice in Dominic Donnelly.'

'You're right, Lady Mary. I understand he's been drawing a

salary from the marquess's estate for almost a year. Where is the plan, the scheme of work, the invoice for the equipment he needs? I hate to ask, but has the marquess been monitoring Donnelly closely enough?'

'My father has wasted months trying to answer Donnelly's pointless questions. He's challenged the viability of the project, its financial backing, and whether Mr Joseph Gage will manage him. Why did he accept the position if he had so many doubts? Why on earth has my father not terminated his contract?'

Gallwey's eyes narrowed. 'I doubt if any of Donnelly's concerns were legitimate, from what I've heard of him.'

'Yet my father remains convinced he's right for the job, that he's worth waiting for.'

'We can make up our own minds,' Andrew replied. 'Let's regard our first meeting with Donnelly as a second interview.'

'Did you manage to track him down?' Mary asked.

'Eventually. Almost everyone knew of him but not in the best light. It wasn't difficult to find the alehouses preferred by the Irish. I'm afraid he's already drunk and in no fit state to talk to us, so I've arranged to see him first thing tomorrow. I've some business here in the port, but afterwards I'll go straight back to our lodging and ask the innkeeper to set up a room where we can be private. We don't want Donnelly to have the benefit of an audience.'

'Shall we meet for some dinner tonight, plan our campaign?' Mary replied.

'Of course, if that is your wish. We should think about the questions we need to ask and the minimum we're willing to believe from his answers.'

Mary paused. 'Thank you,' she said. 'I don't want to eat alone.' She remained standing, studying the men in chains. Andrew hesitated, as if waiting for permission to leave.

'Mr Gallwey,' she said. 'Who are these men?'

Andrew hesitated. 'They're slaves, my lady, taken from the west coast of Africa. Most are shipped to Portuguese colonies, but some end up here in the port.'

'I must seem very ignorant,' Mary said, 'but I don't know where Africa is. I don't know what you mean by a slave.'

Andrew stared into the shimmering water at the dockside before answering.

'I can only describe a slave in terms of what they have lost. They have no home, they will never see their family again, they're not paid for the work they do. Every country in Europe is involved, our own homeland is one of the worst.'

'But what can be gained from treating men this way?'

'Why, wealth of course, the engine of every single economy. As a businesswoman, you fully understand the need to make a profit. The capture and exploitation of these men increases margins.'

'Is there no benefit at all for such people, these slaves?'

Andrew laughed, but his expression showed no sign of humour.

'The Portuguese baptise slaves, guaranteeing their reward in heaven. Britain doesn't even do that.'

Mary felt bile rise in her throat. She swallowed, turning away from the activity on the dockside, and linked her arm through Gallwey's.

'Heaven is no reward, Andrew. Let's walk away. What you have told me is beyond my understanding. This is a hateful, false place and after tomorrow, I cannot bear to stay another day. We must hurry back to Spain.'

Mary and Andrew Gallwey sat on one side of a table, facing a chair that had remained empty for at least half an hour beyond

Donnelly's appointed time. Gallwey again looked at his time-piece, a habit that Mary was beginning to find annoying, when the door swung open and a tall man swept into the room, dressed more like a gentleman than an artisan, with wig, tailored coat, and breeches. He sat down in the empty chair, without bowing to Mary, and appeared preoccupied with licking his thumb to wipe a speck of dust from his knee-length boots.

'Mr Donnelly,' said Andrew, 'we expected you to arrive in Cadiz, not Lisbon, and where are your workers? Surely you have brought with you a team of experienced miners?'

Donnelly raised his head from close inspection of the fine leather and stitching of his boots and stared at Andrew with an intensity that Mary found uncomfortable.

'The team is on its way. They'll arrive in Cadiz in a couple of weeks.'

Gallwey banged the table. 'Then why are you in Lisbon? Surely you should be in Cadiz to meet them.'

'I thought I should make the acquaintance, independently, of Count Cogorani. Study the lie of the land if you get my meaning.'

'No, we don't get your meaning, Mr Donnelly,' Mary said. 'What are you trying to tell me?'

Donnelly continued to stare at Gallwey, ignoring Mary.

'I don't trust this scheme. I've never hidden my doubts about the project. Perhaps if I met the count myself, saw what needed to be done, I might be able to work with him directly. I would, of course, pay Lady Herbert for the introduction. If we can settle on an amount, would that free me from my obligation to her?'

Mary stood. Words dropped from her lips like icicles.

'You are an employee of my father, the Marquess of Powis, but you are contracted to work in Spain under my direction. I will not tolerate your tone or your suggestion that you can buy your way out of your contract.'

Donnelly finally turned to look at Mary, his eyebrows folded into an expression of sadness.

'I understand that a woman of your age might have expected to have a husband and children, but that does not permit you to play at business, funded by your pappa, of course. I am offering you a way out. With my contacts, I can finance this scheme and make it work. You, on the other hand, are doomed to failure.'

Briefly, and to her shame, Mary wavered, tempted to accept. Despite his rudeness, Donnelly had seen right into her heart. It was true, she was out of her depth. If she could negotiate a decent sum, perhaps she might return to Paris, forget all about the mine at Guadalcanal and be freed of some of her debts. It would be a relief. She hesitated before replying, torn between defending her honour or bargaining with this arrogant man.

Without warning, the door opened, slamming against the wall. In the seconds of shocked silence that followed, a stream of plaster dust trickled to the floor.

Joseph Gage crossed the room in three strides, lifted Donnelly out of the chair by his lapels and threw the man against the opposite wall.

'You will never, ever, speak to Lady Mary Herbert like that again,' Joseph yelled, banging Donnelly's head against the plaster in time with each word. Dragging the beaten man towards the open door, he threw him into the yard, causing hens innocently pecking in the dust to scatter in alarm.

'Get to Cadiz,' Joseph shouted at Donnelly. 'Meet your men, start your work. We will follow behind and check on your every move.'

Mary turned to Andrew and said: 'Mr Gallwey, please meet my... my...'

Joseph slouched in Donnelly's vacated chair, his hair covered in dust and sweat, his clothes torn and filthy. He leaned across to offer a grimy hand to Andrew.

'I'm Joseph Gage. I'm Lady Herbert's husband in every way that counts, except in the eyes of the church. Looks like I arrived in the nick of time.'

CHAPTER 17
1728/29

Mary pulled the rough blanket over her shoulders and circled her knees with her arms, trying to orientate herself in this whitewashed room with seabirds calling from just outside the window. She eased her legs onto the floorboards and walked towards the open window, dragging the blanket behind her. The river was just visible, and ships leaned into the wind as they tacked towards the port. A breeze that tasted of salt, with the added smell of rotten fish and tar, tugged at strands of hair escaping from under her cap. Mary thought how much improved Lisbon seemed this morning, but she couldn't linger. She and Teresa were to follow the men in the carriage, as soon as they had breakfasted and packed.

Joseph left early on horseback, with Andrew, both men determined to follow Donnelly to Cadiz. All that remained was a furrow in the pillow and his earthy scent on the blanket. Her muscles ached after last night, but at the same time her skin tingled, and her limbs felt heavy and relaxed. Joseph and she had talked, of course, and quarrelled, which was typical, but her resentment of his long months of absence vanished beneath the feel of his skin, the soft hair on his neck and remembering their pleasure in each other.

Joseph was not willing to account for the missing year, other than boasting of his success at harassing their litigants, including Richard Cantillon. It was better that Mary knew nothing, he said, and she saw the sense of this. Their argument arose because of his insistence that only his forceful action had saved her from Donnelly's bullying but draining the mine at Guadalcanal increasingly felt like a fantasy. If Joseph had not interfered, she would have gained some time to consider the Irishman's offer.

'But Donnelly's a drunk,' Joseph argued, rolling his eyes. 'Nothing he says can be trusted.'

'He would have paid me,' Mary replied, 'both for my time and the opportunity I'd given him.'

Joseph snorted. 'Rubbish. You wouldn't have received a penny.'

'Any day now, my heroic saviour, we can expect to be pursued by Count Cogorani for our lack of progress. I'd rather he was chasing Donnelly, instead of me.'

Joseph pushed her back onto the pillows and kissed her.

'Don't give up yet,' he murmured, 'I think we can make this work.'

Mary's unwieldy coach was exchanged for an expensive post-chaise, using ready cash Joseph had earned in Parisian gaming salons. The rear wheels were higher than those at the front and because it was driven by a single postilion, riding on the left of their two horses, Mary and Teresa were able to draw the blinds but still see ahead, their view uninterrupted. Teresa chattered about people she had met in Lisbon, telling stories rich with intrigue and detail, forgetting that her mistress had only a basic grasp of Spanish. Mary struggled to pay attention and allowed her mind to drift. The chaise sped past rolling hills, peppered with rocky outcrops until they reached the town of Beja, on the summit of a ridge rising from the plains. Here, they stayed in an inn close to the convent. Teresa's enthusiasm for romance encouraged their landlady to spend too long sharing a local myth about a young nun who had been abandoned by her lover. Mary was able to hide her boredom behind a lack of Portuguese, but Teresa's grasp of the language was impressive. Her genuine tears at the end of the tale so delighted their host, they were treated to the best of rooms and food. The landlady and Teresa's exchange of gossip about people neither knew, nor would ever meet, seemed utterly pointless. She could only marvel at Teresa's technique, but such niceties of social exchange were well beyond her understanding.

From the town of Tavira, close to the Spanish border, their coach travelled through mudflats towards the coast. High cliffs encircled wide, sandy beaches, with natural, stone arches stretching far into the sea. Once in Spain, the landscape merged into low hills, covered by a patchwork of olive groves. Pockets of habitation were scattered like discarded handkerchiefs. The coach rattled past whitewashed villages, the wheels throwing up pebbles and tossing hens, cats and stray children into the ditch. After Huelva, rough brush dissolved into miles of shimmering wetland, edged by long beaches backed by dark, forested dunes. At last, they reached Cadiz.

Andrew Gallwey and Joseph were already waiting at the inn where they would stay the night. In her room, Mary wiped her face, hands and neck, holding the damp cloth to her nose and inhaling the scent of aromatic oils of oranges and rosemary. Free from the clatter of the chaise and Teresa's mindless chatter, every part of her body relaxed into the silence. Reluctantly, she joined the others, surprised to find Teresa already seated with the men around a table hewn from the trunk of a single tree. Mary knew she should dismiss the maidservant to her room but felt so weary; Teresa's ill temper seemed a greater threat than the risk of the maid overhearing their conversation. The girl proved her worth by finding the landlady, and in a stream of high-handed commands, ordered food and wine for them all.

Andrew looked over at Joseph, who gave an almost imperceptible nod, as if permitting his companion to speak first. Mary guessed it was not good news.

'We've been making enquiries in Cadiz and the surrounding area, Lady Herbert,' Andrew said. 'Donnelly's reputation preceded him, and people were more than happy to talk to us. We believe he's holed up in an Irish drinking establishment called Plunket's. Some of our workers from Wales have turned up. We've spoken to a few and he's either tried to recruit them to work for him instead of us, or he's dissuaded them from staying. We believe some have already left for home. Naturally, they're angry and want payment for their wasted journey.'

Joseph coughed and stared at the wall before joining in. 'There's another thing,' he said. 'Donnelly's been spreading rumours about you. To anyone who'll listen, he's telling them about your financial problems and debt. I'm concerned this may reach Cogorani. I should head over to Guadalcanal as soon as I can.'

'There are rumours about me.' Andrew spoke again; a flush spread from under his cravat, crawled through his beard, and settled just below his eyes.

'A rumour about you?' Mary asked, turning to Andrew. 'What on earth is Donnelly saying?'

'I have a friend, my lady, a military man. He's staying here with me, in this inn. The situation has been misunderstood.'

She nodded. 'That is unfortunate. It's bad enough when rumours are true, as these are about me, but to have to listen to lies...'

Andrew glanced at Joseph, and then at Mary, his brow creased.

'You are in debt, Lady Herbert?'

'Of course she's in debt,' Joseph interrupted. 'Who isn't, these days? You can't imagine that setting up an enterprise to drain a mine can be done without borrowing large sums of money. Don't worry, you'll be paid what you're owed.'

Andrew's lips parted in a smile, quickly hidden, as if matters which had troubled him now made sense.

Teresa had been following the conversation more closely than Mary had thought possible and said: 'Will I be paid too?'

Everyone turned to look at the maid. It was a good question but one that had no definite answer.

'Yes, yes, of course you will,' Joseph said, 'but what's important right now is to find the disgruntled miners. Gallwey, I want you to round them up, and I'll take a team with me to Guadalcanal. That'll look as if we mean business. First, I'm going to find Donnelly and with luck, send him packing. I have some legal papers to support his dismissal, drawn up this morning by a lawyer in Cadiz.'

Mary raised her eyebrows. 'That was quick work.'

Joseph grinned. 'A bit of... erm... pressure usually means that time can be found in any lawyer's busy schedule. Mary, I need you to sign the papers as proxy for your father. You must also write to the marquess, before a team of angry men turn up at Powis Castle. Let him know that Donnelly is a fraud. We have firm evidence he knows nothing at all about draining a mine. The miners say he questioned them about how it could be done.'

'How could my father have made such a mistake?'

Joseph frowned. 'I'm fond of your father but he's no judge of character. I expect that Donnelly saw an opening and always intended to take the project on for himself. Your father trusts too easily and was ripe for manipulation. He's kind but lazy, never checking or monitoring his decisions or other people's actions. Look at how easily you have manipulated him.'

'That's so unfair!' Mary protested.

Joseph grimaced, drawing his lips wide. 'Possibly, but we haven't time right now for an analysis of you and your father's relationship. We must act.'

The following afternoon, Joseph and Andrew Gallwey prepared to ride to Plunket's Tavern to serve Donnelly with the legal papers. Once Donnelly had been spoken to, and accepted his dismissal, Mary would travel to Seville with Teresa to find lodgings. She watched each man sharpen what looked like a dagger, using the innkeeper's grindstone and hang this from a belt strapped across the shoulder, but hidden beneath their coats.

'What is this?' she asked Joseph, pulling back his lapel to reveal the small sword. You only need to serve Donnelly with papers. Once he has them in his hand, he's dismissed.'

Joseph drew together the edges of his coat. 'It's best to be ready. Donnelly's not likely to be alone. Things could get lively.'

'All that matters is the dismissal,' Mary argued. 'If you believe there might be a fight, then surely it's best to meet Donnelly alone.'

'Has to be done today, I'm afraid,' Joseph said. 'My information is that he's already at the inn.'

Mary's temples began to throb. 'You're losing sight of what's important. If you're injured, or worse, the dismissal might not happen. Why do I suspect you're looking forward to this fight?'

Joseph rolled his eyes. 'Trust me, Mary. Gallwey and his companion are waiting for me; we must leave now, or Donnelly will be in no fit state to hold the document, never mind read it.'

He walked away, heading for the door but hesitated at the entrance, turning back to grasp her shoulders. 'Don't worry,' he said, his tone low and soft, 'by the end of the day, Donnelly will no longer be our manager. I promise.'

Mary's driver pulled up under the shade of a gnarled olive tree growing within Plunket's courtyard. The tavern was a low building, indistinguishable from a farmhouse and the yard seemed unusually quiet, apart from the usual stray dogs. She stepped down from the chaise and crept towards shutters staring wide open, despite the heat, and tried to peer into the gloomy interior. She could hear Donnelly's loud brogue above all other voices and as her eyes adjusted, she picked out Andrew and Joseph leaning against the opposite wall, sipping at jugs of ale, surveying the room. As well as Irish voices, she heard some of the men speaking Welsh. These were her father's missing miners.

Sensing he was being watched, Donnelly glanced behind him and noticed Joseph and Andrew.

'Well, well,' he bellowed. 'The short-arse and the bardajo. Didn't think he'd be to your taste, Gage.'

From the opposite corner, a tall man, most likely Andrew's companion, strode across the earth floor and punched Donnelly with one strike to his jaw. Through the window, the crack of knuckles meeting bone carried above any other sounds. Irishmen immediately came to Donnelly's aid, flailing out at the military man and anyone else within striking distance. Mary gasped, pressing her back against the wall, afraid to witness what might come next. Her two men were easily outnumbered but if Joseph pulled his sword, Donnelly or one of his compatriots would come to serious harm. She felt her heart leap in panic and was desperate to go inside. This should not be happening – they risked losing everything if Joseph and Andrew were arrested.

An Irish voice called out: 'Welsh bastard,' and Mary guessed that the miners would regard this as a call to arms. At least Joseph and Andrew would not be fighting alone. She dared to peer around the shutter and saw the entire room brawling, including the publican and a woman, who must be his wife, swatting at whoever she could reach with her broom. Insults mingled with cries of pain and the thump of fists on flesh. No one had yet drawn swords, but it would not be long.

Behind her, the cobbled yard rang with the sound of hooves and four Spanish guards dismounted, forcing their way through the low tavern door. This was a turn for the worse; an arrest would keep her men safe from harm, but they would be useless to her in gaol. Mary crept from the open window to warn Teresa, instructing their coachman to hide the chaise behind the tavern. Whatever happened, she could not risk becoming involved and tarnishing the reputation of the Herbert family.

Tiptoeing back to her viewpoint, Mary saw the guardsmen haul the injured from the floor by the scruff of their necks and draw swords on any man trying for a final blow. The publican cornered the guards, gesticulating that a good-natured brawl had simply got out of hand. In evidence, his wife appeared with jugs of ale and platters of bread, cheese and ham. The guards sat down to eat with the men they had intended to arrest, and the atmosphere soon became convivial. Mary glowered at Andrew and Joseph, who were sitting opposite Donnelly, chatting as if they were old friends. She tried waving, to remind them of the actual reason they were there, but they appeared oblivious.

The guards sat back, patting their bellies and surveyed the amicable scene while the publican poured everyone another tankard of ale. Singing and back-slapping revived with fresh enthusiasm. The guardsmen finally rose, somewhat unsteadily and with threatening gestures, gave the publican what looked like a final warning.

At last, Joseph leaned across the table and handed Donnelly the papers. Mary held her breath. All eating and conversation paused while Donnelly scanned the document, his lips moving as he sounded out every word. He rose, threw the document aside, and bellowed:

'You fools think my services are no longer required—'

'We don't think, we know,' Joseph interrupted. 'Your so-called services are worthless. I will take over the mine and you will crawl back under the stone wherever you were found hiding.'

Joseph and Donnelly both stood, glaring, fists clenched. A miner cheered, an Irishman told him to shut up and the Welshman retaliated by pouring ale over the Irishman's head. The melee erupted again and Andrew drew his sword. With his sailor friend, they protected Joseph's back.

'Get out of there,' Mary yelled, beckoning. Andrew saw her and rested his hand on Joseph's shoulder but Joseph did not attempt to break from Donnelly's stare. Instead, he responded to the agent's touch, by inching backwards. The three men held the crowd back with their raised swords, fielding blows with their arms. Donnelly tried to follow, but his passage was blocked by a group of furious miners. Joseph, Andrew and his companion escaped through the low door into the courtyard and gathered behind the wide trunk of a spreading oak.

Mary ran across the yard and Joseph wrapped her in his arms. Forgetting decorum, he kissed her on the lips in front of his fellow combatants. She smelt his sweat, fresh and sharp, felt his muscles tense with excitement. He pulled back from the kiss but kept his arm firmly around her shoulders as he barked out their next orders.

'Off to Seville, Mary. I'll join you whenever I can. Gallwey, return to Madrid with Teresa and bring Lady Anne Carrington back to her niece. After that, your services are no longer required. I will be Lady Mary's manager, overseer, agent, whatever title we choose to give me. I will take control of the mining project.'

Mary pulled out from under his grip. 'Am I not to have a maidservant? If I am to lose Teresa, surely you must come with me to Seville.'

Joseph shook his head. 'It's no distance to Seville and you will have the driver to keep you safe. He knows where inexpensive lodgings can be found. Until we start to make money, a maidservant is an unnecessary expense. Anyway, Teresa wants to go home, and she must be paid. We can't keep her here against her will.'

Teresa nodded and gave Mary a satisfied smirk.

'Hang on!' Gallwey interrupted. 'Without me, you might have been killed in there.'

'We don't need a fighter,' Joseph said. 'We need someone who can run a mine and that will be me. You'll be well compensated for your work, provided you return safely with Lady Carrington. Without that, you won't see a penny.'

Andrew exchanged a glance with his friend and both men left, striding towards the horses, their heels kicking up dust. Behind them, Teresa hurried to keep up.

'Andrew Gallwey is my employee,' Mary argued. 'It was up

to me to dismiss or retain him. We don't need to make more enemies.'

Joseph returned his annoying grin. 'Management decision, I'm afraid.'

'You took a huge risk in there,' she said, her voice rising. 'You ask me to trust you, but you lost sight of what was important. How can I be convinced you have the steadiness of character needed to manage our project? Andrew Gallwey is a capable, serious man; one I can rely on.'

'No one was hurt, and Donnelly is no longer your employee.' Joseph enunciated each word, his teeth bared and unsmiling. 'I think thanks are in order, not more criticism. As for trust, what option do you have? You've admitted your heart isn't in the Guadalcanal project, yet you're legally obliged to complete it. If I don't take over, what hope is there? You can't afford Gallwey. Who else but me will work for nothing?'

Mary's stomach lurched. Joseph spoke the truth, but she was about to be despatched with her aunt to some godforsaken place, left to survive on her wits. This was the very same trick Joseph had played on her last year. Worse, he enjoyed his power over her.

From inside the inn, she heard the roar of fighting men drift through the open window.

Joseph's brows creased and he tipped his head back, listening.

'I'm going back in. I have to rescue our miners. We can't have them turning up at Guadalcanal all bruised and bleeding. Enough time has been wasted. We need them fit for work. You must leave for Seville – now.'

Lifting his sword above his head in farewell, Joseph ran back to the inn, abandoning Mary to the care of her coachman.

CHAPTER 18

1729

The happiest three years of Winifred's life had passed living in a comfortable house in the countryside outside Bologna, with sole responsibility for the two princes. The king soon left the boys behind, preferring to establish a court in Avignon, where his presence might be more of an irritation to George II. It had been easy to convince James that the boys were settled in Bologna and should not be moved again.

Life in the villa was as close to normal as any royal child could expect. There were ponies and picnics, play-fighting and hugs, and Winifred tried to mix their learning with active games and play. Even at eight years old, Charles could not focus or sit still for more than a few minutes. If he was forced to read or write, he threw ink, stabbed his brother with his quill or hurled his book into a corner. Henry had just turned four and was a quieter, more biddable child, but one who watched his older brother's outbursts with fascination and respect.

Winifred's role as head of the boys' household was much improved by having Alice working alongside; a woman who modelled for the other women an unquestioning acceptance of orders but who knew her mistress well enough to share, in private, any reasonable complaints from the other servants. Once the children were in bed, they often sat in the gardens and talked. Winifred could never hear enough tales from the years she had missed with her daughter.

On this summer evening, Winifred strolled through the quiet house, the news that they must soon return to Rome causing her to pause and look afresh at the frescoes that decorated the walls of the airy, central hall. She surveyed the gardens from the top of a wide sweep of steps, seeing the countryside exactly as it was portrayed on the walls inside; evergreen oaks, columns of cypress trees, olives and vineyards fading into pastel shades of pink, ochre and blue. Winifred liked to sit on a stone bench, as the warmth of the day drifted into the cool of night, listening to the rustle of deer and the night cries of peacocks. Every week, she met her husband on this bench. It was their time to talk about the kind of matters that preoccupy the parents of adult children.

Maxwell had arrived in Bologna late last year with the queen. Klementyna's health and strength had slowly returned within the convent's care and James hoped she might agree to travel to Avignon to be at his side. Klementyna refused but compromised by accepting her removal to Bologna if Mrs Sheldon could remain as her companion. The household fretted about the queen's imminent arrival, fearing her unpredictable demands, but she had remained within her rooms, protected by the Earl of Nithsdale and her own choice of women. Apart from the kitchen staff, who grumbled about Klementyna's fickle appetite, the villa's routine continued without interruption.

Once Klementyna was settled, Winifred's duties included preparing the children to meet their mother. She helped Charles practise standing still for a few minutes, with his arms at his side, and showed him how to speak to the queen without shouting. Henry was easier, but he had to learn how to sit quietly, without sucking his thumb, for the length of the visit. Once the princes were ready, her husband took the boys to see their mother for an hour every day. To Winifred's surprise, he reported that the queen usually preferred to hold the placid and rather plump Henry on her knee for the entire hour. This left Maxwell free to occupy Charles with pretend sword fights and chasing games, which Klementyna was able to tolerate.

As Winifred waited for Maxwell, from the distant woods beyond she heard the bark of a fox and pulled her shawl around her shoulders. More than fearing the disruptive presence of the queen, she had been troubled by living again with her husband. But steady work for them both had resolved any need to quarrel about money and being on call to Klementyna, every moment of every day, meant that Maxwell could no longer drink heavily. Her husband had been given back his pride; his life had purpose and a young and very pretty woman adored and trusted him. Who would not thrive in such circumstances?

Winifred pulled the letter from the pocket of her petticoat. Her sister Anne needed money, why else would she have bothered to write? Grace had already told her about the mining venture. Anyone with sense could see it was nothing but a ridiculous fantasy. Anne made a further request, asking Winifred to influence the king into making Mary Herbert a Jacobite duchess, since being a duchess would make it possible for them to borrow more money.

She saw Maxwell pause at the glass doors that led from the hall into the garden. Spotting her, he waved and skipped down the steps like a younger man. Striding towards her through paths edged with box, he skirted around statues of nymphs and sea creatures, until he reached the bench where Winifred sat. He dropped down heavily beside her and nudged her elbow in greeting. They both remained silent, watching a servant flame the torches used to light the garden, creating pools of secretive, elongated shadows.

'Busy day?' Winifred asked her husband.

William grimaced, rubbing his chin. 'James is arriving soon. He plans to stay only for a few days before he goes on to Rome. She's not pleased.'

He always called Klementyna 'she'; it was a code between Winifred and her husband, meaning that he respected his special role in the queen's life, but didn't take her complaints or demands too seriously.

'So, we must all prepare to leave with him?'

'I think we should, but not immediately. She'll stick with convention and refuse, try to keep him hanging around for ages.'

'Maxwell...' Winifred hesitated before continuing, '... my sister Anne has written asking us for money. I'd like to send her something. She's living in Seville with Mary. Reading between the lines, they haven't got a penny.'

'She wasn't too keen to help us when we were desperate,' Maxwell said.

'I remember only too well. Grace and I visited them in Paris and begged for help. But she *has* paid for lodgings and education for our daughter, over many years. For the first time in our long marriage, we have enough money. I'd like a chance to be the one who gives, not the one who begs.'

Winifred waited for her husband to reply, watching bats emerge from crevices in the walls of the solid, red-brick house.

'Okay,' Maxwell agreed, 'but don't send them much. Think about our future, what might happen when we go back to Rome. I'll still work for the queen, but the princes are old enough now to no longer need a governess.'

'Yes, I'd worked that out for myself. We'll easily manage on your income, and I'll have a pension. With luck, we'll live in the

Muti Palace as part of the queen's household. It will be very different from before.'

Maxwell tugged at her sleeve. 'I can't stay long. She needs me to read to her before bed. Was there anything else in your sister's letter?'

'Anne wants me to ask the king to make Mary a Jacobite duchess. They think it will be easier to borrow money.'

Maxwell shook his head. 'No, no, no, don't do that. Even making the request would humiliate us and embarrass the king.'

'I agree but what shall I say to my sister?'

'Ignore it. Send them some money but don't mention the other matter. It's a whim.'

Maxwell shifted in his seat. 'I do have to leave. Was there anything else? You don't look as though you're finished with me.'

'Our daughter can't remain at the convent any longer,' Winifred said. 'She's finished school and there's nothing for her in Paris. Since the king is coming back, we have an opportunity to ask if she can join us here.'

Maxwell roared with laughter. 'How strange that will be, having Anne living with us. We'll be a family once more. I'll have to find her a husband.'

'For goodness' sake,' Winifred argued, 'she isn't nineteen yet.'

Maxwell stood and faced her, his feet shifting from side to side, smiling down at his wife.

'I'll arrange a meeting with James. He owes me a favour for persuading her majesty to leave the convent.'

Every day, Winifred and Alice waited for Anne's coach. The king and his household were already present, crowding the limited space, with many of the retinue lodged in Bologna itself. James had immediately given his consent for Anne to join her parents, so overwhelmed and delighted had he been by an unexpected welcome from his wife, including permission to share her bed. The citizens of Bologna were every bit as excited by having royalty in their presence, even an exiled king with little hope of regaining his throne, and parties were thrown in every aspiring household. In their evenings together, Maxwell and Winifred whispered about Klementyna's puzzling and unexpected enthusiasm for her husband, an eagerness that had stretched to new ballgowns and dancing.

At the request of the king, poor Mrs Sheldon was dismissed to a local convent. Winifred suspected that the young woman had decided to lose this battle in favour of winning the war, which was to remain alone with her sons in the peaceful villa in Bologna without James. When Klementyna announced that she was expecting another child and could not possibly be expected to return to Rome with her husband, she knew her intuition was correct.

One hot afternoon, the children ran across the terracotta floors of the house in bare feet, trying to hide from being dressed in the stiff, formal clothes expected by their parents. They shouted as they ran, taunting Winifred, and in the melee, she missed the sound of a coach on the drive. Out of breath and pink with excitement, Alice found her.

'She's here,' Alice shouted above the noise of the children, 'Lady Anne is here!'

Winifred picked up her skirts and ran through the gardens towards the driveway in front of the villa. At the sight of the carriage she stopped, brushed down her robe, and tucked untidy strands of hair behind her ears. Hardly daring to breathe, she grasped her own hands as the carriage door opened, and the coachman raised his arms to help a young woman down the steps.

There were no words. At the sight of a tall girl, so like her father but with the carriage of a Herbert woman, Winifred froze, as if made rigid by sorcery. She had not seen Anne for ten years, but this was indeed her girl, her daughter.

Anne saw Winifred waiting and ran forwards, drawing her into a deep embrace.

'Mother, my dearest mother,' she whispered.

Winifred shook her head, tried to smile, but nothing could hold back her tears. Anne's eyes were also bright, but she hid her face, bending down towards two children who clutched her mother's robe. The girl knelt, level with their faces, helping Henry to buckle his shoes without mentioning that he wore them on the wrong feet.

Lifting her head, Anne asked her mother, 'Who are these fine boys?'

'These are the royal princes, Charles, and Henry. I'm afraid I abandoned their game when I heard of your arrival. They were left for too long in their hiding places and now, they don't want to let me go. Children, say hello to Lady Anne Maxwell.'

Of course, they both refused.

Winifred linked arms with Anne and led her to the room she would be expected to share with Alice, the princes trooping behind still holding her skirts. The girl's trunk already stood open at the side of her bed and a jug of fresh, scented water and cloths sat on their shared dressing table. Alice waited by the bed, trembling, and seeing her beloved friend, rushed forward to grasp her hands.

The boys started jumping on the beds, so Winifred decided to leave the younger woman alone, allowing Alice the chance to share, in private, the quirks and idiosyncrasies of this excep-

tional royal household. They had shared so much, their relationship would always be stronger than a maidservant and her
mistress, just like herself and Grace. She had the luxury of
months ahead to speak to Anne and her duties had already been
neglected. The children, late for a visit to their parents, had
already vanished.

～

The reunited Maxwell family ate together every night and Anne
amused her parents with stories about the nuns and the visits
to Paris from her brother, Will, whenever he managed to escape
from La Flèche. Maxwell and Winifred spared their daughter
the details of their years in Rome, the debt, the humiliation, the
rows, and as expected, she did not ask.

Anne was popular in Bologna, since there were few girls her
age in either the king or queen's household. Winifred helped
her dress for parties, with Alice attending as chaperone,
remembering the balls hosted by the French royal family at
Saint-Germain or Marly. Memories of those sensual nights
made it hard to look her daughter in the eye and she hoped
that Anne would have the good sense not to behave like her
mother.

The king and queen soon tired of their boys, especially
Charles. James professed that he was too old for young children
and Klementyna claimed to be exhausted by the rigours of early
pregnancy. Any hope that Anne might help with the children
proved fruitless; her daughter was quite unsuitable as a
governess. The boys loved her, for all the wrong reasons. She
was willing to roll in grass, climb trees and chase them through
every room in the house, leaving the children hot and overexcited, with the simplest of duties or tasks left unfinished.
Winifred even suggested that Anne teach them some French, or

208

painting, or show them how to sew, but the girl groaned, rolled her eyes, and said: 'Oh, Mother!'

One afternoon, when William had taken Charles and Henry for tea with Klementyna, Anne flopped onto the grass, stretching out at her mother's feet.

'I'm so bored here,' she announced.

'Bored? You're out every night. How can you be bored?'

'It's the same old people at every party. Mother, the king leaves shortly for Rome. Can I go with him?' Anne pleaded. 'I've heard the balls in Rome are like nothing we've seen here.'

Winifred hesitated, taken aback by this unexpected request.

'I don't see why not, if Alice goes with you. Your father and I will follow if the queen can be persuaded to leave at the same time as her husband. If she doesn't, I'm afraid we'll have to stay behind.'

Anne rolled over and faced her mother. 'Thank you, it's wonderful that you trust me to live in Rome without you.'

Winifred considered her words. 'Although my parents were with me at the royal court of Saint-Germain, I was given a lot of freedom. After your grandmother died, the queen took me under her wing, and I went to memorable parties given by Louis XIV and his wife. I can't deny you the opportunities I had, but your father and I will watch you closely. My own father was busy, and I think he left me too much to my own devices.'

Anne sat up, wrapping her arms around her knees. 'Please tell me. I can't wait to hear more.'

'No, it will never be spoken of again. But check if your father is also happy for you to leave.'

As they ate dinner, Maxwell asked his daughter if there was a certain young man she hoped to follow to Rome. Anne blushed but shook her head.

'Don't leave it too long to get married,' he teased. 'Your mother almost left it too late; I was all that was left.'

'Don't be ridiculous,' Winifred interrupted, giving her husband a look that said this conversation must end, right now.

Disregarding his wife, Maxwell bulldozed on. 'She was with child, expecting the birth of your brother. Don't make the same mistake.'

Anne gave a sharp, indrawn breath and stared at her mother.

'Your father has had too much wine, I'm afraid. Yes, it's all true but we loved each other and were betrothed. These things happen when young people are left too much alone. If you need to talk to me about your feelings for a man and you're afraid of giving... giving too much of yourself, I can help.'

Anne's frown relaxed into a deep smile and she rested her hand on top of her mother's.

'Thank you,' she said.

A week later, James's household left for Rome, taking with him Prince Charles and Lady Anne Maxwell, with Alice seated beside the prince's new governor. Klementyna refused to leave, pleading the discomfort of such a long journey when pregnant. Charles had to go – he was a royal prince; it was time for him to be with men and learn to be a king. In the days before the boy left, Winifred sobbed when he lost his curls to the barber, and the childish clothes she had sewn for him, garments made to survive mud and spilled food, were left discarded on the floor of the nursery.

After the last royal coach left Bologna, and she and William were alone with Klementyna and Prince Henry, a letter arrived from Alice. Charles cried himself to sleep every night after long days of being forced to sit still. His tutor tried to control the child by shouting, or worse, and the boy was becoming harder to manage by the day. Left behind, Henry was lost without his brother. His hard-won toileting skills disappeared the day Charles left, and he only wanted to sit on Winifred's knee, sucking his thumb. She felt desperate. The children she loved were in distress; she must go to Rome and take Henry with her. It was unreasonable and a bit ridiculous for Klementyna to use a phantom child as an excuse to delay. There was no sign of a gently swelling belly. She would confront the queen about her pregnancy; if she was not brave enough, who else would?

Winifred paced outside the queen's apartment, biting on the edge of a fingernail. Klementyna had all but owned her husband for over three years and she had not complained. Didn't that give her some rights, some authority? Maxwell had schooled her in the best way to approach the queen, but she feared her own impetuous nature might sweep aside her good intentions.

'Ah, the Countess of Nithsdale.' Klementyna held out a hand to help Winifred rise from her low curtsey, with all the grace of a younger woman noticing an older woman's awkward discomfort. 'How can I be of help?'

'Your Majesty, I would like to enquire whether you need my services for the baby? The winters can be cold here. We should start planning if we're expecting a December birth.'

Klementyna looked puzzled, as if the birth was something she had forgotten, but this was quickly replaced by a capricious smile.

'I thank you for your foresight, Lady Nithsdale, but I have decided I must return to Rome where I will have the best available care for the confinement. Of course, I expect you to continue as Prince Henry's governess, but I plan to find someone younger for the baby.'

This was Klementyna's manner, always unfailingly polite but with an undercurrent of hostility. Winifred struggled to reply, hurt by the queen's blunt dismissal of her services on the grounds of age, but satisfied her oblique approach had worked. Faced with having to make plans for a baby who did not exist, a return to Rome was the queen's only option. Winifred guessed that very soon, Klementyna would sadly 'lose' the baby she was expecting.

The queen's household was the last royal coach to leave the villa, with Maxwell, and Prince Henry accompanying his mother. Winifred followed, with the women from the prince's nursery. Within days of arriving in Rome, Klementyna suffered a minor accident, and was no longer with child. The reaction of the court was muted, confirming that most suspected the child had existed only in the queen's imagination.

The Earl and Countess of Nithsdale were given rooms within the Muti Palace, since they both retained their royal appointments. Unlike the reception rooms and bedrooms on the first floor, their rooms on the third floor were dark and plain, with simple wooden beds and unpainted furniture. Anne brought gaiety into their dark corner of the palace and whenever they were both free, Winifred walked with her daughter through the streets of Rome, finding the shops, squares and fountains that had brought comfort during her years of poverty. Her son wrote that he had married his cousin, Lady Catherine Stuart, and they planned to restore Terregles Castle as their own family home.

Winifred shared her disappointment with Anne. 'I'll never see their children. I won't ever see Terregles again. I'd love to see how he and Catherine restore the old place.'

Anne snatched the letter from her mother's hand. 'For goodness' sake, Mother, stop moping. You and Father have made a success of your life here. I'm proud of you both. Let's focus on the future, the princes, the queen and of course... me.'

Without care of the children through the day, Winifred made a nuisance of herself monitoring the schoolroom, on the pretext of helping Henry adjust to formal lessons.

At almost five, Henry was an enthusiastic learner and had no need for a governess at his side, but she wanted to stay there for Charles, who was punished daily for his inability to sit still or remember anything he had been taught.

Every day, without embarrassment, Winifred intervened, first flattering the inexperienced tutor for his success with Henry, before guiding him how best to teach Charles.

'That's a good choice of story,' she said, when Charles had again been made to stand in the corner for throwing his book. 'Why don't you teach Henry for a while and I'll help Charles to understand what's expected. I always found it best to read to him first, then allow him to act out the story. He can learn, but he needs a different approach.'

The tutor had been chosen from within the ranks of the exiled court by the king, keen to spend as little as possible, despite the young man's limited background, in education or anything else.

When he replied to Winifred, he sounded on the edge of tears.

'Thank you, Countess. I've come to rely on you. There's so much to teach these boys; Latin, Italian, French, literature, religion. I don't know where to start and Charles doesn't want to learn.'

'Punishing Charles is useless,' Winifred said. 'It will make him even more unwilling to try. I have found that play and practical activities help, with lots of breaks for running around. He will learn, I promise, but you need to watch me for a while. You're going to be a good teacher but first, practise your trade with Henry. I will take over Charles's lessons for now but we'll tell no one.'

This pact continued for months, with the tutor assuming responsibility for Charles's education in small steps. Winifred arranged to meet her young colleague in the evenings and together, they planned the following day's lessons. She engaged a monk from a nearby teaching monastery to cover the boys' religious education, since this was an area where they both felt useless, but she sat through every lesson, to prevent any physical chastisement and to remove Charles whenever he was rude, which was often. With the security of her constant presence, in time, both children became the happy boys she had known in Bologna.

CHAPTER 19

1730

T he early morning sun was warm but mist lay like gauze over the parkland and forest, stretching beyond the castle towards the horizon. William walked with Grace along the top terrace, their arms linked, both disregarding propriety in favour of friendship.

William turned to face Grace, his eyes looking down into hers. 'I want to finish this terrace before I die. My mother started it, and my ambition is to complete her vision.'

Grace indicated a bench, further down the path. They settled onto the cane seat, side by side. For a while, studying the green and grey of the landscape was enough and nothing more was said.

'My lord, you have plenty of time ahead of you,' Grace said at last. 'You're in good health. There is no reason to think that the gardens will not be finished long before you die. If for any reason this happens, I will make sure your son completes them.'

William tapped his cane on the stone flags.

'I feel so ashamed about that man Donnelly. He charmed me at his interview and seemed to have all the right skills, but I didn't check, at least not enough. What a waste of time and money! I've shown no better judgement about Joseph Gage. I believed he was a dilettante, but it seems he's putting his back into the Guadalcanal project, managing hundreds of miners, men who are no fools when it comes to respect for supervisors.'

'Anyone would have made the same mistake, my lord,' Grace argued. 'Donnelly was determined to deceive you. Your decisions have been absolutely sound over your own lead mines. Bringing in a German manager was a stroke of genius. Against all expectations, you've achieved some financial security for the castle, the estate, and your family.'

'But most of the debts go unpaid. I send Gage everything I can spare. Someone must support the Spanish ventures until they're profitable, and I don't believe it will be too long before they are. Unfortunately, I have nothing left to provide for Mary, or my sister Anne.'

Grace held a silence for a few seconds, then sighed, as if she needed to weigh her words before speaking.

'Your daughter does not deserve any more money, but I agree, you cannot see her destitute.'

William shook his head. 'I'm afraid I have been blind, quite unaware that Mary is unlike other women. There are things she doesn't understand, which makes her unusual, but she has a self-belief that is hard to ignore. She has put herself in a position where she cannot leave Spain. Her contract with the Espanola Company included a legal obligation to remain until the Guadalcanal project is finished, a contract she willingly signed, but now regrets. She has asked me to write to the Pope on her behalf, to free her from this agreement. I will not write to the Pope, of course, but why can't she see that asking me to do so is madness? Why would the Pope care about her situation?'

Grace nodded. 'Your daughter has little perspective. She believes her problems are everyone's responsibility, as much a concern to the Pope or royalty as they are to her. I have most concern for your sister, who is an elderly woman. Winifred says that Lady Carrington and Lady Herbert are living in poverty in Seville, unable to mix in society and spending many days without enough to eat. Yet they need to maintain a carriage in case an invitation comes. Lady Carrington sits all day in a linen smock, without any undergarments, so I am told.'

'You're right to bring this to my attention,' William said. 'I had no idea things were so bad. I'll send them whatever I can spare but remember that my sister has a husband who should provide for her. Another visit to Mr Kenneth Mackenzie is long overdue. Was there further news from Winifred?'

'Your niece, Anne, is to marry. The wedding is in Lucca, this month I think.'

For William, who thought of his niece as forever thirteen, this was unwelcome news.

'Who on earth is she marrying? She's just a child,' he protested.

'The marriage is to Lord Bellew. It seems to be a love match and both families are happy. She *is* still young, but there's no future for her in Rome and I think Winifred was keen to limit her daughter's freedom to mingle at court with the younger Jacobite men. She remembers only too well her youth in Paris, we both do.'

William patted her hand. 'Memories best kept to yourself, in my opinion.'

With difficulty, he eased himself up from the seat, using his cane for support.

'Walk with me, Grace, and see me up those dreadful steps into the castle. There are things I must do in London; the sooner the better.'

❧

Once again, William was kept waiting outside Mackenzie's office, without a comfortable seat or refreshments. He could hear the man's irritating voice from behind the door but was unable to make out what was being said. At last, a clerk gestured that William should join the solicitor, and he made his way towards the only available chair, trying to pretend that he was untroubled by aching knees after his long wait.

Mackenzie remained seated behind his desk and made no effort to rise or shake hands.

'Ah, the Marquess of Powis,' he said, his tone betraying his contempt. 'Congratulations on the return of your title and estates. When I heard the news, I was glad for your daughter and your sister, for you will now be able to support them.'

The lawyer looked even more prosperous than before, but success did not suit him. Mackenzie was red-faced, with broken veins across his nose and cheeks, and there was an unhealthy sheen of moisture on his skin.

'My sister's well-being is the purpose of my visit. I have heard, on good faith, that she is living like a pauper. You are not providing her with even a small part of what she is due.'

'Lady Anne Carrington, a woman who will not even take her husband's name, has drained me of every penny she is owed as my wife. I cannot provide her with anything more.'

'But she is still your wife,' William reminded him, 'and you have a responsibility for her until the day she dies. She does not need much, only enough to live decently amongst British society in Seville. You must send her regular payments and I will not leave this office until you have drafted a suitable agreement.'

Mackenzie fell silent, and in the quiet that followed, William noticed a tapping sound from ivy, encroaching upon the windowpanes.

'It suits you, doesn't it, that my sister does not reveal her marriage,' William continued. 'If the British in Seville knew that your wife lived in such poverty, word would soon reach these shores. What would your reputation be then? I understand she starves and lives without decent clothing. She cannot leave her rooms.'

Mackenzie tugged at his fashionably short cravat.

'I repeat, sir, I cannot spare anything more. Your daughter and that rogue Joseph Gage own a mine. Let them support my wife.'

William mocked the lawyer's inflection. 'Well, well, well,' he said. 'Now we see the man. In that case, I will arrange for Lady Anne Carrington to be transported to London and will deposit her here in your office. You wish her to acknowledge you as her husband? I can make that happen, just give me a few days.'

Without warning, Mackenzie rose and began to shout words of abuse.

'You cock-sucking gollumpus,' he bellowed. 'You gibfaced lobcock!'

The man roared and ranted with rage, shaking his fist, and thumping on the desk, spittle flying from his lips. The outburst ended, every bit as suddenly as it had begun and Mackenzie fell backwards into his chair, his head resting on his chest.

William waited for the lawyer to rouse, hearing again the tapping of the ivy in the breeze and the far-off voice of a clerk. Many moments passed before William rose, and using his knuckles for balance, edged his way around the desk to lift Mackenzie's head. His eyes were open, staring and a line of saliva hung between the corner of his mouth and the edge of his coat. There was no question, his sister's husband was dead. William left the room to hunt for the clerk, following a distant tinkle of laughter. Down a stone-flagged passage, he found the kitchen, where a clerk pressed a maidservant against a cupboard.

William coughed and the young man turned, red-faced.

'I'm afraid your master, Mr Mackenzie, is unwell and in need of a physician,' he said.

The clerk hurried away, and avoiding the girl's hostile stare, William retraced his steps to the waiting room and found his cloak. Pausing to listen as he tied the cape around his neck, he heard only the sound of his own ragged breathing. He had another appointment, one that could not wait; there was no reason to stay.

In the sedan that carried William to St James's Palace, he had time to reflect on what had just happened. Had he truly killed Kenneth Mackenzie? Should he have stayed behind to speak to the physician? In the actual moment of the man's collapse, the idea that there might be repercussions had not crossed his mind. Perhaps it was best that by tomorrow, he should be back in Wales.

At the palace, William was taken to a rear entrance, the grand hall reserved for those with status. As a marquess, he had every right to be greeted with proper ceremony, but arrival in a sedan chair marked him as back-door material. Frankly, he no longer cared. Visiting his friend George, now the King of Great Britain and Ireland, was honour enough.

The king waited in a comfortable room, warm with wood panelling and wall hangings. William had not seen George for many years and his first instinct was to step forward and embrace him. He remembered, in time, to give a low bow and kiss the proffered hand. Young George had aged, but his friend was approaching fifty. There were new pouches under his eyes and his colour was high, but he still retained his gentle smile. The king was dressed as befitted his title, in a velvet coat of deep blue, edged in gold and silver braid. His stockings were an impractical white and he wore cream, square-toed shoes with diamond buckles, shoes that would never stride along a filthy street in London. William was glad he had worn his wig but was self-conscious of his rough brown coat and breeches, clothes more suited for country living.

The men exchanged their hopes for each other's continuing good health as a servant poured coffee into cups of the finest porcelain. Once they were alone, William saw the king's shoulders relax.

'How are you, Powis? I've heard you've had your troubles.'

'Indeed, I have, Your Majesty, but those pale into insignificance compared to events from this morning. I may have caused the death of a man, without any intention to do so, of course.'

The king's eyes widened. 'Shall I call the guards? Tell me more...'

William took his chance to amuse, embellishing his visit to Kenneth Mackenzie's office, with its unfortunate outcome, until his friend wept with laughter.

The king drew an embroidered cloth from the ruffle at his sleeve and wiped the corners of his eyes. 'It sounds as if he had it coming. Death was waiting for him. It wasn't your fault.'

'How are you, Your Majesty?' William asked, knowing he must wait a respectable amount of time before burdening George with the real purpose of his visit.

'I was so grateful, as you know, that you helped me restore relations with my father before he died, but I'm afraid my family problems continue. My eldest son Frederick was left behind in Hanover when his mother and I followed the king to Great Britain, and I did not see him for fourteen years. Now he is here, fulfilling his duties as the Prince of Wales, but we do not see eye to eye. He schemes with the opposition in parliament and as for his spending, there are no limits to his desires. I have regrets that I treated my own father the same way. It's as if I'm being punished.'

William hesitated. He was unfit to give advice about family matters, given his poor relationship with his own sons and daughters but George was waiting for help, his eyebrows raised, as if expecting some nuggets of wisdom.

'The most important thing,' William replied, 'is to keep talking to your son. Don't do or say anything that can't be undone. Your own father took your children away. No wonder you struggled to forgive him. Admire Frederick's family, praise his wife, play with his children, but let him know when he has overstepped the mark if he sides with your enemies. After all, he will be king one day and such friends may not serve him well.'

'You are so wise, Powis. I'm wondering whether I should try to arrange for you and the Prince of Wales to meet. Perhaps he also needs to hear this.'

'Your Majesty, I will help in any way I can, but unfortunately, I have proved to be a failure as a father. My own heir also robs the family estate of assets, without any regard for the future, and as for my daughter Mary...'

William took some time to tell the king the sorry tale of Mary's financial dealings, her debts and the harm that had befallen the whole Herbert family through allowing themselves to be drawn into her schemes.

'The thing is,' he concluded, 'Mary is trapped in Spain with my sister, contractually obliged to fulfil her responsibilities to drain a mine at Guadalcanal. The project is being well-managed by a man called Joseph Gage – I'm sure you know the family, the Gages of Oxfordshire – so if she left, she would not be abandoning her responsibilities. My daughter needs permission to leave and bring her aunt, my sister, to Paris. My sister is ageing and in poor health, and as I have just recounted, recently widowed. Only the king of Spain has the power to give consent. I am asking, no... begging, that you might intercede with Philippe on my behalf. I would not trouble you, but I can think of no other way to help with her plight.'

'Of course, we can't have a woman of British nobility effectively held as a prisoner in Spain. I'll write to the ambassador, Benjamin Keene, and ask him to sort this out. I'm surprised he hasn't done so already. He's a good fellow, his reputation is sound.'

William knew perfectly well why Keene would have been in no hurry to help Mary, but it was best to say nothing more. If George thought his daughter was a woman who needed rescuing, that could only be to her advantage. He hesitated before raising his second concern, worried that by asking, he might risk the goodwill between them. But time wasn't on his side. Would there ever be another chance?

He cleared his throat and took a gulp of coffee, emptying the tiny cup in one swallow. He grimaced, thinking that the craze for coffee had been overdone.

'One other matter, Your Majesty. Would you consider a pardon for my sister Winifred Maxwell, the Countess of Nithsdale? Her children are married and their future lies in this country. It would give me peace of mind to know that she could return, visit her family and be with her grandchildren, without fear of arrest. Her former home, Terregles Castle, has been returned to her son and his wife.'

George's face darkened and the atmosphere in the room thickened. The king would not meet his eye and William felt his gut twist. That old Achilles heel, misjudgement, had it struck again?

'You must be aware, Powis, that the Jacobite threat remains high. The exiled James Stuart holds on to a misguided belief that he will one day be restored to the British throne. If I pardon your sister, what message will that send out to his supporters? It may well be regarded as an invitation to invade. I am surprised you asked.'

'I'm so sorry,' William stammered. 'I felt I had no choice. Perhaps, we could keep the decision secret. No one need know?'

The king leaned back, looking at William through half-closed eyes.

'You are suggesting that I hide decisions from my government? Hide giving a pardon to a woman found guilty of treason against my father? Your understanding of politics has deserted you, I'm afraid. Out of respect for our friendship, this conversation must end. Now, if you will excuse me...'

George stood to dismiss him and a servant appeared as if by magic to escort William from the palace.

'I apologise, Your Majesty,' he said, making a low bow. 'At my age, I only see the personal, not the political. My request was the folly of an old man.'

The king, his old friend, George Augustus, gave only a slight tilt of his head, indicating that he had been heard. They would never meet again.

CHAPTER 20

1732

Mary's arrival in Seville had coincided with the royal family's removal from Madrid to Seville, which had made the entire city overexcited and absurdly happy. For those excluded from the celebrations, as they were, the royal relocation left only the sour taste of isolation and a sharp rise in the cost of lodgings. Mary had found two hot, airless rooms in the eaves of a narrow house, toppling into its neighbours across an even narrower alley. There was only one earth closet for all the residents, and that was in a small court-yard on the street, populated by rats and spiders. There was no source of water other than a shared well in a nearby square.

From the attic window, they did have a view of the ochre and white walls of a city that shimmered when seen from above but was twisted, dark and secretive at street level. If she stretched her neck, Mary could just see a section of the crenelated battlements that circled the neighbourhoods. Whether this had been built to prevent its citizens escaping, or hinder unlikely hordes of invaders, she could not be certain. Once, she had risked the expense of taking their carriage down to the river and watched the royal household cruise past in richly decorated gondolas. The setting sun, resting on the horizon, had flamed the Torre del Oro with a golden light. Even in her steadfast dislike of the city, Mary could see why some people might choose to live here.

When her father wrote with the news that her aunt's husband was dead, Mary held on to a fragile hope that their financial circumstances might improve, but too much time had passed. Aunt Anne read the legal papers, when they arrived, then stared at the ceiling, as if trying to see the sky beyond their attic window, her chin trembling with the effort not to cry. As Mackenzie's widow, she was entitled to receive only a small subsistence payment, every month.

This was unwelcome news. Anne was now seventy, desperately aged by their time in Seville and it had become clear to Mary that if they remained, her aunt was unlikely to survive. Joseph was fully occupied at Guadalcanal. He returned to Seville whenever he could, but since the mine and its inexperienced workforce demanded his constant supervision, he was never free to gamble for extra money in the city salons. They had nothing to live on, other than what Mary could borrow and whatever her father could spare. Seville was weary of lending Mary money; its citizens now alert to the sad truth that they would never be repaid.

They occupied themselves with fighting their many legal battles through writing letters, or endlessly discussing the progress of litigation either against them or for them. To their list of those pursuing them had been added Dominic Donnelly and more of a surprise, Andrew Gallwey, who believed he had been wrongly dismissed by Joseph. Of course, he had never been paid. To their own lawsuits, Mary and Anne decided to add the family of the late Kenneth Mackenzie.

Sir Benjamin Keene followed the royal household to Seville, and as was his duty, called on Mary and Anne in their rooms.

His visit was long overdue, and in the years that had passed since their last meeting, he had gained the weight that was already threatening his waistline and chin in Madrid. He did not apologise for his neglect or invite them to a single reception or party, nor did he stay for long, keeping a handkerchief pressed against his nose for the entire time. Although Mary no longer noticed the fug in their rooms, she knew they must smell, especially her aunt. There was nothing she could do; neither of them was inclined to do any cleaning and Anne's hygiene had never been a strength. Mary hauled water up to the apartment every day, but if she was to keep her aunt clean, she would have to help her wash. This was not something she was prepared to do.

'Our situation is desperate,' Mary said aloud, looking up from the latest letter from their landlord, demanding payment for months of rent.

Her aunt lifted her head from a doze. 'What did you say?'

Along with everything else, Anne was losing her hearing.

Mary raised her voice. 'I'm not prepared to go on like this, living in poverty in a strange city. I can't speak the language... I can't care for you... not on my own.'

Anne's voice was tremulous. 'I'm not happy either. I didn't choose to live here. I wish you'd left me in Madrid. What are we going to do? You said we can't leave, not until the mine is drained.'

'We must escape, before you are too infirm. Once over the border, we'll be free.'

Anne started to cry, another feature of old age that Mary found infuriating. She struggled to find some reassuring words.

'We're richer than you think. We have me, our greatest asset, along with my courage. We still have the coach and our horses. I've saved a little from the money we're sent by Mackenzie's family. It's not much but should be enough to live on until we reach Paris.'

'But what then?' her aunt pleaded. 'Shouldn't we wait for Joseph?'

'Certainly not. He'll only try to stop me. In Paris, I can earn on the gaming tables. We're leaving, the decision is made.'

One night in April, with bailiffs threatening, Mary helped her aunt down three flights of stairs to the street. Anne struggled with the weight of her bundle, pressing one hand against the damp wall and stumbling as she tried to maintain her balance. Leaving her aunt resting on a step, breathless and panting, Mary carried their few belongings down to the waiting carriage. On her return, rats were already scampering around her aunt's shift, nibbling on scraps of dried food that clung to the fabric. She clapped her hands to scare away the pests and then helped Anne shuffle down the remaining steps. We're leaving not a moment too soon, she thought.

The fastest escape route was to head for the border with Portugal and hence to Lisbon. From there, Mary felt confident she would find a way to reach Paris, if she could sell the carriage in Lisbon. Aunt Anne slept intermittently through the night, but Mary stayed awake, thinking of Joseph and how he would feel, finding her gone. She imagined him searching their empty rooms, but it was more likely he would leave it so long, a different tenant would already be in place. It would serve him right for abandoning her again. He had excluded her from a project that was, in fact, hers. She would contact him once they reached Paris, but until then, he deserved his fate.

At the very moment light began to filter through the cracks in the ill-fitting blinds, the carriage stopped. The coachman opened the door and explained they had reached the village of Santa Olalla. There was an inn, he said, where the horses could be refreshed and they would be able to wash and have some breakfast. The women dismounted, next to a stone cross, with a church behind and a castle resting on the crag beyond. They stretched aching limbs and then Mary helped her aunt hobble down a steep path to the inn where warm water, soap, bread and olives were waiting in a ground-floor room, empty of other customers. The woman who served them stared with curiosity.

In a loud voice, the one she always used when she felt the need to impress, Anne demanded wine. Mary frowned and shook her head, but it was too late. The presence of two British ladies had been noted.

From the door of the inn, Mary saw twelve armed men surrounding the driver and their coach. She hurried across, hoping that an imperious manner and a booming English voice would cow the thugs into a change of heart.

'How dare you,' she challenged. 'Release my carriage at once.'

The armed men raised their swords and moved to form a circle around them.

'I am Lady Mary Herbert, and this is Lady Anne Carrington. We must proceed with our journey. Leave us alone.'

One of the men spoke to her in Spanish. Mary glanced across at their driver for help, but he had turned his back, busying himself with the harness. Traitor, she thought. They were hustled into a cell in the town hall but before the bolts slid shut behind them, she demanded her coachman be brought before her.

He twisted his cap between his hands, not raising his head to look at Mary as she berated him.

'You betrayed us, in cahoots with that woman from the inn. The least you can do is carry a message to Sir Benjamin Keene, the British ambassador. Tell him I demand our immediate release.'

The man did not lift his head or reply. Mary spoke again, her voice shrill.

'Don't pretend you can't understand me. Go now to Ambassador Keene and hurry. We must be freed.'

The accommodation was sparse, but they were treated as important guests and did not have to suffer the crowded, insanitary conditions of ordinary felons. They were fed three meals a day, provided with hot water for washing, and their waste bucket was emptied every morning. Even better, the cell was cool. Compared to their lodgings in Seville, Mary thought, imprisonment had some advantages. Regardless of their treatment, by the end of two weeks her patience was running out, but she had no outlet for her rage other than to shout at the woman who brought their food. It was during such an outburst that she overheard a familiar but unwelcome voice, demanding her release in heavily accented English. It was Count Cogorani.

Mary and Anne were escorted to the home of the mayor, and after washing and changing into simple, clean robes, the British women were shown to the drawing room where Cogorani waited. They paused in the doorway and watched the count pick at an array of Spanish pastries, making polite conversation with the mayor and his wife. All three stood to welcome their guests.

Count Cogorani bowed. 'Ah, Lady Herbert and Lady Carrington, I do apologise for your detention. It was my fault.'

That the count appeared proud of his actions, rather than genuinely apologetic, infuriated Mary and she raised her voice:

'How dare you... how dare you take me and Lady Carrington prisoner.'

The count gestured that the women take a seat. He waved a servant forward to bring them coffee and ensured that Anne was offered a pastry first.

'The king ordered that you be held captive, not me. I simply alerted him to your attempt to escape. Lady Herbert, you signed a contract with the Espanola Company. This contract prevents you from leaving Spain until the mine is drained. If I may remind you, the mine is not drained. It is the king who owns the land. We simply lease the mine from the royal family.'

Mary sniffed. 'King George, the British monarch, wrote to the ambassador asking that I be freed from the contract. He is a friend of my family. I wasn't trying to escape. I assumed it was all arranged.'

Cogorani shook his head. 'Did you hear any word that this was the case? I'm afraid the king of Spain is, how shall we say, not himself. When he is able to turn his mind to affairs of state, you, Lady Herbert, or your affairs, will not be his highest priority. I am sure that Ambassador Keene had every intention of raising your case with Philippe and will do so in due course.'

'The mine is no longer my responsibility. Mr Joseph Gage will finish the work,' Mary argued.

'Gage is your agent and doing a fine job, but he is not legally contracted to complete the task. You cannot walk away from your obligations. Too many people have risked money, and in some cases have lost their lives, to ensure that Guadalcanal is drained.'

Mary raised her voice again: 'You cannot keep me here. I will fight this.'

'Yes indeed, that is your best course of action but you must do that at a legal tribunal, not by running away. You will return to Seville as soon as you have eaten. The carriage is ready and I have found you improved lodgings, which will be paid for by the Espanola Company.'

Mary stood, glaring at her aunt, who had helped herself to another pastry.

'I am grateful for better accommodation, but I regard myself as a prisoner of Spain. I will write to my father. You will no doubt hear from our family's lawyer.'

Cogorani also stood and bowed.

'I would be delighted to have some contact from the marquess. I hear only good things about his mining enterprise in Wales. I regret that my legal contract is with you, Lady Herbert, rather than with him. It isn't easy for a woman to understand such matters and I am sorry you have had to endure so much hardship. Let us try to bring this matter to a close.'

Cogorani eased Anne from her chair, and holding out an elbow to steady her, assisted the elderly woman to the door. Mary followed, and as they walked from the mayor's home into the village square, she felt smothered by the suffocating blanket of another stifling day in Spain. Aunt Anne will not survive this, she thought.

As if he had read her mind, Cogorani leaned towards Mary once Anne had been helped up the narrow steps into the coach.

'I can see your aunt is weak, Lady Herbert, and you are responsible for her. We will try to expedite your release as quickly as we can.'

Their new rooms in Seville were simply furnished but on the ground floor, and therefore dark and cool. They had access to a small courtyard, ideal for sitting out in the early morning or evening and their earth closet was emptied daily by a soil man.

Mary still had to fetch water from the well, but this was so much easier without three sets of stairs to climb.

Their first visitor was not Ambassador Keene, as she had expected, but Joseph. Mary had written to him, explaining that she had found better rooms but thought it wise to avoid mentioning their attempted escape. Mary and Anne had eaten their meal of hard, local bread, olives, and soft sheep's cheese, when they heard his characteristic tap on the door: three knocks and a pause, followed by two more knocks. Joseph stood next to the table, chewing the ends of their loaf, as if he hadn't eaten for days, then he indicated, with a slight toss of his head, that they should walk the streets.

'I thought we should leave your aunt on her own,' he said. 'I don't think she likes me, after the business with de Balfe at the debtors' prison in Paris. She doesn't trust me.'

'We've all noticed a worrying side to you, Joseph. Perhaps she thinks you'll just dispose of her once she becomes a nuisance.'

Joseph turned towards Mary and grinned. 'It can be arranged.'

Mary studied Joseph as they walked, their arms linked. He had a few days' growth of stubble and his hair was longer than usual. There was no longer any need for gentlemen's clothes and he wore a leather jerkin over a collarless shirt, rough breeches stained with ore from the mine, and workmen's boots. Every step reminded her of how much she still desired him.

She tugged at his arm. 'Let's walk down here, it leads to a pretty square.'

Down the alleyway, hidden patios could be seen through wrought-iron gates; glimpses of green shade livened by sunlight on trickling water. In the square, they found a bench and sat in silence, the air scented with the last of the orange blossom.

Joseph was the first to speak. 'I have heard about your flight. Did you not think to talk to me first?'

'I was desperate, and I knew you would have tried to prevent me. What is there for us here? You have taken charge of all the operations at the mine. I only hold the legal responsibility, a duty I can honour from anywhere.'

'Do I mean nothing to you? How do you think I would have felt, finding you gone, your rooms empty?'

As usual, Joseph thought only of himself. 'How do you think *I* feel?' she said. 'You dumped me here, with my aunt, without asking either of us if we wanted to leave Madrid. We spend weeks at a time without any contact from you, or anyone else. We never have enough to eat, we're bored, it's too bloody hot and the place is a sewer.'

Joseph studied his hands, picking out some grime from under a fingernail.

'I thought you understood that my absence is essential. If I don't oversee the draining of the mine, we're in deep trouble. The men need constant oversight and the count's patience is running out. I agree, there was no need for you to leave Madrid. It's just that...'

Mary frowned. 'Just what?'

Joseph glanced up from under his unruly fringe. 'I wanted you nearby. I need you close.'

'For sex, you mean?'

'Not just for sex, although that is always special. You know how much I love you.'

Mary stared fully into Joseph's eyes, seeing the strength of his love. She knew she must not hurt him but was unsure how to respond. She would have to lie.

She reached out to take his hand. 'I love you too, Joseph, and I'm sorry.'

Mary waited for a few seconds, seeing how her words

pleased him. How easy it was, she thought. Keeping her voice low so that the other couples in the square did not overhear, she continued with the matter most pressing on her mind.

'I have written to my father about how Aunt Anne and I were insulted. I fully expect he'll contact the British prime minister and an apology from the Spanish Government will follow. I think we're owed compensation, don't you? There's no date for the so-called tribunal. I think the promise of a legal solution was simply a ruse to force me to return.'

Joseph squeezed her hand, his eyes bright. 'I have important news. I've been bursting to tell you, but I needed to know where I stood. The mine is drained. We've done it!'

'Joseph!' Mary exclaimed, covering her mouth. 'I was beginning to think it was impossible.'

'There still must be an inspection. Once we're certified, the Espanola Company will pay what we're owed. We can then sit back and watch our share of the profits roll in.'

Mary felt something rush through her veins, a feeling which might possibly be love. Perhaps her earlier words had not been a lie.

'I underestimated you,' she said. 'I have been blind. Anyone watching you in a gaming salon would have known. You observe, you learn and then you act. We are saved by your skills.'

Joseph's cheeks flushed at this unexpected praise. 'Almost, but we need to be patient for a bit longer. I must return to Guadalcanal tomorrow and encourage the men through this last test. They're prone to celebrate before victory is in their pockets.'

'Why can't I come back with you? There must be other men who have their womenfolk and children with them at the mine.'

'Your job is to stay abreast of our legal battles,' Joseph said.

'Chevalier de Balfe is doing a fine job in Paris; he's like a stoat after a rabbit in his pursuit of Cantillon. He even had the usurer arrested two years ago but the slippery cheat managed to get himself acquitted. You need to fight on here, against Gallwey and Donnelly, and help your aunt challenge her husband's family over his estate.'

'I can write anywhere,' Mary protested. 'I don't need to be stuck in Seville. A letter from your mining village will have the same impact as one written from here.'

Joseph cupped both her hands into his and held her gaze. 'Indeed, but the miners are a rough lot, as are their wives. They're traditional people too. You wouldn't be welcome since you're not my wife.'

It wasn't difficult to guess at his meaning. This hard-won victory, so welcome in almost every way, might well have rekindled his hopes of marriage. Joseph was the best of men, but he was mercenary. He would expect a reward.

The next morning, the first letter that Mary scratched out, using her twisted quill pen and the remnants of their ink, was to tell her father the wonderful news about the mine. A second letter followed, consisting of just one line: *Father, if Joseph Gage asks for my hand in marriage, say no.*

CHAPTER 21
1732/33

N either Mary nor her driver had any idea how to reach the mine. Their journey required many stops to question passers-by and they made several wrong turns. Once they reached the makeshift village, Mary strode along the main street, kicking up dust from her boots. Her coach stood waiting, guarded by the coachman, with the horses tethered outside what may or may not have been a rudimentary form of hostel. Women stared at her from their wooden porches and called out to their children to stand close. She recognised spoken Welsh and Spanish, but other tongues were unfamiliar.

The noise from the mine became more distinct, and the filth grew deeper with every step, covering sheds, fences and vegetation with a grey sludge that looked like a winter's scene from a nightmare. The mine itself was nothing more than a fenced-off hole in the ground, surrounded by a system of pulleys. Next to it was a row of wooden buildings, where she guessed Joseph might work. The men above ground paused to empty baskets of ore strapped to their backs, watching her as she banged on the doors of huts, calling out Joseph's name. In the distance, she saw a group separate, and one distinctive shape emerged from the dusty haze.

'Did you know about this?' Mary shouted, waving a document above her head, while Joseph was still at least two strides from her. He looked down at his boots, hands in his pockets, but said nothing.

She screamed at him, not caring who heard. 'We're not going to be paid. Cogorani claims the site hasn't been cleared.'

Joseph lifted his head and nodded. 'I'm afraid it's true. He says we haven't complied with the contract.'

Aware that a small group of men had gathered to listen, Mary lowered her voice. 'We passed the inspection.'

Joseph took her arm, steering her towards the tavern.

'Of course we did, and we have smelted silver to prove it. I'm not sure what Cogorani's game is, but he's contesting the inspection report.'

In the tavern, Joseph bought two tankards of ale and sat down on a bench opposite her.

'More litigation I'm afraid,' he said. 'There's nothing more we can do.'

Mary gulped her ale, trying to clear the lump from her throat that may have been dust or unshed tears of frustration.

'I'll tell you what we'll do, Joseph. If we're fighting him in the courts for our share, then we'll stop work. We'll walk away and let the filthy place fill up with water.'

Joseph rubbed his forehead, his damp fingers leaving a streak in the dirt across his brow.

'I suspect the count has decided that Guadalcanal is not going to be as profitable as he'd hoped. He'll try to drag out any litigation. It will be years before we see a penny.'

'He's a twisted, unscrupulous, cheating bastard; a worse fraud than Richard Cantillon. Never mind years before we earn anything, it will be years before I can leave. My aunt will die here.'

'Perhaps we should send for the Chevalier de Balfe?'

'And there would be an unfortunate pithead accident? It's not funny, Joseph. If we must stay, there are other mines. You've gained so much experience, your knowledge will serve us well into the future. We are miners now. We can walk away from this charade.'

Joseph fell silent. Mary watched thoughts track across his face but could not predict his reaction.

'Word mustn't get out,' Joseph said. 'The men will have heard enough today to cause them concern. You're right, we cannot continue here, but allow me time to search out some new prospects, only then will I persuade the miners to come with me. In the meantime, we should keep working, as if nothing has changed.'

'How will we pay them? I was relying on Cogorani fulfilling his promise.'

'Ah...' Joseph drained his ale and drew the back of his hand across his lips. 'I'm afraid we will have to lean more heavily upon your father.'

Mary shook her head. 'That won't work. He's already paid for too much of the work at Guadalcanal. It was difficult enough to get him to agree a meagre allowance for his sister, never mind me, his daughter. We cannot ask for more.'

Joseph pulled on his cap. Looking over his shoulder to check that they were unobserved, he wrapped an arm around her shoulder and brushed his lips across hers.

'Then you and your aunt must use your guile,' he whispered. 'We're mining entrepreneurs now. Your family will benefit, even if your father sees no profit in his lifetime. You must persuade him it makes sense.'

~

One month later, Mary and her aunt had a visitor, the British ambassador. Keene glanced around with approval at their more civilised lodgings, his eager expression revealing that he believed he was bearing good news.

'I have a date for your tribunal, Lady Herbert, to release you from your contract with the Espanola Company. It is my understanding that you might wish to transfer your legal obligation to Mr Joseph Gage. Once this matter is sorted...' he continued, laughing in anticipation of his own joke, 'you and Lady Carrington can leave Spain – no more midnight flits.'

Mary took care to pour the ambassador some wine and tip olives into a bowl before replying.

'Only a year too late,' she murmured.

Keene's mouth turned down, his expression one of regret and confusion. 'My lady, you are not a priority for the British government, nor the Spanish, for that matter.'

Mary lifted her glass to her lips before passing Keene's glass across the table. 'I'm surprised that you, as our representative in Spain, would tolerate the daughter and sister of a peer of the realm being imprisoned and abused,' she said. 'You were no help when we needed you.'

Keene coughed and took a deep draught of wine before replying. 'If I may speak frankly—'

'No, you may not,' she interrupted.

'If I may speak frankly,' Keene repeated, 'you do yourself no favours. A daughter of a peer of the realm would not behave as you have; speaking your mind as you do, running around the country like a madwoman, or trying to run a mine, for heaven's sake.'

Mary struggled to keep her temper in check, feeling her

colour rise and her throat tighten. She spoke slowly and a little louder than necessary, as if Keene was hard of hearing.

'Let's get this straight. You have failed to support me because I behave too much like a man?'

'We can't overlook your reputation, not only your reckless financial dealings, but your unorthodox relationship with that fellow Gage. This is a conservative, Catholic country, where we are guests.'

'This guest has no intention of leaving.'

Keene's eyes were round with surprise. 'I beg your pardon?'

'I must pursue the Espanola Company through the courts. In my experience, legal proceedings are lengthy.'

The ambassador frowned. 'You intend to stay?'

'Of course. What choice do I have? I'm sure you will agree that the only person who has been disadvantaged by your shilly-shallying is yourself.'

Mary wrote to her father. Care of her aunt had become impossible. There was no option, but he must rescue Anne from Spain and take her to the family seat in Powis, for however many years that remained to her. As head of the family, she argued, he was shirking his responsibility for his sister's welfare. He must not burden her with this and consider his duty done.

Her blackmail succeeded. The marquess was persuaded to send a guaranteed sum of money every month, not whatever he could scrape together. When the money arrived, she resented that her father appeared to care more for his elderly sister than her but there was no room for hurt feelings. Cogorani had realised he was still paying rent for two women who were his litigants and had given them notice.

Joseph prospected widely but there was always a need for more funds to pay for equipment and the men's wages. Rumours spread that he was guilty of surveying land without permits, which was sometimes true. In May, Joseph found a neglected copper mine in Casares and persuaded Mary and her aunt to leave Seville to view the site. Anne had again taken to living in her calico shift, without her stays, and passed her days playing solitary card games or writing letters at Mary's dictation. They could not leave until Mary found a seamstress to run up some gowns for Anne, since nothing her aunt had brought from Madrid would fit.

Close to Casares, the coachman halted to allow his passengers to admire the white village clinging to its clifftop setting, before taking a precipitous route down into the valley and then back up narrow tracks towards the church. Mary kept the blinds closed, but whenever the coach stopped or reversed, she covered her face, believing they were on the very edge of a cliff and about to tumble over. The inn where Joseph waited had been built from the remains of a hilltop fort and the streets leading to it were so steep and uneven that Mary and her aunt had to abandon the vehicle. The struggle to help Anne up the remaining passages and winding stairs required the strength of both Mary and the coachman, and it was apparent that once she was safely inside, her aunt would have to remain within the four walls of her room.

Mary made no effort to conceal her irritation. This venture was ill-judged and it was Joseph's fault. Once Anne had been helped to bathe her face and hands with cool water, and the innkeeper's wife brought wine and figs for them all, they left her to rest. Joseph suggested to Mary that they walk around the walls of the hill fort, since the site of the mine was visible from there.

They walked side by side, Joseph explaining to Mary that

the fort had been built by the Moors. In Seville, she had heard much about these people, but she was not interested beyond the fact that they had visited and then sensibly decided to leave. His words droned on. She did not try to feign interest or ask any questions. The purpose of this trip was business, not sightseeing.

Joseph stopped walking and pointed down into the valley, where Mary could see some ruined buildings, all that remained of former mine-working.

'It's perfect,' Joseph said. 'Close to running water, near to habitation, with the potential to yield copper of the highest grade. If only you'd found this one first – we wasted so much time and money at Guadalcanal.'

Mary's ill temper had not abated, and she resented his implied accusation. 'Don't blame me,' she said. 'How was I to know that Cogorani was a crook? I wanted to make some money, and fast, to pay off our debts and get out of here.'

'Listen to me, Mary,' Joseph replied. 'Unlike you, I have no family who care for me. In the past, I've been good for nothing but gambling but through our partnership, I've found mining. I'm good at it. We could have a business here, settle down in this beautiful valley, build a life together.'

She knew this was true. Joseph had sacrificed everything to follow her to Spain. By some miracle, he had found a vocation and a place in the world where he could settle. She sat down on some fallen masonry and stared out over small farms and hills covered in oak woods, the horizon turning pale blue in the late-afternoon light. Somewhere high above, a bird cried like a lost kitten. If he finally accepted she would never marry him, he might see sense and walk away. She had to keep him at her side, which meant more lies.

Mary thought of reaching out to touch him, but she was not enough of an actor to make it seem genuine. Instead, she looked fully into his eyes, shielding her gaze from the sun with her hand.

'I love you, Joseph,' she said. 'You have done so much for me and my family and have shown tolerance, bravery and constancy. If only we could be wed, but I'm afraid I cannot risk saddling you with my debts. If we were husband and wife, you would be responsible for everything I owe.'

Joseph narrowed his eyes. He was not a fool. 'That is the case already. I'm always paying your debts.'

Mary found his stare uncomfortable and looked away. 'But you can choose not to. If we were married, you would not have that option. Besides, my father would expect some sort of wedding settlement. He knows you own nothing and would not consent to the match.'

Both knew this was untrue; the Marquess of Powis would gladly accept any offer to be free of his responsibility. Joseph hesitated, his cheeks drawn and pale under his tan, and Mary guessed that she had stretched the truth too far.

'If a settlement is important to your father,' he said, 'I could ask my older brother to spare me something from the family estate.'

'Yes indeed, why don't you?' she agreed, knowing that this request would give her months to concoct another reason not to marry, one that would seem less like a rejection.

'You do agree we should take on Casares? I think I can make this mine pay,' Joseph continued.

Mary's enthusiasm was genuine now that the tricky subject of a betrothal had been sidestepped.

'Of course, we must. I will write to my father and see if he will agree to underwriting our costs, until we are profitable. We should do it properly this time, make him a full partner.'

'In that case,' Joseph said, looking towards the sky to study the bird that had provided the background chorus for his humiliation, 'I think you and your aunt should leave Seville and return to Madrid, if you will be happier there.'

'When will I see you again?' Mary asked.

Joseph sighed. 'To be frank, after this conversation, does it really matter?'

CHAPTER 22

1735

The Muti Palace was silent, and its dark corridors echoed only with soft footsteps and whispered conversations. The young queen was dead, and the household was in mourning. The physicians had said it was tuberculosis, but Winifred suspected another cause, one that had no name. When she and her husband dined in private with the king and queen, as they had often been invited to do, Klementyna's bright eyes, pink cheeks and stream of chatter masked for all but the most observant, that she ate nothing.

The queen's religious fervour had deepened since they returned to Rome, and she had taken to wearing clothes that emphasised her lack of regard for royal status and possessions. These rough garments, large and unflattering, had hidden her diminishing frame. Winifred had no experience of this condition but had heard it discussed when she served amongst the women of the old queen's household. Some young women, taken from their families and forced to marry someone they did not love, a situation all too common in titled families, stopped eating. She discussed this with Maxwell and her daughter, but it was not a view she could share outside her family. She ought to have tried harder to befriend the queen when she was alive. Her husband had been patient and loyal towards another woman. Had jealousy clouded her judgement?

It was hard for Winifred and Maxwell to be anything but happy. Anne and her husband, Lord John Bellew, continued to live in Rome and the birth of their daughter Frances, now three years old, helped to heal bitter memories of being forced to separate from their own children. The Nithsdale apartment became a place of childish games and laughter, often joined by the princes who had lost their mother. There was little she could do to ease their pain, other than to welcome them with love.

Tonight, Anne and her husband were to eat dinner with them, leaving their daughter in the care of Alice. Winifred guessed what her daughter's news might be, as Anne's growing waistline was becoming harder to disguise, but she resolved to act as if the thought of another grandchild had never crossed her mind.

After the soup, Anne wiped her mouth with her napkin and looked first at her father and then at Winifred.

'Don't pretend you haven't noticed, Mother, but I'm expecting another baby.'

Winifred began to speak: 'That is wonderful news—'

Maxwell leant across the table to fill their glasses with more wine. 'Congratulations, you two,' he interrupted, 'and many more to come, we hope. We always wanted a house full of children, but it didn't happen.'

'Maxwell we—' Winifred couldn't let this pass, but once again, she was stopped from speaking.

Lord Bellew held her gaze, although his fingers continued to crumble the bread on his side plate.

'There is other news, which may not be so welcome. I'm

afraid we are returning to Britain. I need to spend time with my family and my estates.'

'Oh, that is sad,' Winifred replied, feeling her stomach turn to liquid, 'but we do understand, don't we, Maxwell? We've been so lucky to have you here for all of Frances's life. Her other grandparents must be desperate to meet her.'

She struggled to hold her grief in check, not understanding at all. Why couldn't her precious daughter and grandchildren remain at her side, forever? Why was life always about what men wanted. Their voices roared around her, but through the babble, she heard Anne speak her name and tried to focus.

'Mother,' Anne repeated. 'I asked if Alice could come with us? I'm frightened of this birth without you there, but she will be almost as much help as you.'

'Of course Alice should accompany you,' Winifred said. 'With you and your family gone, there is nothing for her here. I will rest easier knowing she will assist at the birth.'

This was not true. Nothing would help Winifred rest easier, except her own presence, with the vulnerability of women in childbirth. Unlike other women here, who were free to return to Britain with their daughters, she would never have that privilege. Her impulsive choice, made so many years ago, flew like a poisoned arrow into the pit of yet another loss.

Maxwell, who never dwelt upon the past unless he was drunk, carried on chatting with the young couple about their plans, indifferent to his wife's distress. There was no choice but to accept their decision, she must not try to come between a man and his wife. No one noticed her silence and in time, Winifred felt her racing heart slow, her breathing become deeper and more regular. There were letters, she reasoned, and Anne would come back to Rome with the children. It wasn't forever.

Anne and her family left within weeks, keen to be settled in

London before the birth of the baby. Winifred remembered her own flight from Paris, desperate to reach Terregles Castle before the winter and the birth of their first child. She tried to recall every detail that might have helped, everything she wished she had known, before giving birth in a strange household. In the weeks that remained before the Bellews left Rome, she drilled Alice about childbirth and copied out her own mother's midwifery notes, even though Alice was not a strong reader. She cornered her son-in-law and begged him not to rely upon his family to deliver the child but to find an experienced midwife, a task that would be easy, but expensive, in London. In the end, reassuring herself that Anne had easily given birth once before, she had to let them go, wringing her hands as their carriage pulled away down the Piazza dei Santi Apostoli.

That night, Winifred wrote a letter to Grace, one weighted with remorse and loss. Her final words were: *As soon as I know where they are living, I will write again. I beg you, Grace, please try to be with her, as you once were for me.*

There were few women in the Muti Palace, no royal nursery, no queen's household, no comforting tasks to fill her day. Winifred resumed her frantic walks around Rome but saw nothing of her surroundings, resisting feelings of panic that she might have missed a message from her daughter. Wherever Anne stopped on her journey, she tried to contact her mother and there had been recent news of the family's safe arrival in London, where they would remain for the birth. Maxwell had been invited to join Prince Charles's household and spent his time keeping up with younger men. Winifred passed many days and nights alone in Frances's nursery, which remained untouched, watching the sun rise and set from the cot bed and holding her granddaughter's rag doll close to her chest, as if she could protect the unborn child simply by willing a safe birth.

Pounding footsteps, quite different from the mournful shuffle the court had learned to adopt since the queen's death, drummed down the passage outside their rooms. A raised voice shouted: 'Nithsdale, Nithsdale.' Winifred drifted into the present from another troubled daydream and held her breath. It was too early for good news. The voice must stop. She would block her ears against the inevitable knock on her door, hold onto the remaining seconds of hope.

It was a breathless messenger, his fist raised to bang on the door again.

Bending at the waist, he panted the words, 'I am looking for the Earl and Countess of Nithsdale. I was directed here.'

'I am the Countess of Nithsdale. My husband is away with Prince Charles. You may share any news with me.'

'I have a letter, my lady, from Lord John Bellew,' the man said, handing her a parchment sealed with the Bellew coat of arms. 'I have ridden from London.'

Shielding herself from the dread to come, Winifred thanked the courier, gave him ale, and led him to the kitchens, where he might find some food. She carried the letter into the nursery and sat on Frances's bed until night fell. There was nothing to fear from this letter. The child may have died, she bargained, but Anne lived and would raise Frances. If her daughter was dead, she would have known.

A maid entered to light a lamp and lay fresh logs in the grate. Winifred waited for her to finish before breaking the seal. Anne was dead. A child named Edward had been born too soon but had not survived beyond a few weeks. Winifred read and reread the letter. The words made no sense, but the world became different, felt different, tasted different.

In the weeks that followed, days still turned, and nights

merged into day but through a flattened landscape, drained of colour. Winifred only wanted to sleep, but when the chance came, she lay dry-eyed on her bed, rehearsing events she had not witnessed. If she imagined Anne dying alone she felt desolate but reminded herself that her daughter had lived with a man who loved her. But what about Frances, a little girl left without her mother and grandmother? Who was caring for the child?

While Winifred's world stopped, Maxwell sought more duties, easily done given the king's retreat into mourning and solitary prayer. The Nithsdales spent more evenings together but spoke little, her husband's fallen expression and distant gaze showing that he felt the loss of his daughter every bit as deeply as she did.

One evening, Winifred broke the silence: 'I feel responsible for Anne's death,' she said. 'I should have insisted they stay in Rome until the baby was born. With me at her side, our daughter and the child might have lived.'

Maxwell stared into the grate, then rose to kick at one of the logs. Sparks flew onto the hearth.

'Such thoughts are nonsense,' he said, his voice barely audible. 'For your own sake, do not dwell upon blame or responsibility.'

'It helps me to do so,' Winifred replied. 'I can't settle, I can't accept Anne's death, without exploring every possibility.'

Maxwell raised his head to look at his wife, hands dangling between his knees.

'It doesn't help me, Winifred. Please don't talk of such things again. Our daughter is dead. We have no choice but to come to terms with our loss.'

Months after their bereavement, Maxwell pulled a letter from his inside pocket, with news from their daughter's widowed husband. He did not immediately pass it to her, but held it aloft, using the parchment to punctuate the air as he spoke.

'He's distraught, as you can imagine, but blames Alice for Anne's death.'

'How on earth can it be Alice's fault?' Winifred said.

'Bellew says he employed the best physicians in London. They left medicines for Anne, but Alice stopped her from taking them.'

Winifred held out her hand for the letter. 'That doesn't mean that Alice caused Anne's death. Let me see what he has said.'

She read in silence, aware of Maxwell watching her.

'His grief is speaking for him,' she said. 'John must find someone to blame, as I tried to blame myself. We should bring Alice home, she must be desperate.'

'What would she do here?' Maxwell argued. 'Anyway, I have sympathy with Lord Bellew. Alice acted well above her station, refusing to follow a physician's advice. Who knows, the potions might have worked, given time. I'm afraid she's not coming back; my mind is made up.'

'Maxwell, she's alone in London.'

'Not our problem, I'm afraid. She's had every opportunity, working for you all these years. My impression of the woman – one I held before our daughter's tragic death – is that she's developed an inflated view of her skills. Let her try her hand at finding another job. The Bellew family won't want to keep her on.'

Winifred fought a drumming rage that felt as if it might blow her skull apart. Then the vile words came, words she had been swallowing for months.

'I know about the blame of grief. I'm afraid I have blamed you for Anne's death, as John is blaming Alice.'

Maxwell's eyes grew wide. 'Me? I wasn't even there.'

'No, but you should have been and so should I. If I was a free woman, I would have been at my daughter's side. If I hadn't saved *your* life, I might have been able to save hers.'

The poisonous words spilled from her mouth, even as she witnessed tears gather in the corners of her husband's eyes. He turned his face away and spoke in a hoarse whisper.

'You remember only what suits you. That night in the Tower, the night before my execution, I asked you not to rescue me. I was ready to die. The choice to free me was yours and I went along with it. What else could I have done? Fight off your friends in my cell and alert the guards?'

'You have rewarded me with debt, with other women, with alcohol. You have had your recompense.'

'Winifred, I have chased my demons in my own way, as you have chased yours. Now, if you'll excuse me,' Maxwell stood and gave a slight bow from his waist, 'I will sleep in my own rooms tonight.'

Within an already grieving community, the depth of their personal loss could not easily be shared. Winifred and Maxwell had no recourse but to fall back upon each other, the secret bitterness at the heart of their marriage belonging only to them. A stream of young men arrived at the palace from Britain and Europe, attracted by the teenage princes and the romance of the Jacobite cause. Winifred saw little of Charles, surrounded by acolytes who treated him as royalty and who encouraged the prince to regard himself as a king in waiting.

She found some occupation, helping their local convent

with the sick and dying, but clung to the hope that no matter how delightful their granddaughter had seemed within a good marriage, to a single man, she would soon feel like an encumbrance. In due course, a letter arrived from John Bellew asking permission to return his daughter to their care. If they agreed, John added, he would send the child immediately, with Alice to accompany her.

As they waited for news of Frances's arrival, neither she nor Maxwell chose to spend any time on errands that took them far from the palace. Every small task seemed to require frequent checks at the entrance and glances into the piazza beyond, for sight of the Bellew coat of arms.

The day arrived. Frances squirmed in the coachman's arms, but once placed on firm ground, the child ran towards her grandparents, then halted, as if uncertain of her welcome. Maxwell strode forward, scooping the child against his chest and carried her away to the nursery. Alice waited by the coach, unwilling to approach, her expression closed but her chin tilted in defiance.

'Let's walk,' Winifred said, and led Alice by the elbow under the portico of dei Santi Apostoli. 'We need to speak right now, or there will be a silence between us that cannot be broken.'

They found a bench in the shade of the church, but before they could sit, Alice began to cry. 'You must hate me,' she said, weeping. '*He* does.'

Winifred pulled Alice onto the bench and rested a hand on her arm. 'Tell me what happened.'

Alice sobbed quietly, resting her brow on Winifred's shoulder. The ordinary sounds of the square; the calls of hawkers, a mother shouting for her child, circled around them. Finding her resolve, Alice sat up and nodded, words following in a rush.

'Anne gave birth easily to a beautiful little boy. He was perfect but too small. I assisted at the birth, but there was a midwife present, a woman who came highly recommended. Everything seemed satisfactory, the child fed well, so the midwife left.'

Alice hesitated and swallowed. Winifred encouraged her to continue.

'Carry on,' she said. 'I'm listening.'

'After a few days, Anne became ill. Her fever was high and she would neither eat nor drink. I tried to nurse her as we did before; remember when she had that fever in France, when she was a little girl? Lord Bellew brought in all these doctors who left many potions. They made her gag, she couldn't swallow, so I stopped giving them to her.'

The dreadful image of Anne fighting for her life almost choked Winifred, but she coughed back her sobs and said: 'He didn't call the midwife back?'

Alice shook her head and lowered her chin onto her chest. The bells of the church pealed above them.

'This wasn't your fault,' Winifred said. 'Those medicines were worthless. I don't have my mother's knowledge, but it sounds likely that Anne retained some of the afterbirth. If the midwife had returned quickly, she might have been saved.'

'Thank you, my lady, you have lifted a great burden from my heart. How can we live without Anne?'

Winifred gave a low moan. 'I've thought of nothing else, but we have Frances with us now and she must be our future.'

CHAPTER 23
1735/36

There were many reasons, William thought, to dislike Henry Saint John, 1st Viscount Bolingbroke, but he was not inclined to ignore a rare invitation. He had been flattered by Henry's request for his company at White's; after all, the man was still influential, if no longer powerful. William was staying at his rooms in Frith Street for a few days and had tickets to see Handel's Alcina at the Royal Opera House. A new young tenor had been offered the role of Oronte, a chap going by the name of John Beard, and William was keen to hear him sing. Although the distance to White's was not far, the area around Upper St James's Park was notoriously unsafe, and he was glad to have brought his carriage and coachman from home. Beyond the walls of the royal park, the countryside was a warren of unplanned development, rising alongside farms still struggling to make a living from the land. It was a haven for London's less desirable inhabitants.

William's view from his carriage window was of the most elegant buildings in London, built along the length of Portugal Street. The Cavendish family had not even started to rebuild the once splendid Berkeley House following their fire last year, and in his opinion, they ought to feel ashamed of leaving its ugly, charred remains. He remembered his fear of fires at night and shuddered. Sometimes, the past should not be visited.

What was puzzling about Bolingbroke, William thought, was why he had supported the Jacobite rebellion in 1715, despite being a Tory politician and a Protestant. It was galling that even though Henry had followed the exiled King James Stuart to France, he had been pardoned and allowed to return to London, unlike his sister and her husband. Even more irritating was Bolingbroke's inexplicable friendship with Richard Cantillon. Since Cantillon had caused the Herbert family so much trouble, it was hard to understand what Bolingbroke had found to like in the man. Cantillon was dead, his end nasty and shrouded in mystery. Perhaps the unscrupulous liar had crossed too many people. The lawsuits had not ended with Cantillon's death, still pursued with enthusiasm both by Mary and his family. Was it not time, William mused, to let the whole matter drop?

The younger man waited for William in the library at White's, standing at a table by the window, examining the day's newspapers. The two men found seats by the fire, welcome on this bitter day in April. William rested on the fender to warm his back and gazed around at walls lined with books, while Bolingbroke ordered coffee for them both.

'I'm glad you could come, Powis. I wanted to let you know that I've had enough of the Commons and will be retiring to France in June, so this is likely to be the last time we'll meet. I was sad to hear about the death of your younger son and your niece. You have had much sorrow.'

William busied himself with settling into a chair and reached for his coffee.

'I was estranged from my son,' he said. 'We never saw eye to eye about finance or the estate. My greatest sadness is never to have met my granddaughter. Barbara was born a few months after his death. I had some care of my niece when she was a child and feel her loss more deeply. Her mother Winifred now has her granddaughter to distract her, which may be some comfort.'

Bolingbroke leaned towards William and lowered his voice. 'Bellew didn't take long to find himself another wife. Mind you, I'm not one to judge. I remarried less than two years after my first wife died. How about you? Any plans to marry again?'

William regretted accepting this invitation, feeling a deep discomfort at Bolingbroke's prying questions and prurient interest, but he was trapped by common courtesy until it was safe to make an acceptable retreat.

He did not smile and kept his answer brief, his tone clipped: 'I'm nearly eighty. I think that's unlikely, don't you?'

'What about all these lawsuits you're engaged in?' Bolingbroke asked. 'I heard a bit about it from Cantillon before his... his passing. It seemed to me that both sides were playing pretty rough. It can't have been easy for you.'

William hesitated, wondering where this conversation was leading.

'The litigation drags on, as these things do, the only beneficiaries being the lawyers. Cantillon's death was timely, in my opinion, but he lingers on in his lawsuits.'

Bolingbroke lowered his voice further and whispered, 'If he's actually dead.'

It felt as if something evil had scratched William's neck.

'What on earth do you mean? He was found burned to death, in the very house next to yours.'

'Indeed,' Bolingbroke replied, his grin revealing his enjoyment at rehearsing this tale, 'but had you heard that the corpse had no head? I witnessed this for myself.'

Reluctant to hear more but nevertheless curious, William asked: 'Are you telling me that the body may not have been his?'

'Exactly.' Bolingbroke fell back in his chair, staring at William. 'There's a rumour he's been seen in Surinam.'

'You're saying he faked his own death?'

'Probably,' Bolingbroke said. 'Knowing how weary Cantillon had become of looking over his shoulder, it doesn't surprise me that he may have decided to disappear. I thought you should know.'

The dark afternoon had become even darker. Bolingbroke may be a man respected for his political analysis, William thought, but he found the man almost as unlikeable as his friend Cantillon. He contemplated this unwelcome news in silence, aware of Bolingbroke's eyes, set deep within a face made longer by a high wig, studying his reaction. If Cantillon was alive, his lawsuit against the Herbert family would continue with a vigour his widow and children could never have matched. If Cantillon was in Surinam, he was beyond their reach, whatever Joseph Gage and his unscrupulous colleagues planned. This thing would not end, not before his own death.

'There's another thing I thought you should know,' said Bolingbroke, interrupting William's rumination. 'Since the Pretender has fallen into a dark place after his queen's death, the older prince, young Charles, has become the focus of a group of young men becoming overexcited by the hope of another Jacobite invasion. I think you should warn the Earl of Nithsdale to avoid getting caught up again. I've heard the Muti Palace is crawling with spies. Your sister and her husband will forever be of interest. My sources suggest it's time they left.'

William spoke his next thought aloud, not expecting a reply: 'Where would they go, Henry, where on earth would they go?'

~

William had avoided London since his uncomfortable meeting with Bolingbroke, deciding with hindsight that Henry's rage over Walpole's re-election and his diminishing political influence had soured the man, turning him into someone who enjoyed upsetting others with unsubstantiated rumour and gossip. Any further pleasure in that visit had been ruined by restless nights, full of irrational dreams of being pursued by a headless corpse, which left him irritable and despondent through the day. Even the opera had been a disappointment with the baritone replaced by an understudy and people chattering during the most solemn moments.

In the year before William turned eighty, his home and his friend and companion, Grace Evans, provided all the comfort he needed. It was summer and he walked the length of the Long Gallery, his favourite room in the castle. In his hand, he held a letter from Joseph Gage, one to which he could no longer delay a reply, but he preferred to remain here, with the past, for a little longer.

Although the gallery was a dark passage, the sun caught the polished elm floorboards and fell through the windows in such a way that interesting shadows were revealed in the panelled walls. In his mind, he could imagine the laughter of his two youngest sisters, always his favourites, as they chased each other down its length. Death was never far from his mind. His eldest sister Frances had been the first of his siblings to die, and by birth order, it was his turn next. His son Edward's unexpected passing had been a shock, and he regretted that their ruptured relationship would never now be repaired. Would he ever learn from his mistakes?

The success of the mine at Casares had encouraged young Gage to write again, requesting that William finally agree to a marriage with his daughter. He sought no settlement or property, all he wanted was Mary. Joseph argued, fairly in William's view, that he had proved himself to be reliable and consistent and could not be expected to wait any longer. That anyone deserved marriage as a reward was arguable, William thought, but it was not this belief that made him hesitate. In secret letters, ones that Joseph would never see, Mary begged her father not to agree to any proposals. In her usual style, as if he was already in his dotage, she drafted the replies he was expected to use.

His daughter's refusal to marry the man she had been willing to spend her life with was a puzzle and he saw no sense in her arguments, but he was a man, and a man born in the last century, so perhaps lacking insight into the ambitions of modern women. In his day, women had jumped at the chance to be married and these unions had always been arranged by the young couple's parents.

Age had mellowed Mary, William reflected, as he walked with his hands folded behind his back, pausing to examine his ancestor's heraldic symbols. At fifty, she did seem more aware that Joseph had sacrificed much to help her and had asked him to reply in a sensitive manner, one that would allow her to finish her projects in Spain and remain friends with Joseph thereafter. That was being hopeful, William thought, believing that a final refusal would exasperate Gage and surely push his relationship with Mary beyond repair. It was unreasonable that he was being asked by both parties to be the arbiter in this long-running saga. Was it any wonder he had not yet replied?

A cough interrupted William's reverie and he turned to face a servant, hovering behind him, accompanied by the German manager of his mines. Of course, he had forgotten his arrangement to meet Henninck. How remiss of him.

The manager bowed, and taking William's cue, walked alongside.

'Henninck, I wanted to discuss my daughter's request that we invest more money in the copper mine at Casares and send them another team of experienced labour. The last crew were not up to the job, I'm afraid.'

'My lord, our mines are performing well, better than expected. We can afford to invest more widely but a word of caution...'

William encouraged Henninck to speak his mind. 'Go ahead, I value your opinion.'

'The mine at Casares has potential and with more invest-ment and skilled labour should do well, but there has been another request from your daughter, concerning a silver mine at Puerto Blanco. It is important not to spread your risks too widely, not at present. We ought to limit our investments.'

William nodded. 'Wise words, wise words indeed,' he said. 'Things are looking uncertain again between Britain and Spain, but my daughter and her business partner seem ignorant of this and are determined to prospect widely in that country.'

'A focus on one mine in Spain would be my advice, to them as well as to you, since the unfortunate situation at Guadal-canal is not yet resolved.'

William turned to Henninck and placed a hand upon his shoulder. This man's expertise had saved his wealth, his estates, and his reputation. He would listen to his advice.

'You are right, as always,' William said. 'Please source miners from Germany and pay for them to travel to Casares, conflict with Spain permitting. Now, if you will excuse me, I have letters to write.'

CHAPTER 24
1737/38

Mary glowered at her aunt, snoring in their only armchair, her head back and mouth wide. If it was not so hard to see clearly, weak daylight fighting against the dirt on their small windows, she guessed there would be a visible trail of saliva stretching from the corner of Lady Anne Carrington's mouth to the neck of her grubby shift. Mary sat at their heavy table on one of the two uncomfortable chairs intended for eating, a pile of letters at her elbow. As a young woman, she had welcomed the opportunity to live in Paris with her aunt, to escape from her mother and ghastly sisters for a few glorious years but had not bargained on a lifetime of caring for an elderly woman in Spain.

Her father expected her to be grateful for the meagre amount he sent to Madrid every month, but surely, as an unmarried daughter, it was her right to be supported by her father. Aunt Anne had a small income from her husband's estate, still the subject of litigation, but they could just about survive. Their former home, the farmhouse on the edge of the city, seemed like luxury compared to these three rooms, leased in one of the poorest neighbourhoods.

To make things worse, the royal family had moved back to Madrid from Seville, and building had started on a new royal palace. The irritating presence of royalty meant they'd had to endure a visit from her nemesis, Ambassador Keene. On sight of Lady Carrington, barely able to walk and with unreliable continence, he had arranged for regular visits from titled British women with too much time on their hands.

On the last visit, Mary had caught a glance between their two visitors as they scanned the table strewn with rinds of cheese and crusts of bread, mouse droppings on the floorboards and the bucket brimming with human waste.

'You have no help, Lady Herbert?' the older woman asked.

Mary did not reply but shook her head. She felt no shame, only rage.

The younger woman exchanged another glance with her companion, and by silent agreement, they entered the bedroom and closed the door. Pressing her ear to the door, Mary overheard the whispered words 'disgrace' and 'neglect', as they bathed and changed her aunt.

To escape their intrusion, Mary carried the slopping bucket down to the gutters and emptied it, ignoring the disapproval of passers-by. This was not a task for daytime; the citizens of this community expected Mary to have more respect for her neighbours.

Unfortunately, the women were still there when Mary returned, sitting erect in chairs, their backs fortified by rectitude, their expressions solemn with disapproval.

'Our role, as identified by the British ambassador, is to help you care for Lady Anne Carrington,' the older woman said.

The younger woman picked up the thread. It was obvious to Mary that this conversation had been rehearsed. 'It is not our role to clean your rooms,' she added.

'On this occasion only,' the older woman interrupted, 'I will send servants tomorrow to clean this apartment.'

'In future,' her companion continued, 'we will expect your living quarters to be clean. You are fit and able, there is no reason for this mess.'

Mary had not shared with her father that his sister was receiving charity intended for distressed gentlewomen. Nor had she told him she had finally sold their coach and horses. It was essential to keep him involved with her projects, to pretend that all was well, or he may decide to stop investing at Casares.

Mary swept the papers onto the floor, where they shone bright against the floorboards, and said aloud: 'God save me from men.'

Anne stirred, smacking her lips, and muttered, 'What's the matter, Mary? What have men done to you now?'

'It's your brother, my father. All he does is complain that the price of lead is falling and he's not making enough money. He goes on and on about the Herbert family debts and how he'll never pay them off, as if it's all my fault. Joseph has found a gold mine in the Sierra Jaeña, which he thinks will make our fortune. He wants me to apply for the lease but how can I persuade my father to back us, in this mood?'

There was no reply from Anne. She appeared to have returned to sleep and gentle sounds puffed from between her lips, the precursor of snoring. Suddenly, she spoke: 'I agree with him. Why don't you take his advice and focus on developing the mine you already have? He's an old man, as I am an old woman. Life makes us weary; the future holds no interest.'

Mary was slow to answer. She knew why Joseph went on with his prospecting; it was the only outlet for his urge to gamble. Each new mine was like the first approach to a gaming table; the assessment, the first move, the waiting for the other gamers to play. Would he be successful? Would he win? She played along, to keep Joseph in *her* game for as long as she needed him.

At last she said: 'He's still going on about marrying me, pestering my father. I wish he'd give up.'

Anne tried to raise herself to sitting and held out an outstretched palm for Mary to help. She used both hands to ease her aunt from her slumped position and placed an embroidered cushion, a present from one of their unwelcome visitors, behind her back.

'I've never understood why you don't marry Joseph,' Anne continued. 'Most people think you are already married.'

Mary crouched to pick up the letters from the floor. 'I've never wanted to be a married woman; to have to give up everything to my husband, to defer to him on every decision, to be expected to have children. The arrangement never seems to be of much benefit to the woman.'

She paused and laughed, returning to her chair. 'Although you seemed to get the best out of your two marriages.'

Anne did not laugh. 'Not at all, Mary. I loved my first husband, Francis Carrington, and it was my greatest wish to have children. Instead, I ended up having to look after my youngest sister Winifred, then take you in and finally, my niece Anne. I agree, I married Mackenzie out of expediency but if I could have had Francis by my side for my whole life, as you have had Joseph, I would have been happy.'

'There is no point in two people, both of whom have nothing but debt, marrying each other,' Mary said. 'There must be some gain, surely?'

'There's companionship, comfort and... dare I say it... there's love. I've not been sure about Joseph, as you know, but he does love you. Is that not worthwhile?'

Mary pushed back her seat, irritated with the drift of the conversation.

'I'm going out. I must buy some food and I think you have a visitor later; someone I'd rather miss. Let me wrap you in a shawl, so you don't completely disgrace yourself by being half-naked when they arrive.'

'Can you help me onto the bucket first?' Anne asked.

Mary rolled her eyes. 'If you must.'

She lifted Anne from the chair, holding her aunt under the armpits, balancing the weight of the elderly woman as she spread her legs and crouched over the bucket. Mary raised her aunt's shift at the back, so that it would not be soiled and as she did so, Anne broke wind. Mary almost let her drop but held on, her back and arms screaming with pain, until the trickling stopped. In silence, she supported Anne back into the chair and wrapped her in a shawl.

At the door, Mary turned back to speak. Anne was already dozing.

'I'll leave the door on the latch,' she shouted. 'Call out when they arrive, and they'll let themselves in. If they bring cakes, save one for me.'

There was probably a puddle of urine on the floor, around the bucket. The interfering visitors would notice and report back to Keene. In her hurry through the narrow streets, shaded by tall buildings, Mary picked her way through the refuse which was still thrown from balconies at night. She imagined the visiting British ladies feigning concern as they described the mess, the smell, the poverty in which Lady Anne Carrington and Lady Mary Herbert lived, all for the benefit of an audience who would pretend to be horrified but grateful for their easy lives, and who would turn away.

She hated her life; hated being trapped in Spain caring for an aged woman without help, hated having no money, or status, or influence. Her aunt was right, she and Joseph should concentrate on the mine at Casares but he seemed driven to go on prospecting, always restless, always searching for something better, each discovery bringing new excitement and hope.

What about her father, sitting in Powis Castle, pretending he was poor and whining about lack of money, when he was surrounded by beautiful objects? Her oldest brother, the one who survived despite his drinking and debauchery, would inherit everything. He had the cheek to sue her, his own sister, for wrongful advice about his financial dealings. Men were so fortunate.

In one of the small squares, almost a courtyard, no different from those discovered around every corner, Mary entered a dark doorway, leading into a storeroom, where she bought bread that was already stale, a few slices of cured ham and some olive oil. She did not intend to hurry home. All that waited for her was the ordeal of trying to help her aunt eat bread soaked in oil and then an attempt to wash before the start of the bedtime shambles. The September sun was still warm on her face. She sat on a stone bench and watched other women huddle around the well, fetching water to scrub their filthy children before bed. There were no men.

She predicted what would happen next: the women would gather around her and ask questions, the same ones she had failed to answer many times before. She had little Spanish, beyond a few words and pointing, but they always asked, where was her husband? Where were her children? She would reply with her habitual shrug, and they would settle themselves around her and chatter, as if she was one of them and could follow their conversation.

The women's questions were reasonable, ones she did not resent being asked. Most people regarded marriage as an obligation, a duty to others, as Joseph believed she had a duty to him. Mary had a thought of such blinding clarity, she wondered why it had never occurred to her before. Joseph should be married, of course. He deserved the chance of a child, a family. She must help him to find someone suitable, or it simply would not happen. That was her only responsibility to him, and it was one she would enjoy.

One of the women pulled a scarf more tightly around her hair to hide the bruising visible on her neck. These women had fulfilled expectations: married, produced children, put food on the table every day, but where had it got them? Her own sisters, two women she could barely remember, had failed in even these basic tasks of life, whereas she, Lady Mary Herbert, the one accused of letting the family down, had vision, owned mines, tried to make a fortune. Neither of her brothers had earned a penny and the only one to have produced an heir had selfishly died before the child was born. Yet her father never complained about how much money those two owed the estate or how they had failed the family. It simply wasn't fair.

The other women left at an invisible signal, like a flock of birds, abandoning Mary to her bench. She realised she had forgotten the water bucket and would have to come back later to the well. Walking home, delaying for as long as possible the misery of their rooms and her aunt's demands, Mary felt better for having a plan. Her mission – no, her obligation – was to find two wives, one for her remaining brother and one for Joseph. Tomorrow, she would start on her letters.

CHAPTER 25

1739/1740

Villiam dozed beside the fire in the small room between the blue and oak drawing rooms. This was where he could be found in the winter months, the tapestries and the generous fire warming his aching joints. Nothing could touch his loneliness after Grace's unexpected death. Her friendship could never be replaced, but he had no choice but to live on without her, alone in his castle. His days passed in conversations with staff, the endless administration of his debts, and the faltering profits from the mines. Above him, on the ceiling, his daughters' faces reminded him of how he had failed them. He had considered spending his afternoons elsewhere in the castle, but he believed he deserved their scorn.

This afternoon, a dark day in November with the lamps not yet lit, he was startled awake by a sharp knock on the door. On his call to enter, James Baker, the estate steward, stood before him, a document scrolled in his hand. Baker seemed breathless and the sheen on his brow glowed in the light from the fire.

'My lord, we have had some unwelcome visitors. You may have heard the hammering on the inner gate.'

William had indeed been aware of some noise but had thought it part of his dream.

'Who was it, James? What did they want with me?'

Baker turned the scroll in his hand.

'It was bailiffs, sent by the Mackenzie family. Here is an account of the money they claim they're owed. They threatened to return tomorrow to remove goods to the value of the debt.'

William reached for the document.

'This is preposterous, I owe that family nothing. In fact, they owe my sister money.'

It was not possible to read the account in the light from the fire, so William sent Baker away to find the boy who lit the evening lamps. Once he had enough light to read, he saw that Mackenzie's heirs had calculated all the money their father had sent to his wife, Lady Anne Carrington. They had deducted the amount they estimated had been used to support Mary and were now invoicing her father to pay this back. The claim was ridiculous and would not stand up in a court of law. The lawyer's money had been Anne's to use as she chose. More worrying, Mackenzie's family were accusing his daughter of advising him on investments and he had lost a great deal. What business of this was his? Only a fool would take advice from a woman with no background in finance.

Reading on, William saw evidence that Mary had borrowed money from Mackenzie to fund the exploration of the mine at Guadalcanal, which she had not paid back. His daughter must have made the request on behalf of her aunt, since Anne increasingly found letter writing difficult.

Not one of these demands is sound, William thought, but he did not have time for the luxury of litigation; the Mackenzie thugs would return tomorrow. He sent a servant to bring Baker back from his home and when James appeared, smelling strongly of the dinner he had left behind, William beckoned to a chair and encouraged the man to sit down.

'I need some ideas,' William said. 'What do you suggest?'

'We have a choice, give them goods to the value of their claims and expect a legally binding agreement that the matter is closed, forever. Alternatively, we resist.'

'What could we give them?' William asked.

Baker passed him an inventory. 'This is a list of furniture, paintings, and tapestries that would meet the debt.'

William read in silence, then tossed the parchment onto the fire. Both men watched the document burn, the ink creating flares of red-and-blue flame.

'They're having nothing,' William growled.

James smiled and rubbed his fingers through his beard. This was a gesture William knew well and usually meant good news.

'In that case, my lord, I've been to the ale house and the men drinking there – farmers, miners, and the good people of Welshpool – they don't take kindly to folk from England coming over here to threaten our marquess. As we speak, they are forming a reception committee for any intruders.'

Emotion gripped William's throat, and unable to form any words, he swallowed hard. Finally, he whispered, 'I don't deserve such loyalty.'

Baker frowned. 'Don't mistake this for loyalty, my lord, it's their way of defending our land from the English. We mustn't waste their sentiments. I suggest we let Mackenzie's men in through the outer gate and have our armed men waiting for them in the courtyard. With such a reception, I think these so-called bailiffs will turn and run.'

William tossed in his bed all night, the mattress seemed unusually lumpy, the bedclothes smothering and sweaty. If Baker's plan failed, Mackenzie's thugs would run riot through his home, helping themselves to whatever they fancied.

Tempers would run high and blood might be spilled. As dawn crept over the battlements, William stood at his window, wrapped in an embroidered robe, staring into the shadows of the courtyard. Before full light, Baker tapped on his door, reminding him to remain in his chamber. As the man left, William called out, hoping to ask Baker to try a final negotiation but a loud banging on the outer gate said this course of action was already too late.

From his vantage point, William saw Baker's shadow approach the perimeter wall. With the help of two boys, James pulled the gate wide open, standing back as ten armed men rushed into the courtyard. From every murky corner, the Welshpool men streamed from their hiding places in the stables, from doorways, from behind statues, holding farm implements or picks above their heads, surrounding their unwelcome guests.

Chanting 'Mynd adref, go home!' and insults about the intruders' parentage and sexual prowess, the Welshpool men parted to allow the bailiffs to retreat backwards through the gate with their arms and weapons raised. As the last of Mackenzie's men ran for their lives, Baker bowed to the final retreating back and locked the gate behind them. He turned, searching for William's face at his bedroom window, and raised his hand in salute.

'That's the last we'll see of that lot,' William said to the girl who had brought him a basin of hot water and some wine.

'Indeed, my lord,' she replied, blushing at having been spoken to by the marquess. 'They'll think twice before they trouble us again.'

The following morning, William met again with his estate manager. He dreamed of a quiet life but his home had been violated. It would never again be possible to walk through his beloved terraced garden, to potter in the grounds or stroll to the village, without looking over his shoulder. Mackenzie's family would never receive a penny, but they had robbed him of everything he held dear.

The tremor that had developed in William's hands over the last few years had become more pronounced overnight. He shook as he tried to pour Baker a glass of wine and the younger man placed his hand over his master's, gently retrieving the carafe and serving wine for them both.

'We won't get away that easily,' Baker said. 'Mackenzie's men had a fright, but they'll be back. It would be wise to prepare for another attack.'

'I feel as if...' William began.

Baker encouraged his employer to finish. 'Feel what, my lord?'

'I feel I'm being pursued by the deceased. Mackenzie and Cantillon are both dead but remain my persecutors. How can I ever be free of them?'

'Three men will patrol the battlements for another two weeks, with firearms,' Baker said, ignoring his employer's plea in favour of practicalities. 'I've already drawn up a rota of volunteers and only need your permission to release weapons from the armoury.'

William nodded but felt his body tremble. Baker noticed and stoked the fire. Before he left, he requested blankets and tucked these around the old man's shoulders.

'Have no fear, my lord,' he said, 'we will deal with your persecutors, alive or dead.'

William took to his bed for two days, fearing a fever, but once he felt stronger, he was informed that intruders had indeed been spotted crawling along the paths of the terraced garden, trying to find another way of entering the castle, but only one warning shot had been required to encourage the strangers to run away. He could see how much his estate manager was enjoying the drama and intrigue. For Baker, these attacks were an escape from their usual quiet and humdrum routine.

'The patrols should continue,' William said, when he learned of this latest incursion. 'Keep the smelting house locked, and a permanent guard on the mine shaft.'

'Of course,' Baker agreed, 'but I think we'll have seen the last of them.'

'Perhaps,' William whispered, 'but not in my imagination. In my worse moments, they are forever present.'

After Christmas the rain started. Day after day, William and his estate manager stood on the top terrace, dressed in their best water-repellent clothing, surveying the sodden landscape. Soon, the farms were more like lakes than fields. The mine flooded, and Henninck stopped all work for six weeks, until the deepest tunnels could be drained.

Nine months later, the fields were dry at last, but the tenant farmers had been late to plant their crops and the sodden fields had produced low yields. James Baker met William at their viewpoint and the two men stood side by side, scanning the rich, brown landscape, fresh from the plough.

William spoke first, sure of what was to come. 'You asked to meet me, James. I expect you want to discuss the rents?'

Baker turned to face his employer.

'You are right, my lord. They can't pay what is owed if they are to keep their animals alive and plant seeds for next year, never mind feed their families through the winter. I have visited many and they are living in conditions you would not be proud to see. Some children are close to starvation.'

'What are you asking of me?'

James studied the toes of his boots, as if he had to search for the courage to say what was needed. 'I'm asking for rents to be forfeited this year. If I may be so bold, the men stood fast at your side when you needed help. Now they need your help.'

William wanted to be the kind of man who would agree to such a reasonable request. A generous answer would reflect his true heart but he was trapped by money owed, the spendthrift ways of his heir and his daughter's never-ending speculation. Every spare penny was needed to service debts or prop up mines in remote corners of Spain.

'I'm afraid that's not possible, Baker. You've seen the accounts. You know how things stand.'

'Exactly, my lord. I'm aware I'm speaking out of turn, but if you perhaps tried to curb the spending of your son, Lord Montgomery, it might be possible. All was well when the mines were profitable, but his lifestyle has become a drain on the estate.'

When was it that servants became so confident they felt at ease to speak to him in a way his father would never have accepted? Was it his age or his reputation as a gullible fool that had led him to this point? Of course, James spoke the truth, but it was far too late to expect William to prevent his son from running up debts against the estate. That horse had bolted, years ago.

He had prepared for this moment, reached the only conclusion that could reasonably be drawn from days poring over the accounts, weeks of sleepless nights and his clawing loneliness.

'I will agree to the tenants being in arrears for a year,' he said, 'but they all must sign an understanding that the rent owed will eventually be paid. I will leave that to you, Baker.'

'That is generous, my lord, but doesn't go far enough to meet the level of poverty I've witnessed. Would you be willing to accompany me on a visit to a few households?'

The thought that William had been playing with for weeks,

solidified and became a firm plan. He felt his cheeks burn with shame, when he imagined his parents' reaction to the mess their only son was leaving behind.

'We will close up the castle and I will leave, forever. This will save a considerable amount of money. The mine should stay open and Henninck will remain, if he is willing, to ensure that we make whatever profits we can. Of course, you will continue to supervise the estate.'

'Oh, my lord—'

William raised a hand. 'Say no more. I am an old man and will fare better in my rooms in London, where I have access to physicians. It's unlikely my son will ever live here, and I cannot say if any member of the Herbert family will be seen at Powis Castle again.'

'We can care for you in your declining years. This is your home,' Baker argued.

'Thank you, but my mind is made up. James, I have been honoured to have you in my service and feel deep regret that the estate is a poor reflection of my time as its steward. My only consolation is that my tenants will be served well by such an honest man.'

Weeks later, William's carriage was ready to leave for London. With James Baker supporting his arm, he walked stiffly past his mother's portrait and down the fine staircase, step by step, constructed by his father. The paintings on the walls were as confusing for an old man as they had been for a young child, like real statues, standing within an actual niche. It was as if they could be lifted out and moved. It was an illusion, it had all been an illusion.

They walked through the terraced gardens created by his

mother, the plants curled and yellowed as autumn encroached and William sat for a few moments, catching his breath, looking out across the fields, woods and distant mountains, inhaling the sweet breath of the turning year. His coach carried him through Welshpool and the countryside of Montgomery, passing Grace's cottage, right next to the church, the new tenants already digging up her flower garden. Pinch-cheeked women stared from cottage doors, lifting their ragged children to wave farewell. Outside the mine workings, a group of men stood in silence, holding aloft their picks. Farmers waited on the edge of fields, standing to attention, saluting as the coach sped by.

He had instructed Baker to use all the food and wine stored, so that nothing would go to waste, and he knew there would be a fine party at the castle that night. He wished he could have left them more. Afterwards, once the debris had been cleared, floors swept and sheets spread over furniture, the castle would fall silent. His bequest to his family was debt and more debt, his bequest to his tenants a life of poverty. He should have done better.

William turned for a final look at the castle, only the turrets now visible. He closed the blinds, slouched down in his seat, and shut his eyes. It was too late.

CHAPTER 26
1741/42

One morning before lessons, Winifred pulled Frances onto her knee to do her hair. Frances wriggled away, regarding herself as too old for such things and slumped in front of the dressing-table mirror, her expression sullen. Winifred spun the child around in the hairdressing chair, making her laugh and brushed the girl's long, dark curls, before twisting the strands into plaits. There was still pinning to come and a ribbon to tie into place, but Frances was restless. She had already slid from the chair, edging out from under her grandmother's grip.

'In Scotland,' Winifred said, trying to hold the girl's attention, 'your mother had a puppy. She was one of a litter born to a strange-looking little dog we had.'

Frances stopped moving, her eyes alert. 'What was the dog called?'

'We called her Bea,' Winifred said, through a mouth of pins.

Frances smiled. 'What a funny name, for a dog.'

Winifred quickly pinned the plaits onto the girl's crown.

'We named her after the queen, the king's mother, Mary Beatrice.'

'That was rude,' Frances said. 'Especially if the dog looked a bit odd. What did my mother call her puppy?'

Winifred paused and frowned. 'You know, I've forgotten. I'll ask my friend Grace, she'll remember.'

Too late, Frances had gone, one partially tied ribbon dangling above her ear.

If her daughter Anne was easy to find in her grandchild, Grace was lost. Her brother wrote to say that Grace had died, but she had already been gone for almost two months. In all that time, Winifred had thought she was alive. So, what was death? Could she not simply pretend that Grace still lived? Anything to avoid this creeping emptiness, this ache, this befuddled mind? She wrote to her sister, the abbess, searching for answers, but Lucy replied that if Winifred could not find solace in the faith of her birth, she must work harder to hold her daughter and her friend in her memory.

If it's any comfort, Lucy had written, *I am certain you will see them both again.* This wasn't any comfort because she didn't believe it was true.

Every day, Winifred passed her free hours when Frances was in her lessons and Alice was busy with mending or laundry, pounding the streets of Rome. Her walks carried her, unseeing, through the dark, cobbled passageways of the poorer quarters, past newly constructed, elegant palaces fronting sunlit squares, or through crumbling ruins. These walks were mostly angry, her steps beating out the unfairness that first Anne had been taken from her, and now Grace. If she gave way to tears, she was left feeling weak and hollow but had to hold herself together for Frances, their only reason for staying alive. Furious walking would not allow her to cry.

The child was now nine years old, studying well with her tutors and a favourite at court. The king had agreed that Frances could take lessons within the palace from the princes' former tutor, but characteristic of James, it was made clear that Maxwell must pay. The money was not easy to find, as Lord Bellew seemed to have forgotten his child and had not once written to ask about her well-being. Winifred feared that if her former son-in-law remembered his daughter, he might ask to have her back.

Today, Winifred climbed the Spanish Steps, completed at last, and sat down under an ancient tree next to the church of Trinità dei Monti. From here, she had a view over the square below and the rooftops beyond. A breeze lifted the sound of water trickling into the fountain and voices carried upwards from the square. Despite her words of caution, when Frances turned seven, Maxwell wrote many letters to Lord Bellew, demanding suitable payment be made for his child's upbringing and education. Bellew had only recently replied, and Winifred carried his letter in her pocket to read through again on her own.

Her worst fears had not been realised; John seemed grateful for their care of his child, apologised for his oversight, and promised to send regular payments. He was careful to ask all the right questions about Frances, as if he was truly the father of a child whose development was of interest. He even requested that she write to him, as part of her lessons. Winifred suggested this to Frances's tutor, but both the child and the teacher stared at her with such uncomprehending scorn that she had not pursued the matter. Anyway, she thought, if John really cared about his child he wouldn't have taken eighteen months to reply. Frances was right; he could whistle for a letter from her.

Winifred hurried back to meet Frances from her lessons,

worrying about the changing atmosphere at James's court. The king had retreated further into solitary and troubled introspection and was rarely seen, even by his sons. The boys, her grown princes, attractive young men with time on their hands, raised in the benevolent indifference of titled families. Charles had taken to calling himself Charlie and could usually be found at the centre of an adoring crowd. The once-silent corridors rang with the braying laughter of men, often the worse for alcohol, and every night there were dinners and parties that ended in pranks and vomit.

The Earl and Countess of Nithsdale were not included in this revelry, but Winifred noticed that younger men did step aside for Maxwell, their faces bright with respect and awe. The grizzled man at her side had become a rarity, one who had seen battle for the Jacobite cause. They did not step aside for his wife. At sixty-nine, Winifred was one of very few older women in the Muti Palace and consequently invisible.

She entered her rooms and adjusted her hair in front of a mirror. While she may live a life unseen by Charlie's friends, she missed nothing. In the palace, Jacobite sentiment no longer lingered in the remnants of the fading nostalgia of aging men but had a new energy, vital and alive for this new cohort of supporters. She worried that pride might draw Maxwell back to a cause best left to younger men and her boys, would the princes be safe? Encouraged by his friends, Charlie had begun to posture as the rightful king of Great Britain and Ireland, and without the guiding hand of his father, had adopted an arrogant, regal manner. Unfairly labelled the Pretender by his enemies, the truth was that King James had turned his back on any hope of regaining his father's crown, but Charlie and Henry saw no other reason for being alive.

The door swung open and Frances ran across the room, throwing herself onto Winifred's bed. She rolled onto her stomach and propped herself up on her elbows, resting her chin on her palms.

Winifred turned to face the child, making sure that a welcoming smile erased the deep worry lines between her brows.

'How were your lessons today? Did you finish all your work?'

Frances rolled her eyes. 'It was so boring. Why do I need to learn Latin and Greek anyway? They're all dead.'

The sense of this was undeniable and it took Winifred a few seconds to reply.

'Well,' she said, 'it's probably because learning difficult things helps your mind to grow.'

'Anyway, I spoke to Prince Charlie today. You used to take him horse-riding, with his brother. Why don't you ever take me horse-riding?'

Winifred smiled and said: 'Ah yes, that was when they were boys, in Bologna. I'm afraid your grandfather and I can't afford a pony.'

'Can my father afford a pony?' Frances asked, her eyes narrowed.

'Yes,' Winifred replied, guessing where this was going, 'I'm sure he can.'

Frances nodded. 'Then I'll write to him.'

Despite the fervour, little changed in the palace for those few exiles old enough to have memories of the court at Saint-Germain, or even Urbino. Many of the old guard had left for home and the remaining survivors had nothing new to say to each other. Letters from Mary Stuart, Maxwell's sister, described her sons as active Jacobite leaders, both working to encourage a group of Highland and Lowland noblemen to fund a Stuart invasion of Scotland. Winifred hoped that her own son would not be tempted to follow his cousins, especially if he felt pressurised by his father's reputation for bravery.

Into this claustrophobic group of aging exiles, desperate for fresh faces and new company, arrived Charles Radclyffe, Lord Derwentwater, his wife Charlotte, their son James, who was seventeen and Mary, who was the same age as Frances. Winifred only felt alarm. Radclyffe was a name she knew well, a name from her past, one she had hoped never again to encounter. Both Charles Radclyffe and his older brother, James, were arrested at Preston alongside her husband. When Maxwell escaped his execution, cruel gossip had circulated, even amongst Jacobite supporters, that James Radclyffe had been executed because of Winifred's treason. Her selfish actions had resulted in another man's death.

The Radclyffe family quickly became the most envied hosts in Rome, holding musical evenings, lunches and parties for a community starved of social contact. Winifred feared she and Maxwell would be excluded, but when their invite came, she fretted about how they might be received.

'We must refuse this,' Winifred said, tossing the letter across the table.

Maxwell frowned as he read. 'What possible reason is there not to attend? he replied. 'I've met Charles and he's keen to introduce you to Charlotte. Mary could be a friend for Frances.'

'How will I be treated?' Winifred argued. 'It's impossible that Charles has forgotten and holds no grudge against me. I was accused by many of being responsible for his brother's execution.'

Maxwell laughed. 'I have no idea what you're talking about. Whatever occurred between our families is in the past. If Charles and his wife had doubts about us, we wouldn't have been invited. We must go, it would seem like rudeness if we did not.'

Winifred was not reassured and watched closely at court for the start of rumours, sideways, shifty glances, and awkward encounters.

On the night of the party, she slipped her arm into the crook of Maxwell's elbow, as they walked towards the villa along a path edged with statuary and lit by flares. Charlotte and Charles met them at the entrance, their faces open and welcoming. From inside, they heard instruments tuning and a roar of conversation, rising and falling. Winifred felt her tension ease as Charles wrapped Maxwell in an embrace and the two men stepped away from the women, patting each other on opposite shoulders. Charlotte smiled and took Winifred's hand.

'Come this way,' she said, leading her through the salon, circled by low settees, where the dancing would soon begin. At the entrance to the library, she scooped two glasses from a tray held aloft by a servant and steered Winifred to a chair.

'I thought we should leave those two to catch up,' Charlotte said. 'There aren't many survivors from the fifteen still living. They have much to say to each other.'

'Goodness yes,' Winifred replied. 'Charles was arrested too, wasn't he? What happened to him afterwards, to you all?'

Charlotte grimaced. 'Charles managed to escape from Newgate Prison – an awful place to be held – but he did rather well in France, where he met your brother, I believe. He's been appointed as secretary to Prince Charles. Our son has fitted in well with the young men here and Mary is to share lessons with your granddaughter. I'm glad we came. I think Charles is so handsome, no wonder the Scots call him bonnie.'

Winifred secretly thought that Henry, always her favourite, was bonnier.

'We love Rome,' Charlotte continued. 'Have you enjoyed your time here?'

Winifred's opinion of Rome, unique to her own privations and losses, could not be shared. Any place you were not free to leave, quickly lost its attraction.

'We are settled here,' she said. 'We're lucky to have Frances with us too.'

Charlotte's eyes softened, and she reached out to take Winifred's hand.

'I was sad to hear about your daughter and the baby. It must have been a shock to learn that Lord Bellew married again and has lost another wife in childbirth.'

Winifred's free hand flew up to cover her mouth. From the salon, she could hear the thump of dancing and the high laughter of women being whirled and tossed between partners. No words would come, nothing that could adequately express her confusion.

Charlotte hurried to fill the silence. 'I can see you did not know. I apologise for my indiscretion. Let's join the dancing and find more wine. Life can be hard for women, don't you agree? We must find friendship where we can. We are friends, aren't we, Winifred?'

Winifred rose and pulled her shawl around her shoulders.

'Of course, Charlotte, I would be delighted to be your friend. The news you shared was indeed a shock, but only because I did not know. My former son-in-law does not believe in staying in touch with us, or his daughter, although he is meeting his financial obligations.'

'That is something, at least.' Charlotte linked arms with Winifred and the women entered the salon, scanning the room for their husbands.

'They're probably off plotting somewhere,' Charlotte said. 'Many here tonight are supporters of the Stuart restoration.'

Winifred stopped and turned to face her companion. 'My husband cannot take part in any action, no matter how keen he appears to be. He is too old, much older than Charles. He must not risk everything again.'

Charlotte let Winifred's arm drop. 'My goodness, I am surprised. We thought we could count on you both, with your history.'

'It's because of our history you can't count on us,' Winifred hissed, aware that the music had paused between dances and her voice carried in the silence. 'If you value your son's life, I'd get him away from here as soon as you can.'

The two women stared, and Winifred felt her stomach contract. She had gone too far, said too much. Any hope of friendship with Charlotte was over. She imagined her husband's fury when he learned, as he soon would, of her behaviour. What if her treasonous words were repeated to Prince Charles? Being right would not feel like a victory in the rough days ahead.

CHAPTER 27

1743/44

Mary won her legal case against the Espanola Company. Not only had she legal control of Guadalcanal but was now the owner of four other nearby mines, including Rio Tinto. On paper, she was one of the richest women in Europe, even without the potential earnings from three further mines she had leased in partnership with Joseph. She was no longer under any threat of imprisonment.

Mary whooped with joy on receiving the news. 'I am free,' she yelled, waving the legal document before his face. 'I'm free to leave all this mining nonsense behind. I can return to Paris.'

'Go back to Paris?' Joseph said, his expression crestfallen. 'We can make a success of these mines. It's our chance to build a profitable business empire. We'll be free of debt, respected, acknowledged by the best of society.'

Mary's excitement flattened into disappointment. 'I thought you would remain behind and manage the mines for me,' she said. 'I believed you had found a purpose and were revelling in your success. I will pay you well, if that is your concern.'

Joseph's lips formed a stubborn line. 'This isn't about money. If you choose to leave Spain, so will I.'

'My aunt can't live in Madrid a moment longer, you are well aware of that.' This detail was beyond argument, surely.

Joseph nodded, as if he understood her point of view. 'Very well, take your aunt home, but you must return. This is where we belong.'

Mary's chest tightened. He was a bully, a controlling and neglectful bully, loyal only when it suited him. She had been right to deny him marriage, he could not be trusted. 'Your so-called enthusiasm for prospecting has been nothing but a superficial and self-serving lie,' she said, her voice rising. 'You tricked me into compliance!'

'I have given you the chance to be a rich woman!' Joseph shouted back. 'You owe me everything. I refuse to be abandoned in this country. I have sweated and slaved for us, for our future. It only matters if you are here too.'

Mary's voice climbed to an unnaturally high pitch. 'Has my suffering over the last fifteen years meant nothing to you? Who has been abandoned, if not me, time and time again?'

Joseph lowered his tone and whispered, his voice weighted with menace. 'Unless you stay here with me, I will not remain. My mind is made up.'

The next day, Mary left Madrid in secret. She didn't believe Joseph's threat, that he would follow her to Paris, but he might try to stop her. It wasn't beyond him to keep her prisoner. Aunt Anne argued desperately to stay, watching Mary throw their few belongings into cloth bundles.

'Why should we leave, just when everything is coming right? It doesn't make sense.'

Mary struggled to control a temper that gripped her throat like a vice. Why did she always have to explain? Wasn't it obvious?

'I have been kept prisoner in this awful country, as have you. We are free to leave, so we must go.'

'What is there for us in Paris? Our life in that city has gone.'

Mary tried hard to swallow down her frustration. Her voice croaked as if she hadn't spoken to anyone for weeks. 'Trust me, aunt, we can earn it back and more. I will make a fortune from these mines wherever I live, as long as Joseph remains as my manager. We can be Lady Anne Carrington and Lady Mary Herbert again, with the finest clothes and carriages. I can gamble in the salons...'

Once her throat relaxed, tears flowed. Mary hated this; she never cried. 'I can't look after you anymore,' she sobbed. 'You need to be somewhere where there is care and friendship. I will buy you the best of help in Paris.'

Anne reached across and patted her hand, a rare gesture of comfort. 'Then we must go to Paris but don't think you have to stay. Once I'm settled, your place is here, in Spain, with Joseph.'

A mule driver was hired, a friend of their maidservant's husband, reputed to be trustworthy and who had already been paid to take a load of olive oil to Paris. Aunt Anne was heaved aboard the hired cart, behind their belongings, where she could sleep, resting her head against their woollen bundles. Mary perched next to the driver, relieved to find him taciturn and silent. For days, they rolled and tossed through barren desert landscapes, over high, mountainous tracks, staying in farm-houses or sleeping in shepherds' huts, until they reached the prosperous farms and vineyards of France. Only then did Mary feel safe to rest in taverns, paying for their board with coins she had saved over months, out of her father's miserly allowance. Every woman must have an escape fund, she decided, as they reached the suburbs of Paris. She had allowed herself to be dominated by a man, even without the shackles of marriage. It would never happen again.

After fifteen years, they were home. The driver dropped them at a convent, where Mary left her eighty-two-year-old aunt to recover, persuading the nuns to accept Anne with boasts of her other aunt, an abbess with an outstanding reputation for scholarly writing and one who could certainly be approached for financial recompense. With renewed energy, Mary tracked down the community of Jacobite emigrés in the suburb of Le Roule, and within a day had persuaded a landlord with Jacobite sympathies to rent a small house to Lady Anne Carrington and her niece, true supporters of the cause. Mary was relieved to have paid some attention to her aunt's ramblings about their family history, using half-remembered truths and exaggerations to encourage the young man to set a peppercorn rent.

Le Roule had a dilapidated church, open sewers and even the remnants of a leper colony cohabiting alongside new villas, such random development typical of Seville and Madrid, but never seen in her natural environment, the wealthier areas of Paris. It was hard to overlook their humble surroundings, but at least they were safe. After a few months, when she had made her whereabouts known to Joseph through a lawyer, she began to receive a small income from the Rio Tinto mine, but this was swallowed up by debts. Life was only marginally more comfortable living in Paris than in Madrid, but that tiny margin mattered.

Mary hoped it would be easier to borrow money, given her new status as a respectable businesswoman and owner of mines. She tapped all her contacts in Paris but banks and financiers refused to invest and her brother did not even have the grace to reply to an opportunity to become a partner. All her mines, even the functioning Rio Tinto, needed serious investment but Joseph stayed silent. When she wrote to her father, begging for funds to pay the miners and replace equipment, his replies were pages of ramblings about pursuit by Richard Cantillon's ghost and threats from the Mackenzie family. Mary wondered if her father had lost his mind, but a visit to London was out of the question.

Aunt Anne recovered from the journey as far as it was possible for a woman her age and settled into their rooms. The climate suited her, although she often complained of the cold, and Mary had enough money spare to hire a girl to help with her care. As letter after letter arrived from her lawyer about lack of money to pay her debts, never mind support the mines, a decision had to be made. She was ready to return to Spain, on her own terms, and check on that no-good Gage.

There was a knock on the door, just as Lucille lit the lamps. Joseph stormed into Mary's sitting room, without allowing the maid to make a polite introduction, carrying with him the smell of Le Roule and the chill of night.

He was not dressed as she had last seen him, in the functional, dirty clothes of a mineworker but wore the best of Parisian fashion. He pulled off his hat and threw his cloak onto the floor, leaving them for the maid to retrieve.

'I found out where you lived from your lawyer,' he said, without a single pleasantry or enquiry after her health.

If that was his game, Mary would play along. 'Have you abandoned our mines, our business?'

Joseph grinned, the grimace he used to threaten, not amuse. 'Of course. We had a deal and you broke it.'

'Who is maintaining the mines?'

Joseph shrugged. 'The men left, they hadn't been paid. I expect the mines are flooded. They're worthless.'

Mary felt a buzzing in her ears and growled, 'That was a stupid, mean act. If I lose everything, so do you. How will you support yourself now?'

He flicked a hand across his clothes, eyes darting around the room. 'As you can see, I manage rather well, unlike you.'

Mary shook her head, pressing her fists against her temples. 'I will have to employ managers, one for each mine. Even if I can recover their profitability, there will be nothing left, not for years.'

Joseph replaced his hat, checking his cravat in the mirror above the mantelpiece. 'It's not my problem. You made your choice, Mary. I will not visit again but if you need to contact me, only for advice about the mines, your lawyer knows my address.'

CHAPTER 28

1744

J oseph was true to his word. The incompetence of the
supervisors Mary was forced to hire meant that within a
year, the Rio Tinto mine ceased to make even a small
profit and the other mines soon fell into disrepair. Unable
to source any financial support and with her father obviously
losing his mind, she tried to bring an end to the drain of
lawyers' fees. If she could only gain immunity from prosecution
in France, as she had achieved in Spain, the many lawsuits
against her would have to end. She told her aunt to write again
to her sister Winifred, a woman who was surely well-placed to
ask the exiled King James, and perhaps even the Pope, to intercede with the king of France on her behalf. Mary herself wrote
to her old friend Fanny, hoping she might have the ear of the
French queen. These pleading letters brought no replies.

As in Seville, poverty stalked every moment of every day. A
maid was essential, she simply could not care for Anne alone,
but it was becoming clear that unless she could earn some
money, the girl would have to be given notice. She was
unwilling to gamble alone, but had she taken the risk, there was
no money spare to place as bets. They had nothing for warm

294

winter clothes, let alone sturdy outdoor clothing, if they were to keep a fire burning in each room and pay for hot food. Mary and Anne took to spending their days in bed, the only place where they could stay warm. Even there, inside the embroidered drapes, her breath was still visible as plumes of frost. She no longer heard anything from her father, other than his meagre monthly allowance, not even rambling letters full of paranoia, and guessed he was nearing his end.

Mary dozed under a deep pile of quilts, her almost-dreams rudely interrupted by their maid.

'My lady, there is a man... several men in fact... waiting to speak to you downstairs.'

'Ask them to go away. Say I'm not here,' Mary muttered.

The girl disappeared for a few moments, but soon returned.

'They won't leave. He says he must see you.'

Mary groaned. 'Who is it?'

'It's a young man called Charles Edward Stuart. He says he's royalty. My lady, he does look royal, the way he's dressed.'

Mary froze. This was not possible. A royal prince should not visit her here. She lifted the bedcovers and sniffed underneath; did she smell, did the room stink?

'Quickly,' she commanded Lucille, 'remove that chamber pot and cut some lemons. Mix them with herbs and bring them in here. After that, show him in, but afterwards, run to fetch a jug of wine from the inn.'

The girl stooped to pick up the chamber pot, holding it with both hands to prevent its contents slopping over the sides. Mary called after her, 'Lucille, don't let our visitors anywhere near Lady Carrington.'

She welcomed the young prince in a trembling voice,

inviting him to sit in the only chair. The prince checked the cleanliness of the seat before spreading his coat to sit down. Oversized men, dressed like the prince in brocade coats and breeches, white cravats tied loosely at their necks, stationed themselves around the room, holding the tail of their cravats below their nostrils.

Mary stammered out an excuse. 'Your Majesty, I would curtsey, but you find me seriously ill. I cannot imagine that I have long to live. You must think it disgraceful for a woman such as myself should be found living in such humble circumstances, but I have no choice.'

'I would not have troubled you, Lady Herbert,' Charles said, studying her from below his fine, arched brows. 'We have been detained on our way to Great Britain and learning that two noble Jacobite women were living in Paris on such reduced means, I felt it was my duty to visit.'

Mary could not think of an answer, other than pretend she was fully abreast of Jacobite affairs.

'I was unaware, Your Majesty, of your journey to Britain. I believed you were in Rome, with your father, King James.'

Charlie glanced around the room, as if he might be overheard, allowing her to see his Stuart nose in profile.

'I will share this with you, but only because your grandfather followed my grandfather to France, after a cruel betrayal by his daughters. He forever remained a loyal servant, as did your grandmother. With such a pedigree, you will be discreet, I'm sure.'

Mary swallowed and nodded, pulling her covers tightly under her chin.

The prince continued. 'I am leading an expeditionary force to restore the Stuart crown, first in Scotland, and beyond into England but for now, we're held up in Paris.'

Mary rarely wasted an opportunity to exploit her heritage

for personal gain but her father had only ever spoken about her grandfather with scorn, belittling his decision to run after a king in exile but there was her Aunt Winifred... hadn't she something to do with the princes?

'I think you may know my aunt, the Countess of Nithsdale?'

The prince seemed relieved to have found some common ground. 'Yes, yes indeed. I'm afraid I have sad news. Her husband, William Maxwell, has recently died. He was one of the few remaining heroes from the earlier rebellion. I admired him a great deal.'

Mary started coughing. She had never met her aunt's husband or heard anyone speak of him. This conversation had gone on long enough. After all, she was meant to be a dying woman.

To emphasise her vulnerability, she allowed her cough to develop into a fit of choking and saw the prince's eyes widen in alarm. 'Your Majesty, if I may be so bold, I have little time left. I would be a very happy woman, in my final days, if your father would consider awarding me the title of duchess.'

Charles rose, his haste of movement betraying relief at being offered a chance to leave, the demands of courtesy intact. His men moved in a pack towards the door and waited for him there.

'Of course I will, Lady Herbert. As soon as I return to Rome I will make the request on your behalf.'

As the door closed behind her royal visitor, Mary said aloud: '*If* you return to Rome, young man, *if* you return.'

It had been a situation so embarrassing, so horribly unreal, that any further introspection would only make her feel more ashamed. Mary dressed and found Lucille, lifting a tray intended for her aunt out of the maid's hands.

'Thank you, Lucille,' she said. 'I'll take this in to Lady Carrington. Not a word to my aunt about the royal visit, that's an order.'

Mary placed Anne's tray on a table next to the bed and drew back the fraying drapes, swatting at dust dislodged from their folds. She perched on the edge of an armchair and gave a theatrical sigh. Her aunt did not stir, in fact she burrowed deeper under her bed coverings. Mary opened the curtains at the window and a grey afternoon light filtered into the corners of the room. Anne turned over, but kept her eyes tightly shut. Her breathing returned to the rhythm of sleep.

Mary repeated her heavy sigh and waited.

'What is it, Mary?' her aunt asked, without opening her eyes.

'I'm fed up with being penniless. We must find more money, from somewhere.'

In time, Anne spoke, long gaps between her breaths. 'You mean you need to gamble with Joseph. Go ahead, you don't need my permission.'

'Why should I forgive him? It's his fault I'm in this mess. If he'd stayed in Spain, I'd be a wealthy woman by now. I can't believe he threw everything away, everything we'd worked for.'

Anne eased herself up against her bolster and looked at Mary through one half-closed eye. 'Your future in Spain was secure. You were both foolish to leave. Now you must live with that decision. I'm only sorry I have to share the consequences, but it won't be for long. Now, please pour me a drink.'

Mary poured Anne a tumbler of ale and passed it to her with a corner from yesterday's loaf. 'I had to bring you home. There was no choice.'

Anne dipped her bread in the ale and sucked the pap

through her few remaining teeth, making her next words difficult to follow.

'Don't blame me. I would have been perfectly comfortable living out my days in Madrid, with all the money you could have earned. It's beyond me why you gave it up, at the peak of success. If you ask me, the pair of you belong together. Who else would have you?'

Without checking whether she had finished, Mary snatched the tray out of her aunt's hands. 'I'm not asking you. I'll get in touch with Joseph and we'll thrash the gaming tables. Heaven forbid, we have to make sure that *you* are comfortable.'

Anne turned over. She pulled the frayed tapestry cover across her shoulders, muttering words that were hard to make out, even if Mary could be bothered to listen and wasn't already escaping through the open door.

'Do what you like,' she heard. 'You always do. Tell Lucille I need to use the pot.'

CHAPTER 29
1744/45

Every morning, William woke with surprise to discover he was still alive. His days at Frith Street were filled with conversations in his head, balancing the charge-sheet of life and making daily adjustments to his will, depending on the credits and debits for that day. When he wasn't talking to himself, his only true conversation was with servants or lawyers. His son still used the estate as his personal bank and Mary had abandoned her mines, confirming his fear that her interest had only ever been a passing whim, without any recognition of his significant investment. The ore from his own mines was now exhausted and James Baker had written to say that the miners were owed wages. He would visit soon, he had said, to withdraw money from the estate's bank in London, but would need a signature.

Recently, William had taken to his bed thinking he might be ill, and there he stayed, sleeping more each day. He was brought food to eat, left on a small table at his bedside, and removed uneaten. It had not occurred to his servants that he should be fed, and he would not ask. He knew it was autumn by the short-ening days, and since no one had yet lit his lamps, the familiar objects in his room had become indistinct. He heard an unusual sound from the street door, followed by voices. Footsteps climbed the stairs; a heavy tread settling twice on each step before attempting the next. This was death, William thought, the grim reaper had arrived. His bedroom door opened, and a servant entered, followed by a tall man. The stranger wore a dark cloak with a hood over his head, and despite the absence of a scythe, William knew that death was a presence in his room.

'Marquess,' the servant spoke, 'may I introduce the Chevalier de Balfe. He has been sent by Joseph Gage on behalf of your daughter, Lady Mary Herbert.'

De Balfe handed his cloak to the servant and William noticed that his wig was stained yellow. His coat, no doubt fashionable in Paris twenty years ago, had been darned many times. Peering over the edge of the bed, he could see that one of de Balfe's legs was in irons. A memory stirred; wasn't this the thug employed by Joseph Gage to threaten anyone trying to sue him?

Not comforted by this thought, William wanted the man gone, but the servant had already left in search of refreshments.

'I am an old man,' he wheezed. 'Tell me your business and leave.'

The chevalier dragged a chair across the floorboards and sat too close to the bed, leaning forward as if William might be hard of hearing. De Balfe's voice was a surprise, the tone unexpectedly soft and high.

'Your daughter cannot be with you, although that is her deepest wish. Gage has asked me to ascertain your final wishes and ensure that... ah... they have not been forgotten in any plans you might have for bequests.'

William felt exhaustion and anger snatch at his breath and whispered, 'How dare you!' He leant back against the bolster, afraid that his last moments might be spent in the company of this monster.

'The very best investment you can make, sir, in these your last hours, is to leave everything to Lady Herbert. With your full backing, she can return to her mines, exploit them to the maximum and earn vast wealth for the benefit of all your family. Mary has given her word that she will pay back the family debts and recompense her brother, if you will give her this final chance.'

William felt as if he was in the presence of one of those snake charmers he had once heard described, as the chevalier's melodious tone reassured and soothed, trying to convince him of the sense of this request.

'Mary has asked me to change my will, against her own brother?'

'Not exactly. It was Joseph Gage who sent me, with Lady Herbert's agreement. Gage has worked tirelessly on behalf of the Herbert family, don't you agree?'

William muttered, his voice spent, 'What do you want from me?'

The chevalier reached inside his coat and pulled out a document tucked into his belt.

'I anticipated you would see the wisdom of my arguments. I've asked a lawyer to draw up a new will. You only need to sign.' De Balfe scanned the room, his gaze searching.

'I will call your servant to bring a pen and ink,' he said. 'Once our business is concluded, I can assist you with some refreshments. Lady Herbert asked me to check whether you are being cared for adequately. Do you need to see a physician?'

The giant of a man stood and thumped back across the bedroom floor, dragging his leg. Through the open door, he called out: 'Help needed up here. Something to write with, and where's that wine?'

More footsteps on the stairs, but fast, two steps at a time. Not a servant at all, but by some miracle, William's estate manager.

'Who are you?' Baker challenged de Balfe. 'What is your business here?'

William cried, 'Get rid of him, James.'

The chevalier raised both hands and took a step away from the smaller man. 'I am here at the request of the marquess's daughter. Lady Mary sent me to see if her father needed help. I arrived not a moment too soon. I see he is being neglected.'

'Out, out!' William flapped his hand, his breath coming in rasping gasps.

James Baker indicated the open door. 'You heard Lord Powis. He has asked you to leave.'

De Balfe threw the legal document onto William's bed. 'Sign it, before it's too late,' he hissed, thumping across the floorboards towards his cumbersome descent of the stairs.

William grasped the hand that James held out to him. They heard the front door slam. 'Thank goodness you were here. Thank goodness you came in time.'

'It was pure chance, my lord,' Baker replied. 'I did write to you about withdrawing cash from the account. I needed your signature and here I am.'

William felt dizzy, heard his breathing falter. The room swung around his bed. It must be the shock, the intrusion. He had to sleep.

'If you wish,' James said, 'I'll sit down and read this to you, in case your visitor was more well-meaning than he seemed. You may want to sign after all, if it's from your daughter.'

William nodded, closed his eyes and Baker began to read aloud.

≈

Days later, Mary arrived in her father's rooms. She wasn't the first visitor, the servants revealed that her brother Lord Montgomery, now the third Marquess of Powis, had already conducted a search, but had left with nothing.

Amongst her father's belongings, Mary found that he had been in the process of drafting a document, detailing everything she owed. Well, no one needs to see that, she thought, pushing it into the pocket of her petticoat. Looking around, Mary tallied what she might earn from his furniture. Most wasn't to her taste, and clearly not her brother's either, but pieces from last century were well made and coming back into fashion. She would arrange for a furniture clearance and see what they would give her.

Mary met her older brother for the first time in thirty years at the reading of her father's will. The funeral had been in Hendon, too expensive for her to reach by hired carriage and her brother had not offered to escort her. An opportunity had been wasted for them to discuss the future of the family and the third marquess's responsibilities, but perhaps her brother had not been of the same persuasion. She would have failed to recognise him, had he not been the only other person present in the solicitor's office. Their father had been tall and slender, in the Herbert mould, with long but pleasant features. This man was short, with broken veins across his cheeks and a reddened, bulbous nose pitted with enlarged pores. He nodded in recognition but sat at a distance, staring straight ahead, as they heard the bequests. Of her sisters, Theresa and Charlotte, there was no sign, but Mary would not have known them, had they chosen to come. To her surprise, she learned that her father had not cut her out of his will, but typical of him, had been unable to resist making a point about how much she had already benefited from his estate and how her debts had destroyed the family wealth. Mary felt her brother's eyes fix upon her and shrugged. Her father asked that she continue to receive an annuity, only a little more than she was already receiving, but it was enough. There was no acknowledgement of Joseph's contribution, nor was he left even a small token of William's affection.

The new Marquess of Powis inherited the title, the castle and the estates, but Mary was pleased to learn that her father had decided to chip away at the actual cash her brother would receive. She enjoyed watching his agitation, as the lawyer disclosed the sum that had been left to William's sisters, to a relief fund for destitute Catholic families and to the tenants of the estate. The list went on, her father clearly desperate to buy his place in heaven.

Her brother waited for her outside the lawyer's office.

'Is this your doing?' he asked, his eyes searching for a distant point beyond her shoulder.

'Of course not. I haven't spoken to our father for years. We only ever communicated by letter and that was never about his will, only about my investments.'

'I heard you'd sent someone from France, a tall chap with a leg iron. Apparently, he tried to persuade the old man to change his will. I wondered if you'd succeeded, since by rights you're owed nothing. Clever work to make it seem like a small bequest, so you don't appear too greedy. A move very typical of you, dear sister.'

Mary hesitated. She knew nothing about a visit, but the story had credibility. If Joseph had threatened her father with the chevalier, then he didn't deserve a mention in the will, never mind even the smallest bequest.

'I know nothing of this,' she replied. 'It sounds to me like one of the servants has made up a tale.'

'Regardless,' the new marquess spun on his heel, emphasising his impatience, 'I am planning to challenge the will. I can't accept that you, or his aged sisters, deserve anything. The charitable bequests I can live with... just. You will hear from my lawyers.'

'Oh, for heaven's sake, William, not more lawyers,' Mary shouted at her brother's departing back. 'Haven't they earned enough?'

CHAPTER 30

1745

L ate one night, a month before Maxwell died, Winifred heard a tap on her door and at her call to enter, a servant escorted Prince Charles into the room.

Winifred curtseyed, but he dismissed her act of respect with an impatient wave of his hand. He asked the servant to leave and sat down heavily in a chair on the other side of the fireplace. In the light from the candles, he looked older than his twenty-four years and for the first time, she saw his dour father in his features.

'Is there a problem, Your Majesty? she asked. Charles had never visited her in these rooms, not since boyhood.

'Please, call me Charlie,' he said, 'and if I may, I'll call you Winifred. I'm afraid I can't call the woman who wiped my backside Lady Nithsdale. It doesn't sound right.'

Winifred nodded and waited for the young man to say more. This would not be good news.

'We leave this week to join a fighting force in France. From there, we plan to invade Scotland. My father will be restored to his rightful place, as king of the British Isles.'

She saw him dead on the battlefield, felt her heart break at the loss of her boy, then an unexpected flare of hope. If this invasion was successful, if a Stuart king was on the throne of Great Britain and Ireland, she and Maxwell would be pardoned. They could go home.

This maelstrom of hope and loss was swept aside by another fear. 'Is Henry going too?' she asked, immediately regretting her obvious favouritism.

Charlie laughed. 'No, I'm the heir and he's the spare. He has to stay behind.'

The questions would not stop, as one fear drove out another. 'What about my husband?'

'Yes, he's coming with us – couldn't leave the old Preston warrior behind – but don't worry, Winifred, I won't let him fight.'

Winifred shook her head, tried to chase away her panic. 'He won't fight, he can't. You must promise me. He'll be arrested for treason the moment he sets foot on British soil.'

Charles smiled with the impatient confidence of youth. 'Then he can stay in France. What's really worrying you, Winifred? I thought I could count on your support, despite what the gossips are saying about your loyalty.'

She hesitated, fighting her well-honed instinct to praise and encourage this young man, a child she had helped raise, a boy too easily set back by criticism.

'Tell me more,' she said, attempting to steady the quiver in her voice. 'I'm afraid I haven't kept up with everything that's been happening.'

In the intensity of his gaze, Charlie's pupils became pinpricks of light. 'The time is right. French foreign policy has shifted. An invasion of Britain means that George will have to pull his troops out of Europe, which would suit France well.

We've been promised enough men and two ships. If we succeed, the Hanoverian imposters will flee.'

Winifred made her decision. She loved this young man, she could not hurt him, but she must speak her mind. 'Charlie, my heart will sail with you and I will not have a moment's peace until you are safe but you must listen. We heard all this in the 'fifteen. I witnessed the betrayal of loyal men, who believed everything they were promised by the French. Too many men were executed, burned, sent to the colonies. Foreign policy turns on a sixpence. What is right for the French now, may not be in a few months. Until you have counted the men yourself, inspected the ships, checked the weather, you must resist the temptation to act.'

'You know me too well, Winifred, I've always been too impulsive. I will try to heed your advice.'

Winifred reached across for his hand. 'Think about what is at stake. This is not only about a throne for your father, but the lives of thousands of men, their wives and families. Let that thought be your guide. I only want the best for you, Charlie, and you can trust you have my support.'

Before he left, Charles kissed her hand, then pulled her into a rough embrace.

'I will keep your husband safe,' he whispered.

They had been married for forty-five years when Maxwell died but since the dreadful evening of the Radclyffes' party, their marriage had all but ended.

That night she had waited for him in their rooms, glad that Alice and Frances were asleep in the nursery, rehearsing what she would say, her hands knotting and twisting in fear. When he slammed into their apartment, his fury hit her like a wall.

'How could you, Winifred!' he roared. 'The Radclyffes are the finest people. I can no longer hold my head up here, in my own community.'

Scheming about a restoration of the Stuart dynasty, passing wine over water at gatherings of drunken men, had been a feature of life at court, little more than a harmless game. Winifred had failed to grasp the moment when everything changed, the day the game was over and Jacobite fantasy became reality.

She tried to explain, her voice struggling to find authority. 'You cannot try this again, to invade Britain. It's nonsense. Prince Charles is barely an adult, and you are an old man. He's a reckless, self-centred boy, being led by sentimental fools. What sort of king will he make, never mind his father? Have you thought of that?'

Maxwell staggered towards her, alcohol fuelling his anger. 'You treasonous bitch,' he bellowed, striking her across the face with the back of his hand.

Winifred staggered, her hand touching her cheek. They both stared at the blood dripping from her fingers where she had been cut by Maxwell's ring. Winifred was the first to speak, her voice toxic with venom. 'I hope you're captured and this time, they finish the job and execute you.'

Maxwell chose to sleep in his own rooms and spent his days with Charles Radclyffe. When she saw him in the distance, Winifred hid in doorways. If he came to see Frances, she made sure she was out. It had always been there, the threat of physical violence, but despite their volatile marriage, he had never hit her before. A line had been crossed and in the febrile atmosphere of the court, it would not be easy for them to reconcile.

Winifred became an outcast. Her cynicism, her outspoken belief that the Stuart cause would never succeed, was no longer tolerated by a community frantic with planning to restore James to his throne. Maxwell, by contrast, revelled in his reputation as a Jacobite legend and spent too many nights than was good for a man of sixty-eight, soused in reminiscence and alcohol. After his sudden death, she felt sure that Maxwell had been the first victim of the campaign, his heart no longer able to endure the excitement, the hope, the late nights.

Since his death, Winifred had nightly dreams of sex with her husband and even now, woke in the morning to reach out for him, only to feel a sick jolt in her stomach when she remembered he was gone. Frances wept often for her beloved grandfather and fuelled by the child's simple grief, she had been able to find her own tears. They had separated many times, with poisonous words and ultimatums, but they had always tried to forgive, if not to forget. This time, he had left her in hate, and would never come back.

Winifred was shocked to discover the scale of Maxwell's debt. He had always borrowed money but in their later years she had believed their income was more than enough to sustain his lifestyle. Alone in her rooms, she found herself shouting at him, as if he stood right in front of her, with his habitual hangdog expression whenever money was the issue.

'Why, Maxwell, why? What did you need? Why did you borrow so much?'

He had abandoned her, left her alone to suffer the shame and regret of their marriage but he had made sure she would share his debts for as long as she lived.

She wrote to her son. He was the head of the family, should he not shoulder some of his father's profligacy? She understood too well when he did not reply. His parents had never been able to save a single coin between them and he had the expense of a young family, a neglected house, empty for many years, and estate buildings in need of repair. There would be nothing to spare and he would blame them, his parents, for their foolish lives and troubled history.

CHAPTER 31

1745/46

M onths passed and there was no news, at least none that was shared with her. The palace became silent and with the young men gone, fell back into its forlorn state of hibernation, perpetuated by James's defeatist nature and eternal sadness. Prince Henry had followed his mother into religion and was training for the priesthood, so any young nobility who turned up at the palace, hearing of its reputation for parties, left sadly disappointed.

By chance Winifred met the king standing in the gallery with three of his men, outside the royal apartments. Seeing that they were deep in conversation, she tried to tiptoe past, but heard James's deep voice call after her. She retraced her steps and waited as the king dismissed his advisors. He indicated that she should walk beside him.

'In case I haven't expressed this as fully as I intended, Lady Nithsdale, I am truly sorry for the loss of your husband. He was greatly respected here, and I cannot forget his kindness to my late queen.'

Winifred lifted her eyes to look at the tall, solemn man by her side.

'Queen Klementyna brought out the best in Maxwell, Your Majesty. I'm afraid I cannot say the same about his feelings for me. We were living apart when he died and he has left me deeply in debt. At present, I can only think the worst of him.'

The king paused. 'Marriage is a difficult thing – I speak from experience. The loss of a beloved spouse where anger, blame, even separation, were present, makes grief harder to bear. I will ask Lord Dunbar to help you with the financial matter. You should not be troubled with debt, as well as your loss.'

Winifred could not believe what she had heard, and in her muddle of emotions, failed to react in any acceptable way.

James noticed her confusion, a misunderstanding he was quick to correct. 'It will be a loan, of course, Lady Nithsdale. Dunbar will consolidate your debts and deduct a portion of your husband's pension every month. We will overlook the interest.'

Winifred felt more comfortable on the safe ground of the king's notorious parsimony but was unsure how her small family could manage on less income.

She noticed that James expected a response, his eyebrows raised and said, 'I am very grateful, Your Majesty.'

The king appeared satisfied and continued walking, his hands clasped behind his back. Winifred kept pace, since she had not been dismissed but had he forgotten she was there?

Again, James stopped and lowered his voice, fixing his mournful eyes upon hers. Winifred noticed his eyelids were pink. 'I didn't want him to go, Lady Nithsdale. I advised him against it. You must understand that.'

'I do understand, Your Majesty. I gave him the same advice. To my shame, I was glad my husband died before he could join the expedition.'

'Please do not repeat this, I beg you,' James continued. 'Charles Radclyffe and his son were captured at sea but I'm uncertain of their fate. I will not inform his wife until I have definite news. Only one ship landed in Scotland and my informants say there is not enough support for my son.'

Winifred steadied herself against one of the many cabinets lining the passage, dizzy with the burden of responsibility the king had passed on to her, keeping this dreadful news from Charlotte.

She had to stay focused on the son, for the sake of the lonely man by her side. 'So, Charles should come home?' she asked.

The king glanced to either side. 'That would be the action of a man of sense, but you know him, he is impetuous and wilful. Charles thinks the Highland clans and Lowland lords will eventually come out in favour of our cause, and France will be shamed into supporting him. But my sources say he has neither the money nor the men to make a success of this.'

Winifred remembered the dreadful impact of James's own delay in 1715, a leader so cautious he only set foot in Scotland once the battle was over and the Jacobite army were prisoners. She heard her husband's voice, as if he stood right between them, raging from his cell about James's betrayal.

Winifred tried to voice some hope. 'Perhaps Charles will have the benefit of surprise. Our enemies will expect him to return to Rome, not invade Scotland.'

James shook his head. 'I wish your husband had not died and was alongside my son. Charles needs mature men around him, not hotheads. He listens to his inexperienced companions instead of me, his father. I fear he may be lost to us.'

'And many others with him,' Winifred said, her voice barely a whisper. 'Many, many others.'

∼

Within weeks of her worrying conversation with the king, news finally reached the court that Prince Charles's army had taken all of Scotland and he was safe in Edinburgh. Frances had been first with the news, bursting into their apartment after her lessons. They both hurried down the long corridors and into state rooms, searching for confirmation that the rumour was true. She heard that the prince's early success had brought out the clans and the Lowland lords, men who would have included her two nephews from Traquair House.

As the palace celebrated, armchair strategists muttered that Charles was wasting his time in Edinburgh, he should move quickly on to England, build on the momentum he had gained. An invasion of England was essential for French support. Winifred felt impatient with such gossip, regretting her own tendency towards cynicism. When had she become so sour and negative? Had she suffered too much personal loss to feel any optimism, she thought, or perhaps she had spent too long living alongside the fading dreams of the exiled court. She ought to have trusted Charlie's instinct, not burdened him with her past. If she had been given the chance, if any of the moaners had sought her opinion, she would have told them so.

It was possible the king also felt regret. In early October, Charlotte Radclyffe was directed to host one of her memorable parties, in the grounds of her home, to celebrate Charlie's victory. They must all enjoy fresh hope of a crown restored, his proclamation decreed, although he himself would not attend.

Winifred was horrified. Since she learned of Charles Radclyffe's capture, the secret had churned inside her, even though she and Charlotte were not friends. She persuaded herself that when Anne died, the weeks when she had not known had afterwards felt like a gift of time. She would do the same for Charlotte and keep the news from her. Charles and his son might well be languishing in comfortable rooms main-tained for peers of the realm, in the Tower of London and worrying Charlotte unnecessarily would be an unkindness.

When her own invite arrived, with Frances permitted to be her companion, Winifred decided to refuse but her grand-daughter's excitement changed her mind. Frances needed company and Charlotte's daughter Mary, who was the same age, would be there. They must attend and Winifred would try to enjoy herself.

Alice and Winifred dressed Frances in one of her mother's robes, a dress that Alice had worked on for days, creating a lace insert at the chest for modesty. They tied up her hair, rouged her cheeks and stood back to admire the girl's beauty. Adolescence, with all its trials, is not far off, Winifred thought, then chided herself for her pessimism.

It was a warm, early autumn evening, and Winifred stood at the edge of the garden with the other matrons, watching Frances and the other young people dance, elongated shadows amongst the garden flares. There was music, distant laughter and the crackle of fireworks. Once it grew cool, the older guests drifted inside, for food and wine and sofas, but the children and young women stayed outside to chase each other amongst the trees, their laughter still audible from indoors.

There was much talk of the campaign. Winifred listened but did not contribute, aware that she already knew too much. She overheard that the delay in Edinburgh had stretched the patience of the clansmen and some had already deserted to attend to their crofts for the winter. She shivered at the memory of her husband's abandonment by the same clans at Preston, remembering the shock of discovering their own blacksmith's apprentice sneaking back to their estate in Dumfries. She had learned that night that a loyalty paid for can never be relied upon.

The evening grew chilly and Alice arrived to take Frances

home. Winifred stayed, finding companionship amongst women who welcomed her, who moved up to make space on a sofa close to a generous fire, patting the seat between them. Servants brought wine on trays and Winifred swallowed too many, enjoying the creeping sensation of disorientation and warmth.

The other women stood to leave and in the wait for her own cloak, Winifred found herself alone with Charlotte Radclyffe.

'Thank you for coming,' Charlotte said, grasping her hand. 'It was such fun and wonderful to see our girls playing together again. I do hope that now victory is in sight, we can be friends. I have felt saddened that Maxwell did not live to see this moment. Your loss has made me desperate to see my son again and Charles, of course.'

The words spilled out, unplanned and forbidden. 'Your husband is a prisoner, as is your son. I heard this from the king. I am sorry you were not told.'

Charlotte stared. Below the thick paste of powder on her skin, colour drained from her cheeks as her neck flushed. 'You are a liar,' she hissed. 'You are a nasty, lying, bitch. I tried not to listen but all the gossip about you is true. You schemed to save your own husband from death, abandoning my husband's brother to be executed in his place. Leave my home, right now, and never return.'

Winifred did not want to be right; would have preferred youth, hope and friendship to have trounced solemn advice and caution. Reports eventually reached Rome that their army had tried to invade England, had even reached Derby, but support promised by English Jacobites had failed. Charlie's inexperienced army had faced war-hardened soldiers, withdrawn from

European battles to fight on the security of their own soil. Her warning about France had been sadly prescient; their fleeting interest lost within the swirling currents of European conflict.

She sat with Alice by the fire, both adjusting Frances's undergarments to allow for her budding breasts and widening hips. Alice shared news from the servants' quarters, always the most reliable source, that the retreat had taken their men through Nithsdale.

Winifred put down her sewing. 'Do you think my son watched the army pass by the estate?'

Alice paused to rethread her needle. 'Of course, my lady. He would have offered Charles rest and sustenance.'

Winifred wondered if this could possibly be true. 'Yes, he would,' she said. She remembered that Alice's home had been one of the cottages near their estate, that the loyal woman at her side had been taken from her parents at only ten years old, as nursemaid for Winifred's first child. This news from Nithsdale would have meant as much to Alice as it had to her. In future, they must talk about Alice's family.

The women sewed quietly together, hearing sounds from Frances as she tossed in her bed and muttered in her sleep. The child had always been a restless sleeper.

'Did you hear anything else downstairs?' Winifred asked.

'They said that Prince Charles had even planned what he was going to wear when he entered London. Everyone laughed but I didn't find it funny.'

Winifred smiled. That tale summed up her charming boy, a young man quite unsuited for leadership. 'I'm smiling because that's exactly what would have been his priority,' she said, 'but you're right, it's not funny.'

After Alice joined Frances in the nursery, Winifred heard a tap at the door and froze. Who was calling on her at this time of night?

Cracking open the door, Winifred saw the haggard face of Charlotte Radclyffe. After her dreadful indiscretion, Winifred had made sure their paths did not cross. She wanted to slam the door in Charlotte's face, anything to avoid another row, but the wretched, dishevelled woman begged to be allowed to enter.

Even before she was inside the room, Charlotte wailed, 'You were right. He was captured and now he's been executed.'

Winifred's heart missed a beat. She gripped Charlotte firmly by the shoulders. 'He was executed?' she repeated. 'Without a trial?'

'On account of his earlier escape from prison, over thirty years ago. The charge still stood.'

Had Maxwell lived, that would have been his fate too. 'I am so sorry,' she said. 'There are no words to soothe your pain. You should have been told he was a prisoner.'

Charlotte sobbed. 'My son is a prisoner too. I've no idea where he's being held. What if he's been tortured?'

Winifred turned the distressed woman to face her, feeling Charlotte's shoulders shaking beneath her palms. 'He will not have been,' she said, hoping in this moment that certainty mattered more than honesty. 'He cannot be held responsible for his father's past.'

'Thank you, Winifred,' Charlotte whispered. 'I had nowhere else to turn. At least you tried to warn me. My daughter and I are alone in this empty place, full of shadows and echoes of past happiness.'

'As I am alone with my granddaughter,' Winifred said. 'My home is yours, Charlotte. You and your daughter must join me here. We will form a new household and provide solace for each other.'

By spring the following year, the residents of the palace shook their heads and muttered in corners about a disastrous defeat at Culloden Moor, the Scots amongst them mumbling that it was a desolate place to die. Then whispers began that Charlie was being hunted through the Highlands of Scotland. When he escaped to France, the community sighed with relief. Winifred knew that Charlie would not come home, his shame would not allow it, although his father would always wait for him.

The sound of shifting embers from a fire nearing its end broke the heart-breaking whimper of Charlotte's stifled weeping. Winifred knew that her friend must have pressed her face into her bolster to protect Mary from the sounds of distress. They had learned that Charles had not been hung, drawn and quartered as befitted a man guilty of treason. Instead, he had been allowed the gift of a sharp, swift blade across his neck. This news was not a relief. Charles's death now seemed more vivid and real. There was better news about James. As a first offender and a boy not yet fully grown, he was being held prisoner but the court's spies did not know where.

Winifred replaced a log and lifted her embroidery from its basket but found she could not find the sense of purpose needed to raise the needle. She stared into the corners of a room she could no longer see but it was not her poor eyesight that stopped her sewing. Beyond those men they knew, friends or husbands imprisoned or executed, she saw in her imagination thousands of other men and women, unnamed and beloved only by their families, suffering punishment from the British government for decades to come. The dream was over for the court in Rome but for their loyal supporters in England and Scotland, the nightmare had just begun.

All that remained for the exiled community was to grow old, tell stories, shrivel away and be forgotten. She would die here too but not yet, not while there were children to raise, free from politics, principles and war. Their days would be comfortable, they would have enough to eat, warm clothes and companionship when they chose. She would help Charlotte to laugh again, even throw a party or two. Frances and Mary would grow, learn, perhaps have children of their own. In this tiny corner of Italy, they would be safe.

CHAPTER 32

1747

It wasn't a surprise to lose her mines at Rio Tinto and Aracena. There was always someone lurking in the background with a counter claim, and she was not in favour with the Spanish courts. When an heir of the original leaseholder decided to sue her, and she lost, she only felt relief at having avoided another expensive round of litigation. Of course, she did not say this to Joseph. He needed to feel wholly responsible for the failure of their dream.

That wasn't to say they hadn't enjoyed making the decision to instruct their workmen to walk off the site, leaving behind no workable equipment, months before the new owner turned up to inspect his empire. He was welcome to it, Mary thought, whatever the mine's potential. Without investment, the site at Guadalcanal remained desolate and stagnant for lack of capital, and she and Joseph decided to allow the leases on their other mines to expire. In Paris, she was perfectly happy to occupy herself with overseeing her legal affairs and arranging a marriage for Joseph.

She had tried not to forgive him, but it proved impossible, in part because Joseph thought there was nothing to forgive. He treated her as he always had, turning up when it suited him, always cheerful, never sorry. In the end, Mary had to accept that he was her only friend in Paris and most importantly, he was content to be her gaming partner.

Mary took up the cause of finding a bride for Joseph with renewed energy. He responded to the idea of a young wife with rather too much enthusiasm and was not willing to leave the matter to her superior knowledge and skills. Only her quick intervention prevented several unsuitable approaches from going any further. Today, a fine day in spring, she was to meet a young woman and her mother, who had travelled to Paris from Nottinghamshire, in the expectation of a marriage contract. She had persuaded Joseph to stay away.

Mary journeyed to their rooms by carriage since her own lodgings were quite unsuitable for guests. In her long absence, Paris had further developed its public transport, and it was now possible for a single woman to travel safely by coach from most areas of the city. She wore her only respectable gown, made for this sole purpose from a deep-blue velvet, embroidered with bronze thread. It was not fashionable, but she hoped it conveyed her maturity and the quality of background necessary for matchmaking between families with pretensions.

The prospective bride and her mother waited for her in a salon cluttered with silk-upholstered chairs, purpose-built for social reclining, competing for space with an assortment of side tables veneered in different woods. Mary introduced herself as the Duchesse d'Herbert de Powis, which was the title she used in Paris, but this exaggeration of her status was wasted on her companions.

Both women spoke over each other, the younger of the two owning a voice that was both high-pitched and grating. The mother was furious to learn that Joseph would not be joining them, making it clear an immediate betrothal was expected.

Both women had dressed for the important event, their Nottingham dressmaker doing her utmost to present her clients in the latest Paris fashion.

After introductions, both women tried to sit down but the daughter's voluminous dress, crushed into the tight armchair, rose to smother her in pink bows and fabric rosebuds and she struggled to see beyond the froth at her neck. Mother was more soberly dressed but this simply meant slightly longer sleeves, fewer frills, and less exposure of cleavage. The chair she chose, angled for ease of languorous reclining, made it almost impossible for her to sit upright.

Once the pair understood they must impress the Duchesse d'Herbert, neither showed any interest in asking questions about the suitability of the groom, but breathlessly regaled her with salacious gossip about people she had never met.

The daughter paused to take a sip of chocolate from a porcelain cup at her side and Mary grasped the opportunity to question the mother about the source of their wealth. She had already researched the family but was interested to see how they presented themselves.

'Of course, we're in sugar cane, we have several plantations in Jamaica. You have heard of Jamaica, Duchesse?'

Mary was not confident exactly where Jamaica was, but she did know, from her days in Lisbon, that sugar plantations ran on slavery.

'So how many slaves do your family own?'

'Goodness, I have no idea, I leave all that to my husband,' the mother replied, easing herself up from an undignified slouch.

'But your business, your wealth, depends on slave labour?' Mary continued.

'I hardly see what that has to do with a marriage between Mr Gage and my daughter.'

Mary had only the vaguest notion about Joseph's views on slavery, but there was something so distasteful about this family, she discovered in the pit of her stomach a deep and unexpected revulsion for them and their business. She had few scruples when it came to money but would not allow Joseph to gain from a marriage dependent upon the exploitation and suffering of other men.

Adopting her most polished, entitled tone, Mary said: 'I must let you know that Mr Gage is unable to marry into a family with connections to the slave trade. That is his view, and he will not be persuaded otherwise.'

The mother flushed, pink blotches crawling from the neck-line of her dress to the roots of her hair.

'That is his loss. My daughter has many suitors, grateful for her attention. We have wasted our time on this journey.'

'And who are you anyway,' the daughter interrupted, finding her voice. 'Why do you feel free to ask us such impertinent questions?'

This girl is brighter than her mother, Mary thought.

'I am Mr Gage's business partner, and since he has no family, I represent him in all matters of personal importance. Now, if you will excuse me, I have financial matters that need my attention. Enjoy your visit to Paris. I recommend an opera at the Théâtre du Palais-Royal.'

The Nottingham family left for home, disgusted by Mary's lack of respect. She had to renew her search, which was not easy given Joseph's age and reputation. There was also the problem of her aunt, now in failing health and requiring care both day and night. Had her aunt's younger sister, Lady Lucy Herbert, not died several years before, the convent in Bruges would have been the answer. Mary felt irritated at her own failure to appreciate this obvious solution. She ought to have sent Aunt Anne there, when she was still fit for travel. Her aunt had deteriorated further and there were times when she no longer recognised those around her. If she spoke at all, it was of the past.

Luckily there was no remaining family, apart from Winifred Maxwell in Rome. No one was left to judge her or question her decision. Lucy Herbert's monastery may not be an option, but her dilemma could still be solved by leaving her aunt in the custody of a religious order. There were many in Paris suitable for distressed gentlewomen without adequate funds, whose family had tired of the relentless burden of their needs. Her father had left his sister a small bequest, enough to cover a basic level of care until she died. The matter was settled.

Moving her aunt was a greater challenge than Mary had anticipated. Normally passive and withdrawn, when Mary and Lucille tried to dress Anne, the aged woman resisted with an energy and tone of voice that was shocking. Both the maid and Mary were hit hard, many times, and Anne used words that Mary would never have guessed she knew. Once dressed in a patchwork of clothing, Anne was held down in a chair, her arms placed backwards through her dressing robe, the sleeves knotted at the back.

Three strong men, including the hired coachman, carried Lady Anne Carrington into the waiting coach. It was a journey her aunt would once have enjoyed, travelling in a vehicle more expensive than Mary could afford, but nevertheless entirely suitable for a titled British woman enjoying an afternoon outing. Anne cowered, pushing herself into a corner as if terrified, crying for her husband, Francis. At the convent, the abbess met them at the gate and Anne was carried into the airy entrance hall, which smelt of cut flowers and wood polish. A huge gilt cross hung from the rafters and the walls were covered with dark paintings of violent Old Testament scenes. Their journey to the cells, Anne carried in a chair by four sturdy nuns, followed a steady deterioration in their surroundings. The plain rooms where the nuns lived, the warm kitchen smelling of bread and the yeasty brewery were replaced by cells with low doors, women screaming and a strong smell of urine. Mary had not visited before agreeing to a place for her aunt, never questioning that the convent's care of the aged would not match the public face of the few religious orders she had known.

The group stopped outside her aunt's room and the wooden door was opened to reveal a cold and sparsely furnished cell. A strange woman pushed into the cell and plucked at Mary's sleeve, using her name repeatedly.

She was startled and pulled back her arm, stating: 'I'm not the woman you're looking for.'

The nun responsible for her aunt's care rolled her eyes and led the stranger from the cell, pushing the woman roughly into the corridor.

'Ignore her,' she said, closing the door behind them. 'She's always on the prowl. We've no idea who she's looking for.'

Mary felt a desperate need to escape from this forsaken world, hearing another woman begin pacing the corridor outside, humming and tapping the wall, back and forth.

'Mary is such a common name,' she said, trying to engage her aunt's carer in some conversation. 'She must be searching for a sister, or her mother. My aunt is always asking for her husband, Francis.'

The nun nodded but showed little interest in such detail. Still bound to the chair and rocking, Anne's eyes sought Mary's, brimming with fear.

'Francis,' she said, 'I want Francis.'

'You heard her,' Mary said. 'My aunt keeps asking for her husband. She doesn't seem to know me.'

'It's time you left,' the nun barked. 'I haven't got all day. They're all the same. She'll settle once you're gone. If you're worried, you can visit tomorrow.'

It wasn't as if she didn't hesitate, she wasn't without feeling, but the fact was, she couldn't stay there a moment longer, with the smell, the moaning, her aunt's pleading eyes. Mary nodded and ran from the dark, squalid rooms, retracing her steps into the cool, civilised entrance to the nunnery, where the abbess waited.

'I assume you're happy with the accommodation, Lady Herbert?' she asked.

Mary's stomach knotted and her throat was so tight, the words emerged in a croak.

'I have no alternative,' she said. 'My aunt has no family other than me, and my father did not make adequate provision for her. I am not up to the task of caring for the aged.'

The nun's smooth, unlined face appeared suddenly aged, and she sighed.

'The very end of life is hidden. When we are faced with the reality, few can cope. Don't blame yourself, but please try to visit, as often as you can. Even if Lady Carrington doesn't recognise you, she will feel your presence.'

In the weeks that followed Mary meant to see her aunt, in fact had intended to be a regular visitor, but hours became days, days became weeks, until months had passed. There was always a pressing reason not to make the expensive journey to the convent. At first, Mary pushed her guilt aside, forbade herself to dwell on that last image of Anne, silently begging her to stay. In the end, she rationalised her neglect. Her aunt no longer knew her, so what was the point? It was a decision that made perfect sense.

Shortly after her aunt had been committed to the convent, a young woman knocked at the door of Mary's lodgings. She did not like visitors at home, a place quite unsuitable for a duchess. Lucille had been instructed to dismiss any callers but the girl said she was a relative and asked for Lady Anne Carrington by name. Unlike her aunt, who had talked endlessly about relatives and made far too much fuss when one of them died, Mary had little interest in family ties but this young woman intrigued her. Catherine Caryll may well be a potential bride for Joseph or have sisters or friends who might be persuaded to overlook his failings.

Catherine was shown into Mary's small sitting room, a comfortable if faded salon, crowded with cheap, end-of-century pieces discarded by newly rich families who sought a lighter touch with decor. Mary instructed her maid to bring them two glasses of wine, indicating with a discreet gesture that these were to be small.

The women sat on either side of a round table and Mary listened as Miss Caryll introduced herself as the granddaughter of Lady Anne Carrington's sister, Frances. She hoped she might introduce herself to Lady Carrington, since she and her sister, Elizabeth, knew few people in Paris.

Mary could not work out how she was related to this girl. Instead, she allowed her expression to fall into one of regret and said: 'I'm afraid you are too late, Catherine. Your great-aunt has lost her mind and is cared for by nuns. You may visit, but she will no longer remember her older sister Frances. You will mean nothing to her.'

Catherine twisted the lace at her sleeve. 'The thing is,' she said, 'Elizabeth and I had to flee to Paris. We were in a difficult situation, pursued by bailiffs for debts we accrued in London. We're alone in a strange city and thought that meeting our relatives might help.'

As the girl spilled her secrets, Mary guessed at the desperation that had led Catherine to gamble on the charity of distant family. While her gown looked fresh and expensive, no doubt bought on credit from the best London dressmaker, like many debtors she would have little money for day-to-day expenses. Catherine's plight was all too familiar.

'But what about your family?' Mary asked. 'They cannot abandon responsibility for you and your sister, whatever your mistakes. You are still a young woman, without a husband to protect you.'

'My brother mismanaged our estates and has had to sell our family home, a beautiful house in Sussex, one which has been ours for generations. When he found out about our debt, it was the final straw. We had to escape his rage.'

Mary sighed and sipped her wine before answering.

'This tale is very common,' she said. 'Your brother has drawn heavily on your family's fortune to gratify his own desires, but he blames you for a debt which I guess is minor by comparison. You have been poorly treated.'

Catherine relaxed and smiled at Mary.

'I'm so glad you understand. It is good to find a friend in Paris, and a cousin, I believe.'

The germ of a plan seeded in Mary's mind. Catherine was pretty, gentle, unassuming, but was there a dowry? To find out something so personal, she must share some confidences of her own. She must try to become a trusted friend, or even better, a trusted cousin.

Mary reached across the table for Catherine's hand.

'I understand so well because I have also been badly treated by my family. My father left me a small bequest on his death, but my brother refuses to pay. He says I owe too much already, yet he frittered away the family fortune and has even failed to produce an heir. In our society, only women's debts count against them.'

Catherine gasped. 'You're right, men have too much power. First our fathers, then our brothers, then our husbands.'

'Listen,' Mary continued, 'this is what we should do. I will negotiate with your brother on your behalf, but first, I need to know if there is anything you are owed.'

'Before they died, my parents arranged a generous dowry for myself and Elizabeth. Of course, my brother can't touch that and nor can we. It belongs to our future husbands.'

Mary nodded. 'Of course it does but it helps to know your dowry is secure. I have a bedroom here, vacated by my aunt. I suggest that you and Elizabeth stay with me while I try to resolve your family conflict. You can trust me, Catherine, I have a great deal of experience in matters of finance.'

CHAPTER 33

1748

Catherine Caryll and her sister Elizabeth moved in to Mary's home that night. As Mary suspected, the more charming of the two had been sent inside to seek help, while Elizabeth waited in the shrubbery with their bags. Catherine, the younger sister, seemed grateful for her rescue but Elizabeth was more distrustful, her eyes narrow with suspicion when she questioned Mary at breakfast about the exact whereabouts of her great-aunt, Lady Anne Carrington, whose bedroom they had taken.

'Our great-uncle, the lawyer Kenneth Mackenzie, was her husband,' she said. 'We heard she lived in Paris. Her committal to a convent must have been sudden.'

This prying is unexpected and unwelcome, Mary thought. How could her family be so entangled with both the Carylls and the Mackenzies? Was it possible Aunt Anne had told her, but she hadn't listened.

Elizabeth explained further, with an innocence that could not be genuine: 'Our late mother was Kenneth Mackenzie's niece. She inherited his estate when he died.'

This is a trap, Mary thought. These young women have been sent by Mackenzie's family to chase me for money, now my father is dead. She decided to feign ignorance, to keep her own plans uppermost.

'Families often keep matters of money away from women. Your brother chose not to keep you abreast of your mother's financial affairs because you should have inherited when she died. You said he was in financial difficulty. Is this another way he has cheated you?'

A glance passed between the sisters and Catherine spoke. 'I'm afraid that may be true. Cousin Mary, you said you would write to our brother and help us fight for what is ours. All we want is to go home.'

'Why should we trust you?' Elizabeth interrupted. 'We came here seeking protection from our grandmother's sister. Instead, we find Lady Mary Herbert, a woman whose reputation is well-known and little admired.'

Mary felt a sudden pain behind her eyes and her throat tightened, warnings of an imminent outburst of rage. She breathed deeply, trying to stay calm. 'You are not a prisoner here and may leave at any time, if you have anywhere else to go. I offered to help because of my own mistreatment by men in my family. I will write to your brother, cousin to cousin, but have no wish to become mixed up in your troubles. As you have reminded me, I have enough of my own.'

From his first meeting with Catherine, Joseph behaved like a fawning puppy. While this irritated Mary and at times, hurt her pride, she reminded herself that she had not wanted him. There was no doubt his feelings were genuine, and despite the difference in their ages, Catherine basked in his adoration and giggled over his unsuitable choice of gifts. Joseph played his part well. He had regained some of his prosperity, using gambling to fund financial investments he chose not to discuss or share with Mary. For Catherine's benefit, he made much of his brother, Viscount Gage of Sussex, and Mary realised that to the unseen and neglected youngest girl in a family who had lost their estates, attention from a man who was almost nobility must be addictive.

Elizabeth did not agree and chaperoned the meetings between the lovers with a stiff back and a sour expression. Mary attributed this antagonism to straightforward jealousy that the younger sister was marrying first. Neither woman was as young as she had first believed, and Mary knew only too well the pressure women felt if they remained unmarried once over thirty. If things had been different, she might have suggested a union between Elizabeth Caryll and her brother, but judged the time was not right.

The scale of Catherine's dowry, combined with the hostility from her sister, made a long betrothal too much of a risk and Mary began to make plans for a wedding. Six weeks later, a letter from John Baptist Caryll rested by her plate on the breakfast table. Mary noticed that Elizabeth had also received a letter, in the same handwriting, which she read in front of Catherine but did not share.

Mary opened her own letter, glanced at its contents, and said aloud: 'Your brother wants to meet me in London next week, at the offices of Kenneth Mackenzie. It looks as if your cousin has taken over the practice.'

Elizabeth's gaze flicked up from the page in her hand. 'He's sending a carriage for me today. She has to come with me.'

'I don't...' Catherine began speaking but Mary interrupted her.

'Catherine will stay, she has a dress fitting tomorrow.'

Elizabeth put down her letter and stared at Mary. 'You know she can't marry Gage without my brother's consent.'

Mary smiled back at Elizabeth, acknowledging this woman as her equal: 'Then I will go to London and secure his blessing.'

Elizabeth was at the meeting, closely flanked by her brother, a lawyer and a clerk. These were the people, Mary thought, who had chased her old father to his grave. These were the same people who had conspired to rob her aunt of her portion of Mackenzie's estate. She would not make this easy for them.

The room was almost dark, typical of a November afternoon, and the group waited while a servant lit the gilt candelabra on the panelled walls.

John Caryll coughed before speaking and shuffled the papers in front of him. 'You chose, Mary Herbert, to litigate against this family on behalf of your aunt but we won the case. You think to pay us back by manipulating my sister Catherine. Elizabeth has informed us of your intent to marry her off to Joseph Gage, for the sake of her dowry.'

Mary removed her glove and stroked the smooth surface of the table with her fingertip. 'My aunt, your great-aunt, was cheated of her rightful inheritance by her husband Kenneth Mackenzie, a crime perpetuated by his family. She lives in a convent and has to be nursed, day and night. It is expensive.'

'Your aunt benefits from a monthly income from this estate,' John said. 'It may not be much, but it is more than she was due, given how you both exploited him to pay off your creditors. Had he not had the foresight to ensure our mother was his beneficiary, he would have lost everything to the sinkhole of your debts.'

'Your mother inherited from him and you inherited from

her,' Mary retorted. 'I don't expect her daughters saw a penny of it.'

It was difficult to see the faces of her antagonists in the candlelight but she noticed that John had glanced at Elizabeth. The younger woman's expression was inscrutable but her knuckles, clasped on the table in front of her, glowed white in the dusk.

'Your mother's inheritance has been spent,' Mary continued, staring at Elizabeth. 'Everything that Mr Mackenzie worked for has gone, because of your brother. He lost the house, the farms... everything. Yet he terrorises you and Catherine for running up a debt at the dressmakers.'

The lawyer pulled his pocket watch from inside his coat. 'I suggest we focus on the matter in hand,' he said. 'You owe this family money, Lady Herbert, and we demand a schedule of repayment.'

Mary gave a snort of laughter. 'Or you will send out bailiffs, just as you harassed my ailing father? In fact, this family owes me money. I have looked after Lady Anne Carrington for over twenty years and can no longer meet the costs of her care. As head of the family, John Caryll, you must pay the convent fees and when the sad time comes, provide expenses for a suitable funeral.'

'She was never part of our family,' John shouted and slammed his open palm against the table.

Mary forced her own voice to stay low and quiet. Everyone leaned across as she spoke. 'As the wife of your great-uncle and sister of your grandmother, you are the closest relatives she has, apart from me, and I am a woman without means. I am happy to return to litigation over this neglect, and I will win.'

John Caryll slouched in his chair and glanced at the lawyer, who gave a tiny shake of his head.

Mary glowed with the quiet satisfaction of having won.

This family could not afford another round of lawyer's fees. Nor could she, but her life was simple and cheap. The Carylls had not yet learned to live with disgrace and poverty. She had seen this before, the panic behind the eyes of those who were still clinging to hope.

Elizabeth's pupils burned, reflecting flames from the candles. She addressed Mary but the message was intended for her brother.

'What about Catherine?' she asked. 'We can't leave her in Paris with this...'

'Forget her,' John snapped. 'She's made her choice. I give my consent to the marriage but our sister is lost to her family.'

The wedding between Joseph Gage and Catherine Caryll took place just before Christmas. Mary surprised herself with recalling details from Fanny's winter wedding, so many years before. She helped her young cousin source a suitable gown and arranged a lavish ceremony, paid for by Joseph with money borrowed on the strength of his bride's dowry.

Only three months later, as Mary and her maid were sorting the rooms for the morning, someone thumped on the door with a fist, a fevered banging and shouting that would not stop.

Always afraid of bailiffs, or worse, Mary opened the door no more than a split, with Lucille close behind her, cupping the flame of a candle behind her hand.

Joseph stood in the half-light, wild-eyed, hair tousled, his clothes dripping with rain that saturated the streets and pavements beyond the door.

'Let me in,' he begged, his voice hoarse. 'Catherine is dead. Her brother is pursuing me. I am not safe.'

Joseph stripped off his soaking garments and sat hunched by the fire, a blanket around his shoulders.

Mary was unable to stop a note of accusation creeping into her first question. 'How did she die?'

Joseph hesitated, his expression alert for blame. 'You think the same as everyone else. I did not harm her, I promise. It was an unexpected infection... progressed without mercy. She died in my arms.'

Mary saw that Joseph was close to tears. He was a strong, resilient man; this was out of character.

'I believe you,' she said, 'but many will not. You have a reputation as a thug, one who could be cruel to those who crossed him. You have used men with even fewer scruples than yourself, to enact the worst of your punishments.'

'I have never been violent to women,' Joseph protested. 'I would not have harmed a hair on her head. I believe Catherine was happy with me. How can I live without her?'

Mary asked another question, hoping he would grasp her meaning without too much explanation.

'Is there any chance you were too rough, without intending to harm her?'

'How could you think that? I have been intimate with you for many years. Have you ever felt threatened or afraid? Have I ever hurt you?'

Joseph had been a considerate lover. She had witnessed no sign of cruelty in his treatment of women. Mary reached her decision.

'You can sleep here tonight,' she said. 'In the morning, you must go far away and remain hidden. I cannot help with your grief. You must survive that in any way you can.'

∿

Ugly rumours circulated, the worst being that Joseph had abused his young bride. Her family sought revenge, and failing to locate poor Catherine's husband, found a victim in the only person left to blame. Mary was issued with more writs, accusing her of scheming with Joseph to murder his bride for the sake of a dowry. Forced back into an itinerant lifestyle, she fled between rooms in Paris suburbs she had never heard of, let alone visited, escaping guards employed by the Carylls. Joseph had thoroughly disappeared, her only contact with him through his lawyer, who gave her control of his financial affairs on Joseph's instructions.

The inheritance from Catherine was considerable, but inevitably challenged by the family, who argued that Gage was owed only a small bequest for the few months of his marriage. Mary made sure the Carylls were given what they were owed, but the small pot paid to Joseph was useful. There was no harm in dipping into it from time to time, was there? She would pay him back. Lady Anne Carrington died only a few months later and bequeathed everything to Mary. The invoice for Anne's funeral, which she sent to the Mackenzie lawyers, remained unpaid and the convent became another of Mary's litigants.

Her remaining brother quickly followed his father and aunt to an early grave. In death, as in life, he cheated her. After stripping the family of its wealth to fund his profligate lifestyle, he named a distant cousin as the only benefactor. Learning that her father's small bequest would never now be honoured, Mary decided his early death was a just reward for dishonouring her, the actual head of the family. She did not attend his funeral.

Mary was alone in Paris but never bored; her lawsuits and her one remaining mine demanded her full attention. The furore about Catherine Caryll passed, as these things do, once the family had been suitably compensated for the loss of their sister, and she returned to living quietly in Le Roule. When a copy of her brother's will arrived from her lawyer, Mary left it unread on a side table, reluctant to allow her mood to be soured by the contents. It was a matter of luck that one evening, after Lucille had lit the fire, Mary chose to idly scan her brother's final wishes before throwing the papers onto the flames.

Mary sat bolt upright, leaning forward to better see the words under a lamp. This could not be true... her brother had briefly been responsible for a ward, a function he had wasted no time in passing on to others. Who on earth was she, Mary thought, this Barbara Herbert. Resting back, Mary sieved though memories of her aunt's ramblings and felt an unexpected sadness for the loss of Aunt Anne, a woman who believed family mattered.

Finally, it came to her. Barbara was her brother Edward's child, a young woman whose claim to inherit the castle and estates was even stronger than her own. Beyond ensuring arrangements for her ongoing wardship in his will, her brother had evidently ignored this girl in her life and in his death.

It was, of course, her duty to rescue Barbara, a child of only thirteen, obviously in need of protection. She could even help her niece regain her inheritance. Perhaps the last of the Herbert women should meet, join forces against the unfair control of men.

This would be her mission. Everything she had suffered, the financial losses, the poverty, the legal battles, led her to this point and she would use everything she had learned to fight for Barbara Herbert. Mary lit a small candle to take upstairs, called out to Lucille to sort the fire, and went to bed, keen for the new day to begin.

THE END

Also by Morag Edwards

The Jacobite's Wife

ACKNOWLEDGEMENTS

A big thank you to beta readers Rebecca Batley, Diane Gilbert, Beth Albright-Peakall, Tracey Madeley, Janet Wright, Christine Eddowes and Suzanne Harrington, as well as editor Barbara Henderson for a thorough structural report, all sourced through The History Quill (Historical Fiction Specialists). Your early advice and insight was invaluable in the development of *The Jacobites' Plight*. I am also grateful to editor Dr Karen Ette (The Writers' Secret Helper) for providing a detailed copy edit at an early stage. The members of Leicester Writers' Club have been consistently generous with their friendship and constructive comments. A special thank you is due to my late mother for giving me a lifelong passion for history and fiction.

I am indebted to my wonderful publisher Bloodhound Books for recognising the worth of *The Jacobites' Plight*, in particular to Betsy Reavley, Director and Founder, for agreeing to give life to this novel. The hard work, enthusiasm, and patience of the team at Bloodhound Books has been essential in bringing this novel to publication, including Abbie Rutherford, Commissioning Assistant and Editor, Shirley Khan, Editor, Tara Lyons, Editorial and Production Manager and Hannah Deuce, Social Media and Marketing Executive. A heartfelt thank you to you all.

ABOUT THE AUTHOR

Morag Edwards has spent over 30 years as an educational psychologist and uses her knowledge of child development to shape fictional characters in both historical and contemporary fiction. She has an MA in creative writing from the University of Manchester's Centre for New Writing and is an active member of Leicester Writers' Club. *The Jacobite's Wife* is Morag's debut novel and is the first in a planned trilogy. The Jacobites' Plight is the second novel in the series. Morag also writes contemporary fiction and has recently self-published the novel, *Broken*. A second novel in this genre, *Crash*, will soon be available.

.

A NOTE FROM THE PUBLISHER

Thank you for reading this book. If you enjoyed it please do consider leaving a review on Amazon to help others find it too.

We hate typos. All of our books have been rigorously edited and proofread, but sometimes mistakes do slip through. If you have spotted a typo, please do let us know and we can get it amended within hours.

info@bloodhoundbooks.com